Also by Ian Wha

The Gif

The Mammoth B
(edite

THE NOISE WITHIN

By Ian Whates

SOLARIS

First published 2010 by Solaris
an imprint of Rebellion Publishing Ltd,
Riverside House, Osney Mead,
Oxford, OX2 0ES, UK

www.solarisbooks.com

ISBN: 978 1 906735 64 7

Designed & typeset by Rebellion Publishing

Printed in the UK

In memory of Bill Whates, who, I like to think,
would have been proud of his son.

PART ONE

CHAPTER ONE

LEYTON CROUCHED BENEATH the wall, waiting for the right moment. Two red dots moved across the inside of his visor, steadily converging: the two guards on their rounds, about to cross almost immediately above him.

As they drew nearer, he stepped away from the wall and raised his gun, holding it ready.

"Another two degrees higher," whispered a voice in his ear.

He hated when it did that, but made the minute adjustment in any case. As the two dots on his visor touched, he squeezed the trigger. The gun featured two grenades built into the unorthodox and slightly bulky base of its barrel. One of these now flipped up, to be catapulted forward, spinning as it flew over the wall and onto the balcony beyond. Brief seconds later, the night's stillness was ripped apart as the shell exploded.

Something flew past, arcing over his head to land wetly on the lawn; it might have been an arm or some other body part, but Leyton didn't wait to find out. He was already racing up the broad stairway, gun levelled and firing as he reached the veranda, sending a stream of pulsed sonics at the glass doors before him. Bullet-proof and reinforced, the glass had resolutely withstood the force of the blast, but the machine-gun-quick pulses set up a resonance within its structure before delivering a sonic hammer-blow. The doors shattered spectacularly, enabling him to run without pausing through a curtain of glassy splinters and into the building beyond.

More red dots; three of them, approaching at a run. He sub-vocalised the word 'projectile' and then moved quickly away from the doors to stand against a wall, relying on the eye-foxing qualities of his shimmer suit to do the rest.

Three more guards came charging from the narrow corridor that emerged beside the stairs. They ran straight past him and then slowed as they approached the gaping expanse of doorway, seeking an enemy.

"Body armour," whispered the voice.

Now standing at their backs, he raised the gun and fired, raking a stream of bullets across the trio at knee level. Body armour protected the torso, but not the legs. All three went down, screaming. One of them let off a burst of bullets from his own clutched weapon, an instinctive twitch of the trigger finger as he fell; enough to turn the face of the man beside him to bloody pulp.

Again, Leyton didn't pause to finish them off but charged on, taking the marble stairs two at a time. Sensors and alarms showed up in his visor as orange beams criss-crossing the stairs. He ignored them. If every alarm in the place wasn't going off already, then these guys had some serious technical issues.

"Automated weapon placement," the voice whispered, and his visor highlighted the centre of a fast-approaching pillar which marked the top of the stairs.

"Best counter?"

"Energy, not projectile."

"Energy!" he snapped at once, then raised the gun and fired. The centre of the post exploded, a fraction of a second before he reached it. Shards of marble stung his legs, slicing through the shimmer suit and damaging its integrity, though hopefully he wouldn't need it to pass close inspection from here on in.

He ordered the gun back to 'projectile', knowing how quickly 'energy' depleted its power reserves. Two more red dots went down as he tore along the corridor. A spent ammo clip was jettisoned and replaced, and then he was at The Door.

The visor reported two occupants, one hiding behind a false reinforced wall in the room's left hand corner, the second pressed against the wall to one side of the door. The latter was armed. No concealed weapons.

"Armour-piercing."

The gun carried just three such shells, tips constructed of a polymer tougher than diamond with sharpened edges that would put a razor to shame. He put two of them through the wall and the man hiding against it, then kicked the door open and stepped into the room.

The readings on his visor confirmed the identity of the surviving occupant. He fired the final armour-piercing round through the false wall and the man behind it, then swapped instantly to projectile and put a dozen bullets through the hole left by the shell. The red dot faded. Mission accomplished: scratch one drugs baron.

But more red dots were converging on this room from both directions in the corridor beyond.

His shimmer suit was still sound everywhere but the legs, so he dropped to his belly when peering out into the corridor and fired to his left from the resultant prone position, instantly rolling over and doing the same to the right, before scrambling back into the room. There were a few bursts of answering fire, but all of it far too late. A couple of the red dots winked out on either side and the others stopped their advance, for the moment at least.

It was going to have to be the window. He raised the gun.

"Opening the window might be quieter," said a familiar voice.

Good point. He pressed the wall control and the glass panes instantly slid upwards, smooth and silent – the system clearly not fingerprint-coded, which made sense in a place with multiple occupants. Besides, the focus of security here was to keep people *out* rather than in. Not that they were doing such a great job of that, either.

He returned to the door and fired a further burst blind down the corridor for good measure, then holstered the gun and dashed across the room, using the noise of the red dots' inevitable response to mask any slight sound as he eased himself out of the window. No red dots outside, thank God. For a brief moment he hung from the sill by straining fingertips, his arms fully extended, before letting go, to roll as he landed on the veranda. He came to his feet and sprinted the few steps to the wall, which he vaulted, pivoting on one hand while gripping the balustrade's top in order to come down in its shadow. He crouched, hugging the wall as he had before entering the house.

Only once he was there, at the very edge of the building's dampener field, did Leyton open up the appropriate frequency and fire off the retrieval signal; a microsecond burst on a very tight beam which would make it impossible to pinpoint should anyone be trying to.

Now all that remained was to wait.

Voices from above him, presumably from the window – the red dots still one step behind. He edged along the wall, crouching low, just in case his exit had been picked up on any security cameras.

Where was his damn pick-up?

Four red dots closing fast, too quickly to be human.

"War hounds," the voice whispered; "armour plating grafted to head and shoulders."

He knew the type: all augmented muscles and steel teeth. They *could* be stopped by a bullet if you were very accurate and very lucky, but there were four of them, and he didn't feel *that* lucky.

"Sonics," he sub-vocalised, reasoning that dogs were sensitive to sound and so might be confused, distressed, or even stopped by it. Though, of course, anything he did was likely to leave him exposed to the guards at the window or elsewhere. Where the hell was that pick-up? He felt a mounting sense of doom, but was determined to fight until the last.

A long bass howl filled the night, sounding as if it came from just around the corner of the house. Seconds left before they arrived. He licked his lips, aware that he was breathing harder than at any time during the mission. Would they come down the steps, over the low wall, or both?

He wanted to step away from the wall and give himself some room, but knew that would leave him exposed. Guards were bound to be hot on the hounds' heels.

Another howl, much closer this time. The red dots were on the veranda, almost on him.

Stuff this! He pushed himself away from the wall, standing upright with gun at the ready. Then came the boom and he felt the push of wind as a craft dropped from the sky to hover above the lawn scant metres away.

"Come on!" yelled a voice.

He didn't need any further urging but was already sprinting towards the gaping hatchway. From the corner of his eye he caught a flash of fur as something large hurtled down the veranda steps. An energy beam sizzled past, fired from the hatchway, and he heard a yelp of pain behind him. But he could hear the other dogs now. It was going to be close.

A machine gun chattered from the direction of the house, though whether aimed at him or the rescue craft he would never be certain. It didn't seem to hit either. Answering fire came from figures crouching in the hatch.

Then he was flinging himself aboard.

"Go!" yelled a voice and the craft lifted, his feet still dangling from the open doorway. Even as someone pulled him in, steel teeth clashed shut a finger's breadth from his ankle, the leaping hound falling back as the craft continued to rise.

Leyton rolled onto his back and let out a whoop of laughter.

"How the hell can he laugh about it?" somebody said.

He sat up, grinning at the soldier who had asked such a stupid question, even though it wasn't directed at him. "I'm alive; how would you expect me to react to that particular revelation – cry?"

A figure loomed forward out of the shadows as he got to his feet. "How did the new visor work out?" That was Benson; the man had no sense of occasion and even less patience, which was typical of government officials in Leyton's experience. He wondered whether they deliberately bred them to be that way.

"Fine; no problem at all."

"And the gun?"

"The same – worked perfectly."

"Naturally," said the gun's familiar whisper. "Did you seriously expect anything less?"

KYLE WAS ON the bridge when the emergency began; which was kind of funny really, because he had just spent the best part of the previous hour moaning to Mac, the ship's captain, about there being nothing for him to do except sit around on the bridge and moan. That and talk about swans, of course.

The only part of the preceding hour not spent on the bridge had been when he slipped away to accost Marie. Marie was petite and cute, with large brown eyes, full lips, a pert little nose and a way of wearing the requisite black and white uniform which seemed to have passed the rest of the passenger service crew by. She somehow made the outfit look sexy, whereas it reduced everyone else to a state of bland androgyny.

You had to admire the young woman's skill and professionalism as well. She never spilled a drop, even when two arms enfolded her from behind without warning.

"Stop that!"

"Stop what?" he said softly into her ear. "I only grabbed you because you looked a little unsteady; thought you were about to fall over."

"Well I wasn't, so you can let go." Her words said one thing, but the way she pressed against him, turning her head to nuzzle his chin with her forehead while grinding her buttocks against his groin, suggested quite the opposite.

"Now why would I want to do that?"

"Because I'm on duty, and I'm holding a tray of drinks... and mind where you put those hands!"

"That's not what you said last..."

"Don't you dare!" Marie stepped away from his embrace and turned to face him, the tray and its liquid burden staying improbably level as she revolved around it. She was evidently trying to look stern but failed dismally; the smile which tugged at the corners of her mouth wrecking any pretence of severity.

He studied her with the sort of quizzical consideration people normally reserve for wall pictures that are hung slightly askew.

"What is it?" she asked, suddenly concerned. "My hair, my makeup...?"

"No, no," he assured her, "nothing like that. You just still look a little... I don't know, unstable. Here, maybe this will help."

He reached forward and picked up two of the chilled champagne flutes, one from either side of the silver serving tray. "Better?"

"Kyle! You know that's for the passengers. I'm not supposed to serve crew."

"Shhh."

"You're unreal."

"Now that's more the sort of thing you said..."

"One more word and I'll throw the whole trayful at you!"

He mimed a kiss, then, grinning, turned and walked the few steps across plush, deep-piled carpet to the door marked 'Flight Crew Only'.

He stared into the retinal scanner and the door swished open. On its far side, the carpet became more practical; harder wearing, but the fact there was carpet at all told you all you needed to know about *The Lady J*.

Contrary to several regulations, the door to the bridge stood open. Nonetheless, he paused at the threshold.

"Permission to enter the bridge?"

"Quit fooling around and get in here with those damn drinks," said a rich, baritone voice. "What took you so long, anyway? Flirting with that pretty brunette waitress, I suppose."

"I wasn't flirting with her, she was flirting with me. And she's not a waitress, she's an In-Transit Passenger Entertainment Officer."

Mac grunted. "She can entertain me any time she likes."

"Ah, but you're not the one she flirts with," Kyle pointed out. He had reached the pilot's chair in which Mac lounged, and now held out one of the drinks.

The slightly older, slightly broader man frowned at the proffered glass. "Champagne again? I thought you were going to get beer." It didn't stop him accepting the glass.

Kyle shrugged. "I can only bring back whatever Marie's carrying. Seems you just can't find the right class of passenger these days."

"Ain't that a fact?"

They clinked flutes and each took a generous swig, the dry effervescence tingling against the back of Kyle's throat as it slid down.

He slumped into the deep leather of the absent navigator's chair. He had no idea where the seat's official occupant, Brad, was at the time – probably cosying up with one of the off-duty service crew. "Now, what were we talking about?"

"Don't care," Mac replied, "so long as it's not swans again."

Kyle had been fascinated by these long-extinct birds ever since he was a kid, when his father had first shown him archive footage of them. He could remember it clearly to this day: a picturesque scene with trees and mountains in the background, a mirror-surfaced lake in the middle-distance and a meadow in the foreground. Perspective had shifted almost at once, zooming in on two white smudges, which started out as mere dots on the water but were now revealed to be magnificent white birds, sailing majestically across the lake as if they owned the place.

Their precise posture, even down to the curve of their necks, could not have been more perfect had they been sculpted by a master aesthetician. It was this deportment that he especially loved, a way of carrying themselves which declared to all the world that these birds were beautiful and they knew it.

Good looks with attitude. Just like *The Lady J*.

Apparently, there had once been a myth that while swans might look serene and elegant on the surface, out of sight, beneath the water, they were paddling away furiously to maintain that image. Which was *exactly* like *The Lady J*. For most of her staff at any rate.

The Lady J was a pleasure cruiser; top of the line, attracting the obscenely rich and famous as well as those with ambitions to become such. In theory, as the ship's In-Transit Systems Engineer, Kyle was one of those responsible for keeping her paddling. In practice, he was barely needed at all; a trophy spaceman to be paraded in front of the passengers from time to time to demonstrate that they were in safe hands.

The ship was just too damn efficient. Or, to put it another way, Kyle was just too damn good. He had managed, in effect, to get himself promoted out of the job he loved. Having cut his teeth in the navy, Kyle found himself at something of a loose end once the War ended. Still a young man, he got a berth as flight engineer on *The Star Witch*, an aged rust bucket of a private trader which should have been sold for scrap long ago. Somehow he performed miracles and kept her engines ticking over. He didn't stay long and there followed a period which saw him flit from one vessel to the next, each subsequent ship being a few notches higher on the evolutionary scale which culminates in 'fully space-worthy'.

Along the way he began to build a reputation as one of the best mechanics around, which brought him to the attention of an altogether superior class of ship owner and eventually led to his current position. Only the best for *The Lady J*; a maxim which extended to her engines and systems – state of the art in every regard, requiring virtually no maintenance whatsoever, which was kind of hard on the man employed to maintain them.

When he first joined the crew of *The Lady J*, Kyle was unable to believe his luck. She had the latest Kauffman Drive, the Mark VI, engines he had never dreamed of seeing, let alone working on. What could be better than this?

That first trip had been the most frustrating of his life. While the cabin crew ran themselves ragged to produce the illusion of effortless efficiency, he could only twiddle his thumbs and look on. His most challenging moment came when a vending machine malfunctioned and started to dispense lukewarm bucks fizz.

The entire ship's systems were subjected to a full diagnostics test at the end of each and every trip. If anything showed up as performing at less than perfect efficiency, that part was immediately replaced. Even the ones that consistently registered as perfect were routinely discarded after a specified time, well within recommended performance parameters. On top of that, multiple redundancy had been built into every conceivable system, leaving Kyle very much the last resort. He found himself relegated from being a hands-on mechanic to simply being on hand in the unlikely event that something should go wrong; but how could it, with a maintenance regime like that?

He didn't really feel as if he was a genuine spacer any more and pined for the challenges of the shit-heap ships of yesteryear. On *The Lady J* he even had his own cabin for goodness sake, and yes, even *it* had carpets.

Despite all this, Kyle still loved *The Lady J*. She was a beautiful vessel. It was just that actually working on her proved to be so utterly *boring*, despite the occasional diversion provided by Marie. He was fast coming to the conclusion that *The Lady J*'s beauty was of the sort best admired from a distance, unless you could afford to be one of her passengers, of course.

Fortunately, he was not the only person on board relegated

to virtual irrelevance by the efficiency of the ship's systems. In Mac, he found a fellow sufferer and soul mate. *The Lady J* effectively flew herself, which meant that her captain's primary function seemed to be to smile at passengers and entertain them at the captain's table during formal dinners. So the pair of them spent much of their time hidden away on the bridge, where they swapped anecdotes about the days when they had been *real* spacemen rather than highly paid back-up systems.

"And what's wrong with swans?" Kyle wanted to know.

"Nothing, nothing." Mac held up a defensive hand. "It's just that I've heard enough about them for today, that's all."

"All right, you pick a subject then."

"Whatever I like?"

"Anything."

"Okay; that little trolley-dolly of yours, are her tits really –"

"– Anything *except* Marie."

Mac snorted. "I might have known."

Further conversation was interrupted by a gentle alarm beep, an innocent 'ping', which was to signal an end to the pair's boredom once and for all. At their failure to respond immediately, the sound repeated, a little louder this time.

"What's that?" Kyle wondered.

"Just *The Lady*'s way of letting me know that there's another ship in this sector," Mac replied, swivelling his chair and sitting forward to view the screens. Once he did so, he frowned.

"Problem?"

"Maybe. Our new companion is surprisingly close, and she seems to be chasing our course."

Curious, Kyle stood up and strolled across, peering over his friend's shoulder to get a better look at the screen. "Coming up on us pretty quickly, too."

"Hmm, I spotted that. Remind me, what's the maximum we can get out of those shiny little engines of yours?"

He knew the answer to that, as did Kyle. "I forget," he said, daring Mac to challenge him.

"Well whatever it is, how about we give *The Lady* a little exercise?" He ran his open palm from left to right over a sensor screen. A line of colour travelled across the crescent-shaped display, following the movement of his hand. The line changed from amber to red as it went, until the previously blank screen glowed a vibrant crimson.

Being *The Lady J*, there was no vibration, no shudder to alert the passengers to the fact that the engines, inert since the minor course adjustments needed as they exited the last jump point, had started up again. The ship's gravity field would protect them from all sense of movement, so, as yet, there was nothing to cause those on board any alarm. Except for Kyle and Mac, of course, and they were beginning to get alarmed enough for the whole shipful, especially when the vessel behind matched their increase in speed without apparent effort, reacting the instant they began to accelerate and continuing to close at exactly the same rate as before.

"The bastard's playing with us," Mac muttered. "Well, I suppose we might as well try being polite." He pressed a control. "This is the cruiser *The Lady J*, out of New Apolis, to unknown ship. Please identify yourself and state your intentions."

To neither man's surprise, the request met with complete silence.

They started to get some telemetry back on the other ship; in fact, they began to get a lot more information than expected.

"Not shy, is she?" Mac commented.

"What the hell *is* this thing?"

"I was hoping you were going to tell me."

"I've never seen anything like her," Kyle admitted, as the figures continued to roll in and the computer started to sketch an image of their pursuer from the data. A bulbous, ungainly craft, bristling with protrusions and arrays.

The weapons systems revealed were daunting in the extreme.

"I take it we're not going to fight." *The Lady* carried a

limited complement of missiles and mines, enough to reassure the passengers that they were not wholly unprotected.

"Are you kidding? Her armament reduces what we've got to the level of a peashooter. If we try to fight it'll only annoy them. I don't even recognise what half that stuff is, let alone what it might do to us."

Kyle peered at the screen. "Those two have to be energy projectors of some kind, but I've no idea what sort."

Mac grunted.

As if to prove the point, twin beams of energy shot forward from their silent nemesis, neatly bracketing *The Lady J* in passing. The ship's systems efficiently analysed their composition and strength.

"Shit," Mac said. "If either of those were actually aimed *at* us and got past *The Lady's* engine burn…"

"Yeah, makes an impressive calling card. It's nice to be proved right and everything, but just this once, I could have lived with being wrong."

Predictably after such a display, the pursuer chose that moment to break her silence. It was a cool, collected, male voice which addressed them. "This is *The Noise Within*, out of your worst nightmares. Please shut down your engines and prepare to be boarded, or face the consequences."

Kyle and Mac stared at each other. Eventually, Kyle said, "I wish he'd stop beating about the bush and say what he really means."

Mac gave a sour smile. "Funny."

"It's at times like this I'm glad you're the captain and I'm just the grease monkey."

"The only grease you've been anywhere near on this trip has been the stuff you put on your hair."

There followed a few seconds' further silence. "I don't suppose we've got much choice."

"Not unless you can think of something I haven't."

Kyle shook his head.

Mac moved his palm across the crescent-shaped screen again, this time from right to left, shutting down the engines. The ship would continue to sail forward, of course, but at a constant velocity, making it easier for their pursuer to match speed and dock.

"We'd better call in the service crew supervisors and bring them up to date before saying anything to the passengers," Mac said.

"I'll wake the other shift as well." He didn't see any reason why the off-duty members of the ship's operational crew – Mac's co-pilot and his own assistant – should miss out on the fun. "And, Mac?"

"Yeah?"

"You know all that complaining I did earlier about being bored? Forget I ever said it, will you?"

"Consider it forgotten."

Kyle saw what Mac was busy calculating and asked, "How long have we got?"

"Well, allowing for her mass and assuming she can perform to a similar spec as *The Lady J*," which seemed unlikely given the quality of their ship's drive, "I'd say we have about ninety-three minutes before she can be in position to board."

The Noise Within managed it in a little under sixty-seven minutes, which went far beyond the limits of being impressive and entered the realms of scary.

The problem the pursuing ship had just overcome so effortlessly was not so much that of overhauling *The Lady J* – she had already shown she could do that – as doing so in such a way that her speed exactly matched *The Lady's* as the two ships drew alongside. If she had continued accelerating at the same rate as when Mac shut the engines down, she could have been there a lot quicker but would have shot past *The Lady* and been forced to turn around and start again. Starships are big behemoths and Kyle knew it took time and deft piloting to slow one down and match velocities with another ship. Much of her final approach would have been spent *de*celerating rather than *ac*celerating.

He was there with Mac, Brad the elusive navigator, and the other two members of the ship's crew – Bryant and Sol – when the main hatch hissed open and six armed and armoured figures came aboard. The armour and weapons were the type of heavy-duty kit that Kyle had not seen since the height of the War, and the boarders operated with clinical, military proficiency. They kept their helmets on and visors darkened, so no one had a chance to see their faces.

The pirates' intelligence was impressive, because they winnowed out who they wanted and didn't want from among the sixty-odd passengers in no time at all, ending up with a party of eight hostages, three women and five men. Even Kyle recognised two of those selected, a politician and an actress, and guessed these would be the eight with the highest net worth.

Clearly it was not just the passengers their captors had designs on, but also *The Lady J* herself, because everyone else, Kyle and Mac included, was herded to the life boats. Fully provisioned and well equipped, the boats would support the whole party for several weeks, and this was not so off the beaten track that they wouldn't be discovered before then, particularly given the strength of the life boats' distress beacons.

A few of the passengers whimpered and one or two cried, but none of them gave the pirates any real problems. In fact, they had given the service crew a great deal more aggravation before the actual boarding, when hysterics and threats abounded, as if the situation were somehow the crew's fault or something they could affect.

At the very last, as everyone was about to be forced into the boats, one of the pirates, his voice turned flat and tinny by the helmet, said, "We're looking for volunteers to join our crew. Anyone interested?"

Kyle was amazed to hear a voice declare, "Yes, me." He was even more amazed to discover it was his own.

*   *   *

PHILIP KAUFMAN WAS not looking forward to this evening. He hated public speaking and avoided it wherever possible, which was ironic when you considered that this was precisely what he was most famous for. Not his ideas, not his achievements, but for talking about them. Though, of course, that wasn't really him doing the talking, and therein lay the crux of the problem.

Three outfits were laid out on the bed, ranging from traditional black evening suit – a one-piece affair with smart trousers that could be adjusted from above-the-knee shorts to full-length longs with a single thought, depending on circumstances and local fashion expectations, to the purple tarlken – a wraparound garment harking back to the togas of ancient Rome, favoured for formal occasions on certain provincial worlds. The suit in the middle, the uniform, had been a mistake and was no longer in the reckoning.

He gazed in the mirror again, picturing himself in each of the outfits in turn. False modesty had never one of Philip's failings, yet at the same time he had few delusions about his appearance; a little taller than average, with a physique that leant towards the athletic but had never been impressively so and a face which boasted pleasant enough features without any that were striking; 'reassuring' was how one girlfriend had described it. His dark eyes were matched by dark brown hair, worn conservatively short even by his own estimate – a habit he'd adopted when first taking control of the company, a deliberate gesture intended to emphasise his maturity and help cement his authority. He smiled into the mirror, revealing a row of even, white teeth, testing what people would see later. The expression helped to round out a face that sometimes verged on being too angular and the result was not too shabby, if he said so himself. Philip was fully aware that the camera liked him even if it would never quite love him.

The truth was, he was capable of carrying off either suit well enough.

He knew what he ought to wear, what he would be expected to wear, but a certain impish side of him was tempted by the tarlken. After all, he was the Guest of Honour, so could get away with being unconventional. Besides, if they would insist that he actually attend their ghastly function in person, let it be on his terms. On the other hand, in the tarlken he would stand out like a sore thumb and that would only make him more self-conscious and, if he fumbled the speech, seem even more ridiculous.

All this fussing amounted to procrastination, and he knew it.

Yet the fact remained that he was about to stand up, open his mouth and disappoint people. It was inevitable. He could never hope to match up to the competition, even though said competition was, in a sense, himself. The problem was that all those famed lectures and speeches had not really been delivered by him at all. Oh, those were his thoughts, his words and they appeared to come out of his mouth, but they had all been delivered by his partial. After all, that was the whole purpose of partials: to do all the things the original organic individual had no time or inclination to do themselves, such as answer the door, take calls, fend off the unwanted, conduct basic research via the infonet, and even deal with routine interviews and deliver lectures if they were sophisticated enough. His was. Of course, the partial was *not* Philip Kaufman as such, but only a reflection of certain elements that made up the actual man.

The thing was, with partials there would always be the temptation to tinker, to tweak ever so slightly. After all, if you could have a lecture delivered by an idealised version of you rather than by an exact reflection of flawed reality, why not go for it?

All the imperfections he perceived in himself had been ironed out from those elements of Philip Kaufman that constituted his partial. It was the perfect orator: suave, confident, never losing its place or pausing for an 'ehm,' each phrase pitched in the appropriate tone, every syllable delivered with exactly the right emphasis. How could the real him possibly hope to compete with that?

Ridiculous but true, he was about to fall short of his own partial.

A discreet tone sounded in his ear.

He sighed. A call was the very last thing Philip needed right now. Though maybe not; maybe this was exactly what he needed: something to while away what little time remained, so that when the call ended he would be forced to make a snap decision, throwing on one of the two garments and rushing down to the waiting limo. A decision he could then regret all the way to the venue.

"Who is it, Phil?"

"Your father."

Oh no, not now. The announcement sent a chill down his spine. This was not his father, of course; his father was dead. It had been typical of the man, though, to ratify his partial; typical of his arrogance. He couldn't have it erased like any normal person, or allow it to fade after a decent interval, no, not the great Malcolm Kaufman. Once confirmation came in that he was dying, he had to enhance the thing, uploading as much of himself as modern technology would allow, so that he might live on in virtual form: transhuman. Usually, such ghosts lasted only until the money ran out – supporting a partial carrying *that* much detail was expensive. Unfortunately, Malcolm Kaufman had enough credit at the time of his death to leave his son comfortably off *and* support his partial for an eternity or two.

That was a decision Philip would never forgive him for.

"I've told you not to refer to him as that." Why did Phil persist in doing so in any case? A display of solidarity among partials, perhaps? He hesitated, tempted to refuse the call, but he knew that if he did so that would only be storing up aggravation for the future. "Put him through. Audio only."

"Mal, I haven't got much time."

"Yes, yes, I know, the Gügenhall lecture," his father's voice said dismissively, "but this is important."

And the Gügenhall isn't?

"Go on."

"You'll need to patch in the visual."

Again Philip hesitated. Hearing his father's voice was difficult enough; watching the man's face as he spoke to him from beyond the grave was too much, so he never activated the visuals when Mal called.

"Don't worry, it won't be me you'll be looking at."

At least that was something. "What then?"

"Go visual and you'll see."

Despite the fleeting conviction that he was going to regret this, Philip complied. Instantly, the 3D image of a ship hovered in the air before him.

"Recognise her?"

Philip frowned. "It looks like…"

"It's *The Noise Within*."

Of course it was. "The pirate ship they've built the latest media circus around?"

"That's the one."

This vessel had already achieved folklore status courtesy of the glamorous coverage afforded it. Despite any suggestion to the contrary by writers and the makers of popular dramas, piracy was not an easy thing to perform. Quite apart from the vastness of space, there were practical considerations which made overhauling and capturing a ship far more difficult than it had been in the days of the Jolly Roger, eye patches and the simple two dimensions of an ocean's ruffled surface. Yet *The Noise Within* was making the act of piracy look *very* easy, first appearing out of nowhere to attack a luxury cruiser called *The Lady J* and then returning three times within as many months, capturing a plum prize on each occasion. All of which was ambrosia to the sensationalist press and reporters desperate to titillate the palate of a jaded public, but what was Mal's interest in the thing?

"Now watch," his father's ghost instructed.

The Noise Within seemed to be anything but coy, leaving itself open to surface scanning with an insolence, a cockiness, guaranteed to fuel the media hysteria. From the resultant telemetry, a detailed picture of the ship's appearance, surface structure and overt, not to mention formidable, weapons capabilities had been produced.

As Philip watched the image before him, elements of the ship's structure began to fade and then disappear entirely. This happened in three stages, with extrusions, bumps, vents, weapon arrays and other parts along the length of the vessel stripped away, layer by layer, to leave a simpler, sleeker shape each time, until it was pared back to a very basic design. One that Philip recognised all too well.

"My God." Of course the design was basic; it had only been a prototype.

"You see?"

"Oh, come on," Philip said, recovering from his initial shock. "You could probably do that with almost any ship; after all, there are only so many basic hull shapes. Knock bits off a million vessels and you'd come up with something that looked like that."

"But this doesn't simply 'look like that' and you know it. This is identical in every respect. I'm telling you, Philip, it's her."

"You can't be certain…"

"Of course I can!" His father's voice rose for the first time. "I designed the fucking thing. Stop being so stubborn, Philip, and trust me on this, will you? It's *The Sun Seeker*. She's finally come home."

The hovering ship faded, to be replaced by an image which Philip had determined never to gaze upon again: that of his father's face.

*   *   *

HE WENT WITH the dinner suit in the end, deciding there were enough distractions already and he could live without *looking* as incongruous as he was inevitably going to feel.

As he sat in the back of the limo en route, it wasn't his choice of clothes that occupied his thoughts or even the imminent speech but rather Mal's revelation about *The Noise Within*. He would be studying the images received in minute detail, yet gut instinct told him that the old man was probably right. Much as he hated to acknowledge the fact, no one knew ships better than Mal Kaufman.

Bad enough that he was about to be upstaged by his own partial's reputation; being made to feel inadequate by *two* partials in the same evening was more than any man should have to put up with, particularly a man reputedly as brilliant as he was.

But such, it seemed, was to be his fate.

CHAPTER TWO

THE CRAFT WAS an odd one. Bulkier than the speedsters commonly used for racing, larger than the one-man exec ships designed for the in-system hopping of business magnates and playboys, and smaller than just about everything else. She was also equipped with more manoeuvring vents and thrusters than any standard vessel had a right to. She needed them.

Jenner, the ship's sole occupant, felt completely at ease as he swooped in on the target asteroid, following its course and rapidly overhauling. He deftly turned his craft through 180 degrees some distance before reaching the rock and fired the engines so that he was accelerating hard against his original momentum. The asteroid commenced to shoot past him, seeming to slow the whole while until the final section drifted past as if in slow motion, allowing him to appreciate the sheer brutal size of the thing as it sailed majestically on a predetermined course, an inanimate leviathan of the spaceways, its irregular surface pitted and craggy, composed mostly of dirty ice. At a little over 12 km, this was hardly the largest asteroid even in this sparse belt, but it was big enough. Soon the entire rock was fully in front of him once more. By the time it was mere tens of metres away Jenner had matched velocities perfectly, to hang behind it like some diminutive, unwanted shadow.

Then he started to ease the ship forward, sliding towards the asteroid's underbelly from his perspective. Jenner had marked the spot he wanted and knew his timing had to be perfect. He also had no doubt that it was.

The rock's steady rotation made the term 'underbelly' inappropriate, since every part of the thing was destined to be 'underneath' at some point, but Jenner always preferred to make his approach this way, watching as one particularly large shadow rolled around the back end of the object. The shadow represented an unusually deep pit, one that was far from natural, and his approach had to be timed perfectly so that his arrival coincided with its. He checked constantly to ensure that it did and that no last-minute adjustments were needed, multiple calculations flying through his brain in fractions of a second.

His craft slipped smoothly into the opening, which was less than double the width of the vessel. Once inside, the fun really started, as he brought the full array of ship's thrusters and vents into play, nudging it this way and that in a lightning-quick series of short, sharp manoeuvres, all designed to match the asteroid's rotation while continuing to move into the chamber hollowed from the rock's innards. The chamber was considerably wider here than at the entrance but, even so, a single miscalculation could spell disaster. Which was fine with Jenner, who had no intention of making any.

In terms of the asteroid's overall size, the chamber was a small one – the rock had not been completely gutted, merely pitted, a cavity gouged into the surface rather than a full coring – leaving enough mass to still be consistent with its size. Jenner eased the small vessel towards the far wall, where a framework of metal braces and mechanical grapples stood ready to receive it. As he felt the ship grasped by the docking mechanism and so made one with the rock, he cut the engines; not with any surge of triumph or flood of relief, but simply with satisfaction at a job well done.

He started to unbuckle his harness and could dimly see movement on the outside of his gel suit as others hurried to help. The figures became clearer as the gel drained away to reveal a trio of white-suited assistants. Then somebody disconnected his head-jack and he forgot all about the figures as reality came crashing down and consciousness fled towards aits central core, withdrawing from the wider world as if it were shallow water draining down a plug hole, or a two dimensional scene folding rapidly in on itself, until all that remained was the limitation of 'me.'

Jenner blinked at the hands which now reached to help with his harness, and squinted up at half-familiar faces which he felt certain would be fully recognisable once he had regained some equilibrium.

One in particular loomed closer as the helmet came off, the air feeds pulling out from his nostrils, a young woman. Pretty, with a small mouth, cute snub nose and large almond eyes – a little bloodshot as if overtired, but still pretty – a face which he categorised as being vaguely oriental.

The headache kicked in; a searing lance of pain which emanated from somewhere deep in his skull and found a focus in the centre of his forehead.

He must have winced, because the young woman asked, "Are you okay?"

"Yes," he lied automatically. The pain had settled now to a throbbing ache. Perhaps it was just wishful thinking, but this time around it seemed less intense than usual.

Gel clung to his face in amber globules, tickling his cheek where a clump slid down, while its antiseptic taste clogged his mouth and nose. "Yes I'm fine, thanks," her name came to him at the very last second, "Lara."

She smiled, and only then did he remember that he loved her.

PHILIP KAUFMAN SUPPRESSED a stab of envy as he watched the young pilot, Jenner, being helped from the simulator. His gaze flickered down to the multiple readings on the desk screen before him, which looked perfect at first glance. No question that this was their best prospect.

In truth, Philip was finding it hard to concentrate on the figures. His thoughts were still preoccupied with everything that had happened the previous evening and that morning. On arriving at work he had cleared his diary for the day, told his staff he was not to be disturbed for anything short of imminent global disaster and then spent the best part of the morning tinkering – dissecting the images Mal had sent through last night, deconstructing them and then building a program which could exactly mimic the stripping away of the ship's hull. After that he refined it, so that the initial three stages occurred in ever smaller steps, until individual attachments could be plucked away at will. Once perfected, he applied the result to a series of standard hull designs, running the program backwards and forwards, adding layers of body kit, sensor arrays, weapons systems and the other accoutrements that *The Noise Within* boasted, before reversing the process and taking them away, only to begin again.

Several times he had ended up with something that outwardly resembled *The Noise Within* but which, under closer examination, never quite measured up; literally. However similar the resultant image might appear to be, detailed analysis would reveal that the actual proportions varied significantly from those of the enigmatic pirate vessel. Only in a single instance was the match perfect in every determinable regard – the very last hull on which he tried the process; that of *The Sun Seeker*.

One of a multitude of pioneering ideas developed during wartime and spawned by the insatiable quest for tactical advantage, *The Sun Seeker* was a unique vessel – it had to be. True, Malcolm Kaufman had begun the design with the specs for a standard ship's chassis, but he and his team had constantly reconfigured them, changing dimensions and proportions as the project evolved. The hull which the shipyards eventually produced for him was not quite the same as anything they had birthed either before or since.

And now Malcolm's son and heir had become completely absorbed in analyses inspired by the ghost of that vessel, attacking the task with an obsessive focus that precluded all else. By the time he had finished that morning, any doubt regarding the true identity of *The Noise Within* had been well and truly swept away. Gut instinct was shown to be right again; his father's partial really *had* stumbled on the truth. *The Noise Within* was definitely *The Sun Seeker* reborn.

Whatever his misgivings where Mal was concerned, the partial had given him exactly what he needed, what they all needed. If this didn't spur on those board members whose resolution had begun to waver of late, nothing would.

Having reached this conclusion he took time to review everything, to ensure that he had considered all the angles and covered every pitfall. Only then did he summon the other board members to an extraordinary meeting.

It had come as no surprise when Catherine was the first to call.

Catherine Chzyski was one of the most formidable people Philip had ever met. He was told that she had been a great beauty in her youth. He didn't believe it.

Philip had seen photographs and holographic recordings of the younger Catherine and he still didn't believe it. Perhaps his perception was too clouded by the image of the hard-faced woman he knew – pepper-grey hair habitually pulled back from her prominent forehead to reinforce the severe countenance – for him to ever see her as beautiful, or perhaps she never had been, whatever reports might claim to the contrary.

"You should have known her back then," one of his father's colleagues – a man who *had* known her in her youth – once told him, "before she partnered, before she had responsibilities, in the days when she didn't have a care in the world. She took society by storm. It wasn't just her looks, you see, it was her spirit – the force of personality which animated the flesh. She had an aura, a genuine presence. Magnificent, truly magnificent." This last was spoken wistfully, with a shake of the head as if to dissipate lingering memories.

Philip was still far from convinced.

Catherine's face peered at him from the viewscreen, her mouth pursed in waspish disapproval, momentarily diverting his attention from her too-sunken cheeks. She had always spurned the temptations of rejuve and instead flaunted her age as if it were some badge of honour, famously destroying one young and pretty reporter impetuous enough to raise the subject in the space of two sentences: "I earned this face and I'm going to keep it. Can you say either of those things about your job?"

After appraising Philip for a second, Catherine spoke. "A meeting, you say. Today. In person."

"Yes," he replied simply.

Her eyes were the only feature that hinted at a glorious past; clear, bright and of a piercing blue. For long seconds her gaze held his, as if measuring his worth, his integrity. It was all he could do not to flinch.

"Very well," and, with a nod of farewell, she broke the connection.

Philip let out a breath which he hadn't even realised he was holding. At least Catherine had not been crass enough to ask *why* he was calling the board together. She for one had the intelligence to realise that he would not be insisting on a physical meeting were he willing to discuss the subject so readily.

If only others were equally as perceptive.

"What the hell's this all about, Philip?" David Benn had demanded.

"I'll tell you at the meeting."

"Don't be ridiculous. I can't simply drop everything just on your say so!"

But he did.

"Well?" demanded a familiar voice.

Philip's reveries slipped away. He hadn't even noticed the

approach of Susan Tan, his senior research assistant.

"Looks pretty good," he temporised, while pulling his focus back to the readings in front of him.

"*Pretty* good? That was fantastic!"

"Perhaps," and his eyes darted across the figures, seeking imperfections and finally focusing on something, "but that approach turn and acceleration would have killed him in real life, if not for the gelsuit."

She snorted. "Oh, come on. That's like saying that in real life he'd have died in the near-vacuum of space without the ship; which is why we build ships and why we've designed the gelsuit. You're going to have to do better than that."

She was right, but at least the banal observation had given him enough time to hunt down more significant indicators. "Look at the stress levels," he said, pointing to the relevant figures. "You're right, that performance was just about perfect, but this was one manoeuvre lasting only a matter of minutes… and just *look* at the strain! If we'd subjected Jenner to a couple of hours of this, let alone a day or two, he'd most likely be dead."

And therein lay their real frustration. No matter what drugs they fed in and cushioned it with, no matter the gelsuit and all the other physical supports they provided, the human brain still struggled to operate at these levels for any length of time; it simply couldn't keep up without burning itself out. Yet they were so close. He could sense it, everyone involved could sense it.

"I know." Susan's sigh was a weary one. "But this is something, isn't it?"

"Yes," he agreed, "it's more than just something. This is fabulous progress." He left the many 'buts' unspoken; Susan could hear them as clearly as he could. Philip checked the time, and was surprised at how much of it had passed. "I have to go."

"Ah yes, this mysterious board meeting of yours. Maybe, if I'm lucky, you'll eventually get around to telling me what it's about some time."

Philip suppressed a smile. Susan's inquisitiveness was legendary. He supposed it went with the territory; after all, what good was a senior researcher who didn't yearn to discover things?

"When I can," he assured her. He gave her shoulder a reassuring squeeze. "You'll be the first to know, I promise."

"I'll believe that when I see it."

He afforded her a wry smile from under raised eyebrows but turned without further comment and strode away.

"More likely I'll be the last, as usual," she called after him.

Philip returned to his office. He knew there were preparations to make before the meeting but was strangely reluctant to begin them. His thoughts kept returning to *The Sun Seeker* and all that the ship meant to his company, his family.

He picked up a statuette awarded him for innovation some years ago, running his fingers distractedly over the familiar contours of the clichéd rocket ship's hull, putting it back only to pick it up again. He couldn't sit down, could not stop fidgeting, while his mind switched incessantly between considering the past and reviewing that morning's work. With a conscious effort he battened down the former and concentrated on the latter, reaffirming its significance to his own satisfaction and making sure that he wasn't allowing his enthusiasm to run away with him and cloud his judgement.

No, this really was as important as he imagined it to be. He found himself near-breathless with an excitement unmatched since the very earliest days of the ongoing project, the latest chapter of which he had just witnessed.

The somewhat blandly named Homeworld may not have been the centre of the universe, or even of that small portion of it claimed as human space, but at least Kaufman Industries had ensured that the planet's name remained prominent on any map. Popular myth had it that the world's underwhelming name came about because this was the world where a base was first established when this section of space was originally being explored. Those early pioneers, weary after protracted time in the cramped confines of their ships, would talk about returning to 'home base' or simply 'home' and the name had stuck, expanding to encompass the whole world. Philip had no idea whether the story was apocryphal or not, but a sentimental part of him hoped it wasn't.

Kaufman Industries had been innovators in ship systems and engine design for three generations, rising to real prominence under the stewardship of Philip's father. Malcolm Kaufman had overseen the development of the Kaufman Drive, a completely new approach to the propulsion systems which powered starships through wormholes and enabled them to sidestep the laws of physics and traverse the gulf between the stars. So revolutionary was the system, so much cleaner and more compact than anything seen before, that the name 'Kaufman' soon became synonymous with all ship's engines in the minds of the general public.

Such success came at a price, and competitors were quick to latch on to Kaufman Industry's meteoric rise, doing all they could to hang onto KI's shirt tails. 'Imitation is the greatest form of flattery; except when it hits you in the bank balance!' had been one of the company's maxims since Malcolm's time. KI's past was littered with lawsuits against the manufacturers of devices with such dubious epithets as the 'Kouffman Drive' and the 'Kautman Drive', all with suspiciously familiar logos.

Yet despite its eminence and despite having branches on over half the settled worlds – including every single one that mattered – the company's roots were surprisingly provincial and their power base remained so. The seven people who joined Philip in the boardroom towards the end of that day represented almost the entire board of Kaufman Industries. Only Daniel Ackerman was absent, being out of town and unable to get back in time.

Philip was well aware of the irony of the situation: only the previous evening he had been cursing the organisers of the Gügenhall for insisting he attend an event in person, and now here he was, dragging seven equally reluctant souls across town to do the same. However, he had examined his own motives carefully. He was wholly satisfied that the situation merited every precaution, and that this was not some form of perverse transference of his own enforced discomfort. At least, not entirely.

He waited while the others took their seats before sitting down himself at the head of the magnificent polished rosewood table – so deliciously retro with its rounded corners and edges inlaid with gold and imported mahogany; so pleasingly incongruous in this setting. The room itself was a functional oblong space with plain walls and a trio of large plate-glass windows. The latter had been treated with a patented nano-coating designed to break up the rhythm of vibration and so prevent their being used as a sounding board by any would-be eavesdroppers. The imposing table with its complement of ten hand-carved and equally impressive chairs – four to either side and one at each end – might have been lifted from another world, another time. Furniture and room provided a jarring juxtaposition between the practical and the ornate, one which Philip delighted in.

"This had better be important, Philip!" Benn growled before Philip even had a chance to bring the meeting to order.

"Now, David, I'm sure our chairman would not have been so insistent we should be here in person if it weren't," Catherine Chzyski said before flashing her disgruntled colleague a misleadingly pleasant smile. "Would you, Philip?"

Her mouth might have been smiling, yet those piercing blue eyes were anything but as they turned towards him. Philip could almost hear the unspoken 'dared to' in her gentle rebuke to Benn. He swallowed on a suddenly dry throat. "Thank you, Catherine. Indeed I would not."

She was the key here. Even within such a small group as this, alliances and cliques were inevitable as people shuffled to gain advantage. Catherine represented the traditionalists on the board, with a history of influence stretching back to long before Philip's time. There were even whispered rumours of an affair between her and Malcolm, which Philip had never chosen to listen to or explore. At least two of the others here would follow Catherine's lead; if he could convince her of the significance of all this and what it meant to their project, he would all but have won the day. Philip took a deep breath and began.

"I apologise for dragging you here in person, but, as we all know, any form of electronic or virtual conferencing is susceptible to interception, no matter how sophisticated the security safeguards, and what I have to show you is far too sensitive to risk a leak before we're ready to go public." He didn't mention that electronic communication was precisely how *he* had learnt of the matter in the first place.

A holographic image of *The Noise Within* appeared, to take station above the centre of the table.

"I take it we all recognise what this is?" he enquired. Judging by the nods and murmurs that went around the room, they did.

"*The Noise Within*," someone muttered helpfully.

"Indeed, but you may be surprised to learn that she's far more than just that." The image began a slow horizontal rotation.

This time around the transformation was far more impressive than the dry simplicity Mal had presented the previous evening, which had resembled an academic teaching module. Philip had designed his version for maximum effect; taking full advantage of the larger scale and his own revised program. As the ship turned, gaining speed by imperceptible increments, individual arrays and attachments floated away from the hull one at a time, only to disappear as they departed. This happened slowly to start with but gained speed to match the image's rotation. Soon parts were detaching in rapid succession. Choreographed as if it were some elegant dance, the process was initially regal and restrained but built towards a flailing crescendo of disappearing parts, stripping the vessel down to its basic hull in the space of a few moments.

Philip surreptitiously studied his fellow directors as the show unfolded, pleased to see that all of them were absorbed by the metamorphosis and delighted to hear a sharp intake of breath from more than one as the slightly stunted, uncommonly bulbous form of *The Sun Seeker* began to emerge. A few seconds' stunned silence greeted the ship's full unveiling.

"You can't be serious," someone said – Pete Bianco, judging by the pinched, nasally whine of the voice. One of Catherine's lackeys.

"Oh, but I am. This much-fêted ship, this latest cause célèbre of the media, is none other than *The Sun Seeker* reborn."

A babble of voices erupted

"But where has she been all this time?"

"… can't be!"

"And where did she get the armament and the modifications?"

"Preposterous!"

Philip waited until the initial reaction began to wane before holding up a restraining hand. "Please!" The babble died away completely. All eyes were on him. "I have no idea where the ship has been or what has happened to her in the meantime, but that's not the point. Am I the only one here who's able to grasp the significance of this?"

Catherine had sat silent, watching him throughout. He suspected that she at least understood the implications.

"That long-ago experiment which everyone assumed had failed *hasn't*," Philip continued. "The proof is out there right now. Think about it. This ship, which we've all heard so much about, this vessel which pops up out of nowhere to run rings around the space service, making the authorities look like a bunch of inept fools in the process, is *The Sun Seeker*!" These last words were almost bellowed.

A few calculating glances flickered around the table.

Philip's voice was again calm and controlled as he resumed speaking into the silence. "What further proof does anyone need that we are very much on the right track? The project puts us light years ahead of the opposition. We've always had our detractors and I know that even some of you in this room have harboured doubts of late, but what are they going to say now – those people who called the project folly, a waste of money and resources?"

One or two of his colleagues looked fleetingly uncomfortable. Philip avoided looking directly at David Benn, whose overheard comment he had just quoted, but hoped the man felt as discomfited as he deserved. Realisation was starting to dawn on a few of their faces, but Philip pushed the point home in any case. He was beginning to enjoy himself. "Who else are the government going to turn to once the truth gets out? Who are the only people equipped to pull their collective arses out of the fire? Us! Nobody else has anything even remotely resembling the project in development. Since Shippeys pulled the plug on their own parallel project five years ago, we've been the only players in the game; which means that only Kaufman Industries have any hope of producing a system that can go head-to-head with *The Noise Within* and win."

He paused and stared at each of their faces in turn. Then he continued, very deliberately, "We are the only people *anywhere* who might stand a chance of actually beating mankind's first AI-controlled starship."

CHAPTER THREE

A FEW SEATS away to his left a marine snapped open the magazine compartment on an oversized cannon of a gun which was currently perched on his lap – the type of weapon that Leyton would never dream of carrying into battle in a million years; too heavy, too restricting. After a few seconds' close examination, the man slammed the flap shut again in a dramatic gesture which was clearly designed to emphasise his macho credentials and reassure anyone interested that he was not in the least bit nervous. A sure sign that he was. The soldier caught Leyton watching him and glared, as if inviting a comment.

Their destination, Holt, was a grubby ball of rock at the fringe of human space. Fourth planet out in a solar system which boasted several smaller worlds and one more distant gas giant, it was a little smaller than Earth and a little denser, with marginally less gravity and a day–night cycle which was fractionally longer. This was a barren, inhospitable world for the most part, the only exception being around its equatorial belt, where a few humans scratched a living. It boasted just a single major town – a former mining settlement.

Holt had a port, a trickle of exports from the few mines which stubbornly refused to close down, an abundance of drinking houses, a relaxed attitude to the law, and a dislike for the new order. Holt had been on the losing side in the War. Memories lingered in this region and resentment ran deep. It was a place where terms such as 'resistance' and 'piracy' were easily confused. In short, this was a perfect bolthole for the freebooters and opportunists who plied their trade in the gaps, the gaping holes which were inevitable in the fabric of a society still knitting itself together following more than a century of conflict. This was one of several fringe worlds to declare independence at the end of the War, and the newly constituted government, the United League of Allied Worlds, had too many other priorities at the time to afford it much notice. A situation destined not to last. Leyton suspected that the name 'Holt' appeared on a long list somewhere and it was only a matter of time before the ULAW authorities turned their attention this way. In the meantime, the current situation gave the authorities all the excuse they needed to teach this rebellious world a lesson.

Until a few hours ago, Leyton had never heard of Holt. Now he knew far more about the place than he ever wanted to – the terrain around their projected landing area, the layout of the town centre, approaches and entry points to the spaceport's admin and control centre, the strength of opposition they were likely to face from local militia, population density...

He felt a little punch-drunk, as if he were being shunted from pillar to post without the chance to catch his breath. Everything was being done in a rush. They hadn't even paused to give him a proper debrief following his last mission, but instead had thrown him straight into this one. In place of the usual detailed preparation, he was being force-fed the lowdown on the target world through his visor-gun link while in transit. Diagrams, schematics and 3D mock-ups flashed across his vision, while the gun's placid voice unveiled detail after nit-picking detail. No formal briefing, no opportunity to get a feel of the situation, just a constant flow of facts on the run. Until, that is, he put a stop to it by saying, "Enough!"

"Know thine enemy," the gun admonished.

"I now know plenty, thank you."

"The condensed information has been carefully calculated to..."

"... drive me nuts. I said 'enough'!"

The woman in the seat opposite smiled sympathetically, as if to indicate she knew exactly what he was going through. But he didn't trust that smile. It was easy enough to twitch the corners of your mouth upwards, but when he looked beyond that surface expression at the eyes which watched him from beneath a visor identical to his own, they seemed mocking, suggesting that she was laughing *at* him rather than with him. He allowed his gaze to slide away, feeling indifferent to the assumed superiority he had sensed in the woman from the first. Leyton had no idea if she had a problem with men in general or just with him specifically. Nor did he care.

He knew most of the other eyegees – after all, there were as yet only a dozen or so of them in total – but she was new to him. She had been introduced as Boulton, and was perhaps a year or two younger than him. Her body was as fit and well toned as he'd expect in an eyegee, and she was pretty enough in an austere sort of way, but there was a coldness about her, a frostiness which precluded attraction. They'd exchanged polite banalities on meeting, enough for her to make it clear that she preferred their interaction to remain at this sort of superficial level. Surprisingly, despite the rarity of encountering a fellow intelligent gun-toter, so did he.

He wondered whether Boulton's gun had been lecturing *her* en-route. Probably not; doubtless she had been afforded the luxury of a proper briefing.

Having dismissed the girl, his gaze settled on the other members of their 'team'. Tellingly, they all sat a little away from the two eyegees, even the soldiers. It was subconscious, he felt sure, but there was a two-seat gap between Boulton and the rest of the group; three on his side of the craft. Along from Boulton, one of the two techs fiddled with laptop equipment of some sort, forehead creased in a frown as if unhappy with something. His older colleague appeared oblivious to any problem and was currently leaning forward, nattering to the trooper who sat nearest to Leyton. She wore the black flashes of special forces on her suit and her ginger hair was little more than freshly cropped stubble, lending her head an angular, block-like severity. Despite that, she looked to be barely out of her teens. Beside her, one of the other troopers sat back with eyes closed, saving his energy for when it would be needed. The man seemed skinny, barely bulking his suit out at all. His relaxed posture might account for some of that, but not all. Opposite him sat the marine with the cumbersome gun. He was staring away from the two eyegees, towards the front of the shuttle. The gun was now propped against an empty seat beside him, its butt resting on the floor while the business end pointed towards the ceiling. It stood as tall as its seated owner. Leyton just hoped the marine had remembered to leave the safety on. Beyond the two techs sat the soldiers' commander, a Sergeant Black. He was evidently absorbed in checking his shimmer suit's various sub-systems for the umpteenth time. An obsessive-compulsive, but presumably that didn't interfere with his efficiency or he wouldn't have been there.

The stubble-haired girl glanced across at Leyton. They locked gazes for an instant – long enough for him to note how pale a blue her eyes were; almost grey. She nodded before turning her attention back to the tech – an expression which conveyed respect but no hint of warmth. There were special forces and special forces, it seemed.

Leyton decided to emulate the example of the skinny trooper and sat back, closing his eyes, but found himself overly aware of the woman in the seat opposite. He couldn't shake the feeling that she was staring at him, though he resisted the temptation to open his eyes again to check.

It was rare for members of the so-called Intelligent Gun Unit to work together. The technology involved in creating the guns and the human-weapon pairings was prohibitively expensive and still in its infancy, which was why there were so few of them. As a result, demand for the gun–human partnerships, across a spread of nearly three hundred inhabited worlds, moons and stations, far outstripped their availability. Besides, the eyegees were invariably loners by nature.

So why did this smug cow remind him so much of Mya?

Leyton knew that elsewhere in the sector, at that very moment, a stealth shuttle similar to this one was dropping towards another planet bearing its own hand-picked team which likewise boasted two eyegees. For the powers-that-be to commit as many as four of them to a single venture spoke volumes about the importance they placed on the mission.

No question, *The Noise Within* was the hot topic of the moment, though all this seemed like complete overkill to him. After all, pirates were hardly the usual concern of eyegees. What was the navy there for, for goodness sake?

They came in hard and fast, shedding velocity as the craft tore through the planet's atmosphere. How in the name of heaven this qualified as a 'stealth' shuttle was beyond Leyton.

He must have sub-vocalised the thought, because the gun responded. "Circumstances dictate this particular approach; the craft *is* capable of far more subtle atmospheric insertion. Currently, much of the energy generated by our entry is being absorbed and stored by the hull, and this will be used after landing to maintain stealth functions. Velocity, heat signature and other indicators have been carefully calculated to match those of a meteor smaller than the actual shuttle. Meteor strikes are not unknown in this region."

The eyegee let the words wash over him. Half of this he knew already, while the other half undoubtedly consisted of leftovers from the aborted briefing. If the gun was really this determined to impart its programmed knowledge, best to get it out of the way now rather than later on when they were groundside and into the mission proper.

Without warning the craft shuddered and all on board were thrown sideways in their harnesses. Leyton knew this must mark the release of the 'cannon ball', which meant they were nearly down. A lump of iron fired from the craft to smash into the ground a short distance from their designated landing site, the cannon ball served two purposes: the act of firing would rob the shuttle of some of its momentum and, just as importantly, the impact would be consistent enough with a meteor strike to keep any groundside seismologists happy. Almost immediately on the heels of this jolt came the landing itself, which, theoretically, was 'cushioned', the shuttle's passengers spared the worst effects of accumulated g-force as the craft dumped a significant amount of residual velocity at the very last minute. Leyton had experienced plenty of 'cushioned' landings in the past so knew what to expect. A huge weight pressed down on him, as if determined to grind his body into the seat. One of the techs let out a muffled whimper, so presumably he was that lucky individual for whom this was a whole new experience, but everyone else bore the brief seconds of intense discomfort with stoic determination. Thankfully, it really *did* last for only seconds, and the pressure was guaranteed not to be beyond the body's ability to cope; though Leyton had yet to discover who issued said guarantee.

The weight lifted. They were down.

Leyton slapped the release and the seat straps sprang open. He was on his feet instantly and was first across to the door, arriving even as it hissed open to allow the landing ramp to unfurl. A wall of chill air greeted him, sucking the comparative warmth from the confines of the shuttle's interior and stinging his cheeks. Before the sun had a chance to warm the world, temperatures here tended to hover just a little above freezing. Breath plumed around his face and Leyton shivered, even though he was ready for the cold. Fortunately, there was no time to hang around. Without waiting for the ramp to fully deploy, he crouched and dropped to the ground – actions made only marginally awkward by the armoured shimmer suit. Boulton was out a second or two behind him, dropping from the shuttle on the other side of the ramp.

Leyton pulled the hood of the shimmer suit up, sealing it around his visor and activating the suit itself. He always left this to the very last minute, feeling one step away from reality once the suit was sealed and ears and nostrils were confined to the same limited space as the rest of him. Oh, the suit's sound system was excellent, but it was still hearing once removed and provided an oddly disassociated sense of being.

Around him, the marines were doing the same; sealing their suits in preparation of moving out.

The gun stayed silent, which meant there was no obvious danger close enough to worry about. Nonetheless, Leyton scanned the terrain, examining every nook and cranny for sign of potential threat. The area was a barren one, depicted in shades of listless grey, probably not helped by their choice of landing time – a few minutes before dawn, intended to catch as few of the locals awake and alert as possible. They had come down behind a low bluff of rock which hid them from the town. The terrain in the immediate vicinity seemed to consist predominantly of loose stone, mosses and sparse tufts of scruffy grass, as if more complex plants struggled to establish themselves here.

The ULAW strategists who planned this mission reckoned that stealth was likely to prove more effective than force, so their party had deliberately been kept small. The idea was to ghost in, grab the information they needed and get out again before the locals even knew they were there – less complicated and decidedly less messy than a full-blown military assault. Personally, Leyton could have done with the group being smaller still. A total of one would have suited him perfectly.

Their progress was to be aided by the navy, who were supposed to provide a distraction at the appropriate time, but the eyegee knew better than to count on such things.

Their actual deployment had been settled in advance. Leyton took point, moving out immediately while the soldiers organised themselves in protective formation around the two techs. Boulton would lag behind and act as rearguard, so maximising the cover provided by the two eyegees.

"On the way back, we swap," Boulton had insisted, apparently accepting Leyton's authority but still determined to underline her own at the same time. He was not about to argue the matter; so long as they got the job done. Besides, if it meant there was as much distance as possible between him and her, he was more than happy. If he were honest, Leyton hated having to work with other people – not just Boulton, *any* people. The gun and he were used to operating as a self-contained independent unit; the need to consider others while in the field could only hamper his choices and compromise his effectiveness.

A wave of very welcome heat washed over Leyton's entire body as soon as he began to move – the suit doing its job. The heating system was something else developed during the War. Throughout human history conflict had always offered one silver lining: while focusing the human mind on trying to find ever more efficient ways of killing one another, useful by-products tended to emerge, as technology took giant leaps forward in all sorts of unexpected directions. The stealth shuttles and the shimmer suits were the product of deliberate design, but the heating system perhaps less so. For this outing, the party had been equipped with the latest model of shimmer suits, which were both armoured *and* wired. The latter meant that so long as they kept moving they would never freeze, despite the worst that the local climate might throw at them.

A web of fine, flexible wires lay beneath the suits' outer skin, concentrated around muscles and joints and supporting a host of storage cells – miniature batteries. Use of muscles generates excess heat, which the system was designed to capture, absorb and store, feeding back into the body when required. Not sweltering, not fireside hot, but enough to banish debilitating cold and keep the body functioning even in extreme conditions.

Leyton's suit also had a few other advantages, courtesy of its smart nano-coating. Did Boulton's boast the same? Probably.

"All clear?" he sub-vocalised.

"I would have told you otherwise." True, the question was redundant, but being responsible for others was putting him on edge. "There is nothing larger than a medium-sized rodent in the immediate area," the gun continued, before adding unnecessarily, "and said rodent is not armed."

"Point taken."

Timing was crucial, with speed the essence of this mission, so Leyton didn't hang around worrying whether or not Black could organise the techs and his squad of half a dozen troopers in short order, trusting that the man was capable of doing so. As the eyegee rounded the bluff the sun chose to put in an appearance – a watery crescent peeking over the horizon and gracing the world with pallid light. It failed to make the place seem any less grey.

Between Leyton and the sliver of sun stood the town – irregular pillars of concrete interspersed with blocks of squat stone whose severe edges and corners were cast in stark relief by the sun's wan glow. Closest of all stood the spaceport, the reason they were here.

Blocking his path to the port there was a fence, of sorts. The thing looked to be more symbolic than functional; a statement that 'this is ours' rather than a barrier intended to keep any determined interlopers out. No harm in checking though, just on the off-chance it had been deliberately designed to give that impression.

"Defences?"

"None."

As he'd thought; presumably 'determined interlopers' were not especially common on Holt.

Leyton holstered the gun, not needing it for this and, besides, just because the fence was unsophisticated did not mean that the whole base was. The chances were that an energy weapon's discharge would register somewhere with someone. So instead, the eyegee took out a small metallic tube from his belt; an object which resembled an oversized pen. Holding his breath, he pointed it at the fence and depressed the trigger, moving his arm to trace the shape of a broad archway as he did so. Pressurised liquid shot from the tube. The fence's metal links bubbled, steamed and melted as the stream of highly corrosive acid struck home. By the time the tube was exhausted, Leyton's hand was pointing towards the very foot of the fence. He waited a few seconds and then kicked the section of meshing in front of him. It gave way, catching at the bottom on the uneven ground but, with a little more persuasion, it swung open like a reluctant gate.

A sudden high-pitched wail interrupted the silence and he froze, afraid that he had triggered an alarm despite the gun's assurances. His head snapped up towards the sound and his hand automatically reached for the gun, but it was only a night bird, or rather the local equivalent. A translucent form sailed past overhead – tapering body and wide-spread wings which rippled as if made from some form of gelatinous material. The splayed wings were completely see-through. The creature sailed gracefully on with its mouth gaping open. The screech seemed to be less a call and more the product of air passing through its body in what looked to be a crude form of jet propulsion. Leyton was tempted to ask the gun whether it had any info on the strange avian, but resisted, fearing another lecture.

As the creature vanished from sight, his attention returned to the job in hand. A series of green dots appeared in his visor, showing that the rest of the party hadn't hung around and were now close behind him. All the more reason for him to hurry onward. He set out at a steady trot – a pace he could maintain for hours if need be, even in an oxygen-light atmosphere such as this. The ground here was hard, compact and uneven –

rutted by tyre tracks from long ago – but that didn't slow him.

A cluster of amber dots appeared towards the left of his visor, the colour indicating that the gun had yet to determine whether they represented a threat or not.

"Dogs," the voice supplied.

Leyton cursed. A shimmer suit might deceive the eye and obscure a heat signature, but it did nothing whatsoever to disguise scent. "Augmented?"

"No, completely natural."

Which still didn't answer the question of whether these were guard dogs or simply a pack of feral hounds living within the spaceport compound. He looked, but they weren't yet visible.

He kept a wary eye on the visor as he drew level with the hounds' position. One dot detached itself from the globular mass and began to move towards him. He looked again and could see it now. The pack must be lying down, either in a deep rut or simply hidden by the grass. But this one had stood up and so exposed itself. Leyton saw a tawny coat, long legs and spindly body. Not your regular guard dog type, that much was certain, and the dog's approach was tentative, as if inspired by curiosity rather than being an obvious attempt to intercept. Despite this, the visor dot's colour deepened towards the red as the hound drew nearer. Leyton didn't really think this represented a threat, but he readied the gun in any case. The animal stopped approaching and simply stood with neck extended and head lifted, scenting the wind. Leyton relaxed as the dog made no effort to pursue. As anticipated, curiosity, not attack. After he moved past without any further reaction, the dot slipped back to amber.

Then, behind him, he heard the sibilant *phut* of silenced weapons and the inquisitive amber dot winked out. He cursed, wondering if he was the only one here concerned about concealment, but he didn't want to risk using the radio and so carried on, hoping the other dogs wouldn't come any closer and that the soldiers weren't *too* trigger-happy.

To Leyton's relief the rest of the dots moved away, causing him to wonder whether this wasn't the first time the dogs had been shot at. Perhaps port security took pot shots when they got bored, which was probably most of the time in this miserable place.

The hulk of a derelict shuttle loomed ahead of him, the back part of its fuselage blackened by what he assumed to be a calamitous drive malfunction, but may equally have been combat damage. Leyton kept the wreck between himself and the fast-approaching buildings as much as possible. Their path had been planned to bring them through an unused part of the port, but now that he was getting close to the hangars and terminals contact with the natives was inevitable. Shimmer suits were all well and good but they worked most effectively when their wearer was stationary. Leyton was more than happy to hedge his bets by utilising whatever cover the surroundings offered.

Red dots now. In the buildings beyond the shuttle. Not many – skeleton crew only at this hour – and no indication that any of them were patrolling, so probably just your average Holtan employees doing whatever Holtans did. Why bother with security in a place like this? Leyton paused by the craft's charred fuselage, taking a moment to catch his breath and get his bearings. Two concrete blocks, each uglier than the other and each containing a handful of red dots. His path lay between them. He jogged on, passing the two buildings but stopping at their far corner, to wait for the main party to catch up with him. The control centre was in plain sight, another ugly box, five storeys high. A wide avenue separated him from it. The green dots drew closer, though two remained by the shuttle husk, presumably to provide cover for their retreat if it were needed. Good move. Leyton's respect for Black grew.

There were half a dozen red dots showing in the target building, all bar two of them in the room they were headed for.

One of those two appeared to be stationary, while the other was on the move. The control centre was the one building sensitive enough that it probably *did* merit guarding, no matter how theoretical any threat might be. Those in the room were most likely systems operators and admin, but the two outside it were almost certainly guards – one on patrol and the other at a monitoring station. An important part of Leyton's job was to ensure that nobody in the control room had the chance to sound the alarm and summon reinforcements, while Boulton was tasked with running interference and ensuring that, if any reinforcements were dispatched, they didn't get as far as Leyton and the others.

His visor stripped the shimmer suits of their camouflage and he watched as Black led the two techs and the other soldiers up to him.

"Two guards," he whispered to the sergeant. "I'll take care of them. Wait here and watch the door." He then crossed the intervening avenue.

"Locked and alarmed," the gun told him as he approached the front door. Neither were problems in themselves, but the red dot at the security monitors was bound to be alerted immediately if he broke in or even opened the door, so it was just as well he had other plans.

"Windows?"

"Secured, but no alarms."

Good enough.

The building was brick-built and looked solid. He pressed the palm of one hand against the wall as a test, waiting for a second to make sure the smart skin had melded before tugging. A little dust resulted, but otherwise fine; the glove had stuck firm. Satisfied, he lifted his wrist in an exaggerated movement which pulled his palm free from the wall while pressing fingers against it, ensuring that the smart skin pulled out of and away from the bricks and cement. Then he began to climb; hand first, then opposite leg, other hand, then other leg, going up the wall like a cross between a rock-hugging lizard and some outlandishly splay-limbed monkey.

The presumed security station was on the first floor, so he was up to the window in seconds. It was also towards the centre of the building, away from any windows, a sensible precaution which denied Leyton the simple solution of shooting the guard from his current position. The window's lock was of the usual electric type, easy to short with a standard piece of kit. Clinging to the surrounding wall with toes, knee, inside of a leg and one hand, he simply placed the small device against the area of frame that corresponded with the internal latch-mechanism and waited for a click. Old-fashioned manual locks presented far more of a challenge; not that Leyton was complaining.

Once inside he moved forward along a deserted corridor, lights dimmed to the point of mimicking the greyness outside. The passageway soon turned right, taking him past a series of elevators, none of them in use at this hour. A little further and the floor opened up into a mezzanine-style gallery, with a modest flight of steps leading down to a small lobby area and the front door. Set a little back from the top of the stairs was a broad horseshoe-shaped desk, behind which sat the guard, his profile to Leyton. The man was leaning back in his chair. By the look of him, he didn't have a care in the world. In fact, had he been any more relaxed he would have been asleep.

The uniform was charcoal-grey. Now there was a surprise.

Twin banks of monitor screens bracketed the desk and inane music chuntered from a speaker somewhere beneath it, which made the eyegee's task all the easier. Holstering the gun and drawing a serrated combat knife, he slipped behind the seated figure, steadied himself, and then struck.

In one coordinated movement, he reached forward to cup the guard's chin in his left hand, covering the man's mouth in the process while pulling the head back against his own chest. At the same time, his right hand drew the knife's blade swiftly across the exposed throat, applying sufficient pressure to sever every major blood vessel.

The unfortunate guard had enough time to stiffen in shock at the sudden assault and then twitch once as he died, but that was all. Leyton eased the body out of the seat and onto the floor. One good thing about standing behind a man when you cut his throat is that the blood sprays forward and not over you. The bad news from Leyton's perspective was that in this instance a considerable amount had spattered over the control panel, and he was going to have to use that shortly.

Not before taking care of the second guard, however.

Even though his visor showed the current whereabouts of the wandering red dot, he instinctively checked the bank of security monitors in any case. On one he noted the control centre. Three figures sitting at desks, intent on their own screens. Three, when the visor reported four in the room, so that might indicate another guard, perhaps stationed by the door.

Worth noting, but not his primary concern just then. He turned his attention to one of the other screens, which showed a grey-suited figure strolling down a semi-darkened corridor.

One floor up. Leyton headed for the fire exit and its stairway, ignoring the more convenient elevators.

He came out into an empty passageway ahead of the guard's route, chose a convenient bit of wall to stand against and waited, allowing the shimmer suit to do its thing. Moments later the oblivious guard sauntered past and Leyton stepped forward, reaching out to grasp the man's jaw from behind and repeating the performance of earlier. Then it was back to the monitor room, where he deactivated the alarm, ignoring the blood that now marred the control panel, and opened the door to allow Sergeant Black and the rest of the party to enter.

He watched as one man stayed to cover the front door while another peeled away to cover the building's side entrance.

Black, the two techs and the two remaining troopers hurried up the stairs to meet him.

Again foregoing the elevators, Leyton led them to the fire stairs, ascending swiftly but silently and cursing under his breath at the amount of noise from behind him – the scuffing of shoes and slap of feet on uncarpeted concrete stairway sounding all the louder in the enclosed confines of the stairwell. The gun evidently recognised the cursing as not being directed at it and stayed mercifully quiet.

Then, unexpectedly, one of the red dots on the floor above moved their way.

Leyton held out a restraining hand, emphasising the gesture with a hissed "Wait!" He was relieved at how quickly the sound and movement behind him ceased. They were spread out along a stretch of stairs between the second and third floors. On the fifth, the red dot kept coming. The third guard, perhaps, drawn by some slight noise from the stairway?

Ignoring his own instruction, Leyton hurried upward, treading as lightly as he could. He knew he had to be in position before the door on the fifth floor opened, after which movement would be risky, not only because any noise he made would be amplified in the confines of the stairwell but also because the slight distortion of a shimmer suit on the move might be enough to give him away. Particularly to a guard already suspicious enough to come looking. Yet, before he could even reach the small landing to the fourth floor, he heard above him the telltale creak of a door opening. Leyton froze, fully aware that he was still a dozen paces short of where he needed to be and that there was little chance of taking the guard out from here before the man could raise the alarm.

CHAPTER FOUR

A VOICE CALLED out from somewhere above, drawing a "Yeah?" from the guard.

In his visor display, Leyton saw that one of the other red dots had moved away from the main group, presumably stepping from the office to the corridor. The door above was only half opened, the man delayed and his attention temporarily elsewhere. Leyton risked moving forward again, hurrying as silently as he could past the door to the fourth floor and onto the stairs to the fifth.

He was still a few paces short of his ideal position when he heard the guard above say, "Will do," followed by the squeak of oil-thirsty hinges as the door opened completely. He stopped moving at once, gun pointed towards the emerging man. He just hoped those below him, the two techs in particular, held their nerve and remembered how effective the shimmer suits were so long as you stayed still.

Thankfully, the guard didn't even look their way beyond a casual glance. Instead, he reached inside his uniform and withdrew a small but bulky pen-shaped object, which he thrust against his stiffened left arm, not bothering to lift his sleeve, and held there for a handful of seconds. Leyton smiled – the man had *not* been alerted by any noise they made at all, but had slipped away to shoot up! A narcotic micro-spray fired through uniform and skin alike; possibly a stimulant, much needed towards the end of a long shift when energy was flagging, but definitely something not allowed in the job description, or he wouldn't have sneaked away in the first place. With a sigh, the guard relaxed his arm and slipped the applicator away again.

He stood for a few seconds, breathing deeply and puffing his cheeks out, before straightening his uniform and turning, obviously preparing to go back to his post. Leyton made a quick calculation. The guard's hands were now empty and there was nothing obviously loose about the uniform, nothing to clatter noisily should he fall. Could Leyton reach him in time to catch the body and prevent it from tumbling down the stairs? Probably.

He squeezed the trigger. Fully silenced, the gun made little more noise than a person spitting. The eyegee was on the move even as the bullet smashed into the guard's skull.

He made up the distance easily, catching the guard's body as it began to wilt towards the stairwell and laying it gently down onto the small landing, being careful not to block the door.

He waved the others forward, exiting the stairwell with Black close at his heels. There were now three red dots left in the control room.

Against all sense the room's door stood open, perhaps left that way by a guard who expected to be returning soon. Leyton, Black and the remaining marine ghosted into the room, each taking station behind one of the three civilians – two men, one woman – intent on their work. One of the men was just finishing a conversation, apparently with somebody aboard one of the two ships parked in orbit around Holt. The trio waited for him to break the connection and then struck. These were civilians, so they applied a non-lethal approach. Three stun guns, weapons using electro-muscular disruption, fired simultaneously. The three Holtans collapsed, to be dragged away and quickly bound and gagged.

Black's remaining marine took station by the door, looking alert and ready for anything, while the two techs came into the room, gratefully pulling back the hoods of their shimmer suits. They both sat at one of the terminals, and the older man sighed. "Oh well, I suppose it was too much to hope for."

"What was?" Leyton wanted to know.

"Oh, nothing. We just hoped that by catching them with screens running it might give us an easy way into their systems, but no such luck." He placed the valise, carried with him throughout, on the workstation and popped it open. "Not a problem, it'll just take us a little longer, is all."

Hardly the most welcome news, but it couldn't be helped. "Quick as you can."

"I know, I know. You do your job, we'll do ours."

"An alarm has been sounded," the gun's placid voice informed him.

"How? We didn't give any of them a chance to touch anything."

"More a case of what has not been done rather than what has. The alarm was caused by inactivity at one of the work terminals."

Really? That was interesting, and seemed remarkably sharp of the locals, which came as something of a surprise given what they'd encountered here so far.

None of which altered the situation they found themselves in. "Look lively," he said to everybody; "an alarm's been triggered, so we can expect company sooner rather than later."

He looked across at Black, who nodded his understanding. At the door, the trooper adjusted the grip on his gun and somehow looked even more alert.

A tense moment passed, with the techs working silently and Black fiddling with something on his suit.

Then came the chatter of automatic gunfire from outside. Leyton was a little surprised at the speed of response, but red dots were suddenly blossoming from two directions. So many that the visor apparently gave up trying to represent them as individual dots and settled for expanding red smudges.

"Shit!" Black said from the window. "There's a small army out there,"

Leyton crossed to join him. The sergeant was right. Where the hell had this lot materialised from? Well-disciplined troops advanced towards their position, covering each other in classic style and utilising the available terrain effectively as they converged on the front door. Difficult to judge numbers, even with the visor, but he estimated half a platoon or more in each direction, perhaps as many as fifty in all.

What was it he'd been told to expect? 'A poorly trained and inadequately equipped militia; slow to respond and unlikely to offer significant resistance.' That was one part of the briefing he *had* listened to.

Where was his fellow eyegee? "Boulton?" He broke radio silence; little point in maintaining it at this stage.

"Not now. I'm busy!"

She had better be. They only had one man guarding each entrance, and neither stood a chance against this many hostiles.

Black seemed to have reached the same conclusion. "Pull back to the first landing," he ordered, presumably speaking to the two soldiers guarding the doors. He then turned to Leyton. "I hope you eyegees are all you're cracked up to be, because at this precise moment we don't have a clear way out of here."

Leyton made no response, but instead looked across to see how the techs were doing. What he saw was far from encouraging. The younger tech had gone white as a sheet; in fact he looked petrified. His colleague just looked resigned. Neither seemed to be doing a great deal except staring at the screen.

"Problems?" He hurried over to them.

The older man nodded, staring at the screen before him as if it had tried to bite him, while his companion looked up to flick a wide-eyed glance towards Leyton. "This has much higher-grade defences than we were told to expect."

The eyegee snorted. He was beginning to sense a pattern here. "Which means?"

"Which means that I can't guarantee we can get inside its safeguards and blocks before every scrap of useful information is erased."

Black chimed in, before Leyton could voice a suitable expletive. "But you can still recover it even then, right? I mean, nothing on a computer's ever irretrievably lost, is it?"

"Don't believe everything you hear," the older tech replied. "Given the right equipment and enough man hours, we *might* be able to get to it, depends on how the erasing was done, but I wouldn't like to bet on it."

"Besides which, we don't *have* either the equipment or the time," the younger man added.

"Right," the first tech confirmed.

There had to be something they could do. Leyton's inherent stubbornness wouldn't allow him to give up on any mission so readily, especially one which was shaping up to be such a total pain in the butt as this. "What would make the difference?" He addressed the more experienced of the two, who at least seemed to know what he was doing.

"Sorry?"

"What would you need to breach the system's defences in time to preserve the info, to prevent it being erased?"

"More computer power than we have here." The man tapped his valise.

If it was computing power they needed... "Could you help?" Leyton sub-vocalised to the gun.

"Perhaps, but it would mean shutting down all higher defensive and offensive capabilities while I did so. I would just be a simple chunk of inanimate weaponry."

Leyton digested that, a little surprised at how vulnerable the prospect made him feel, but he knew that, if the mission were to stand any chance of success, he had no choice.

"I might be able to help you there," he told the tech, and conveyed the gun's offer.

The man looked dubious but said, "We'll give it a go."

"Make sure you're on projectile and do it," he instructed the gun.

"We'll need to hook it up to my gear," the tech said, holding out his hand. Leyton hesitated and then passed the gun over.

His visor went dead. Red and green dots disappeared to leave just the room and its occupants.

The gunfire seemed suddenly louder, closer. The sergeant had crossed from the window to take station with his man by the door. Both were braced with weapons drawn. Leyton felt abruptly lost, impotent. His hand itched to be clutching a gun but he didn't carry a spare – why would he? And he resisted the temptation to ask either of the soldiers if they had one, which would have sounded too much like an admission of weakness.

As he watched, the stance of the two soldiers altered – a subtle readjustment but a telling one, as both sighted along their guns and started firing. Bullets hammered into the door frame above Black's head, causing the sergeant to duck back inside. Only for an instant, then he was leaning out and shooting again, but this time in the opposite direction. So the attack was coming from both sides, the local troops must be emerging from the stairs and the elevators simultaneously, which didn't say much for the chances of the marines designated to guard the building's doors and stairwell.

Leyton looked around the room, futilely searching for a weapon. Then the marine beside Black spun half around, stumbling into the room and clutching his shoulder. Leyton started forward, intent on claiming the injured man's gun and replacing him, but as he went to do so, a voice whispered, "Did you miss me?" and at the same instant the tech declared triumphantly, "Got it!"

The world came alive again. Doubtless only a matter of seconds had passed but it seemed far, far longer to the eyegee. Red dots appeared in his visor, concentrated in the corridor outside. Leyton snatched the gun up, almost yanking the tech's still-attached unit from the desk as he did so before the connecting lead fell free. The walls to the corridor were partition, which, to a gun of this calibre and at this range, might as well have been tissue paper. The eyegee squeezed the trigger and held it flat. Chewed-up shards of wood and plasterboard flew in all directions and screams came from the corridor beyond as the bullets tore into soldiers who had been attempting to storm the hard-pressed sergeant's position. Leyton moved his aim steadily along the wall, away from the door. Several dots winked out while others withdrew. The clip emptied, was ejected and replaced. He was at the door now, peering over Black's shoulder. The charge had been halted from one direction, but soldiers were edging forward from the other, using office doorways as cover.

Where the hell was Boulton? She was supposed to be ensuring this sort of thing didn't happen.

"Explosive," he sub-vocalised. At the first squeeze of the trigger one of the built-in grenades spun away down the corridor, at the second, with the gun held at a slightly greater elevation, its twin did the same. He grabbed Black and pulled him back into the room, clipping a replacement brace of explosive shells onto the gun even as the first explosion shook the building. The second followed an instant later.

"Energy," he sub-vocalised. He hated running the risk of depleting the gun but they had to force a way out of here, which meant clearing at least one direction of enemies, and 'energy' offered the precision needed to do that.

He tapped Black on the shoulder and pointed in the direction of the elevators, where the two shells had just exploded. "Cover me that way."

The sergeant nodded. The injured soldier pushed himself upright, as if determined to help, but Leyton waved him back.

As Black started laying down covering fire in one direction – his automatic chattering through the bullets – Leyton took careful aim in the other, using a combination of eyesight and visor to pick out even those targets hidden from view. With great deliberation, he squeezed the trigger, releasing it as one red light winked out before moving on to the next. He was a little surprised there weren't more of them, based on what he'd seen from the window. Perhaps Boulton had done some good after all. Either that or the other marines had sold their lives dearly.

After Leyton took out his fourth target, the remaining Holtan troops must have realised that staying where they were just enabled him to pick them off one by one. While two laid down covering fire of their own, causing Black to duck hastily back into the room, the others – five in total – again attempted a charge.

"Explosive."

The blast left one groaning, the rest unmoving and silent.

After the eyegee reverted to 'energy' and killed the soldier nearest him, the final defender chose the better part of valour and ran for the stairs.

"Glad you're on my side," Black murmured, with more than a hint of respect and perhaps a similar measure of envy.

The techs had gathered their equipment and were now crouching by the wounded marine. Leyton turned to them, whispering, "Ready?" Nervous nods all round. "Sergeant, lead the way to the stairs on my order. I'll cover. Be careful – one of them made a break for the stairwell."

Black grunted his understanding. The others clambered to their feet and bunched forward.

Leyton leaned out, catapulting his final explosive shell in the direction of the lifts, where some dozen red dots still showed.

"Projectile." He started firing even before the shell had landed, saying, slightly louder, "Now!" The others charged past him.

Leyton backed out, still firing. Contrary to his instructions, Black lagged behind the others, crouching where Holtan troopers had stood seconds before and firing towards the lifts and the remaining enemy. Needing no further urging, Leyton turned and ran, leaping over the bodies that littered stretches of the corridor, until he was past Black and able himself to stop to provide cover for the sergeant in turn.

There was now very little fire coming back at them. Leyton noted that only four red dots were showing on the visor, and there was no telling how many of those might be injured. Maybe they were going to get out of this after all.

One of their own troopers lay dead at the top of the stairs. The shimmer suit must have been damaged when the soldier was hit, because the body was clearly visible to the naked eye. Leyton saw the black shoulder flashes and realised this was the stubble-haired girl who had sat nearest him on the shuttle. Strange, but in the brief second they'd locked gazes he had felt a connection, professional to professional. He'd never even spoken to her, which was a fact he now briefly regretted.

He was about to move on when something caught his eye. One of the local soldiers sat slumped against the wall, blood staining the front of his uniform from a row of bullet holes. The man wore an unusual visor which had a faintly orange tinge. In fact, all the local troops seemed to have them. On impulse Leyton reached for the nearest one, pulling it off the dead soldier's head.

He slid his own visor up and held this orange one to his eyes, and cursed. "Sergeant!" The man glanced back from the top of the stairs. "These visors negate the effect of our shimmer suits."

"Shit!"

Which just about summed up his own feelings. The goggles on shimmer suits were designed to allow wearers to see each other, but intelligence hadn't suggested that Holt's defenders were equipped with anything as sophisticated as this. Either somebody had got things badly wrong in the preparation for this mission or there had been some major changes around here very recently. Whatever the case, their intel was clearly screwed across the board as far as this outing was concerned.

It was beginning to look as if cutting short the gun's crash-course mission briefing during their approach had been the best decision he'd made all day; most of it would have been even more worthless than he'd feared. He didn't blame Black in the least for broadcasting the news about the visors over the radio for the benefit of his surviving men.

Now he thought about it, there was somebody Leyton wouldn't mind contacting as well. "Boulton, are you still with us?"

"Still here, still busy," came the clipped response.

Doing what, he wondered.

The number of bodies sprawled across stairs and on the landing below paid testament to how hard the stubble-haired girl had fought. They had to carefully pick their way around the fallen to avoid tripping over. Hampered by the wounded soldier, the two techs had not gone far ahead and Black was soon able to resume his position at point. Leyton stayed at the back, keeping a wary eye on the red dots on the fifth floor, but they made no attempt to follow. No sign of the one who had fled down the stairwell, either. In fact, the visor showed no other hostiles in the building. So, had they successfully dealt with everything the locals had to throw at them? Judging by the occasional burst of gunfire from outside, not yet. Who were the Holtans engaging? Was it the two men Black had assigned to cover their retreat or had Boulton finally decided to pull her weight? They'd find out soon enough, no doubt, as the sergeant led them from the fire exit stairs towards the front door. Again, a good choice; the side door was almost bound to be smaller, less easy to escape from and the perfect place at which to get pinned down. The more Leyton saw of Black the more he approved of him.

It looked as if the marine left to guard the front entrance had chosen to make a stand behind the security desk on the gallery floor. At least, that's where they found his body. A big man, whom the eyegee remembered from the shuttle due to the smashed remains of an overlarge gun which now lay beside him on the floor.

Black was already halfway down the front stairs, the others behind him. The visor didn't show any hostiles in the immediate vicinity but Leyton still felt uneasy. There could be a ring of snipers outside the visor's range all targeting the front door for all he knew. Gunfire still sounded sporadically, a reminder that they weren't home and dry yet, as if any were needed.

"Boulton, what's your status?"

"Bruised and dirty, with a compromised shimmer suit. You?"

Compared to her previous communications this was almost a speech. Leyton didn't respond immediately. He joined Black who had paused at the front door.

"Think I saw some movement out there," the sergeant told him.

The visor agreed. Now that the eyegee had moved forward to the very front of the building it showed a cluster of red dots at the extreme reach of its range. "You're right," he told Black. "Looks as if they've set up between the two buildings across the avenue, waiting for us to come out."

"Figures. What do you reckon, should we try the other door?"

Even as the sergeant asked the question, the visor showed a mass of red dots streaming up to and into the other entrance.

"Too late. They're already coming through that way in force. We just ran out of options."

"If we ever get out of here," the sergeant muttered, "I'm gonna kill whoever drew up the intel for this mission."

"You'll have to stand in line." He switched back to the radio. "Boulton, we need some of that interference of yours to clear our path, and we need it now!"

"I'm on it."

Seconds later an explosion from within the ranks of entrenched local soldiers suggested that she actually meant what she said. Black meanwhile was talking calmly into his radio, instructing the two soldiers he'd left to cover their retreat to move up and support Boulton.

"Come on," Leyton urged, pushing through the door himself and firing as he emerged. An armoured truck had been parked across the gap between the two buildings they'd used in their approach. As the eyegee watched, the truck lifted slightly and rocked on its wheels, while the top peeled back like an opening seed pod to vent fire and fury, the accompanying roar only slightly muffled by the truck's armoured hide. Red dots winked out. Gunfire came from the wrecked vehicle's vicinity and the dots kept fading. Only a few in that direction now and it looked as if Boulton had their attention, so Leyton directed Black and the other survivors that way – the quickest route back to the shuttle.

At that moment, the still-murky sky was lit by a bright flash from somewhere high in the atmosphere. The navy's diversion. Better late than never.

When they arrived at the outskirts of this system, two vessels had been spotted in orbit around Holt. Both were identified as freebooters responsible for assorted acts of piracy and both had 'shoot on sight' directives logged against them. The plan had been for the navy to destroy the two ships at roughly the same time as the team on the ground made their incursion, so distracting the authorities' attention. It seemed unlikely that taking out ships in orbit would have produced such a spectacular display, however, so Leyton presumed this was the navy's way of being additionally helpful by triggering attention-grabbing incendiaries in-atmosphere; either that or they had just taken out a shuttle or something of the sort. Leyton didn't really care, explosions in the sky were fine by him whatever the cause – anything that increased their chances of getting off this rock alive had his vote.

They reached the smouldering truck. No red dots showing here now. Behind the wrecked vehicle, a dozen or so orange-visored corpses and a clutter of dropped weapons, beyond which stood Boulton, flanked by a single marine.

Black looked at the man and asked, "Cutter?"

The marine shook his head. Four down.

Red dots again, coming out of the control centre – the soldiers who had gone in via the other door.

"Move!" Leyton urged.

They all ran to the derelict shuttle, where Leyton squatted down, preparing to cover the others' retreat, but just then the air reverberated with the sound of engines and he looked up to see a fully operational shuttle, *their* shuttle, coming in to land on the field beyond, so he turned and sprinted with the rest. A few optimistic shots pursued them but little else. The locals appeared to have lost heart. Somebody seemed to step up and take responsibility, however, as the shooting suddenly became more accurate. Leyton almost stumbled as one shot ricocheted off his left side – unable to penetrate the body armour at this distance – while, another found a softer target. As Leyton caught up with the younger tech, the man jerked and cried out. Blood spattered the eyegee's uniform and he watched the red stain of it blossom on the man's lower arm, immediately below the body armour's seam. It was hardly a fatal wound, but the surprise and abrupt pain were enough to cause the tech to stumble and fall. Leyton pulled the man back to his feet and helped him onward to where the others were already piling onto the waiting craft.

They lifted immediately. Shimmer suits powered down and hoods were pulled back to reveal relieved smiles mingled with wide-eyed surprise at still being alive. Now that they were out of immediate danger, Leyton had time to think about the mission itself. He caught the older technician's eye. "Well, did you get anything?"

The older man tapped his valise. "There's a lot of data in here and it'll need to be analysed, but from what I saw... I don't think so. There was no mention of *The Noise Within* as far as I could tell. Wherever she's set up base, I don't reckon it's here."

So all this had been for nothing. No, not strictly speaking true. The powers-that-be would doubtless claim that a negative told them something, that it ruled out a possibility; but that seemed small return for all that they had been through.

AS THEY SLUMPED into seats against either wall of the shuttle, it became apparent that the dynamics in their little group had shifted. Black chose the seat immediately next to Leyton, the two techs sitting opposite – the younger of whom looked to be teetering on the edge of shock, even though his wound had been cleaned and gel-skin sealed. The injured marine was strapped into a seat between the other remaining soldier and Black. He was at best semi-conscious and dosed up to his eyeballs with pain killers, while his shoulder boasted a fresh white dressing.

The older tech caught Leyton's eye and, at this late stage, chose to introduce himself, as if the eyegee had passed some sort of test which qualified him as worth knowing. "Name's Ed, by the way. Thanks for getting us out of there." The comment pointedly excluded Boulton, who sat apart, several seats removed from the rest of them. Nobody spoke to her or seemed keen to even look in her direction.

The journey was conducted in almost total silence. Leyton suspected each one of them to be preoccupied in reliving what they had just been through, remembering the fallen and reflecting on the fact that it could very easily have been them lying there dead on a grim little world called Holt.

For his part, the eyegee's thoughts had already moved on from there.

He kept thinking about how quickly the local troops had reacted to their incursion and in what force; about the clever alarm setup which was triggered by a computer terminal's inactivity, and about that alarm not prompting an initial enquiry to see if everything was all right but bringing an immediate armed response. Then there were those orange visors – not standard issue anywhere as far as he was aware; a very specific piece of kit designed to counteract shimmer suits. He was just grateful that the centre's security guards hadn't been equipped with them, or things might have gone very differently. No matter how he added all this up, it amounted to just one thing.

"They were ready for us," Black murmured beside him, too quietly for anyone else to hear.

The pair exchanged grim, knowing glances. The sergeant's thoughts were obviously following similar lines to his own. Holt might not have known *when* an attack was due, but there seemed little doubt they knew one was coming. Someone had tipped them off.

Leyton promised himself that one day soon he would take the trouble to find out precisely who.

THE DEBRIEFING HAD been fractious, with no one about to take responsibility for the flawed intelligence or even willing to admit that it was flawed in the first place. Seething during the process and frustrated afterwards, Leyton returned to his cabin in a foul mood. All of which meant that he was spoiling for an argument even before someone knocked sharply on the door. When he opened it to see who stood there, he was almost too surprised to be angry.

Fortunately, he remembered himself in time. "If you've come to apologise, forget it!" he told the startled woman.

"*Me* apologise?" Boulton replied, looking as furious as he felt. "I'm here to ask what the hell you thought you were playing at, leaving me stuck out there facing a whole fucking army on my own while you minced around in that little building with your soldier buddies dealing with a couple of security guards!"

"It was never a competition," Leyton told her, his anger hardening to cold menace. "The mission had nothing to do with counting how many locals each of us killed, but it had everything to do with getting information, and you were supposed to cover our backs while we did so."

"And that's what I did; without any help from any of you."

"*Help?* You're an eyegee for God's sake. You shouldn't *need* any help!"

"Exactly! An eyegee, not a wet nurse for a bunch of incompetent arseholes who can't look out for themselves."

He came close to losing it then, close to hitting her, but he kept control and instead forced the anger down. "Face it, Boulton, you screwed up. You weren't where you were supposed to be and you could have got us all killed as a result," he said.

"*I* could have got us killed?" She was clearly on the edge herself, perhaps pushed there by a sense of guilt, or perhaps it was frustration at the fact that she *had* done all she could yet nobody seemed to believe her. "I took out one patrol, then scooted over and pinned down a second. What were you doing at the time, chatting to your new buddy the sergeant?"

"Ensuring the mission proceeded. *You* were supposed to secure our perimeter. You're a fucking liability." But he said this with less conviction than he'd felt earlier. Perhaps part of him was starting to believe her, or at least wanted to.

Without warning her hand shot out, striking before he could react, stinging his cheek with an open-palmed slap. His own hand moved almost of its own volition to deliver a similar blow to her face. She jerked her head back but at the same time clasped the top of his shoulders and pulled herself to him, her lips clamping onto his, tongue thrusting into his mouth.

He hooked his fingers into the neckline of her top and tugged, ripping it away. Her tongue withdrew and she bit his lip, drawing blood; her fingernails dug into his back through the thin material of the shirt and raked downward, before finding their way under his shirt, claws stripping flesh as they descended towards his waist. Clinging, grasping, biting, their limbs and bodies entwined, the two of them tumbled towards the sofa, him twisting around so that he would land on top, his hands clasping her to him as they fell, his mind aware of how taut and unyielding her body felt beneath his fingers and how hot her skin.

More of her top tore away, revealing a small, firm breast, which he bent to kiss, biting the prominent nipple before encircling it with his tongue. Her hands forced themselves between their bodies, reaching for and undoing the front of his trousers. He lifted his hips to accommodate her, taking the opportunity to pull the remnants of her top away to reveal her other breast.

When he entered her it was brutal, fast and uncompromising, with her teeth biting into his shoulder, his back stinging beneath her nails. She screamed obscenities at him, squirming beneath his body and jabbing her heels against his buttocks, while he reached for her arms, pinning them down with bruising strength to hold her still, and drove into her for all he was worth, conscious of her thrusting back at him, the jarring impact as he rammed against the thinly cushioned bones of her pelvis. Making love never came into it. This was an explosion of pent-up energy and lust that burned fiercely to leave both of them bruised, bleeding and drained once it was spent.

HE WOKE TO find his back stiff with a multitude of stinging scratches and the bed sheets bearing the occasional small smear of blood, though not as much as expected given the violence he remembered. The bed was empty. Boulton had left while he slept. Her shredded top lay on the floor and he allowed himself a smile, wondering what she might have worn to cover her modesty as she scooted back to her own cabin. He pictured her scurrying down the corridor, clutching a strip of cloth to her breasts and furtively peering round corners to ensure the coast was clear, but dismissed the image as absurd; mere wishful thinking. Truth to tell, he couldn't imagine her scurrying anywhere.

Then he saw the note. Hand written on a sheet of paper, how quaint; presumably to avoid disturbing him by making a voice recording.

He picked up the flimsy white sheet and read the brief text. Two lines; no signature.

Mya was right about you. Next time I see her, we can compare notes.

She knew Mya? *She knew Mya?* He balled his fist, screwing up the sheet in the process, and punched one of the metal poles supporting the bed's headboard.

That hurt; but not enough.

CHAPTER FIVE

PHILIP BREEZED INTO his apartment, still riding high on an adrenalin buzz that had carried him through the morning and resurged during the board meeting, which could not have gone any better had he scripted the whole thing himself. At that particular moment he felt as if he could take on the world. Thankfully, all those present seemed to have been caught up in his enthusiasm and swept along. By the close of the meeting, every single one of them was fully behind him. Nor did he have cause to doubt their sincerity, since the deceptively old-fashioned chairs they were seated on had recorded the physical responses of each board member throughout the meeting. Subsequent biometric analysis confirmed the honesty of their responses within an acceptable degree of certainty.

Despite lip-service to the contrary, it was a long time since he had enjoyed the whole-hearted support of the entire board. The prime reason for his little show had been to ensure that there would be no more dragging of heels. In recent weeks Philip and his team had been thwarted by minutiae. The exasperating thing was that he knew they were close; for months the project had teetered on the verge of a major breakthrough, yet it had been stalled by niggling issues which could have been readily solved if only everyone had remained committed and focused. Now, barring some unforeseen disaster, all the frustrations should disappear overnight. Given a clear run he was confident they could finally deliver a triumphant conclusion. The example of

The Noise Within was exactly the impetus needed to push them over the finishing line.

Perfecting the long sought after human/AI interface would be an achievement which history itself would take note of; one to rival even the wondrous Kaufman Drive.

As important as anything his father had ever achieved.

Philip needed to calm down. Doing his best to ignore the black box sitting on a shelf – reminiscent of the sort of flat oblong jewellery case which might house an expensive necklace, if a little too large for that purpose – he poured himself some chilled water from the fridge, closing his eyes at the first sip in order to savour the coolness as it spread through his body. He forced himself to pause, to breathe deeply and to relax. He continued to drink the water steadily while glancing in distracted fashion at the list of calls Phil had handled during his absence. Most seemed to be from those wishing to congratulate him on the Gügenhall speech: platitudes delivered because duty required them to be – all hail the great God of Etiquette. None of them had been flagged by Phil as requiring his personal attention, so he dismissed the list without bothering to review any of the individual messages.

No calls from Mal; though in fairness he would have been disappointed if there had been. The real Malcolm Kaufman would have been patient, waiting for Philip to call *him*, confident that he had provided sufficiently impressive a revelation to ensure that such a call would come, as indeed it might... eventually. Evidently there was enough of the man in the partial to elicit at least that much behavioural accuracy.

Last night's lecture had passed in a blur, his mind preoccupied with the implications of *The Sun Seeker's* possible return, with planning what he would do to the images in the morning. Perversely, the talk had gone all the better as a result, at least to judge by reactions immediately afterwards. When people had sought him out to press the flesh and congratulate him they seemed genuinely impressed, if, in some cases, a little surprised. He made a mental note: should a similarly daunting engagement ever arise in the future, arrange a momentous revelation immediately beforehand so that he would be too distracted to get nervous.

Philip's gaze kept being drawn back towards the black box. Going to watch Jenner's run in the simulator had been a mistake. Oh, he'd needed the distraction, but the visit had awoken an old itch, an irritation he had been struggling not to scratch for days. Leaving the box in such a prominent position was deliberate: a calculated challenge to his resolve, one which he had been confident of resisting at the time. Perhaps a little overconfident, or so it now seemed, as the itch threatened to develop into full-blown hunger.

If asked, Philip would have denied vehemently that he envied the trainee pilots as such. Yet, despite the inconvenience of having software grafted into their skulls, there was a part of him deep down which hankered to sample the incredible expansion of consciousness that each of the subjects experienced when linked to their AIs, but which they all struggled to describe.

Therein lay Philip's greatest disappointment. He was desperate to know what that super-human communion felt like, wanted it so badly that at times the desire screwed his insides up into knots and turned every bit of progress they made with the project into incremental torture. Only at times, thank God. On the whole he had learned to live with his frustration, and certainly it hadn't prevented him from throwing all his efforts behind the project; which was just as well, since he was very much the driving force behind the whole thing. Yet he knew that when they finally achieved their goal – when, not *if* – the sweet taste of success would arrive with a hint of bitterness on the side. Sometimes, Philip entertained the suspicion that his desire to experience the human/AI commune was so strong precisely *because* it was denied him when so few things were, but he had analysed that argument and rejected it. The plain truth was that he saw this communion with another form of advanced intelligence as the pinnacle of intellectual achievement, possibly even of human existence, and he seemed doomed to merely watch while others experienced it, to bask only in the reflected glory of facilitating the process.

Their understanding of the principles involved grew almost daily, and it was this fact which enabled Philip to carry on, to harness these conflicting desires and push the project forward. He had to believe that one day they would find a way to allow even the likes of him to experience the joy of full gestalt, no matter how unlikely this seemed at present.

The brain is a delicate organ, and even though man prided himself on knowing virtually all its secrets, it remained a fragile construct. Despite the latest stem cell technology enabling them to coat the necessary implants in a film of organic material cultured from the recipient's own cells, forty percent of all such operations still failed, sometimes with fatal consequences. The insertion of the bionic augments had the potential to traumatise the brain no matter what precautions were taken, and they had yet to devise a way of completely avoiding this. They *had* learned, however, to recognise which brains were most likely to reject the augs. Unfortunately, his was one of them.

So he was barred from experiencing the union of organic and artificial mind which had become the focus of his life's work, and that fact frustrated him more than he would ever dare admit to anyone; which was where his latest hobby had sprung from, his illicit pleasure. No, barring miraculous development, Philip would never be able to experience the full revelation of human/AI communion, but he *was* in a position to grant himself an approximation of what that must be like, a tantalising glimpse of the ultimate – not so much second best as several leagues removed from the real thing, but better than nothing, surely. Ever the pragmatist, Philip accepted this as the closest he was likely to come to his personal Holy Grail, yet even this pale imitation was proving insidiously addictive.

Philip knew that his relentless pursuit of a dream which originated with his father but had long since become his own was a source of great amusement to many, but Kaufman Industries was strong enough both financially and technically to withstand any slight tarnishing the company's reputation suffered as a result. As time passed and KI continued to be at the forefront of engine and systems designs, despite the distraction of the project, the matter was relegated to the status of an endearing foible – something for competitors to smile indulgently about when they could find little else to smile over. Philip had long ago accepted that most saw the project as his attempt to expunge the one glaring blot on Malcolm Kaufman's record – his greatest perceived failure: *The Sun Seeker*.

And perhaps there was an element of truth in that, but if so it was by no means the whole truth.

Philip's father had been born into a time of war, a time when every human territory had been caught up in a lumbering conflict which monopolised resources and attention. By the time Malcolm was growing up, few people if any could remember what the War was about, it was simply a fact of life. KI were heavily involved in the design and development of new warships for what proved to be, in effect, the winning side. Although both claimed to be such when the conflict eventually ground to a stuttering conclusion, only one side dominated the 'unified' government – the United League of Worlds. By this time, every new ship which rolled off the production lines and into the War boasted engines built by Kaufman Industries. Competitors survived by outfitting the trickle of merchant and private vessels which were still occasionally commissioned, but only the best was good enough for the military, and the best meant the Kaufman Drive.

Yet Malcolm genuinely believed it was not his engines that posterity would remember him for but rather *The Sun Seeker*, his pet project, which he saw as being the *real* revolution in interstellar travel.

An AI-controlled ship would be faster, nimbler and more capable than anything seen before. Conceivably, if it worked, this was the innovation which might just win the War, and that would be only the beginning; the potential was enormous. Except that it hadn't worked; at least, not as intended. Perhaps, given the advantage of hindsight, some might think that it had actually worked *too* well.

There had been a crew, of course, even though theoretically the ship could operate without one. Somehow, Philip doubted there would ever be a time when AI ships flew without crew, even if *The Sun Seeker* had delivered Malcolm's dream – there were too many things on board a ship which human hands could do more readily than any automated system, particularly in the event of repairs being needed. Then there were mankind's deep-seated insecurities to factor in. Would any government *ever* be ready to let an AI ship go anywhere without human supervision? Personally, Philip couldn't see it.

Besides, those had been very early days and *The Sun Seeker* was only a prototype, so a crew was inevitable.

Malcolm had told his son more than once that, even decades later, he could still hear their calls for help as the ship disappeared, swiftly building up acceleration to a level which no human could survive.

In the middle of a series of test flights, *The Sun Seeker* had gone AWOL, somehow circumventing every safeguard and managing to lock out the captain and officers who were on board with failsafe protocols – theoretically guaranteed to return control to human hands if necessary. Oblivious to every override and precaution, the ship had abandoned its predetermined course and made a dash for the nearest wormhole jump point. The move was timed to perfection, calculated with clinical efficiency to ensure that the experimental vessel arrived as far ahead of those ships attempting to intercept as it possibly could have done.

The Sun Seeker had never been seen again. Until now. Was it pure coincidence that the long lost vessel had reappeared at this particular time, when the project was so close to a conclusion?

Philip stepped out of the dryshower, his skin tingling from its ministrations and feeling as invigorated as the rest of him. Yet, even after slipping into fresh clothes, that insidious black box continued to call to him. No matter what distraction he attempted to conjure he couldn't escape its allure and eventually he bowed to the inevitable. With great deliberation, he took the box down and carried it with a steady hand through to his office.

Philip sat in the familiar chair, a recliner which instantly reacted to his presence, adjusting its contour and angle to accommodate his maximum comfort; but he didn't sink into it immediately. Instead he sat forward, placing the box on the desk and pressing gently on a deceptively decorative panel with thumb and index finger, in that order. The hinged lid lifted slowly and smoothly, a breath of cool air flowing out to touch his hand as it did so. The box maintained a steady temperature of seven degrees – ideal for storing the two drugs it contained.

Viewed from one perspective, the project could be seen as little more than a series of apparently insurmountable obstacles which had been solved either by flashes of inspirational genius or by outrageous good luck. Syntheaven was very much in the latter category. It seemed ironic that one of the most lethally addictive products to emerge from the illicit narcotics factories, which had been a bane of police forces for more than a generation, should prove so crucial to a project aimed at benefiting mankind.

The discovery that Syntheaven greatly increased the human brain's capacity to cope with expanded consciousness and to accept association with artificial intelligence came as a real breakthrough at a crucial time. The details of quite *how* the discovery was made and which of the pilots had been indulging between sessions remained deliberately obscure. Since then, the drug had been constantly refined, adapted to remove some of its less pleasant side-effects, such as the loss of bowel control which frequent users often experienced and the unfortunate neural implications, while its mind-expanding properties were enhanced. Unfortunately, one thing they had not been able to eradicate was its highly addictive nature, which was where the second drug in Philip's precious black box came into its own. A bespoke narcotic developed specifically to counteract the addictive properties of Syntheaven.

Two rows of small perspex bubbles occupied the bottom section of the moulded interior, each snug in its individual slot. Symbolically, the Syntheaven ampoules were the devil's own colour – red – while those containing the inhibitor were green – the colour of grass, of healthy growing things, of nature itself. Alongside the colour-coded bubbles lay the dull grey length of the applicator, which would fire a high-pressure dose of the loaded narcotic through the skin and directly into the bloodstream.

His fingers ran lightly over the applicator but settled on the other item contained within the box, a collapsed web of metal wires and beads beneath which rested two bizarrely pirate-like eye patches. Strangely appropriate, given the fact that official Kaufman Industries records showed this equipment had been destroyed as obsolete.

He lifted the delicate-seeming web out of its housing and it immediately assumed a more rigid form – a bowl -shaped cradle of wires, with the two patches at one edge. He fitted this mesh dome partway over his head, with two significantly larger beads dangling near his ears and the eye patches resting on his forehead. Already, as always at this point, he felt as if his consciousness were expanding, though he knew this was self-delusion. Without the Syntheaven and without pushing the cradle fully home, the nodes would not yet have connected with the targeted areas of his brain, and this early, crude product of the project could not be having any effect. But the feeling persisted, as if he had to consciously resist leaping into the darkness before everything was ready.

With exaggerated care, he picked up the applicator, slipped one of the red ampoules in place and pressed it to his throat. There was no sound to indicate the narcotic had been dispatched and no pain, just a cold tingle to confirm that the dose had been administered.

Quickly now, Philip put down the applicator, slid the headpiece fully into position, pressed home the ear studs and eye blinders and lay back, the recliner reacting instantly to his new requirements.

Phil, are you there? he thought rather than said.

Yes, I'm here, his partial responded and so, reassured, he let go, entering another world.

The apartment block which Philip called home for the majority of the year was one of the most exclusive and desirable in the city. As a consequence, it boasted a sophisticated computer system to oversee the micro-climate, security arrangements, staff deployment, garbage recycling, maintenance and delivery schedules – all the mundane administrative and technical minutiae which enabled the building to function as a community.

This was not self-aware, not an AI, but it was still a sophisticated piece of kit. Even granting that what he experienced here, via prototype equipment incapable of facilitating full gestalt even if this were an AI, fell a long way short of the real thing, Philip still felt a thrill of anticipation as he embarked on his own unique form of joy-riding the building's information highway.

Philip's career path had never been an issue. He showed an aptitude for computers at an early age and a quick grasp of all things mechanical. His intelligence registered at far above average and following in his father's footsteps had been the natural choice. He quickly excelled at design and research and few begrudged Malcolm's decision to groom him as his successor. Philip had never for one moment questioned that decision, had never seen anything he would rather be doing; until, perhaps, recently.

Oh, he recognised that his position was one of privilege and knew at an intellectual level that his life could hardly be better, but even so...

These illicit excursions were his way of assuaging the occasional bouts of curiosity and wistful regret that he was prone to.

He settled back, dismissed all peripheral musings and concentrated on the experience that awaited him.

It always began with a peculiar sense of dislocation, a split second of disorientation which never failed to catch him unawares despite his knowing what to expect. Just as his mind began to adjust to this new state it was blown wide open by the wonderful feeling of expansion, as if some barrier in his head had been swept away, allowing his consciousness to flow out in a way it had always been intended to. That was the part that invariably left him feeling a little in awe afterwards – the lingering impression that this state of consciousness was *right*, for him and perhaps for all humanity.

Fully attuned to his surroundings, he began to take note of what else occupied this adjusted reality. As ever, he experienced things in a strangely skewed manner, as if he were an observer rather than a participant, like somebody dipping their face into a lake and peering beneath the surface. He was fully aware that this was the big difference between his experience and that of the pilots. They were fully immersed in this reality, the swimmers to his pond-dipper. He suppressed the comparison and concentrated on what awaited.

The first thing to confront him was a list of tasks, things which the computer had earmarked for attention both overnight and during the next day. There was no writing, nothing so substantial, but rather a sequence of meanings which drifted through his perception, insubstantial veils brushing his consciousness and each leaving an impression – a camera on the blink here, interference in a resident's comms unit there (indicating faulty insulation), erratic climate levels in two adjacent apartments on the thirteenth floor – suggesting a faulty processor unit – a loose service hatch on the ground floor which a departing electrician had failed to secure properly following his visit, a dead area in a corridor on the twenty-third where the sensors had completely failed (this latter flagged as a top priority) and a further dozen or more minor maintenance issues.

Fortunately, his own apartment was blissfully free of any problems, which saved him from one temptation in that direction, but a corner of his mind snagged on a familiar name: Cindra Broughton, a willowy young blonde with an apartment on the floor below who had warmed his bed on a regular basis for a while. They had parted on good terms and remained casual friends. Evidently she was having problems with the security system, her front door not always releasing and opening at the first time of asking. He bumped the issue up towards the top of the list from its former position near the bottom, for old times' sake.

To Philip, this reality was not something he experienced in any physical sense. There was no avatar or other analogy of self, nothing to centre awareness on and claim 'this is me.' It was more the case that anything he wanted to reach which stood within the computer's compass of being he could summon instantly before him, or perhaps it would be more accurate to say that he directed his awareness to them. It was as if he were already touching everywhere and everything, and merely focused attention on any given point. Since the computer governed all aspects of the building, what lay open to him were its residents, their apartments and *their* computers, which invariably communicated with the building systems for all manner of requirements on a daily basis. He could have taken it beyond the building but resisted the temptation, conscious of this system's limitations and wary of over-extending himself. Besides, there was plenty here to keep him occupied.

Of particular interest at the moment was a resident by the name of Pelloy McGovern, who had the type of security system built into his PC which a government department would have been proud of. Some people might have seen this as a warning to stay clear. To Philip, it was a challenge.

During recent visits he had familiarised himself with McGovern's defences. The first time he risked actually breaching them had been nerve-wracking as hell, though he knew it was all a question of perception. No matter how formidable these protective programs might be, they still permitted communication with the wider world, allowing information to flow to and fro across them and only coming into play when something was perceived as a threat or unfamiliar. All Philip had to do was ensure they saw him as an impulse they were configured to accept, so that they presented themselves as a porous mesh rather than an impenetrable wall.

Confident in his disguise, he had pushed his consciousness towards the barrier. He'd never tried breaching a system this sophisticated before, so remained alert for the unexpected.

As it turned out, he simply slipped on through without drawing any reaction at all.

Once inside, he discovered a wealth of encrypted information and locked files. On that first visit he had simply studied them, familiarising himself with the structure of McGovern's records as much as possible and deciding which files to target first. Now he returned, ready to take on the encryptions themselves and discover what secrets lay hidden behind them.

He couldn't have cared less what those secrets might be, it was the challenge that drew him, that and the thrill of doing something illicit and getting away with it. The problem was that he *had* been getting away with it, and was a sucker for the temptation to push the boundaries that little bit further. As a result, Philip had begun to think of himself as invulnerable;

a trap he would never have fallen into in his professional life.

So when he began to unravel the code to a particularly tempting packet of information and the alarm went off, it caught him completely by surprise. There was no sound, it was more a sense of awakening around him, the realisation that something here had been alerted to his presence. Belatedly, Philip considered that maybe this time he'd pushed his luck too far. He immediately abandoned what he was doing and fled. Was it just imagination, or did the defences resist his departure far more than they had his arrival? If so, too little too late; as he successfully pulled his awareness free of McGovern's systems.

Yet it wasn't over. Something touched him; cold, implacable and deadly, and he knew that whatever this was, it was coming after him. A search program, a virtual hound tailor-made to seek and destroy, and doubtless one bristling with nasty surprises.

Philip had long ago learned to differentiate between taking a chance and being reckless. The first equalled excitement; the latter was more likely to prove either painful or expensive. His father probably had a maxim to cover this as well, but, if so, Kaufman junior had done his best to forget it.

He'd had the foresight to take a few precautions when first indulging in these night-time excursions, establishing and installing latent counter measures of his own. Now, as his consciousness fled for all it was worth along a predetermined route, he was more than grateful of them. Ghost programmes rose up at his back, presenting the hound with false seemings designed to confuse systems and cause delay – fractional, but that was all he needed. Next a myriad of misleading trails blossomed in his wake, so that his was suddenly one of hundreds of pathways that sprang from a single point, some of the others linked to genuine locations while many were complete fakes, leading nowhere and disappearing almost as soon as they were birthed. Behind him, his own trail was vanishing in much the same way, erased by his passage.

This was a desperate flight and one which Philip had never truly expected to make. He knew his safeguards were good, but he had a feeling so was the hound. Even so, as his consciousness returned fully to his physical body, he dared to hope that he might just have got away with it.

Philip sat up, gasping for breath and conscious of his pounding heart. He pulled the studs from his ears and ripped the mesh cage away from his head, dragging the blinders off his eyes in the process, before flinging the whole contraption down onto the floor. Philip Kaufman was rarely fazed but the past couple of days were proving eventful, to say the least; few things scared him, but what he had sensed pursuing him just then did.

"Phil, is there anything attempting to trace me?"

"Not as far as I can see."

"So the indications are…"

"… that you got away with it, yes."

Hardly a cast-iron guarantee, but better than nothing. No harm in double-checking, though. "Run a systems check. Any trace of intrusion, or of anything knocking on the door during the past five minutes, I want to know about it."

"Checking now. I'll get back to you."

While he waited for his partial's report, Philip reached for the applicator, a little dismayed at how much his hand shook. He took a few seconds to steady himself before jettisoning the spent red bulb and replacing it with a green one. He then lifted the applicator quickly to his neck and positioned it over the carotid artery before triggering, so that the addiction inhibitor was delivered to the brain as swiftly as possible. He sat there with eyes closed, waiting for the temptation to load another red ampoule to fade, while fearing, as ever, that this time it wouldn't, that the inhibitor would have no effect at all. Slowly the craving subsided, not disappearing entirely but at least reaching a point where it was manageable. He knew that from here it would soon slip away until he could pretend not to notice it at all.

When Phil did report back a few seconds later, it was to confirm the same thing as before: there was no sign of any continued pursuit. So why did Philip still feel so uneasy? Why did he have the nagging sense that perhaps he hadn't escaped as cleanly as he seemed to have done?

CHAPTER SIX

PHILIP TENDED TO work from home most of the time, dropping into the office whenever a significant sim-run or other important event was scheduled – once or twice a week at most. But things were suddenly different. Life had acquired new zest and nothing could have kept him away from the office just then. Not for any rational, quantifiable reason. Had he bothered to sit back and analyse it, he could almost certainly have worked as effectively and achieved as much from the 'virtual' office at home as he could from the physical one across town, and saved the transit time to boot... but that would have meant missing out on so much. 'Job satisfaction,' Malcolm would have called it. All Philip knew was that he wanted to hang on to the previous day's buzz for as long as possible, and that could only be done if he were at the heart of things, able to feed from and also contribute to the collective energy and vibe rather than merely sip from its edges.

Besides, there were other reasons for going in. The latest variant of bastardised Syntheaven should be ready for testing later that day, and they had high hopes of this one. Then, too, there was a call he needed to make, one which would look far better coming from the office – presentation might not be everything, but it counted, and he wanted to avoid any suggestion that this was a casual or social call.

"Philip, good to see you."

"Hello, Geoffrey, thank you for sparing the time to talk to me."

Geoffrey Hamilton was more than a decade older than Philip, though you would never have known it to look at him. He possessed the sort of youthful vigour, not to mention the permanent yet subtle tan, which seemed reserved for politicians and other public performers. Philip had yet to catch him with a single strand of his sandy brown hair out of place, no matter what the hour. As reigning global president and a member of the wider star-spanning government, he was also nominally the single most powerful person on Homeworld, commercial interests aside.

"Not at all; always available for you, Philip."

Total bollocks and they both knew it. Though, as one of the man's principal supporters *and* head of Kaufman Industries, Philip knew he was pretty hard to ignore.

"How secure is this signal?" he asked.

The president smiled. "As secure as anything can be, or so my people assure me."

Philip had known as much but was keen to impress upon Hamilton a sense of gravitas. "Good. I'm going to send you through some images, with your permission." Or without it, for that matter.

"Go ahead. Care to tell me what I'll be looking at?"

"Sure. *The Noise Within*. We've discovered her identity," Philip said casually, as the familiar image materialised in the air before Hamilton.

"You have? About time someone made some progress on that front, but I wasn't expecting it to be you…"

The president's voice trailed off as the image began to rotate and shed attachments, in a repeat of the previous day's performance.

"What you're looking at is *The Sun Seeker*," Philip explained as soon as the display reached its conclusion, and before Hamilton could admit his ignorance by asking.

For a moment the older man looked blank, but then realisation seemed to dawn. He stared again at the image, then at Philip and back. "*The Sun Seeker*? That old wartime experiment? You mean this *Noise Within* business is all your friggin' fault?"

"Hardly," Philip assured him, prepared for such a reaction. "I wasn't even alive at the time and all Kaufman Industries were doing was carrying out a government commission, so if anything it's *your* friggin' fault, or rather your predecessors'." He knew the man well enough to talk to him like that, and had no qualms about doing so. He had always half-suspected that Hamilton appreciated such straight talking – something he was unlikely to hear from those around him, most of whose jobs depended on the president's goodwill.

Hamilton waved a dismissive hand. "We can apportion blame later. I'm more concerned with the here and now. Don't think I'm not grateful for your information, it's all very interesting, but how exactly is this going to help us stop the wretched thing?"

"Well, I could harp on about knowing your enemy being the first step to understanding him, and understanding him being the first step to defeating him..."

"But you're not going to."

"No. Because, you see, there's more..."

Philip sent across the second parcel of images. The stripped-down ship was replaced by a three-dimensional map showing a section of space. Within that map, shaded elliptical areas appeared, depicted in pale blue.

"These are the areas of space in which *The Sun Seeker's* test flights took place." Four red dots followed, each pulsing so the eye couldn't miss them. "These are the locations of the four attacks to date which have been credited to *The Noise Within*."

The four red dots all sat squarely within a blue-shaded section.

The president nodded. "So she's sticking to the areas she knows." He looked up towards Philip suddenly, accusingly. "How come no one else has spotted this before?"

"Because nobody else was looking. Why would you, unless

you'd already made the connection with *The Sun Seeker*? But now that you *do* know, this should make the job of anticipating where she's going to strike next a hell of a lot easier."

The president stroked his chin before nodding again, very deliberately.

"There's something else."

"Not a 'but', I hope."

"No." Philip laughed in what he hoped was a reassuring manner. "Actually, it's a bit of good news for a change. Give me a month and I'll be able to deliver you a system which can take on *The Noise Within* at her own game."

The president's stare gained new intensity. "You're that close?"

"We are," Philip assured him, crossing metaphorical fingers.

The president absorbed that for a second. "You'll need ships."

"Already in production."

"Good... good. So, just to make sure we're both completely clear about this. You're assuring me that a month from now Kaufman Industries can deliver to the ULAW government battle-ready units capable of stopping *The Noise Within*."

Philip had to be careful not to get carried away here and promise the impossible. He chose his words with great deliberation. "I'm telling you that a month from now I expect to deliver you a squadron of at least a dozen ships and pilots which will be able to face up to *The Noise Within* and will stand every chance of beating her. They won't be battle-hardened, won't be experienced beyond simulator level, but they *will* be ready."

The president held his gaze. "Good enough. If you need anything to make this happen, anything at all, just ask. This gets top priority."

Yes. Philip kept the elation from his face and voice as he said, "Thank you, Geoffrey."

"No, thank you, Philip. I owe you one; we all do."

"Any time, Geoffrey, any time."

Philip let out a long sigh after the call had ended. He'd just secured his team near limitless federal resources to supplement the not-inconsiderable ones Kaufman Industries already had at their disposal. In exchange, he had also given the project something it had never had before: a deadline, committing them to a schedule that was by no means certain. Yes, they were close, but after all these years, a *month*? But he had sensed Geoffrey would not have responded to anything longer.

Susan Tan was going to kill him.

Yet he saw this as a positive step. There was nothing like a deadline to focus the mind, to spur them on for that last big push, which was precisely how he intended to pitch this to Susan and the team.

She was still going to kill him.

Philip chose to delay contacting the media to tell them about the *Sun Seeker / Noise Within* link for another couple of hours. That would give Hamilton time to set wheels in motion and to prepare for the media onslaught that was about to come. He'd then make sure that the man *knew* the reason for the delay. It never hurt to have a president in your debt.

"Doctor Kaufman?"

Late afternoon and he was on his way home. At the sound of his name Philip glanced back over his shoulder, to see something which made the decision to come into the office seem worthwhile all by itself.

She was a vision of porcelain perfection; her pale skin managing to radiate vitality rather than anything wan or sickly, with a suggestion of icy strength underlying it, while the lustrous night-black hair, though worn comparatively short, was meticulously coiffured into full-bodied waves with two elegantly crafted strands curling in to kiss her high-boned cheeks. Yet by far the most striking features were her eyes, which were large and of a brown so dark that they seemed to mirror her hair. Onyx orbs set against virgin snow, they lent her gaze a directness guaranteed to skewer any man's heart.

Philip knew without doubt that here before him stood the most beautiful woman in this or any other world.

"Julia Cirese, Universal News." She held out her ID but he barely glanced at it, unwilling to tear his gaze away from that face.

"Sorry to pounce on you like this." If only, he fleetingly thought. Her voice matched her appearance: strong but with a musicality and a surprisingly high pitch that hinted of the girl she must have been not so very long ago. "But I've been trying to reach you for weeks. Your staff do a great job of protecting you."

He recovered enough equilibrium to smile and say, "It's always a relief to know that, Ms Cirese; after all, that's what I pay them for. But you've got my attention now." And how!

"I'm glad to hear that; and it's Julia, please." The smile she returned was dazzling. "I won't keep you long; I just wanted to schedule an interview with you, assuming you're willing. I'm doing a series on the most significant entrepreneurs of our time, and you're top of my list."

An interview? He hated interviews and usually left such things to Phil. Yet he said without hesitation, "Of course. Send the questions through to my secretary and I'll..."

The way she screwed up her face and dropped her gaze for a second showed exactly what she thought of that idea. "Sorry, it wasn't a pre-recorded answer session I was after. I know it's old fashioned of me, but I really do prefer the spontaneity of conducting my interviews face to face. That way I can get a better feel of who you are and can bring so much more texture and presence to the report. Of course, I can forward the main thrust of the questions in advance so you can prepare and you'll have power of veto on the piece before it goes out, but I was hoping to sit down and do this somewhere with just you, me and a mini-cam."

All of which suited him down to the ground, but why stop there? "That could prove to be a little tricky," he said with what he hoped was a suitable level of regret. "I'm well and truly snowed-under at present. Unless, perhaps," he added, as if it were sudden inspiration, "we could find some time outside of working hours...?" Did this come across as transparently as it felt?

"That sounds good to me."

If so, she clearly didn't mind. He took a deep breath and went for broke. "Perhaps over dinner?" He knew exactly where, as well: Piérre's – an intimate table in one of the bay windows overlooking the harbour; exquisite food complimented by an equally impressive wine, which he would carefully select from their famous list....

"That would be lovely, so long as you don't mind a fly cam hovering over the table throughout."

An intrusion like that might well be enough to get even *him* ejected from Piérre's, or any of the exclusive restaurants he preferred to frequent. "Ah yes..." Could he invite her to his place for dinner instead? No, not impressive enough and too much hassle. "Perhaps not, then. How about if we have dinner first and then do the interview afterwards?"

"Even better; when did you have in mind?"

He resisted the temptation to say 'how about right now?'

"I should mention that I'm due off-world on an assignment in a few days," she said into the silence of his pause. "We could always do this after I get back, if you'd prefer."

Off-world? That could take weeks. He *had* to see her before then. "Right... well, we might as well get it out the way sooner rather than later. Are you free tomorrow evening?"

"I am now. Do you want to wricme?"

Philip was caught off guard by this vaguely recognised expression, a reaction which made him feel suddenly old and out of touch as its meaning belatedly dawned. "Sure," he said, hoping she hadn't noticed his hesitation but certain that she had.

He touched the side of his wrist information centre or wric – the 'personalised companion no civilised man or woman can do without' or so the advertisers insisted. Programmed to respond to him alone, the screen pulsed once with luminous green light behind the digital time display, to show that it recognised his touch and was receptive.

"Actually, it's probably easier if I wricu…"

"All right, mine's receptive."

She touched her wric, which squirted her ID across to Philip's. The screen on his pulsed once, indicating it had just logged a new 'friend', which meant it would now accept messages from Julia. He activated his own ID, repeating the process but in reverse.

She touched her unit again and the face of Philip's wric pulsed a second time, to confirm that it had received a fresh parcel of information; doubtless Julia's standard contact package, which could include all manner of things, usually a brief bio, selected photo images, plus details of food preferences, musical taste, hobbies, preferred drinks etc., maybe even her favourite colour – all the information which most people would have no interest in until they got to know you better, if then, but which the manufacturers reckoned should be available in any case. Except that in this instance, Philip might just take the trouble to look; even at her favourite colour.

A small green envelope would now reside in the top left corner of the wric face until he opened the message. The wrics were independent units, isolated from other systems and loaded with security safeguards so that all information received could be vetted and 'cleaned' before being downloaded elsewhere. Now that they were established 'friends', he could reach her at the touch of a button or a word to his partial.

"See you tomorrow, and thanks." She gifted him another dazzling smile and then turned to leave.

He hadn't noticed her figure until she walked away, too captivated by that face, that smile, but now wondered how he could possibly have failed to do so. In theory, even the office's car park was a secure area, but Julia Cirese struck him as a very determined lady. Watching her now, it didn't surprise him in the least that she had managed to get in here. In fact, Philip suspected that she could gain access to just about anywhere she wanted.

Philip continued to his car – a black coffee bean of a vehicle, shining like some newly minted medal. At his approach, a seam appeared in the car's side, a split which gradually widened to become a door, the surface to either side seeming to ripple as the opening appeared. Philip sat into the car and the door immediately sealed itself.

"Good afternoon, Doctor Kaufman. Destination?"

"Home."

The two-seater car began to move as soon as he was comfortable. The pod-like vehicle provided perfect visibility on all sides, even though the exterior appeared to be a uniform glossy black. Philip could have had the view opaqued, but he preferred to watch the city slip past around him, particularly when the alternative was to be cocooned within a private cell, oblivious to the world outside.

"Music, sir?"

He thought for a second; "Tydell's *Solar Flare*." Raucous in parts, but it began soothingly enough with some wonderful moments, and he would be home before the louder sections arrived.

The first part of the journey took place underground – only a couple of minutes but it carried him nearly halfway home; a direct, straight route at an even pace, which ate up the miles far more effectively than would have been possible above ground, where buildings and other obstructions kept insisting on getting in the way.

Happy coincidence saw *Solar Flare* hit a section in which the music swelled to a minor crescendo at the exact moment the car emerged into daylight once more, so providing a fittingly dramatic accompaniment to one of Philip's favourite views of the metropolis. The towering buildings at the city's heart seemed to emerge from the ground like primordial giants, and from this lowly vantage point you were treated to their full sweeping grandeur as they exploded upward, stretching towards the heavens. A little ahead and to the right stood the Skyhall hotel with its twin glass spires, which at present sparkled with sunlight, as if in reaching for the stars they had somehow each snatched one and brought them back to the ground. Beside the Skyhall was the contrasting grey solidity of the Mirayla building with its crenellated crown and, beyond that, more imposing buildings still. Surely it was impossible not to marvel at such a sight?

Just as he was craning his neck, imagining he could see the multi-levelled crenellations which he knew to be high above him, the car's computer spoke, shattering his pleasure.

"There is an unauthorised vehicle behind us."

"Unauthorised in what sense?" Philip wondered, more than a little irritated at the interruption.

"A vehicle not regulated by the city's traffic control system."

"What?" That had him sitting up. "Where? Show me."

The dashboard screen dutifully displayed the traffic around them. His own car appeared as a blue stretched oblong with rounded corners, while other vehicles were depicted in beetle black; except for one, four cars back and in the same lane, which was singled out in red. The shape and colour reminded Philip of the Syntheaven ampoules and he felt a familiar stirring, but hot on the heels of that association came his recollection of the previous evening's unfortunate episode.

He gave an involuntary shiver and concentrated on the image before him. There was no reason to think this unregistered car had anything to do with him at all, but it never hurt to be cautious. "Take the higher lane. Let's see if it reacts."

He watched the screen intently, the Syntheaven craving having subsided to the merest whisper at the edge of thought, easily ignored. After a few seconds a gap duly appeared in the stream of vehicles outside them, as the request to change lanes was accepted, allowing his car to slip into the outermost and fastest moving lane of traffic.

Shippeys, who for so long had attempted to challenge Kaufman's in the race to perfect a human/AI interface, were responsible for the automated traffic systems which now governed the flow of vehicles in major cities across much of human space.

That suited Philip just fine. They were welcome to design all the traffic systems for every world they wanted to as far as he was concerned.

Homeworld had been among the first to embrace the system and Philip had even been a strong supporter. "Stick to what you know," he muttered.

"Sorry, sir?"

"Nothing."

Philip had to admit that Shippeys had done a fabulous job. Since their traffic supervision system had been adopted here, with interconnecting arterial highways between all the population centres involved, major snarl-ups were a thing of the past and road traffic fatalities had been reduced to virtually zero. The 'virtually' could be explained by such factors as freak natural disasters, rebellious free spirits who still insisted on driving manually along unregulated rural roads outside of the towns, and very rare systems failures.

Nobody really drove their cars any more. They simply got in, logged onto the traffic system's grid, stated their destination and sat back, surrendering control to central and joining the stream of computer-directed traffic which flowed constantly throughout the city's streets, as smoothly as blood feeding a body. Perfect, really, from the state's point of view. The road system had in effect become another form of public transport, though one in which people's 'space' was never invaded and their privacy was maintained, while the public shared much of the burden of cost by financing their own vehicles. Add to that the freeing-up of resources previously dedicated to traffic control or dealing with accidents and their consequences, and it was no wonder Shippeys' system had proven to be so popular on so many worlds.

None of which allowed for the presence of an unregulated vehicle on the urban roads. Philip chewed at his bottom lip, never having heard of anything like this before. Memories of his helter-skelter flight from the building's computer system came back to haunt him, along with that nagging fear that his escape had not been as clean as it seemed. Paranoia, surely; it was ridiculous to think that last night's events were in any way related to this rogue vehicle.

He had just about convinced himself of that when the red lozenge changed lanes, moving out to join the string of beads his own car was a part of.

"Get me Phil." Normally, the in-car computer was adequate for its purpose, but in a situation like this Philip preferred to have access to a higher level of insight and resource.

"Here," the summoned partial said, almost at once.

The suspect car had changed lanes as smoothly as you like, which meant a suitable gap in the traffic must have been created to accommodate it, yet the system was apparently oblivious to the vehicle's presence. All of which suggested that somebody was manipulating things very deftly.

"How's he doing this?" he asked the air, not bothering to check if Phil was up to speed – he would have been as soon as he arrived.

"Not certain as yet. I'm working on it. The system has myriad elements and a host of perfectly legitimate sources of input – it has to, in order to remain flexible. Trying to trace one source that shouldn't be there, or one that should but which is doing things out of the ordinary… took me a while."

"You *have* found it, though?"

"Of course." Phil might not have represented as

comprehensive a personality download as Mal, but he was well on the way and was certainly a good deal more sophisticated than the standard 'protocol partial' which most people created and employed. Phil was Philip's closest ally, able to access places and information which the corporeal Kaufman could never have reached and martial resources in an instant which would have taken Philip considerable time and effort. The perfect assistant – unflinchingly loyal, and he always knew what Philip was talking about.

"It's as if the whole system is in denial – accommodating this unregistered car but refusing to acknowledge the fact," Philip murmured.

"Actually, that might be a better analogy than you realise. They're hacked deep into the system, to the point where not only are they able to manipulate it, they're then able to erase their own tracks and all record of the vehicle as they go. Ingenious, really."

This still didn't prove the rogue had anything to do with Philip, but he never had been a great believer in coincidence. Assuming it really was after him, he still didn't see what those driving the car were hoping to achieve. Due to the inevitable slight delay in its response to Philip's lane change the rogue was now three cars further back than it had been, and they were now both in the fastest lane. So how was it ever intending to catch him?

Perhaps this was simply a joyrider out to buck the system and Philip was being over-sensitive following the previous night's narrow escape. Mind you, if so, this had to be the most expensive and sophisticated joyride in history.

He watched uneasily, waiting for the unregulated car to *do* something.

He didn't have to wait long.

The suspect vehicle moved out to straddle the two lanes – both the one they were in and the slower one they had recently left. As it did so, the cars ahead of it all shifted sideways a little, the two lines drawing away from each other to leave a clear path between Philip and the rogue.

"Can *we* do anything like that?" he wondered.

"No chance," the partial replied. "I don't have that sort of access to the traffic system, let alone control. I might be able to find a way given enough time, but –"

"We don't have that time," Philip finished for him. He watched as the rogue began to accelerate, easing towards them. "Can we at least patch through what we're seeing to traffic central to show them what's really going on out here?"

"That much I can do."

"And give me a wing mirror, will you? So I can see what's happening back there for myself."

The car duly extruded a mirror from its seamless exterior. Glancing out, Philip could see the maverick clearly enough. A gleaming silver pod on wheels, moving steadily up through the corridor which had so conveniently opened in the traffic to accommodate it. The corridor extended as far as his own car. The fact that in front of him the other vehicles remained stolidly in the centre of their lanes effectively banished any doubt.

He was the target. And a damned easy one too, as things stood.

"Phil, take us off the grid and switch to manual drive."

The dashboard before him immediately split open and a steering wheel unfolded, the column supporting it gaining instant rigidity. At the same time, straps appeared from the back of the seat, which he automatically clipped into place. Philip grasped the unfamiliar wheel tightly, wondering whether this was really such a good idea. It was years since he had driven anywhere, let alone through a crowded city thoroughfare. One further glance at the sinister silver shape in the wing mirror convinced him that he had little choice.

Slowly, he turned the wheel and thumbed the accelerator. His car drifted out of lane and he began to close on the vehicle in front. There didn't look to be enough room to pass between that and the car immediately beside it, but he was going to have to try and squeeze through anyway… and if by some miracle he managed that there would be the next one and then the one after that. He was bound to hit one of them. But what choice did he have?

A warning light which he hadn't even known existed flashed at him from near the top of his viewscreen and a soulless female voice repeatedly asked him to abandon manual control and return to the grid. Ignoring her, he pressed a little harder on the accelerator and closed in on the two cars.

He found he was staring, his eyes wide, when all he really wanted to do was close them tight. His gaze darted between the pair of vehicles, and then focused on the seemingly tiny gap between, which grew smaller the more he stared at it. Finally he decided to concentrate on the space itself rather than the sides of the cars which defined it. He took a deep breath and committed himself, thumbing the accelerator another notch.

At the very last instant, as the snub nose of his vehicle entered the gap and he felt certain he was about to hit one or the other, the two cars ahead of him veered apart.

"Traffic central," Phil supplied. "They might not be able to see the renegade but they *can* see you, and have made room to avoid you causing an accident."

Philip felt a huge surge of relief and pressed his thumb down as far as it would go, feeling the car surge forward in response, shooting between the twin lines of other vehicles.

But the silver car continued to close. The two of them were racing down the same corridor. There had to be a break at some point, even allowing for the fact that this was 'rush hour' when those who still physically went to work were liable to be travelling home, but there was no sign of one yet. Ahead of him stretched twin lines of cars, appearing to be strung together like beads on a wire, creating boundaries which defined his world at present. This was a straight race – a hound and a hare; and it was immediately apparent that the pursuer had the legs on Philip's hare.

The bordering cars were passing in a blur, the speed of his passage robbing them of definition, so that they seemed to be almost solid barriers. His concentration was fixed on the road ahead, on keeping the wheel steady. The silver nemesis continued to edge nearer, until it loomed close behind him, filling the rear windscreen as if intent on ramming his vehicle. Was that the plan – to shunt him into the other cars at high speed?

If so, Philip didn't see how he could prevent it. There was no way out. He could *feel* the presence of the other car so acutely it might as well have been breathing down his neck.

A reckless impulse gripped him. If this really was the end, then let it be on his terms, not the pursuer's.

Before he could analyse the concept and think of all the reasons why this was such a bad idea, Philip lifted his right thumb off the accelerator and at the same time pressed his left down hard on the brake. He had read about, heard about and seen dramatisations that involved the squeal of tyres, but had never experienced the effect firsthand before. The sound struck him as suitably dramatic. As the skid began, the car held remarkably steady – a testament to the quality of the design – for all of that split second or two before the rogue slammed into its back, throwing him violently forward in the restraints, the straps biting into his shoulder.

Impact cushions inflated on all sides. The car seemed to slew and rock. Philip lost track of what was happening. The straps around him became implements of screaming agony, gripping, biting and squeezing him as his body was flung this way and that, its momentum struggling against them.

Finally, mercifully, the chaos stopped.

For long seconds he simply sat there, breathing deeply, raggedly, feeling his bruises and his aching neck and not quite able to believe he was still alive.

A sense of danger did not so much seep back as slam back into his thoughts. Yet the impact cushions still engulfed him and he had no idea what was going on beyond them.

"Phil, get rid of these stupid bags, will you!"

"Those stupid bags just saved your life," the partial's calm voice reminded him.

He felt a huge surge of relief that at least this much of the car's systems still worked. "That's as may be, but if I can't see what the hell's going on, they might yet cost me it as well."

The foam-filled bags were deflating even as he spoke, their contents dissolving to liquid smears, and he was already able to see past them. The first thing that struck him was that nothing was moving. The cars on both sides were stationary; traffic central must have shut this section of the grid down. Then he looked behind, primarily to see what had happened to the rogue, but what he first noticed were the dented, partially buckled forms of several cars in the 'wall' on his left, and at least one badly scraped vehicle to the right.

"Central had stopped all traffic before the actual crash," Phil told him; which explained why the cars had seemed to flash past so quickly. "You were pushed into one car, scraping along its side, then caught the back corner of the next, which brought the back of your car around and sent you sideways. The back struck a car in the opposite side and you rebounded to hit a further four cars on the left. It's a miracle you didn't roll."

Phil made it sound so simple, so clinical. "Did I hurt anyone else?"

"Unknown."

Then he saw the silver car, which lay on its side, the crumpled front wedged between two of the cars in the right-hand lane, which themselves had been pushed out of traffic central's nice neat line. Both looked to have sustained a fair bit of damage and the nearest had half-mounted the car in front, causing it to now rest balanced at a precarious angle.

Sirens were sounding somewhere in the distance.

As Philip took all this in, he saw movement from the rogue. He saw first a black-clad arm and then a head emerge from the skyward side of the stricken vehicle. There was something odd about both. They seemed ill-defined, like hastily drawn sketches of a head and limb.

First one and then a second black figure clambered from the stricken car, to drop to the ground, presumably keen to make their escape before the police arrived. Although he was looking straight at them, Philip found it frustratingly difficult to actually see the pair; it was as if his gaze kept sliding past them every time he tried to focus. All he was left with was the impression of vaguely human forms in a fuzzy smudge of black, which was a very bizarre and unsettling sensation.

"What the hell are they wearing?"

"Matts," Phil replied. "They utilise similar technology to the military's shimmer suits but aren't as effective. A poor man's version of the real thing."

Philip knew about shimmer suits; their outer coating consisted of thousands upon thousands of interconnected microprocessors and receptors, all constantly communicating in order to produce an ongoing illusion. Anybody looking at someone in an activated shimmer suit would only see what lay beyond the wearer, no matter which angle they were viewing from. The result was convincing enough to fool even man's perception of depth of field. Standing still, a wearer became invisible to all intents and purposes. On the move, the result was less perfect, as the system had to constantly adapt its illusions to keep up with the movement, but it was still damned impressive. Generally there was just a slight shimmer reminiscent of a heat haze to give the wearer away – hence the suits' name.

"Why not simply get a shimmer suit and be done with it?" he wondered.

"Because shimmer suits are rarer than computer shit on the sidewalk and, in the unlikely event you should ever find one, it would carry a price tag which reflects the fact. Matts are not exactly cheap, but they are compared to a shimmer suit and they're much more accessible. Besides, they do have their uses, confusing a shape or outline enough to make most people pause, while if somebody wearing one stands in deep shadow you'd never know they were there unless they moved."

"Shit!" Philip's exclamation came as he realised that the two figures were not fleeing the scene as anticipated; far from it. They were coming towards him and one was carrying what looked to be an impressively large gun. As Philip watched, the gun swept up to point his way.

Philip grasped the steering wheel again and thumbed the accelerator, praying that the thing would respond. To his relief, the car leapt forward instantly, though the steering seemed shot. He careened into one of the motionless cars in front of him, to half bounce, half scrape along its side before lurching past.

"Sorry," Philip mumbled, pointlessly.

A shiver ran through his body, quite unexpectedly, and he felt the hairs on his neck stand on end. At the same instant, the windscreen in front of him turned opaque; it was only for a second, but that was long enough for Philip to slam on the brakes with a squeeze of his index finger, as he found himself driving blind.

The screen cleared again, the darkness withdrawing rapidly to the edges before disappearing completely. But a large hole, roughly the size of his head, now punctured the screen, just left of centre, as if that section had simply melted away – reinforced or not.

A quick check confirmed that the back of the car now sported a similar hole. A shock of fear coursed through Philip's body as he realised just how near a miss that had been and how close he had come to dying.

He made no effort to see where the two black-clad figures might be, his only concern was to get away from here, to run as quickly as he could. Already the attacker might be adjusting his aim, ready for another shot.

Philip jammed the accelerator down until his thumb hurt. The car shot forward again, jolting him back in his seat, but almost immediately the power died and the vehicle started coasting towards a halt.

Horrified, Philip pressed again and again, while the car continued to slow. "Come on, you bastard," he yelled, "come on!"

But there was no response. The power had simply gone. Phil was trying to tell him something, but the partial's words didn't register. The car came to a complete halt. Philip knew with a horrible certainty that he was about to die, without ever knowing who had killed him or why. Somehow these anonymous attackers had immobilised his car and they were now coming to finish him off.

Even as he thought that, the seam of a door appeared beside him, where none had a right to be without his say so. It widened to become a door and Philip found himself staring down the barrel of a gun. He shrank away, waiting for the end.

Yet seconds passed and he was still alive. The man behind the gun was yelling, and gesturing with the barrel for Philip to come out. Perhaps they wanted to take him alive. Renewed hope energised his limbs and he started to comply, undoing straps and moving his feet towards the door, but the man evidently lost patience and reached in to pull him out.

Belatedly, Philip registered the uniform; not the black matts of his attackers at all but rather the dark blues and black of the police. Men were shouting and a cruiser hovered above his head, lights blazing down despite the daylight, while other uniformed figures swarmed around. Sanity began to return. He stood still, pressed against the side of his car while a scanner was traced with steady proficiency across every contour of his body, presumably checking for weapons or other concealed equipment.

Philip didn't care.

"Thank God," he murmured, too relieved to be ashamed of his fear, reckoning he had every right to be afraid.

The police must have thought him either mad or intoxicated, because as he stood there, with their glowers and at least one weapon still trained upon him, all he could do was smile.

CHAPTER SEVEN

THE POLICE AND the hospital seemed to want to fight over him, but in the end his lawyers ensured that neither got their wish and he was permitted to return home. Not before having pain killers administered and a sub-dermis neck brace inserted – one which he'd hardly know was there until it dissolved in a few days' time. Extricating himself from the police proved to be a little harder, primarily because at least one of the officers involved refused to accept that Philip wasn't somehow responsible for the whole thing, despite all evidence to the contrary. Presumably the prospect of arresting such a high-profile figure had gone to the man's head and he simply couldn't bear to see the opportunity disappear. Plus, of course, Philip was the only person the police were physically holding following the incident. The men in the matts had managed to elude capture, which came as no great surprise.

Fortunately, other wiser heads were on hand to ensure that Philip was exonerated and granted the status of victim rather than suspect. He'd still violated a fistful of local laws, but it was accepted that he'd done so only in reaction to a genuine threat and in order to preserve his own skin. This plus the influence he was able to muster ensured that he was released, pending further investigation, though this all took time. It was late in the evening before he was able to return home, with the sage advice that he should 'be especially careful over the next few days' still ringing in his ears.

The police had promised to increase patrols around his home and be ready to respond if he needed assistance. Knowing something about local funding issues, Philip took this as code for 'we'd love to help but we don't really have the resources'.

Philip vowed not to watch the news for the next day or two, confident that the incident, and presumably his face, would be all over it.

In accordance with standing instructions, Phil had refrained from reporting on messages until he was safely indoors.

"Eight calls from different reporters, all requesting to talk to you personally," the partial informed him.

"Are any of them Julia Cirese of Universal News?"

"No."

"Then they'll have to make do with your eloquent self."

"I have a call coming in right now from your fath –"

"Phil!"

"…from Mal," the partial swiftly amended.

Philip was almost disappointed. He would have expected the old man to have more patience than this. It seemed his father's partial simply couldn't resist the opportunity to gloat. Any burgeoning disappointment, however, was soon sidelined by his sense of satisfaction at having successfully out-waited the old goat.

He composed himself before instructing Phil to patch Mal through, determined not to allow any smugness to creep into his voice.

"Mal, what can I do for you?"

"It's more what I can do for you. Again. In case no one's told you yet, you've been listed."

"What?"

"Your name's been posted at *The Death Wish*."

Philip thought this through for a second, turning the words over to see if they might reveal some hidden meaning in the process, but other than a realisation that, to judge by the words 'Death Wish', this probably wasn't good news, he drew a blank. "I'm sorry?"

"You've never even heard of *The Death Wish*, have you."
This wasn't a question, more an expression of disbelief.

"I can't say I have, no."

"Now why doesn't that surprise me?" Definitely a question
this time but a rhetorical one, so Philip kept quiet and waited
for the old man to continue. "It's a bar, a sleazy heaving CGR
bar, one which is frequented by those with certain... skills."

Philip was not in the mood to suffer another 'slow reveal'
from Mal, so there was a distinct edge in his voice as he said,
"Namely?"

"Do I have to spell this out for you? Doesn't the name
suggest anything? It's where assassins and thugs on the make
congregate between jobs – where they go to pick up new
commissions. Thrill seekers too; in fact, anyone who wants to
sample the taste of life at society's shadier fringes."

Really? Now that did pique Philip's curiosity; he had no idea
such a place even existed. "Lowlifes, you mean."

"I couldn't possibly agree with that description, even as a
generalisation, since I hang out there a fair bit myself."

"You do?" Philip was genuinely surprised. This didn't sound
the sort of place he could imagine either Malcolm or Mal
frequenting. "Why?"

"To be prepared, of course, to stay one step ahead of the
game. How else am I ever going to know if somebody's posted
notice on me?"

Which might go some way to explaining why his father *used*
to go there, but was hardly relevant any more. "Okay, I'll buy
that for days gone by, but what's your excuse now?"

"Force of habit."

Or maybe the desire to look out for a son who still numbered
among the living. Philip quashed the thought; somewhere
down that route lay the path to madness, or at least to thinking
that this obscene recording really *was* his father. Then the
context of their conversation sank in. "So you're trying to tell
me that there's a contract out on me?" There went any hope

that today's car problem was a one-off incident.

"Ah, reality bites at last! Yes, that's exactly what I'm telling you."

"Whatever happened to simply hiring a hit man?"

"That's illegal."

"And this isn't?"

"What could the law possibly object to in someone posting a person's name on a message board? And the fact there happen to be some numbers nearby is a complete coincidence."

"But surely the intent...?"

"... is difficult to prove," Mal assured him.

"Look, the authorities do know all about the place."

"Then why haven't they shut it down?"

"Too few resources too thinly spread. And besides, shutting it down would only drive all the lowlifes underground. Who knows, maybe one day the police will have the budget and the backing and the will to take that sort of step, but for now they simply monitor *The Death Wish*. At least this way they can keep up-to-date with who's being targeted."

"Wonderful." Philip shook his head. Even in this day and age nobody seemed to have enough resources to do everything, not even all those things that *needed* doing. "So how come I've never heard about this Death Wish place?" he asked.

"Don't ask me, I thought everybody had; everybody who's wealthy enough and successful enough to make enemies, at any rate. If pushed, I'd guess that you're so caught up in your own personal definition of reality that you never thought to look for it."

Philip ignored the jibe and instead turned his thoughts to another matter; after all, he couldn't help but wonder: "These numbers you mentioned... add up to a lot, do they?"

"Enough that I'm almost tempted to come after you myself."

"That much, huh?"

"Oh yes. Look, I don't know what you've done to piss off whoever it is and I don't want to know, but my advice is to get in touch with them as soon as you can and do whatever it takes to get them un-pissed. Otherwise you're going to have every killer, glory hunter and wannabe in the system making a beeline for this city and, more specifically, for you."

"I'll bear it in mind."

"Make sure you do. Oh, and I'm sending something through. Fifteen wishits."

"*Wishits*? What the hell is a 'wishit' when it's at home?"

"Currency. What you buy drinks with at *The Death Wish*. There, I've credited you with them." The image of three small piles of gold discs appeared in the air before him, five to a pile. "They're transferable, not identity-specific, and you can also use them to pay for membership. Ten will get you in, which leaves you five to play around with."

Philip snorted. "You don't seriously expect me to actually visit this 'Death Wish' place, do you?"

"No, of course not; silly me. Remember what I said, though."

"I will."

Philip wasn't entirely certain what to make of that conversation. He had never before been the subject of a 'contract' or a 'Death Wish', and had never expected to be, but that was not what caused him to sit there for long minutes after ending the call simply analysing his reaction. The uncomfortable truth was that this was the first time in the two years since Malcolm died that the lingering partial had reminded him so strongly of his father.

As for the *Death Wish* itself, Mal had offered some sound advice, no question about that; just a shame it was so impractical in this particular instance. After all, what could he say to the pissed-off individual in question? "Hi, I'm the neighbour who snooped into your private records, but don't worry, I didn't actually *see* anything, so you can rest easy and call off the hounds."

Sure, who wouldn't believe a story like that?

Of course, that didn't mean that contacting McGovern was

a bad idea in principle, it simply wasn't enough on its own... During the conversation with Mal, Phil had fielded a call which he deemed important enough to bring to Philip's attention. It was from the local head of police, Commissioner Kincaid. Philip had met the man briefly at a function but would hardly claim to know him, so he didn't bother returning the call in person, simply reviewed it. Essentially, Kincaid wanted to warn Philip that the police had 'information' that his life was in danger and stressed that, while they would do all they could to provide assistance, they couldn't guarantee his safety against a determined threat. The man closed by suggesting that Philip should consider spending a period off-world, if only for his own safety.

Philip was just digesting this when Phil interrupted his train of thought once more.

"I have a call for you from Catherine Chzyski. She insists it's urgent."

Philip sighed, banishing all consideration of assassins and plans for the moment. This was bound to be about *The Noise Within*. Adjusting his mindset accordingly, he said, "Put her through."

Not for the first time in their association, the canny old shrew managed to surprise him. As her image formed, she said, "I gather from the news feeds that you had a somewhat interesting journey home."

"That's one way to describe it."

"Well I think I can explain why. Were you aware that a Death Wish has been posted against you?"

She knew about this Death Wish site as well? Was he the only one who didn't? Maybe it was a generational thing.

"One offering a sufficiently impressive pay-off that it's bound to attract considerable attention," Catherine continued. Perhaps his face gave him away, because she second-guessed his thoughts by immediately adding, "I've been around a lot longer than you have, Philip. Checking on things like this ensures I'll be around for a while yet. Trust me, the threat is very real and not to be underestimated."

He hardly needed convincing of that. At the same time, if he were to seek advice from anyone, he could do a lot worse than Catherine Chzyski. After a few seconds' thought, he said carefully, "Assuming everything you say is true, what would you do about it if you were in my shoes?"

She raised her eyebrows and the corners of her mouth twitched as if threatening to break into a smile. "What's this, Philip Kaufman asking for advice? Life is still capable of producing surprises it seems, even when you reach my age."

He took the dig with a polite smile, accepting that he'd probably earned it. "Even so…"

All hint of humour vanished. It was the shrewd businesswoman he knew so well who now stared back at him. "Two things. First I'd do everything I could to get the Death Wish lifted, and second I'd run as far and fast as I could, just in case the first part failed or word of its success didn't circulate quickly enough to those who had already seen the posting."

More sound advice; he was beginning to sense a theme here. Philip had plenty to think about once Catherine's image faded. With the project so tantalisingly close to fruition he was loathe to go anywhere, yet the idea of saving his own skin was not without its appeal. He determined to try and follow the first part of her advice at least, and trusted that this might prove enough for now.

He remembered what Mal had said about *The Death Wish* and had to admit his curiosity was piqued. His thoughts turned to those intriguing 'wishits' Mal had sent him…

THE DEATH WISH proved easy enough to find. As with so many things, it was all a question of knowing the place existed in the first place. Philip had thought long and hard about how best to approach the situation, and even toyed with the idea of simply hacking into the site's systems and erasing his name entirely. He was confident of his ability to hack into almost anywhere and could probably even enlist Mal's help if needed, but in the end this seemed more trouble that it was worth. After all, his name would already have been seen by many and once somebody noticed it had disappeared they could, presumably, simply post it up again.

Besides, there was the potential backlash to consider should his meddling be noticed. Did he seriously need the sort of aggravation a place like this could undoubtedly direct his way? Definitely not, particularly given the current situation.

In the end, he decided that rather than sneak in via the back door he would use the front, and simply join the site. He had no real idea what he intended to do once there, but he had to *see* this board and his name upon it. Only then would all of this seem real. Yet part of him was reluctant to take such a direct approach, not only because Mal had seemed so confident that he would, but also for more pragmatic concerns to do with security. Could he really afford to trust this site with his personal details? Then he chided himself for being daft; after all, his address was a matter of public record and hardly difficult to find if anyone were determined enough. If registration required other more sensitive details... well, he would face that when he came to it.

His concerns were proven to be groundless as no intimate details were needed; nor for that matter were his name and address. After seeing two of the small piles of wishits disappear, all he was asked to provide were a username, password and avatar name – with a stipulation that the latter *had* to be different from his user name. After some deliberation, he opted for 'Seeker', which struck him as fitting. Unfortunately, somebody had evidently beaten him to it and he was asked to choose again. Not wanting to spare this process any more thought, he went for 'Seeker2', and was relieved to see it accepted.

Then, things turned difficult. He was required to select his avatar's appearance, being offered a bewildering selection of standard characters or the facility to upload a customised avatar of his own choosing.

For goodness sake! All he wanted to do was satisfy his curiosity and actually gaze upon this wretched board for himself. Once he had seen his name up there he intended to leave and had no expectation of ever coming back.

He gazed at the proffered list with a growing sense of hopelessness, only to enjoy a flash of inspiration. He smiled, suddenly knowing *exactly* which form to adopt, and chose accordingly.

As soon as he did, his living room was transformed.

At the back of his mind, Philip had long suspected that he lacked a little imagination; not in terms of his work and seeing the potential for the technology and concepts he played around with, but in certain other... less structured areas. When Philip let his imagination run wild it rarely did, but instead tended to stay within safe, clearly defined parameters.

He had no real idea of what to expect from *The Death Wish*, so perhaps anything would have come as a surprise. Certainly what awaited him did.

In place of his living room a darker, dingier place appeared. Philip had to admit, this was one of the most convincing examples of CGR – Computer Generated Reality – he'd ever seen. He was familiar with the principle and knew that the program was using his own systems to produce a virtual setting, one which now overlay the real-world room that still existed beneath it. The real test of such things was how well the program coped with the varying topographies of the solid rooms which it covered, while maintaining the illusion for each and every participant that they were interacting within the same, consistent virtual environment.

He stepped forward, a little warily; not only because of the unfamiliar surroundings but also for fear of bumping into a piece of his own furniture now hidden beneath this all-too convincing illusion. The room seemed considerably wider than his lounge, disappearing to his right into dimly lit corners. Figures were to be seen, their features indistinct due to the deep shadows and the partitions which conveniently sectioned off small booths of seating; leaving more the impression of people rather than an actual presence. Dark wood predominated – even the ceiling was panelled with the stuff. On the polished bar top it shone with the deep, rich russet of rosewood, but elsewhere a slightly menacing dimness prevailed, courtesy of the wood's sombre influence and some tastefully subdued lighting.

Taking a deep breath, he continued into the room.

Not quite everybody looked up as he entered, though enough did to make him feel even more self-conscious than he already did.

Discounting the shadowy lurkers in distant corners – whom Philip tended to dismiss as embellishments of the program – the place was still pretty busy; though it hardly deserved the term 'heaving' as described by Mal. Nearest him, sitting at a table which he was fairly confident coincided with the position of his own, sat an unlikely looking pair of drinking companions: one appeared to be a large, shaggy-haired bear, sporting a red neckerchief and a bandolier of outlandishly large bullets slung over one shoulder, the other a fearsome Amazonian warrior, with bulging biceps and bare breasts, the nipples of which had been stained gold and pierced. He tried not to stare as he walked past, though they clearly possessed no such qualms and seemed perfectly happy to stare at him.

He squeezed past a bare-torsoed man of delicate, boyish frame who boasted a mane of orange and yellow flecked hair sprouting from just above the waist and growing in length and thickness as it climbed his back, to form a tall, proud crest on his head, and, as he continued towards the bar, saw a knight in full black body armour, a space warrior with garish ray gun, a stick-thin woman with bulging multifaceted eyes, a red-cowled monk from under whose habit jutted the pommel of a sword, an angular, bulk-bodied robot of a design which could only ever work in fiction, a green-tailed dragon lady, at least two horned demons of similar type but differing detail, and a man who appeared to be built out of cabbages.

So the androgynous individual standing by the bar whose face and hands looked to consist of silvered fish scales – where they showed beyond the neck and cuffs of an iridescent grey suit – came as no surprise at all.

The fish man glanced at him with mild interest. Philip nodded greeting, and then caught sight of himself in the long mirror behind the bar, its edges decorated with mock scrolls either painted onto the glass or stuck on, while in one corner a cartoon caricature blonde with fishnet legs and unlikely cleavage held out a bottle of beer, a brand he had never heard of. Staring back at him from the mirror itself was a classical pirate, no less a caricature than the mirror-bound blonde.

His face was unrecognisable. Long and thin, with a waxed moustache and prominent nose, the whole framed by a tumble of black-haired ringlets – far darker than his own natural brown – which fell to his shoulders from beneath a quite startling hat.

At least there was no eye patch.

Looking at his avatar and comparing it to the others present, he realised that he stood out like a sore thumb. While everyone else appeared to be exotic and highly individual, totally at home in their assumed personas, he wore his with an awkwardness that shouted of inexperience. Nothing about him suggested this was anything other than a clichéd and uninspired off-the-peg avatar chosen in haste; which, of course, it was.

He dragged his attention away from his face to what he was wearing: off-white almost ivory shirt with puffed sleeves, over which sat a waistcoat of an indeterminate colour which he settled on as being aubergine. The garment boasted some elaborate embroidery and overlarge buttons, none of which were done up. The look was completed by a sash belt, jauntily tied to one side... and that hat. Philip toyed with the idea of taking the latter off, but decided that was a ridiculous notion; after all, it came with the persona. Part of him did wonder, though, how the simulation would cope if he attempted to.

"You're new here." The barman stepped across, blocking his self-inspection. His words did little to improve Philip's confidence. The man was bald and large, with no apparent neck, just a domed head emerging from improbably broad shoulders like some over-ripe pimple. Philip wondered whether he was part of the simulation, a fellow member of the site, or even one of the people who owned the place. Now there was a thought.

"You drinking?"

Philip remembered Mal saying that wishits could be used to buy drinks. How far did this simulation go? "Beer, please."

With a grunt, the barman lifted a glass to a wall tap and proceeded to fill it with a suspiciously dark liquid before placing it on the counter before him. Definitely an avatar, Philip decided. The man's upper arm bulged with muscles and looked to be broader than some girls' waists he could think of.

Philip reached for the beer, half-expecting his hand to travel straight through, but it didn't, instead encountering what felt like a solid, chilled glass.

Beneath the illusion this was *his* living room, and no matter how complex the programs running *The Death Wish* were they were being channelled through *his* systems. He had no idea they were capable of producing something like this. He was supposed to be an expert at such things and being presented with this evidence of his own ignorance was annoying, not to mention embarrassing.

"That's one wishit," the barman said. "You got a name?"

He passed over a gleaming, solid-feeling coin. "Seeker2."

Silver Scales looked up sharply at that. "Seeker2, huh?"

Philip did his best to look nonchalant, wisely deciding that menacing was beyond him at present. "What about it?"

"Oh, nothing. Permit me to introduce myself: the name's Seeker."

Now *that* was what 'nonchalant' really sounded like. Philip blinked, searching for words and coming up with, "Really?" What were the chances of that, for goodness sake?

The other laughed, shaking his head. "I knew it wouldn't take you long. Seeker2... I should have guessed."

Philip was feeling increasingly uneasy and out of his depth here. "I'm sorry."

"It's Mal, Philip."

Seeker. Of course it was Mal. Who else would call himself *Seeker*?

"I've been waiting for you," the fish man continued.

"Lucky me."

"Glad to see you remembered your wishits."

"Yes... thank you." Damn it! Showing gratitude to this lingering afterthought was the last thing he wanted to do. Lately, he seemed to be doing nothing but.

"Nice tri-corner."

"Pardon?"

"The hat; it's a tri-corner."

"Oh, right. Came with the persona; glad you like it." There was no way he was going to say 'thank you' again.

"And you can take it off if you want. Seeing as you're inside now."

Philip simply stared. Then asked, quietly, "Do I look as out of place as I feel?"

"Pretty much." Mal was clearly enjoying himself. "But I shouldn't worry about that. They all do – the newbies I mean. You'll soon get used to the place. After a couple of visits you'll simply blend in like the rest of us."

"There aren't going to *be* any more visits. This is a one-off."

"Right; of course it is."

Even here, in these bizarrest of surroundings, the man had smugness down to a fine art.

Philip looked at the silver-scaled being beside him. "So, where is this notice board anyway?" There seemed little point in beating around the bush. They both knew why he was there.

"I thought you'd never ask. It's the other side of the bar." Mal nodded in the appropriate direction.

Philip grunted and sauntered over that way, Mal keeping pace.

If anything, the board came as a disappointment. It was simply that. A board. An oblong piece of spongy wood, or perhaps even cork, fixed to the wall. Secured to it by coloured plastic-ended pins were scraps of paper, with names hand written or rather scrawled upon them. His was cast with red ink in blocky, untidy letters. There were pins skewering three corners of the paper, one white, two yellow. The bottom left corner hung free and lifted slightly from the board. Philip didn't recognise the other three names.

He shook his head.

"What?" Mal asked beside him.

"I don't know, I just expected this to be…"

"Grander? More dramatic?"

"I suppose so. This just seems such a sorry, squalid way to have your life ended."

"Then make sure this isn't how it ends. I take it you know who posted this?"

"I've a fair idea, yes."

"Have you decided what you're going to do about it yet?"

"More or less." Mal could fish for information all he wanted – a thought perhaps inspired by his choice of avatar – Philip had no intention of elaborating.

"Well, much as I'd love to hang around…"

"… you've got things to do," Mal finished for him.

"Precisely."

Only when he had left *The Death Wish* and seen his home return to normal did Philip realise that he had never even checked the amount being offered for his head. He'd been vaguely aware of further scraps of tattered paper at the bottom of the board, but hadn't thought to glance at them. He almost succumbed to the temptation of returning to the virtual bar, but determined not to, reasoning that Mal might still be there, and he had suffered enough of the partial's company for the time being.

So instead he concentrated on finding the best way to get his name off that wretched board as swiftly as possible.

PHILIP COMPOSED HIMSELF, rehearsed what he intended to say for one final time in his head, and then said, "All right, Phil, make the call."

There was a noticeable delay, and he could imagine Phil making his case, and doing so as well as he could have done it himself. Whatever the partial said must have worked, because after a few uncertain minutes, his calm voice announced, "Mr McGovern."

Pelloy McGovern was a bloated goat of a man, at least to judge by the image that appeared before Philip at that moment, and he couldn't imagine that anyone would choose to disguise themselves by looking like that. In fact, Philip wondered why the man hadn't resorted to reduction work in order to *avoid* looking like that. Which was hardly the most important issue at that particular time.

Philip attempted to combine his most disarming smile with his steely 'I'll brook no nonsense' stare.

"Mr McGovern, thank you for sparing me the time."

"I nearly didn't, but curiosity got the better of me."

Nothing like being honest; Philip decided to employ the same policy. "Mr McGovern, I don't have any more wish to speak to you than you do to me, but I do have something to say which I know you'll want to hear. You see, last night, while pursuing a... *hobby* of mine, I stumbled upon some information regarding a certain individual. *Sensitive* information, you might say – the sort of thing which the person concerned would *not* want to see in the public domain. Now, personally, being a great believer in the principle of 'live and let live', I could not care less about any of the things I found, but I can understand why someone might want to keep this sort of thing private.

"Interestingly, since this incident, my name has appeared on a notice board in a place called *The Death Wish,* and do you know what, it seems that people are trying to kill me. There has already been one inept attempt."

The big man was doing an excellent impression of looking bored. "Fascinating, no doubt, but what does it have to do with me?"

"Bear with me, please. Obviously I can't allow this situation to continue. I sincerely wish that I could turn the clock back and 'unsee' what I saw, but failing that, I've taken steps to protect myself. The information in question has been recorded and stored in a *very* safe place. And, if you know who I am, you'll understand why I say that with confidence. It will stay in that place, undisturbed, until the day I die. As I say, I have no interest whatsoever in the material in question. However, in the event of my death, a copy of all this information will appear at every law enforcement office and media centre on the planet, and quite a few beyond.

"Doubtless the individual this information relates to has influence in many of these places, but I guarantee not all of them. Now clearly I have a vested interest in living a long life and for this information to never see the light of day, but for that to stand any chance of happening, my name would need to disappear pretty quickly from that wall in *The Death Wish* and not reappear."

McGovern's stare had grown ever more stony. "It seems to me," he said, very quietly, "that the poor schlep whose information you ran off with is in one hell of a bind, with the threat of exposure hanging over him forever and his having to rely on both your honesty and your continued good health."

Philip shrugged. "What can I say? I intend to live for a

long, long time and as for my honesty, I know full well that if I ever *did* reveal what I know, I wouldn't live to enjoy whatever satisfaction that might bring me. I'll behave myself. There's nothing like a glimpse of your own mortality to keep a man honest." That was the stick, revealed and extravagantly brandished; now it was time for the carrot. "Having said that, I do recognise the misfortune this individual has suffered and the part I've played in it, so I was thinking of offering him something to soothe his hurt... And this is where I was hoping you might help me."

"Go on."

"Well, knowing you to be a man of experience in the business world, I was seeking some advice. Do you think a quarter of a million Universal Standards would be suitable recompense for the situation?"

"Well, there's a question. It's difficult to put a price on this sort of thing, of course, but I would have thought a half a million US might be nearer the mark."

"Half a million?" Philip feigned dismay. "I hear what you're saying, but I really *do* want to sort this out as soon as possible and I couldn't lay my hands on that sort of sum immediately. I *could* probably scrape together 400,000 if I needed to... Do you think that would be enough to make my case?"

McGovern stared for long seconds before saying, "I think for 400,000 US, any man would have to take your sincerity very seriously indeed."

Philip smiled as guilelessly as he could manage. "That's a relief. I knew you were the right man to ask. Thank you so much for your time, you've been a great help."

The man's smile was even more chilling than his stare. "My pleasure."

"I really appreciate this, and don't worry, I won't trouble you again. In fact, if you ever *do* hear from me after this, it will most likely be from beyond the grave."

Philip cut the connection.

Well, that had been intense. 400,000 US: painful, but manageable. He'd expected to have to go to half a million, so when viewed from that perspective he was ahead of the game.

Philip gave it an hour before he ventured into *The Death Wish* again. When he did so, there was no sign of Mal. More importantly, his name had vanished from the infamous board.

He went to bed feeling extremely pleased with himself.

"WE HAVE AN intruder." Phil's voice was calm and softly spoken, but still managed to convey a sense of urgency.

"Wha...?" Philip's voice on the other hand seemed distant and confused, even to his own ears, as he surfaced from the oblivion of sleep.

"Coming in through the lounge."

He hauled his body into a sitting position on the edge of the bed, toes curling into the warm carpet while he stretched his shoulders and neck, which ached spitefully. The meaning of the partial's words began to percolate through the muzziness, but not quickly enough.

"Give me a shot of number one, Phil," he said, lifting a reluctant arm and pressing his wrist against the dispenser built into the bed's headboard.

There was a slight tingling as the micro-spray permeated his skin, while he took a deep breath, waiting for the stimulant to kick in.

He could almost feel the woolliness lifting from his mind. "All right, show me."

An image appeared in the air a metre or two in front of him. He recognised his own front room, looking out towards the panoramic window. A dark shape could vaguely be seen beyond that window. It seemed to be in the process of cutting a large circle in the glass, using a laser, the brightness of which effectively masked the wielder. Philip squinted, trying to make out more detail.

"What the hell is that thing?"

"Initial readings suggest it to be a remote-controlled shell," Phil told him. "I'll be able to tell more once it gets inside."

"Sophisticated enough to bypass the alarm, by the look of it."

"Granted. And whoever's directing it knows enough to come in through the lounge rather than the bedroom." The apartment boasted heavier night time defences in the master bedroom than anywhere else, since that was where Philip slept and so where he was at his most vulnerable.

The circle was almost complete. "Another assassination attempt, I presume." Philip sighed. That was the problem with this 'Death Wish' system: how could you tell people who had already seen the notice that the contract had been cancelled? How could you even know who they were? He wondered whether McGovern would still pay out should the assassin prove successful. Probably.

He was feeling fully awake now, the stimulant doing the job it had been designed to do. "The police?" he wondered.

"Would never be able to get here in time."

"Building security?"

"They might make it, just."

"But would they be of any help?"

"I shouldn't think so."

Philip grunted. "And I don't suppose anything we've got in place is likely to stop it."

"Difficult to say until we know more about the intruder, but I wouldn't count on it."

He caught his first proper glimpse of the threat now, as a peculiar, squat mechanism floated in through the circle of missing glass. About half the height of a man, maybe a little less, or so Philip reckoned, it was shaped like an irregular sphere; the symmetry marred by bumps and lumps and a pair of three-fingered claws, one digit opposable to the other two, which were now flush to its body but which Philip guessed were extendable. He was on his feet now, watching with morbid fascination. He pulled on some clothes, for no good reason other than habit suggested he should.

"Armament?"

"Impossible to evaluate with any accuracy, it's too well insulated; but a cutting laser for certain, and I would imagine at least one high-calibre gun and a blade or two. That would be standard for this type of modified unit."

"They have standards, do they? That's reassuring." The almost comical-looking machine was now flying into the room and towards the hall, managing in the process to neatly avoid the smart carpet strips which would have glued to the floor anything that actually walked or rolled across them.

Philip frowned. "It's a survey drone, isn't it?"

"Originally, yes. Designed for extreme environments and now modified in some pretty extreme ways as well." One huge advantage a partial had over a physical original was instant access to information.

The intruder had reached the door, which stood temptingly open.

"It's a sneaky so and so, that's for sure; the doorframe isn't even detecting it," the partial observed. "Luckily, I am." The drone drifted through the door, to be met by a curtain of energy which lanced in from three sides as Phil triggered the frame's defences – an electrical discharge which danced across the thing's shell, so that for a brief second it was limned in light. The unit didn't even slow down.

"Tough little bastard, isn't it?" Philip murmured.

"Very – designed to be; that's what makes survey drones ideal for this sort of assignment."

"Thanks, you're filling me with so much confidence. Have you got the frequency pinned down yet?"

"Almost. It's not that simple. The carrier wave is switching frequencies constantly, not oscillating to a set pattern. Key codes carried within the transmission itself alert the receiver in the shell to the shifts, causing a microsecond delay in the unit's response time, and it's that microsecond I'll have to try and take advantage of in order to jam the transmissions. First, of course, I have to break the codes."

Whoever was directing this thing knew what they were doing. For the first time, Philip began to worry. There was no emergency exit, no other way out of this room. His hopes of surviving the next few minutes rested entirely with the partial. Phil had *his* knowledge and the not-inconsiderable computing power of the building to call on – all of it if need be – but even so... Would it be enough?

"How sophisticated is this, Phil?"

"It's pretty impressive, but we're not talking military-grade tech here."

"Can you crack it?"

"No sweat."

"Not for you, perhaps. After all, you don't." He glanced uneasily towards the door, which was firmly shut and had been securely bolted since the intrusion first began.

"How long is this likely to take, Phil?"

"Another minute or so."

"That's fine, take your time. I mean there's a whole door standing between me and imminent death."

"Patience."

There were times when he wondered whether Phil contained a little too many of his own less desirable traits: arrogance, for example. Perhaps the partial was overdue for a serious overhaul.

His attention returned to the image still being projected in front of him, which showed the mechanism's progress along the short hallway as it approached the bedroom. It was a little weird seeing the same door simultaneously from both sides.

The drone came to the end of the hall and stopped. Once again its laser came into play. The bedroom door was bolted in three places – top, bottom and middle. Rather than make three separate assaults, the drone went for the very centre of the door, apparently intent on cutting out another disc, as it had with the window. Built of multiple layers of carbon-fibre nanotubes sandwiching a steel alloy centre, the door was of the same type they installed as the innermost barrier to the bridge on starships, and a lot tougher than the reinforced window. Presumably this shell was packing a good supply of power, but it would need to be in order to cut through this. Which would give out first: door or power? The analytical part of Philip's mind was fascinated to see the outcome of the contest, while the rest of him began to edge from concern towards fear, especially when a spot on his side of the door started to smoulder and smoke. The spot slowly developed into a curve.

Now ignoring the projected image, Philip stared at the black curve, seeing it creep steadily towards a crescent. He knew there was nothing in the bedroom capable of stopping something like this, but he couldn't just stand around and wait, so he started opening drawers in search of anything that could be press-ganged into service as a weapon. He examined the comms unit and scrutinised the crystal statuette beside it, hoping for a flash of inspiration. Pointless, all of it, but at least this beat simply watching the scorch line spread.

When he dared to check again, the circle was a little over half complete.

"Come on, Phil!"

"I'm there."

"About time!" Now that he knew the primary danger could be contained, Philip's thought turned to potential secondary threats. "What if they've set up a reserve frequency to fall back on?"

"That's possible, but it won't be as complicated as this sequence and, besides, I intend to throw them enough feedback to make their ears and eyes bleed!"

Philip nodded, his mind accepting this but still examining other implications.

"They could have programmed the shell to act independently if transmissions are interrupted."

"True, but these things are designed to be operated remotely, on the slightly questionable basis that only the human mind is flexible enough to deal with the unexpected conditions and situations a survey drone is likely to encounter. So any back-up program would have to be pretty basic and would offer a greatly reduced chance of a successful hit." The charred disc had progressed to the three-quarters stage. "Far more likely they'd program it to simply explode and hope to take out the target that way."

"Oh well, that's all right then." An *explosion*? Philip was pretty certain the containment field which the door boasted as a final defence would not have been enough to hold the drone, but it might just be able to blunt the force of an explosion. "Might be an idea to hold off from jamming the transmission until the drone is in the containment field, then."

"Why do you think I haven't done so already?"

"Can you send whoever's directing the shell a message, telling them they're too late, that the contract's been cancelled?" Transmission had to be going both ways, since whoever was directing the drone needed to see what was going on.

"Already taken care of," Phil assured him, with a hint of impatience. "If the feedback I've lined up doesn't fry whatever equipment they're using entirely, a message to that effect will be recorded there when they pick up the pieces."

Sometimes it was easy to forget that the partial was designed to think like him, and to act independently.

"Now," Phil continued, "in case this thing *does* decide to explode, perhaps you might want to step back a little."

Or a lot, for that matter. Philip moved away, heading for the en-suite, which, reassuringly, was not directly in line with the door and so seemed unlikely to feel the full force of any blast. There was no telling what type or quantity of explosive the shell might be packing. For a bizarre second he entertained the thought that it could be carrying a small nuke, which would make his current retreat pointless, but that seemed a bit over the top for the assassination of one man, *any* man. He paused on the threshold, watching in fascination as the cutting laser completed its task and the disc of door fell away. He peered through the resulting space despite himself, but ducked fully into the side room as soon as there was a hint of movement.

Philip crouched down, bracing himself, glad that David Benn couldn't see him now, nor anyone else for that matter. Seconds ticked past with no sound, nothing at all to disturb the silence. Impatience began to win out over caution and he was just reaching the conclusion that nothing was going to happen, that Phil had cut the transmissions guiding the drone and it had simply gone dormant, when there came a deafening bang and the floor beneath his feet seemed to buck, to ripple, while the whole room shook. Something tumbled off a shelf to smash on the floor close by, but he was too preoccupied to notice what.

Then it was over.

The world was as it should be once more – silent and unmoving. Even as Philip registered the stillness it was interrupted by what could only be sprinklers coming on. He stood up and stepped back into the bedroom. The smell of burning and of chemical retardants filled the air. A corner of his mind noted with numb regret the shattered remnants of a Leiarian figurine, one of the few 'frivolous touches' he allowed in his bedroom, as a fondly remembered ex, Annalise, had noted one dreamy, long ago morning. Yet the sight that greeted him wasn't nearly as bad as he'd feared. The door was completely destroyed, the wall to either side charred and streaked with burn marks. A widening strip of carpet, fanning out from the door to the centre of the room, had likewise been blasted away, and this was the part of the room which the sprinklers were dousing, the few bits of carpet and wrecked machine that still smouldered quickly submerged in a frothing foam of chemicals and water.

"So, a bomb after all."

"Yes," Phil confirmed, "But pretty much contained as anticipated. There's no structural damage and, let's be honest, you never much cared for that carpet in any case."

Philip laughed. "True."

"Oh, and security are on the way up."

"Better late than never."

Security; the implications were nearly as daunting as what he had just been through: red tape, repetitive statements and interminable bureaucracy. Again. But Philip was resigned to that. What concerned him now was the dawning realisation that he had done all he could, succeeded in getting the Death Wish lifted, yet it still hadn't stopped the assassins. He looked at the shattered shell of the survey drone, or at least the largest surviving chunk of its dull metal carcass, which rested just inside the door where it lay half-buried beneath a mound of still-bubbling foam. He had been lucky this time, but sooner or later his luck was bound to run out.

Now there was a cheery thought to cuddle up to when he was eventually allowed to return to his bed.

CHAPTER EIGHT

KYLE WAS MORE than a little confused by *The Noise Within* and had to admit that in volunteering to join the ship he had probably made the biggest mistake of his life. To date, at least; he would never rule out the possibility of making an even bigger cock-up at some stage, but this would do to be getting on with.

He began to regret this impetuous leap into the dark almost as soon as he came on board, and started missing *The Lady J* at once, not least because nothing about his new ship was remotely what he had expected. In fact, it made no sense at all.

Bizarrely, *The Noise Within* brought back memories of his childhood and of his Aunt Tamzin, whose home he had been required to visit as a kid once or twice a year in order to play with two cousins who were a few years younger than him, whom he had never really liked and whom he had barely spoken to since the onset of puberty. Except that it had never been the *same* home. Aunt Tamzin and Uncle Andrew moved a lot, for reasons he hadn't thought to question at the time, so each visit was to a new address, or so childhood memories insisted. Little about those visits stayed with him, but two things definitely did.

The first was his aunt's disapproving glower. She never told him to stop fiddling with this or asked him to leave that alone. She didn't need to. She would sit there in a high-backed chair, which remained unchanging even though the house around it had morphed so frequently. Rigidly upright in her elegant yet austere dress, she simply turned towards him. One glare and his hands stopped moving of their own volition, while all energy and the will to fidget would drain away from him as though sucked out by a leech.

The worst glower he ever received had come as a result of his dismembering one of the cousins' toys – a remote-control starfighter which wobbled erratically when asked to hover. All it needed was a slight adjustment to the gyroscopic sensor and everything would have been fine, but would anyone listen to him?

No, of course not. He was taken home in disgrace that day, leaving behind the disconsolate wails of cousins and the dismantled parts of a toy which he could easily have fixed and made as good as new – better, in fact – if they had only given him another ten minutes.

The second thing that lodged firmly in his memory was the fact that none of Aunt Tamzin's homes seemed complete; he didn't mean this in terms of the buildings as such but rather in terms of their function as homes. There may have been no unfinished walls or gaping holes where a roof ought to have been, but there *was* a sense that the family had not yet fully moved in, that they hadn't completely unpacked either their belongings or their emotions and that before they did so it would be time to put everything away again, ready for the next move. His own childhood home had a solid presence, a comforting sense that it would never fail him; whereas, by contrast, Aunt Tamzin's always reeked of impermanence, as if they were transient pauses in some ongoing journey rather than genuine homes. They never benefited from the care and attention that a real home deserves.

It was this remembered impression from childhood which came flooding back when he first clapped eyes on the interior of *The Noise Within*. Kyle had served on many ships, most of them possessing a distinctly lived-in quality; even the naval vessels, though they were invariably cleaned and maintained to rigorous standards, while *The Lady J* might always have been pristine and sparkling, but she still felt occupied and she still fitted together as a whole. *The Noise Within* didn't.

At first Kyle couldn't put his finger on what was missing, but then he started to notice the little things. He recognised the ship's general type immediately, and could probably even have named the shipyard that built her if he put his mind to it, but the closer he looked, the more he found it hard to believe that any yard would have launched a vessel in this state. She was a ship put together in a hurry, without due care being taken over the details and a noticeable absence of finishing touches. Welds were still clearly visible – ripples of congealed metal at the base of walls which normally would have been smoothed out long before the ship was unveiled, and rivet heads remained exposed without any attempt to mask them. The walls were bare metal, the flooring likewise in many places. The precision he had come to take for granted on any ship simply wasn't there. It was as if this were a first attempt at something, a working life-size model that was intended as a template rather than an actual spacegoing vessel. Just like Aunt Tamzin's series of homes, *The Noise Within* fell short of the real deal, as if the ship were little more than a mock-up of what she was supposed to be.

Perhaps the most disconcerting aspect though was the lack of human touches, either personal or corporate. There was nothing anywhere to suggest that people lived aboard or that they ever had. Kyle was willing to bet that, internally at least, she looked little different now from the day she had rolled off the production line.

Nor did she *smell* like any ship he had served on before. No matter how much a ship was cleaned and polished or how many times the air was refreshed and recycled, there was always the ghost of human odour, of sweat and scent; all but intangible smells which had been absorbed by fitments and bulkheads or simply lingered in the air. Kyle had never really considered it before, and he only recognised this background odour of human habitation now by its absence. *The Noise Within* smelt new and unlived in, yet, conversely, the air also carried with it a hint of mustiness, and perhaps even of death.

From his very first moments on board, with the luxury ship he had so wantonly abandoned only a short distance away – a captured trophy now slaved to *The Noise Within's* systems like some cowed lapdog – he began to wonder what the hell he was doing. Never before on any ship had he felt so completely alone.

The most disconcerting thing of all was the existing crew. All right, perhaps he shouldn't have expected too much banter as they all scrambled along inside the hastily attached umbilical tube which connected the two ships, all suited up and helmet sealed – a manoeuvre that took him back to his navy days. But once safely back on *The Noise Within* surely *anyone* would want to celebrate. Even one whoop of elation or relief would have satisfied him, but nothing. No excitement, not even a slumping of military-stiff shoulders to indicate a degree of relaxation. Instead, everything continued with the smooth efficiency the boarding party had displayed aboard *The Lady J*. They didn't even take their helmets off.

Kyle had served with all sorts in the days immediately following his discharge. When he deserted *The Lady J* in favour of *The Noise Within* he had expected to be joining a gang of merry adventurers; treacherous and deadly no doubt, but nothing he couldn't handle – a group who would be happy to accept him as one of their own, to welcome him onto the 'gang'. In retrospect, such expectations might have been a little naïve, doubtless spawned from his growing sense of frustration and boredom. Perhaps he also missed his days in the military more than he realised and had seen joining *The Noise Within* as an opportunity to regain the addictive spirit of camaraderie which he had only really encountered during the War, when lives – including his own – were being put on the line for the sake of others.

If so, he was destined to be sadly disappointed. Kyle was not exactly held prisoner, but there were certain sections of the ship which were out of bounds, such as all the areas where the rest of the crew spent their time. And, even after *The Lady J* and the selected passengers were returned in exchange for the equivalent of several princes' ransoms, he still was not allowed to see any of his new shipmates with their helmets off. They claimed this was for security reasons, a temporary measure until he had proven himself, but as time went by he began to wonder whether there was more to it than that. Kyle was fast reaching the conclusion that he might be the only real human aboard *The Noise Within*.

Drevers' arrival came as a Godsend. After several days of kicking his heels in growing frustration, Kyle was notified that the ship was about to embark on a second attack. He wasn't allowed to participate but *was* given a ringside seat, with full audio and visual feeds which enabled him to follow everything that went on.

As far as he could tell, this was more or less a repeat of the attack on *The Lady J*, with the target vessel standing about as much chance and offering a similar lack of resistance. From his perspective, the chief gain from this raid was a second new crewman: Drevers. Finally Kyle had some company.

If *The Noise Within*'s original crew had proven to be something of a disappointment, Drevers proved to be anything but. His uniform might have been shiny white and spotless but his spirit looked to be as dark and twisted as anyone could have wished for.

As soon as Kyle saw the twinkle in the man's eyes and heard the newcomer's opening words: "So, what the hell does a man do for entertainment on this tin heap?" he knew that life aboard *The Noise Within* was about to get a great deal more interesting.

THE MESS HALL was a functional, soulless place, the food served there only marginally less so, but, looking on the bright side, at least nobody was shooting at him. Leyton spotted someone he recognised and steered his feet that way. Carver was stocky but strong, not an eyegee but still a useful man to have by your side in a scrap. His face bore a scar running from ear to mouth across the left cheek – not an angry mark, simply a crease in the skin which shouldn't have been there but which the man had never bothered to get removed. Leyton could understand why. It broke up the symmetry, banished the 'cuteness'. In basic training, Carver had been nicknamed 'baby' due to his round face, clear complexion and innocent expression; not a comfortable label for someone who valued his cred.

Leyton recalled spending one semi-drunk evening long ago trying to persuade the younger Carver that this could work to his advantage, that by building up a reputation for toughness and cockiness he could turn the situation on its head and wear the cutesy nickname as a badge, an ironic antonym of who he truly was, but Carver never seemed to buy into the idea and remained determined to leave the belittling nickname behind. As far as the eyegee was aware, he'd succeeded.

Carver grunted a greeting as Leyton placed his plate on the table and dropped into the seat opposite him. The man looked up without raising his head, intent on shovelling the next forkful of slop into his mouth. One of the things that Leyton tended to miss out on, being an eyegee, was the 'barrack room' gossip. For the most part, this was something of a blessing, since the majority of it tended to be bullshit and outrageous hot air, but every now and then the grapevine brought along something worthwhile, and Carver had always possessed a knack for separating the wheat from the chaff. He also couldn't resist showing off if he *did* know anything of value, so Leyton didn't bother pushing him – not wanting to give Carver the satisfaction – but instead kept quiet, waiting for the other to speak first.

"How's life with the high-fly-gees, then?"

One thing Leyton had forgotten, or perhaps deliberately

blanked out, was the man's puerile sense of humour. "Busy, as ever."

"Not likely to get much quieter anytime soon either, from what I hear."

"No surprise there, then." Leyton still refused to bite, but instead concentrated on his plate, trying to decide what the long, green, listless stems might have been before they were irradiated into anonymity. Vegetables of some sort, certainly, though their elusively faint flavour offered no clue.

"Big op coming up," Carver said. "There's going to be a mass briefing called tomorrow, or the day after at the latest. All hands freed up for this one, you eyegees included. Least, that's the word."

Leyton's turn to grunt. He shifted his attention to the meat, lumps of which stood proud from the gloppy brown gravy like islands in a swamp. The lumps were no easier to classify than the vegetables.

A mass briefing for a major op? To Leyton that had the promise of him riding shotgun on somebody else's mission written all over it. He also had a terrible suspicion that this would have something to do with that pirate ship again – a prospect which produced a sinking feeling in the pit of his stomach; an effect caused by something more than the muck masquerading as food before him. Having failed to glean any useful intelligence from the series of raids on freebooter friendly bases and planets, the authorities were bound to try something else at some point, though he hadn't reckoned on them organising anything this swiftly. Suddenly Leyton found he'd lost his appetite, and pushed his plate away into the centre of the table.

Carver looked up, his gaze switching between the eyegee and the rejected food. "If you don't want that..."

"Help yourself." The man always did have a cast=iron stomach.

Carver grabbed Leyton's plate, as if afraid someone else

might claim the 'food' ahead of him, tipped it up and slid the contents onto his own.

Leyton shook his head, then pushed his chair back and stood up. "See you, Carver."

"Yeah, have fun."

The eyegee walked off towards his quarters, very much doubting that he would.

IT WAS OCCASIONS such as this that reaffirmed Leyton's faith in human nature, or at least his faith in Carver's ability to tell the difference between nuggets of worthwhile information and bilge swill. The meeting was called for first thing the following day.

At the front of the room stood Commander Roberts, all neatly pressed uniform, gleaming buttons and razor-sharp creases. He had obviously drawn the short straw and been given the task of delivering the briefing. Behind the uniformed officer stood two men in civilian suits: Benson and another man, whom Leyton failed to recognise; a fact which surprised him. He made a note to find out who the mystery man was. He liked to have a handle on everyone in a position of command, particularly those whose pretensions of authority might affect him in some way.

Leyton barely heard the opening words of the address; he was too busy concentrating on the other two men. Typically, Benson stayed in the background, content to watch from the shadows. The newcomer stood beside him, the pair exchanging occasional whispered words which Leyton was unable to catch; cupped hands hiding mouths, or said mouths barely moving when uncovered, rendering his lip-reading skills useless.

The room was packed, with well over a hundred field operatives in attendance. There were a few faces he recognised, though not many. He exchanged nodded greetings with some of those he knew, including Carver, who gave him a smug 'told you so' grin in response. As he quickly scanned the crowd he counted a total of six other eyegees – a good half of the total unit – though neither Mya nor Boulton were among them. The thought did occur to him that if some dissident group knew enough to smuggle a bomb into this place, they could cripple the government's intelligence and black-ops capabilities for years.

Purely from a selfish perspective, he hoped that no one had.

"As you know, it was initially assumed that the reason these 'boarders' kept their faceplates opaqued was to hide their identity," Roberts was saying, "but analysis of readings taken from the first two raids confirms that, in actual fact, they don't have faces to hide. The suits are empty. They're nothing more than remotely controlled shells."

The Noise Within. Again. He was beginning to hate that wretched ship with a passion. Surely there were more important things he could be doing, such as bringing down crime lords and preventing rebellions; though judging by the size of the assembly for this briefing, others clearly didn't think so. Perhaps there was more going on here than met the eye.

The commander was still speaking. "At first we assumed that the suits were being operated by the real crew who were back on their own ship keeping their heads down, but recent intelligence suggests a different possibility: that there *is* no crew. It appears that *The Noise Within* may be an AI-controlled starship."

Murmurs rippled round the room.

"We're now confident that she is, in fact, an old Wartime experiment called *The Sun Seeker*, returned to haunt us." Roberts' next five words were spoken precisely and a little more loudly, effectively quieting the residual mutterings. "It Stands To Reason, Therefore… thank you…" he continued in his usual voice, "… that the same AI is operating the shells. Lack of a human crew would certainly go a long way to explaining the ship's manoeuvrability and the adroit way she handles such impressive acceleration and decel. All of which begs the question, why has *The Noise Within* set about recruiting a human crew?

"It might beg the question, but, to be frank, I couldn't give a damn. What I *do* care about is the fact that with a human crew on board the ship is going to be hampered. She'll have to take those humans into account in all sorts of ways; not being as fast or as agile is only the start of it. Will the crew be allowed downtime? It's all well and good that they're earning enough Standards from the raids and the ransom monies to buy a planet or two each, but where will they go to spend it? If they're not allowed to let off steam at all, how long before they start creating trouble for the ship? Let's face it, they're only human, and the sort who jump at the chance of joining a pirate vessel are unlikely to be the most disciplined of men. Clearly the AI wants them around, but how far is it willing to go to accommodate them?

"These are the questions which *The Noise Within* is going to *have* to find answers to, whoever or whatever's running the ship, and that gives us a real shot at her.

"We're mounting a determined campaign to either capture or destroy this pain-in-the-butt ship; make no mistake, this is the number one priority until further notice. That means decoy ships masquerading as cruise liners, security patrols in the systems we know she's hunting, and operatives among the crew of ships, all eager to join *The Noise Within* if invited. You lot here have the easy bit – the cherry among all those jobs. You're going to be haunting every leisure district, every watering hole, whorehouse, casino and dive within staggering distance of a spaceport that falls within these sectors.

"Congratulations, boys and girls, this is the assignment of your dreams. I'm ordering you to go and hang around bars and to drink!"

The announcement was greeted with predictable guffaws, muted cheers and mumblings of delighted disbelief from around the room.

"But," the commander spoke over the din, repeating himself once the chatter subsided, "but, woe betide *any* of you who are found to be drunk on duty *without* having first managed to gain a berth aboard *The Noise Within*!"

PHILIP FOUND HIMSELF almost regretting the stimulants he had pumped into his system after the broken night which had started with such adventure and been followed by such bureaucratic tedium. At that particular moment he could have done with being a lot less alert. He hadn't been lectured to like this since childhood.

"I get the message, Catherine."

"Good; it's about time you listened to somebody…"

Philip held up a restraining hand. "You've made your point. You want rid of me."

"It's not a question of 'wanting rid'. It's more the desire to see you out of harm's way. Your father was a genius, Philip, and you take after him." That had to be the nicest thing Catherine had ever said to him, even if it did amount to a second-hand compliment. "Granted, you're not without fault, but you remain the closest thing to Malcolm we've got and you're far too important to be put at risk. All I'm proposing is that you go as far beyond the reach of this threat as possible until we're certain it's been well and truly dealt with.

"I can handle the business side of things until your return and from what I gather, the project itself is now moving very nicely under its own momentum again. Your research assistant, Susan Tan, seems to be more than competent…"

"She is," he said quickly, "a great deal more."

"Would she be able to take the reins from here on in?"

Philip had to admit that, with the new Syntheaven variant panning out so well, she almost certainly could. He found himself nodding, if reluctantly.

"So why do you insist on staying around on Homeworld waiting to be shot at?"

He had to give Catherine credit: she knew how to frame an argument. So did he, yet in this instance he was finding it difficult to contradict her; particularly as, for once, he was a step or two ahead of the old witch.

"Would it help if I mentioned at this point that my ticket off-world has already been booked?" he asked innocently.

She stared at him for long seconds. "It would; although perhaps you could have mentioned this a little earlier in the conversation."

"True." He smiled. "I suppose I could."

Catherine shook her head, as if exasperated by the behaviour of an irresponsible child, but there was no reprimand in her voice as she asked, "When do you leave?"

"This afternoon."

"*That*, I'm sure, is a relief to us all. Have a good trip, Philip. I'll make certain everything's in order for when you get back."

"I know you will," he said, but Catherine had already ended the call.

Philip took time to sip some chilled water. It might have been a little cruel to let Catherine sound off before telling her of plans already in place, but after the experiences of the previous night he felt he deserved a little indulgence. Next on the list was Susan Tan. He headed to the lab, reckoning she deserved to hear the news in person. For some reason he was looking forward to this even less than the conversation with Catherine, perhaps because he wasn't at all sure how Susan would react to his abandoning her at such a vital time.

Kaufman Industries could afford the best and Susan was up there, but she had been part of the project for a long time. Yes, she ran the team on a day to day basis, but she had always relied on Philip for direction and occasional flashes of inspiration when the need arose; perhaps a little too much. Philip was fully confident that she could oversee the project's final stages in his absence despite being lumbered with the new one month deadline, but would she be?

In the event, Susan took the news of his trip 'to visit some of the company's facilities on other worlds' in her stride, inevitably not believing a word of the official line.

"I've seen the news feeds, Philip. I might not know exactly what the situation is but I can deduce that you have good reason for wanting to make yourself scarce, and I know you wouldn't be leaving right now unless you had to." She then added, with obvious embarrassment, "If there's anything you ever want to talk about... well, you know where I am."

He smiled, genuinely touched by her concern, which was patently sincere. "Thank you, Susan; I appreciate it, really, but the situation you're referring to has been taken care of, hopefully."

"So your going away is..."

"A precaution, that's all. Me making myself scarce until the dust has settled. And besides, this gives me the opportunity to do a few things I've been hankering after for a while but have been too tied up with the project to pursue."

She smiled, clearly able to appreciate that sentiment. "Well, have fun then, but make sure you come back safely. I don't want to be fronting the research end of things on a permanent basis."

"Nor would anyone on the board want you to, I can promise that much."

"What?" She looked up sharply, as if taken aback by the implied slight.

"It would mean we'd have to pay you more, for starters," he explained, his face deadpan, though he was grinning broadly by the time she jabbed him on the arm with her balled fist.

There remained a series of necessary calls to make, including those required to ensure Catherine's authority would go unchallenged in his absence, yet in a surprisingly short time he was left with just the one outstanding. He left this until last because it was the call he begrudged making the most, almost as if he hoped something would delay his departure and render this unnecessary. There had been a distinct temptation to stay one more day, but he couldn't face another night like the last, and the assassin responsible for that was still out there somewhere, so...

He found himself talking to her partial, disappointed yet at the same time relieved when it informed him that Julia Cirese was indisposed. The partial promised to relay his message, sound and vision, as soon as she was free to take it.

"Hello, Julia; I really hate to do this, but unfortunately I'm going to have to postpone this evening. Something urgent has cropped up and I'm going off world, leaving today. So I'll get in touch on my return and, ehm, rearrange; if that's all right. Sorry again; can't tell you how much I was looking forward to this evening. Anyway, goodbye for now."

He cut the connection before the opportunity to babble further caused him to make a complete fool of himself.

Damn! He hoped fervently this didn't turn out to be one of those things that were destined to never quite happen.

Then he stopped and analysed that thought. Was he really so attracted to this Julia Cirese, a woman he'd barely met? Honest answer: yes. She was stunning and he was totally hooked, not by her depth of character or personality – which as yet he knew next to nothing about – but purely by her looks. Was he really that shallow?

All the short term relationships which he had flitted in and out of over the years, growing bored and moving on before anything serious could develop; he had always blamed the breakups on shortcomings in his lovers and perhaps, by inference, on women in general, telling himself that each was too limited, too shallow. Had he been wrong; did the fault lie with him rather than them? Was he guilty of projecting his own shortcomings onto any partner who threatened to get too close?

The thought was an unpalatable one and he dismissed it instantly, blaming it on the unsettling events of recent days.

Julia Cirese was a beautiful woman. What man wouldn't be attracted to her? There was no need to analyse anything beyond that.

Having reached that conclusion, he did his best to forget about Julia Cirese; for now at least.

Philip had scant minutes in which to gather his thoughts before heading for the port. He would be driven there in an unmarked company car and was travelling under the anonymity of the Kaufman Industries corporate banner, as many did every day. This struck him as preferable to the alternative of surrounding himself with heavy-handed security. The latter would be the equivalent of hiring a marching band and waving a flag that read 'I'm over here, assassins, come and get me', or so it seemed to Philip. This way, he felt there was every chance of his slipping away unnoticed.

It felt odd. Not just the rushed manner of his leaving and the unfortunate timing, but everything. The project had been the centre of his professional life for so long that he was finding the idea of its not being there surprisingly hard to contemplate. Somehow, with the end in sight, he was already suffering from a sense of impending anticlimax.

Was this it? Was his work essentially done? The project's conclusion would leave a whopping great hole in his life and the truth was that this prospect frightened him, because he had absolutely no idea what he was going to fill it with.

PART TWO

CHAPTER NINE

KETHI KICKED OFF, flinging herself along the tube at a shallow diagonal. Her left hand snaked out ahead of her to grab one of the handholds which were spaced out in a long line throughout the chute's length – the fifth one to be precise, the one she always went for. She did so not for support but rather to gain a little added momentum and make a slight course adjustment. As soon as her fingers clasped the cold metal of the flattened hoop, she used it to drag her body forward and push herself onward again; this time straight along the tube.

This procedure was now so familiar that she had long since passed the point of feeling proud at not needing to make any further adjustments to either speed or direction, at not having to reach for any more of the handholds to correct even minimal rotation. She simply took all that for granted.

Unlike some of her colleagues, Kethi felt no discomfort in zero g; in fact, she positively revelled in it. Her destination, the observation pod, was coming up fast, though not too quickly; as ever, she had judged her approach to perfection. Grasping the bar guard with both hands, she used it to stop her upper body even as her legs swung underneath to slip into the pod, which was essentially a transparent bubble built around a comfortable chair and a mess of equipment.

By entering this way, Kethi was able to slide feet first into the chair and grab the arms to stop herself from bouncing off again, then fasten the seat ties to ensure there would be no floating around while she concentrated on other things.

There it was: the quickest, simplest way to get from the habitat to here; and she still held the record. No one could shoot the chute faster. Except for Demahl, of course. He *had* managed to beat her time. Once. But in doing so he'd overdone it, coming in too quickly. The dislocated shoulder suffered as a result of stopping himself with a combination of the bar and the pod's wall at the end of his run had rendered the time null and void. So Kethi still reigned supreme.

She always looked forward to her shifts out here. Solitude was a rare and precious commodity. Besides, the sense of wonder that gripped her the very first time she gazed out at the universe had never diminished, and there was nowhere in the whole of the habitat where that sense was sharper, more immediate than here.

Kethi relaxed, settling into the chair and focusing her concentration before she opened the feed. A bewildering array of information flooded her awareness, playing across her lenses as she reviewed and correlated the data from a battery of different sensors to create a rapidly drawn digital picture of how the surrounding universe appeared from this vantage point at this specific time.

"Kethi," the voice was a murmur at the edge of her awareness, "could you please meet me at the hub right away?"

She kept the mild irritation from her voice as she replied, "Nyles, I've just arrived to do a shift at the pod. Can this wait?"

"No, it can't. I'll assign someone else to take over from you. This is a matter of some urgency."

"Very well. I'm on my way."

Kethi blinked twice in rapid succession, wiping the data from her lenses and shutting off the flow. So much for a few hours' peace and quiet out here. It would be weeks before her next pod shift came around.

With a sigh, she unfastened the seat ties and then carefully positioned her feet preparatory to stretching up through the semi-solid barrier of the pod's door, in order to grasp the bar guard beyond and haul herself outside.

A simple enough manoeuvre when you knew how, a nightmare the first couple of times you tried it.

As she sailed back along the chute scant moments after having travelled it in the opposite direction, she wondered what was so urgent that Nyles had seen fit to pull her away from a duty. None of the alternatives she came up with were in any sense good or reassuring, whichever way she looked at it. This would prove to be something to do with ULAW no doubt; perhaps a newly announced policy which Nyles and his people saw as an opportunity, or a trend which they chose to interpret as a sign of undue influence. Nyles seemed incapable of realising what most people here had recognised long ago: this place and its population were a complete irrelevance to the rest of humanity. Ever since the founding of the habitat and their decision to withdraw from the arena of politics, and indeed society in general, their community had been dismissed and forgotten about by the wider populace.

Stubbornly refusing to acknowledge as much, Nyles and his more ardent supporters continually scoured news feeds and data flows in search of some whispered snippet or rumour that they could cling to in order to justify the habitat's existence. This latest summons was doubtless another example of his clutching at some cosmic straw or other.

Kethi knew her history, and was aware that William Anderson, the habitat's founder, had once been a significant political figure. Anderson's position as head of one of the largest resource conglomerates of its time had provided him with extreme wealth and the influence to match. At one point, the food synthesis wing of his empire alone was said to have fed nearly a quarter of all the people across human space. Yet his apparently extraordinary claims at the height of the War that ULAW were not the real enemy, that there was a bigger, darker threat waiting in the wings, had caused outrage and widespread condemnation. Hindsight was a wonderful thing and it seemed extraordinary to Kethi that anyone would have expected otherwise. How naïve were Anderson and his people? Of course nobody was interested in the 'evidence' he claimed to have to support his assertions. The only enemy claiming people's attention at the time was the one whose armies and warships were arrayed before them.

'The Prepared' Anderson and his followers had styled themselves. 'The Pre-Scared' some media wag had dubbed them, a tag which quickly degenerated to 'The Scaries' – they became a joke. Worse, they stood accused in some quarters of being ULAW sympathisers, of collaborating with the enemy and attempting to undermine the war effort. Discredited, humiliated and frustrated, Anderson gave up any hope of being listened to and chose to withdraw from public life. It was then that he decided to lead his followers to the fringes of human space and establish the habitat, a safe haven where they could continue their work and ensure that they at least would be ready. The project all but exhausted their leader's personal fortune, but it was a price he had been more than willing to meet.

From her own studies of the man's life, Kethi concluded that Anderson never believed the habitat would become such a long-term home but rather viewed it as the platform from which he would relaunch his political career, returning as society's champion in its hour of greatest need.

Yet that hour never came. Little more than a decade after the War ended Anderson had died, leaving his aging contemporaries and their successors, the next generation, to continue his dream and live the lives he had shaped for them. There was a growing feeling of restlessness among the younger folk, some of whom resented the great 'founder' for his legacy and a few of whom even harboured misgivings about the habitat and what it stood for.

No such concerns troubled Nyles, that much was certain. As a man who had actually fought in the War he had been one of the very first to convert to Anderson's cause, and believed in it as fervently now as he ever had. It was a level of zeal that Kethi was finding increasingly hard to feign, let alone emulate.

She arrived at the end of the chute and entered the habitat proper; surrendering to the pull of gravity once more. As she stepped across the threshold and felt her body's weight again, she reflected on how easy it was to take such things for granted and wondered how many here even noticed the technology which allowed a limited-area gravity field to be so accurately focused. Few, she suspected.

"Kethi!" The shout came from behind her as she neared the hub. She knew who it was even before turning around to see the familiar, slightly gangly form of Simon running towards her, narrowly avoiding collision with a startled pair of elders in the process. He skipped past them, oblivious to their disapproving frowns.

His boyish grin as he reached her was as infectious as ever, and she couldn't help but smile in response. Simon was one of her closest friends and her greatest worries. He was besotted with her. He knew it and she knew it, just as they both knew that she could never love him in return.

He held his crippled hand close to his stomach, a habit that was entirely subconscious, cradling it as if to protect its imbalanced combination of organic and prosthetic digits.

"Thought you were at the pod this shift," he said, a little out of breath from the quick sprint.

"I was; until I got a call from Nyles. He's summoned me to the hub."

"Oh wow, that means you'll be one of the first to find out."

"Find out what?"

"Whatever it is that's going on around here. Something's up but nobody seems to know what, or if they do know they're not saying."

"Really?" This must all have been very recent; she hadn't noticed a thing before heading out to the pod.

"Yes, *really*! Nyles's cronies are running around as if they're expecting a visit from someone really important at any minute. It must be what he wants to see you about. Let me know, Keth, won't you – as soon as you find out what's going on."

"If I can," she assured him, and laughed, all too familiar with Simon's appetite for gossip; being out the loop when there was the prospect of something juicy going down for once was guaranteed to drive him nuts. She started to walk away from him. "Gotta go."

"I know. Remember, though, call me," he yelled after her.

"We'll see."

Predictably, Nyles was already at the hub waiting for her, pacing across the auditorium's polished floor with its emblem of a cause long lost in a war which the wrong side had always been destined to win. The Allies were never more than a gathering of grudgingly cooperative states which lacked the focus and all round unity of the United League of Worlds. The concession of inserting an 'A' so that it was the 'United League of Allied Worlds' which seized the reins of humanity's fractured society in the War's aftermath hadn't fooled anybody. Only the stubbornest of die-hard supporters could possibly view the outcome as anything other than a ULW victory.

Kethi wondered whether anybody even noticed that symbol any more, though if anyone did, it would be Nyles. She also wondered, not for the first time, whether the 'Prepared' might just have been able to turn the tide of the War had Anderson chosen a different course. A redundant question; this was all ancient history now, and their only option was to deal with the present that faced them.

She banished her heretical musings as Nyles stopped pacing and turned towards her. Seeing him now, he looked anything but the hero he was, instead seeming tired and old. In recent years his face had steadily grown into that prematurely greyed hair which had been his hallmark even during the War.

"Ah, Kethi, there you are."

"Sorry to have kept you waiting, Nyles."

"No matter," he assured her, smiling to prove the point. Being Nyles, he'd missed the sarcasm entirely.

"So, what's up?"

"I'll show you. Image." He spoke the latter to the empty air.

A bulbous and ill-conceived starship appeared in the space between them.

"Ugly so and so, isn't she?" Kethi observed.

"*The Noise Within*. Have you heard of her at all?"

Kethi shook her head, wondering what all this was leading up to. "No, sorry. Should I have?"

"She appeared out of nowhere and has been wreaking havoc with ULAW's luxury-end shipping – preying on cruise ships it would seem, but choosing her targets with great care."

"A pirate?" Kethi snorted and began to wonder whether Nyles was losing the plot. "Come on, Nyles, do you seriously think I have the time to take an interest in this sort of thing?"

"No, of course not; nor the inclination, I'm sure, but you might be tempted to after you've had a look at her weapons systems."

On cue, a component of the hovering image started to glow bright orange, then another did the same in red. Both were systems connected to the ship's exterior but which lay largely hidden beneath her hull.

As each section glowed an enlarged cut-away version appeared beside the full image, showing greater detail.

"Where did the intelligence for this come from?" Kethi asked, as her gaze flickered across the cut-away.

"You'd be surprised. Our little pirate is far from modest about her assets. This sort of thing's all over the media streams. Obtaining it was hardly a challenge."

Kethi looked more closely as another array lit up. Something about these components looked uncomfortably familiar. Then she had it. "Sanctity!" She felt a chill shiver course through her body.

"Recognise them?"

Of course she did, as he well knew.

Deep down, she had always hoped that nothing like this would ever happen, that these sort of arrays wouldn't be seen again; at least not in her lifetime. She felt a vast pit of dread open inside her. This was what she had been preparing for, almost since she was born, what the whole of the habitat was established to face. Yet now it was actually happening she felt anything but ready. For a few numbed seconds Kethi was grateful to fall back on her training and, operating on automatic pilot, opened the feed so that figures and equations poured in, enabling her to study the information in greater detail. The raw data started to pan across her lenses as a sequence of further elements within the ship glowed in differing colours. The familiar flow of information provided the anchor she needed, and she was able to haul her emotional responses back under control.

A detached part of her mind realised that she would remember this moment forever. The Kethi who was shortly destined to walk out of the hub would be a very different Kethi from the one who had walked in; different expectations, different ambitions.

That went for everyone in the habitat after they had seen this, not just her. They were no longer waiting for something to happen – it just had. Now they were faced with the far more challenging prospect of having to do something about it.

Then, on the heels of the numbness and the dread, an odd calm settled over her. "So," she said, "it begins." She was aware of Nyles watching her intently, so made sure that she didn't flinch, didn't waver, and was proud of how steady her voice sounded as she asked, "When do we leave?"

"In two hours."

Two hours? She knew the ship was kept at a state of permanent readiness, but even so... Yet she nodded and said calmly, "See you aboard *The Rebellion*."

CHAPTER TEN

EMILIO KNEW ABOUT life, knew that 'fair' didn't come into it. Life was all about taking whatever you could whenever the opportunity presented itself. People who chose to hang around waiting for 'fair' to lend them a hand were never going to see old age. Not Emilio, who had already made it as far as his teens.

His people might refer to their world as *Paraíso* but that was only because they enjoyed having something to laugh about; though with the passage of time the joke had lost its flavour. Frysworld was a cesspit; a stinking mire of human misery in which desperation had taken on almost tangible proportions. Oh, sure, that wasn't what the tourists saw, but it *was* what the people here had to live with. You could see it etched into the faces of those around you and burning deep within their eyes – everyone who hadn't already given up, at least. Desperation was a taste that tainted the air. Young tigers on the make; twitching, calculating, sizing everything and everyone up while searching for a way out, for a route to a different world and a better way of life. The pretty and the young selling their bodies and their souls to the tourists for a handful of Standards, they could tell you about it. Without desperation, there was only despair.

Which was where the stranger came in. He was Emilio's ticket out of here.

Pure luck that Emilio saw him at all, which went a long way

to convincing him that fate had finally chosen to turn a smile his way. He woke up to the sour smell of vomit and the sickly smell of urine, all interwoven with the heady smell of sex. The incessant buzzing of a fly drew him back to consciousness. More than one. He tried to raise a hand and swat at them, but his arm was pinned. Something soft but heavy also lay across his crotch and bladder, pressing down uncomfortably on the latter. A leg.

God, he needed a pee. And a drink – his throat was as dry as sand – but the pee came first. The leg belonged to his sister, Juana, younger than him by a year – her leg cocked around him, the mound of her sex hot and moist against his hip – while his arm was pinned beneath the buttocks of his best buddy, Caz. Both of them were as naked as he. Shards of memory came chivying each other in splintered flashes – his sister's sweet face contorted with agony or ecstasy, her eyes screwed tight and teeth gritted as she pushed back fiercely to match the rhythm of his thrusts, rough male hands pumping his cock, the familiar hot searing pleasure-pain of something pushing piston-like in and out of his arse. He rubbed his eyes as if to banish the fractured images. The *Giazyu* which Caz had brought round last night must have been some *seriously* powerful manna, and it had taken all three of them on one hell of a ride. Emilio couldn't remember with any clarity how long they had fucked or how many times or who had done what to whom; all he knew was that his bum felt raw and his prick throbbed, while his head was pounding fit to die.

And he still needed to pee.

Moving as slowly as his bladder would allow, he managed to untangle himself from the assorted legs and body parts, tenderly lifting his sister's thigh to fully free his legs. She mumbled something as he sat up, but she didn't wake.

For a few seconds after he made it to his feet he simply stood there, making sure he could. Daylight streamed in through the cracks in the planking of their clumsily built shelter and he wondered idly what time it was. Tentatively, he moved towards the door, pulling aside the curtain and stumbling outside. Late morning he judged, squinting upward to gauge the sun's position.

After shuffling a few steps away from the doorway, he grabbed his cock and relaxed, allowing his bladder to empty into the weeds and the dirt. This brought such blissful relief that he sighed, closing his eyes until the aching pressure eased.

It was when he opened them again that he first saw the stranger.

The man didn't belong here – you could see that straight away – but at the same time he looked different from the usual *forastcerdos* who thronged to Frysworld the year round – the pampered and gluttonous tourists who were only here to eat, drink, gamble, patronise and fuck as much as they could. After they were sated or had run out of money they would go, feeling good in the face of others' misery and leaving behind everything they'd fucked and abused to sink back into the *pocilga* and again become part of the rich cultural mire of *Paraíso*, the real Frysworld – the place the tourists never saw and never wanted to see.

Yet the stranger was here. Not strolling down the broad streets ogling the local *cabronas* or stuffing his face with 'authentic' native delicacies, but here where he had no right to be, where if he wasn't careful he'd get more of the authentic culture than he ever bargained for.

After he'd stopped peeing, Emilio turned to face this newcomer. He saw that he wasn't the only one watching him. Curious gazes followed the man as he walked confidently, now seeming to head directly towards Emilio.

"Hey, bambino, put that thing away, or are you hoping the sun will make it grow some?" Carla called from across the street.

She seemed the only one paying attention to anything other than the stranger.

"Carla, sweetheart, gimme a minute and I'll come over there so you can feel it and judge for yourself if it's grown any." But his commitment to the banter was half-hearted and his gaze only flickered away from the stranger for a second.

The man moved with a purpose and apparent self-assurance which no *forastcerdo* ought to have here. Pale skinned and muscular, he wore one of the feather-light shirts that were supposed to keep you real cool. Not bad looking either, in a rough, pasty-faced sort of way. No question now, he was making a beeline for Emilio.

The boy assumed he wanted a fuck and was already calculating how much he could take him for.

"You're Emilio."

Mierda! The *bastardo* knew his name. That put a very different, almost sinister spin on things. For the first time Emilio began to worry. He tried to keep all of this from showing in his voice though, as he said, "Who wants to know?"

Chasing hard on the heels of his initial panic came the realisation that somebody had most likely recommended him to this man as a good lay. After all, why else would a *forastcerdo* be looking for him? The thought caused his best 'come on' smile to spontaneously materialise, lifting both his eyebrows and the corners of his mouth upward, while at the same time the price he had been thinking of demanding went up a few notches.

"Look, kid, I'm not in the mood."

"You sure about that, mister?" Emilio asked.

He stood facing the stranger with hands on hips. This close up the man was far more imposing than he had first seemed; Emilio registered just how well toned his body was, not like the usual flabby *forastcerdos* at all. He pictured this stranger naked and, at the thought, felt his cock starting to stir. Making sure the smile never stopped dancing around his lips, Emilio gyrated his pelvis slowly, provocatively.

From across the way, Carla wolf-whistled.

For his part, the stranger pursed his lips and shook his head as if losing patience. Emilio knew the sort. In denial; not wanting to admit what he had come here for.

Suddenly the stranger moved, so fast that Emilio couldn't even think to react.

He felt a vice-like grip close on the back of his neck and what could only be the barrel of a gun press against his head, just above the ear. *Fuck!* The stranger was behind him. *How had he got there?* Panic blotted out all thought and caused his knees to wilt. If Emilio hadn't squeezed every last drop out of his bladder already, he felt sure he would have wet himself. From what seemed a long way off he heard Carla shout something, but he didn't catch the words.

"Into the hut," a voice hissed in his ear.

The boy half stumbled and was half propelled back to the doorway and through the curtain, his feet scrabbling to prevent him hanging from the stranger's grip like some dangled mannequin.

Coming back in from outside the hut's stink was even worse than it had been when he first woke up. Caz still looked to be out of it, but Juana was beginning to stir – perhaps disturbed by the commotion and Carla's shouting, or perhaps having simply metabolised enough of the *Giazyu* to allow her body to start functioning again.

"What the fu..." Juana began as they burst in. Presumably the sight of her brother dangling from the stranger's fist like some gutted *conejo* hung out to dry must have had her wondering if she'd really woken up at all.

The stranger spoke across her, demanding, "Tell me who this is." The gun barrel jabbed at the side of Emilio's head, causing him to wince and pull away, in as much as he was able to. What if the man's finger twitched? What if the gun went off, even by accident? *It couldn't end like this!*

Juana blinked stupidly, as if in the hope that her eyelids could wipe this apparition away. Caz finally showed signs of life, rolling over and groaning.

"Tell me!"

"Tell him, Juana, for fuck's sake!" Emilio heard himself scream. He no longer cared what the stranger was here for, he just wanted that gun away from the side of his head.

Juana presumably concluded this really was happening, or at least that she might as well act as if it were. She stared at him. "Emilio... bro... what's goin' on?"

"Good enough." The pressure of the gun finally lifted, though Emilio would have sworn he could still feel it pressed there even after he saw the weapon waved in Juana's direction. "You two, get out."

Neither Juana nor the still-groggy Caz made a move to go anywhere.

"I said out! Or first I shoot this piece of shit and then the two of you!"

That got through to them. Juana scrambled to her feet and helped the bemused Caz do the same, almost dragging him past them and out the door. Emilio wanted to cry out again, wanted to plead with her not to leave him alone with this maniac, but he was too scared to articulate the need and the fear, too terrorised to form the words, so instead simply screamed them inside his own head.

Then it was just the two of them.

The man threw him down onto the sleeping mats – the same ones that had been vacated by his sister and friend mere seconds ago. At last that crushing hold on his neck was gone and he felt able to think again, to act. Except that the gun was still there, resting on one knee as the stranger squatted in front of him.

"Right, Emilio," the man said slowly, casually, as if they were old friends, "I'm told you're the stud with his ear to the ground and his cock in every club, that you're 'The Man' when it comes to knowing what goes down around here. Am I right?"

"Sure." Emilio forced a grin, recovering a hint of his usual cockiness. "I hear things, everything." At that particular moment he was ready to say whatever the stranger wanted to hear, anything to keep that gun away, but in this instance he didn't need to lie. It was true.

"Good." The man produced something, a sheet of four photos. "You recognise any of these?"

Emilio looked. Four *forastcerdos* but he hadn't seen any of them before. He was tempted to joke that all *forastcerdos* looked the same to him, but thought better of it, both because they didn't and because the stranger did not strike him as the joking kind, so he simply shook his head.

The man grunted. Suddenly money appeared in his hand. Not the local shit printed on paper which could disintegrate if you stared at it for too long, but genuine 'live through a couple of washes' Universal Standards. Maybe the bastard did want to fuck him after all.

"If you should see any of these four, call me, at once. The stranger pulled a tiny comm from his pocket and passed it to Emilio, along with the pictures. "This is preset to my number only. Remember, call immediately at any hour, day or night, if you see them."

"Yeah, yeah, I get it." Emilio's gaze was still transfixed by the money.

"Here's 50 US to make sure you do."

Fifty? For that much, this *forastcerdo* could have had him for the rest of the day. He reached to take the money, but the stranger didn't let go. "This is just the down-payment. There's twenty times as much again in this once you lead me to one of these four. That's 1,000 Universal Standards." The man spoke each word very precisely, as if Emilio were some kind of simpleton. "Do we have a deal?"

"Hell, yes!" Emilio could hardly believe his luck. This was enough to buy passage off of this God-forsaken dung heap for good. "For 1,000 US I'll find you all four of these *forastcerdos* if they're anywhere on the planet and will even throw in a night or two with my sister as well, if you want her."

The stranger simply stared and then stood up, before heading for the doorway. Emilio didn't care; he was grinning from ear to ear, partly from relief and partly because of the 50 US clasped in his hand. The best thing about it was that he hadn't even needed to bend over and drop his pants to get it.

He grabbed a pair of trousers from the floor and pulled them on before following the stranger outside; mainly because this gave him a pocket in which to stash the money and the pocket comm. No point in advertising his new found good fortune. A small crowd had gathered in front of the shack, some with makeshift clubs and even a knife or two, though Emilio noted that at no point had anyone tried to rush in and save him. They looked like a bunch of people who reckoned they *ought* to be doing something but deep down didn't especially want to. Caz and Juana were there, the former seemed indignant, while Juana just looked vulnerable and scared – she was particularly good at doing 'vulnerable' – earned a living that way. She had somebody's shawl clutched around her in an effort to cover her modesty; as if she had any.

The stranger was facing up to the gathering with a nonchalance that suggested he did this sort of thing every day. He stood there with arms folded and feet firmly planted. In fact, it looked to Emilio as if the man was amused by the whole thing. Emilio put on his best swagger as he left the hut, coming up to stand by the stranger.

"Hey, thanks and everything, but me an' my man here were just talking a little business, is all."

"You sure, kid? He didn't force you?"

Absurd, really; had someone raped him on one of the dingy back streets off Strip, no one would have cared less, they would have snorted and said that it served him right, but because this stranger had dared to enter their world and walk down their streets, suddenly everyone came over all concerned and neighbourly.

"Nah, everything's good."

There were a few mumbled curses and black looks as people drifted away, the glares mainly in Emilio's direction rather than at the stranger, which was crazy. Not as if anything here was his fault.

The stranger walked away as calmly as he'd arrived.

Carla was still there. She came towards Emilio while everyone else steadily disappeared.

"You all right, Emilio, really?" Her hand rested on his shoulder. Her touch felt warm against his naked skin.

"Sure, you know me. Invulnerable."

Carla was quite a looker for an oldie, no doubt about that. The two of them had always flirted with each other in a half meaning it half joking sort of way. She might have been a decade or more older than him but this woman still had a good figure and a nice ass for all that she'd had a couple of kids, and there was no grey yet in that long dark hair of hers. The main reason Emilio had never put a move on her was because Carla had one mean bastard for a husband, and he valued his own good looks too much to risk having his face beaten to a pulp. This morning, though, Emilio was on a high, both from the residue of *Giazyu* still floating around his system and in reaction to having survived what had been a shit-scary incident, so he chanced pushing things a little further than he usually would and placed a neighbourly arm around Carla's slender body, his hand resting casually on her butt.

"So where's Miguel?" The muscle-bound brute worked security at one of the rougher clubs off Strip.

"Oh, he's already gone for the day. Won't be back until the early hours."

Emilio closed his hand slowly as the woman spoke, grabbing a good handful of one of Carla's buttocks and squeezing. It proved to be pleasingly firm. He then began to massage her cheeks with his finger tips. She didn't pull away but instead smiled in a deliciously sexy way and pressed her hip against his.

"Really?" They were of similar height. Her hand drifted down from his shoulder to his waist and Emilio felt his cock semi-harden. He began to walk, steering her towards her home. "And the kids…?"

"Huh! As if I ever know where they are."

He didn't doubt his ability to perform, to do Carla justice, despite the previous night's heavy session; though he would probably have to sleep the afternoon away or he'd never be ready for work that night. "Shame…"

And then they were stepping inside, away from prying eyes. He stopped walking and pulled her to him, savouring the pressure of her breasts against his chest and the feel of her warm, soft lips pressed to his.

FRYSWORLD WAS BASKING in the sort of warmth guaranteed to generate both heat hazes and scanty clothing – the type of climate preferred by holidaymakers throughout human history. Sleeveless neckless legless backless and sideless dresses skirts shirts shorts sarongs and thongs were in evidence throughout the central thoroughfares, in a bewildering array of styles and colours which defied the rainbow.

The frequency of balmy days such as this was just one of the reasons why Frysworld had become so popular as a resort destination. Certainly the Strip and its attendant districts offered everything a vacationer might want – at a price; and that price wasn't even all that unreasonable if you knew the right places to go. The vacation experience was made all the more enjoyable by a dark-skinned, slightly exotic featured and invariably eager to please local population.

After two days on Frysworld, Leyton was bored stiff.

It might have been different if this were a real vacation but it wasn't; he had a job to do, which meant he could not even relax and immerse himself in the pleasures that surrounded him but instead felt compelled to stay alert. Nor was the mission proving as simple as he'd hoped. On the face of it, finding out whether specific individuals were here or had ever been here should have been pretty straightforward. After all, both the ports kept records, there was a well-resourced local police force to call upon and all the reputable bars, clubs, casinos, hotels, brothels, racetracks, combat arenas, games centres, flying zones, safari cruisers and restaurants were equipped with surveillance systems. Not only that but their owners were, for the most part, falling over themselves to cooperate; if only to demonstrate they had nothing to hide.

But the keyword there was 'reputable'. For every place that could claim to be, there were half a dozen or more which held no such ambitions. The further away from the Strip you went the less reliable the various establishments tended to be, until you reached those where a 'surveillance system' equated to a peephole into the boudoirs and the dungeons.

Spacers being spacers, Leyton had a fair idea which type of place the four who had defected to *The Noise Within* were likely to go for, should they ever come here. So he had to establish a network of informants to cover the sleazier areas – locals who had their fingers on the pulse and were desperate enough and greedy enough to do what he asked. To find such people, Leyton was prepared to leave the safe and cosy environs of the Strip and its attendant tourist districts and risk stepping into the far edgier world of *Paraíso*, where *Giazyu* reigned supreme.

Giazyu was the primary reason – climatic considerations aside – that Frysworld had gained such notoriety as a resort destination. Native to this world, the plant grew in abundance, and its root and leaf, even the bark of some of the more mature specimens, contained a substance with highly hallucinogenic properties. The local people had grown incredibly resourceful when it came to processing and utilising the extracts from different parts of the plant. *Giazyu* was commonly available to tourists around the Strip as sanitised pills, the colour of which were uniformly coded to depict the strength and origin of the dose, but here in the slums of *Paraíso* it was to be found in far rawer forms. The natives tended to inhale, smoke, inject, chew or swallow their *Giazyu*, depending on what part of the plant had been subjected to which preparation process.

The pungent, slightly acrid stench of the drug lay heavy in the air as the eyegee made his way between the squalid hovels of the native quarter. That was how the area appeared on official maps: 'the native quarter'. In fact it was a vast sprawl of land carved out of the surrounding jungle, far greater in size than all the tourist districts put together. If the part he was currently crossing was typical, he could well appreciate why the maps tended to decorate the native quarter with ominous warnings and discouragements. There were guided tours into the districts, he understood, conducted aboard air-conditioned vehicles; though he couldn't imagine what anyone would want to come here to see.

Poverty. That was the inescapable, overriding factor that governed life here. Closely followed by *Giazyu*. Slip over and land face down in a puddle and the water was likely to be infused with so much of the drug that you'd stand up and find yourself in a different world.

Not that there was any evidence of puddles at that particular time. Leyton walked calmly through dusty streets as he crossed this depressing shanty town, oblivious to the stares and the glares, allowing all the malice and the need and the jealousy which those looks embodied slide off him. He had long ago learnt that confidence and an air of purpose were the keys to an untroubled passage in such threatening places. It was the timid and the uncertain who invited malicious intent to manifest as physical threat.

In the visor's absence, the gun chattered incessantly, warning of potential dangers on all sides, until he instructed it to stay quiet unless the threat was an immediate one.

Fortunately, the boy he was looking for lived only a little way into *Paraíso*, as those who relied for a living on the Strip and its surrounds often did. In fact, if Leyton's information was correct, he should be more or less there by now.

He saw a naked boy relieving himself outside a hut; noted the lithe, athletic body, the size of the lad's manhood and the sunburst tattoo on his right buttock, all of which tallied with the description he'd been given, so the eyegee felt pretty confident that this was the kid he was after. But he wanted to be certain before flashing any money about. Once they saw the colour of his Standards, any given local would undoubtedly be happy to claim they were Emilio, their own grandmother, or anyone else Leyton might want them to be.

So he used the gun to bully the kid into the hut, the inside of which nearly made him gag; it stank even worse than the air outside. Using the gun for such menial duty might have been akin to using a sledgehammer to crack a nut, but the performance at least secured confirmation from the two young *Giazyu*-heads he found inside – barely into their teens by the look of them – that this really was 'Emilio'. He then scared the pair out of the room. Only then did he flash the cash and recruit the kid to the cause.

Leyton knew that *Paraiso* could be a dangerous place for the unwary, so he came fully alert as he stepped out of the hut to find a reception committee of disgruntled locals waiting.

"Thanks for the warning," he intoned.

"Just obeying instructions," the gun responded. "They weren't an immediate threat until you stepped outside."

In fairness, they were barely that even now. The group looked more nervous than menacing, as if they were embarrassed to be there at all. Emilio appeared from inside the hut before anything beyond posturing was required; their relief at seeing him was almost palpable and he soon defused whatever threat there might have been, leaving Leyton free to head back towards tourist town, where he belonged.

That was it; the final piece. If any of *The Noise Within's* recent recruits turned up on Frysworld, he now felt confident he'd hear about it.

Of course, from a purely statistical viewpoint the odds were against that, but if Leyton were looking for some R and R and money was no object, this would be one of the first places he'd think to head for, which might just tilt those odds a little in his favour. Who could say?

Whether they came here or not, all he could do for the foreseeable future was wait, while doing his best not to die of boredom in the process.

CHAPTER ELEVEN

DREVERS WAS NOT Mac by any stretch of the imagination, but he was sharp, no question about that, devious even. After a little jockeying, Kyle had settled into a banter-based friendship with the man which seemed to suit them both, even if it didn't yet encompass anything as profound as trust.

Drevers was a lot more vocal in his complaints about the situation on the ship than Kyle had been, making the latter wonder whether perhaps his time in the military made him prone to accept authority a little too readily. If so, clearly Drevers had never been a navy man; a fact Kyle was soon to be eternally grateful for, as the newcomer's frequent gripes and protestations appeared to have an effect. The two of them were even permitted to take part in the next action, the one that saw them recruit Blaine and Hammond. Kyle was convinced their presence was the reason *why* the latter pair defected to *The Noise Within*, a point which fully deserved to be emphasised.

"Let's face it," he said to Drevers later, when they were back on the ship, "our smooth talking and irresistible humour has to be more appealing than the usual blank-faced delivery of the zombies." The words were as much for the benefit of whoever was directing the ship as for Drevers himself.

Kyle had reached the conclusion long ago that everything they said and did was being observed. Without openly discussing the subject, he and Drevers had come to a mutual understanding about it. At first the thought of being spied upon irritated the hell out of him, but then he began to view it as a challenge and had determined to convince whoever the ship's real masters might be that he was a valuable asset, indispensable even, and certainly of far more use than the 'old crew', the zombies, whom he was increasingly convinced were not crew at all but uninhabited remote-operated shells.

Neither he nor Drevers were averse to manipulating the situation to their advantage.

"You see, they've got it all wrong," Drevers insisted, clearly playing to an audience. "Currently, we're treated little better than prisoners."

Kyle nodded vigorously in agreement. "Exactly. All four of us joined this crew because we *wanted* to, so you'd think they would be trying to make sure we were keen to stick around rather than making us regret we ever came here."

"Right. I mean, this place isn't exactly a holiday camp, and a man has needs..."

Kyle was nodding agreement. "What I wouldn't give for a really good meal, some decent beer – properly chilled – and a few hours alone with a willing woman."

"You and me both; anyone who could offer a package like *that* would have my loyalty forever."

"I'll drink to that!" And they clinked together their identical plasti-dure mugs, guaranteed to bounce and not shatter, before each taking a gulp of the near-tasteless recycled and alcohol-free beer which was the closest to a real drink *The Noise Within* provided.

During the years he had spent in the shipping wilderness following his discharge from the navy, Kyle encountered just about every type of decrepit and malfunctioning drinks dispenser and neglected unhygienic autogalley that man had ever devised; servicing and repairing each one with loving care, if only to prevent them from poisoning himself and the rest of the crew. When he first saw those carried by *The Noise Within*, it was like a reunion with old friends. These were exactly the same models he remembered from his navy days.

In the long period of unrelenting tedium following his arrival on *The Noise Within*, Kyle kept himself busy by taking apart, inspecting, cleaning, and then reassembling each and every unit the ship boasted, piece by piece, ensuring that they were all operating at optimum efficiency.

Evidently, his proclivity for such things had not gone unnoticed.

When the hulking form of Zombie Number One loomed over Drevers and himself, both assumed this signalled another raid, despite it coming so soon after the last one. However, the suited figure soon made it clear that on this occasion only Kyle's presence was wanted.

"You have technical expertise which is needed," was the anonymous figure's sole effort at explanation.

Kyle had no idea whether this was the genuine reason he was being singled out or not; his imagination went into overdrive and started painting sinister alternatives. Perhaps he had said too much in his criticism of the situation, perhaps he was being summoned to be punished, condemned to the brig or jettisoned from an airlock... In the absence of any explanation from his blank-faced escort, paranoia born of bizarre circumstance ran riot.

To compensate for his nervousness, he talked. "So, did you always want to be a pirate? Bet you did. I reckon your mum was a pirate before you – a lady corsair of the spaceways – and you grew up thinking: 'One day I want to be just like my mum'; though wearing different underwear, obviously."

Kyle was babbling, spouting nonsense, and he knew it. In truth, he didn't expect a response from the zombie, so could hardly claim to be disappointed when none was forthcoming. He read stoicism into the resultant silence, on the part of those guiding the suit if nothing else.

At first Kyle was hoping to be taken to the bridge. He'd been itching to have a look at the control systems ever since he first caught a glimpse of *The Noise Within's* weird adaptations and weapon arrays from the bridge of *The Lady J*. However, it soon became clear that he was being directed towards the lower decks rather than the more central areas where the bridge would be.

So, assuming he was not about to be thrown into some previously unsuspected dungeon room hidden deep within the ship's bowels, it had to be the engines. That prospect intrigued him only marginally less than being able to tinker around on the bridge itself.

At least he was being led to a bulkhead door and not an airlock, so, on the plus side, he wasn't about to be forced to 'walk the plank' without a suit.

Being around the silent, inhuman-seeming zombies was an unsettling experience, and Kyle had quickly come to view his original separation from them as a blessing. The mechanic in him was hoping to be let loose on one of those suits at some stage to see what made it tick, but at the same time he was grateful that his current guide walked ahead of him, so that he didn't have to continually stare into that opaque faceplate, which he was increasingly convinced hid only emptiness.

They finally arrived at the engine room; the ship's internal layout familiar enough that Kyle could happily have found it on his own had he been trusted to.

The sense of familiarity ended the instant he stepped through the door. Not that the Kaufman Drive units were anything other than he had expected; it was everything else.

The business end of the engines lay in shielded compartments beyond this room, where titanic energies were generated, clashing to produce the violent forces needed to power a starship; where those same energies were channelled and harnessed and regulated into useful form. What confronted Kyle was the control element of the process, the governing systems which kept those furies tame and prevented them from ripping the fragile ship apart.

The familiar sleek banks of moulded metal which housed

the monitoring arrays and adjustment interfaces sat upon their plinth towards the centre of the room as usual, but on their far side was... something else. Kyle struggled to identify the thing that stood there, even in the most general terms. It was unlike anything he had encountered before and his mind baulked at trying to allocate any label to what his eyes reported.

Dark, pulsating pillars which rippled with energy and on which he was finding it impossible to fully focus – their edges ill-defined and blurred. It literally hurt to stare at them for too long, causing his eyes to water, but the afterimage when he blinked the tears away left him with a sense of deepest purple shading into onyx black, of scarlet sparks glimpsed at the very periphery of vision and hints of other colours he couldn't even begin to identify. Beyond the pillars sat something else, sensed as a bulk but so dark that it was beyond his capacity to identify any details of form. He had the impression that whatever he was seeing was not wholly there, that by merely trying to look at this thing he was gaining a glimpse of somewhere else, of a place other than normal reality.

The Kaufman Drive console was linked to this outlandish object by several veils; which was the only way Kyle could describe them. He was uncertain whether these shifting, inconsistent curtains had any substance at all or whether they were composed purely of energy.

"What the hell...?"

"The engines have been augmented to enhance performance."

Augmented? Not in any way Kyle had ever come across. He stared at the zombie in disbelief. "You don't honestly expect me to go near that, do you?"

"It is necessary. Drive systems are marginally out of synch, enough to drop engine performance to little more than ninety per cent of optimum. Due to the nature of the engines' augmentations, recalibration cannot be accurately achieved from the bridge, only from here. You have the skills to do this."

True – at least as far as the Kaufmans were concerned. Kyle

looked back at the pillars and the hidden bulk of the mechanism beyond and licked his upper lip, feeling less than thrilled at the prospect.

What about radiation? "Is it safe even being in here?"

"Brief exposure will produce no discernable detrimental effect," the zombie responded.

Kyle grunted. As reassurances went, this fell a long way short of ideal. Not that he had much choice in the matter. He briefly considered refusing to do as asked and wondered what would happen if he simply turned around and walked out of here. Would the zombie move to stop him? And what then; thrown off the ship, perhaps? He wasn't prepared to find out. Besides, the sooner he was done here the 'briefer' his exposure would be.

"The necessary equipment has been provided," the zombie said.

Sure enough, a standard set of diagnostics and repair tools sat at the foot of the console. With a sigh and a muttered, "I must be mad," Kyle stepped forward.

Ignoring the shifting, almost seductive lure of whatever occupied the room's far side, he concentrated on the familiar Kaufman units before him, initially running through a series of diagnostics so that he could get a feel for these particular chunks of hardware and judge exactly how well they were running. As ever, he could not help but admire the sheer beauty of these machines which, presumably, had not been properly maintained or supervised in a fair old while, yet still they performed with quiet efficiency.

The zombie was right; they were slightly out, but not by anything like the margin suggested. He was relieved to see that it would be a comparatively simple task to recalibrate and correct. As Kyle worked, he was careful not to touch the enigmatic, veil-like intrusions which were fused to the console's far side. Those apart, it was easy to become absorbed in the job at hand and forget about the surreal aspects of the situation.

After a gratifyingly short period of time he was done, but he didn't give any indication of that fact just yet. A vaguely rebellious thought had occurred to him. In the early days, before mass production made the custom impractical, each and every Kaufman Drive console had two pieces of apparently trivial information coded into their registration signature: the date the unit was completed, and the name of the ship it was destined for. This was not a practice that had lasted long, as the engines proved their worth and demand for them grew exponentially, but seeing as these were Mark Twos, it seemed worth the effort to check.

As Kyle gave the system one final run-through, he brought up the registration details, without any real expectation of learning much. He made sure to keep his features impassive as first the completion date and then the ship's name appeared on the display. The latter sent a chill running down his spine; it was a name which nobody with a serious interest in anything to do with starships could fail to recognise: *The Sun Seeker*.

He had no idea whether he managed to prevent the shock of this particular revelation from showing or not. He was too stunned to think about it for a second.

Suddenly, a lot of things fell into place – *The Noise Within's* odd variance from the classic military vessel she was clearly based upon, the unfinished nature of many of the fittings, the vessel's uninhabited feel, and the mystery of the zombies. No question in his mind now that the 'original crew' were simple husks, operated by the controlling AI. From everything he had heard, there was little chance anyone unfortunate enough to be on *The Sun Seeker* when she went rogue could have survived the breakneck multi-g acceleration of her escape.

Remembering himself, he banished the display and made a big show of stepping back with a relieved, "There."

"A job well done," the zombie said. Praise indeed, but only after brief hesitation, as if it were consulting with someone or confirming something.

If the animated suit realised what he had discovered it gave no sign, but instead turned and led the way out of the engine room. Kyle could not get away quickly enough and was convinced that what he had seen and felt in that room would haunt his dreams for many a night to come. Not to mention what he had learned.

He recalled the stoicism he had attributed to his escort's silence on the way down here, and smiled to himself, realising that this could only have been a product of his own imagination, since it seemed unlikely that either the zombies or the intelligence guiding them were capable of anything that flirted so closely with emotion.

The walk gave him time to think, to take stock of the situation. He was on board arguably the most infamous ship in the history of space flight. That fact almost overshadowed the awe he felt on discovering the unfathomable and extensive modifications that had been made to the ship's engines. The realisation that these were not the product of any technology he was familiar with – and he was, after all, something of an expert on the subject – was a particularly sobering one, the implications of which he shied away from grappling with at first, as if unwilling to face them until the shock of recent experience had grown a little less immediate.

Yet his curiosity started to win over his disquiet, and he began to wonder exactly what those bizarre 'augmentations' were and what they were supposed to achieve. Clearly they were revolutionary in concept. The thing that puzzled him most was exactly how *The Sun Seeker* had become *The Noise Within*, and, perhaps most intriguingly of all, why. If this was an example of what an AI could achieve when left to its own devices for a few decades, what did *that* mean for the future of poor little organics like him?

The brief visit to the engine room had one further unforeseen consequence. As Zombie Number One led him back to the unrestricted sections of the ship, Kyle found himself reaching a newfound resolve, one which surprised even him.

His growing sense of regret at joining *The Noise Within* had now been swept away, and any thoughts of jumping ship should the opportunity arise were completely banished. Irrespective of what lay ahead, this was history in the making, and he was at the very heart of it. Sure, he had taken part in the War, but so had a few billion others. This was different, more concentrated and more personal. The return of *The Sun Seeker*, and *he* was there to see it, to live it. His rashness had just gifted him a once in a lifetime opportunity to witness momentous events which were bound to reverberate throughout human civilisation, and there was no way he was going to miss out on something like that.

Drevers was nowhere to be seen on his return, nor were either Hammond or Blaine, for which he was grateful. He determined to keep what he had learned to himself for the moment, and at that particular point preferred the company of his own thoughts. One thing above all else was troubling him, and, perhaps because it was the most mundane issue as well as the one which most directly concerned him, this was the mystery he concentrated on. Why would an AI be so determined to recruit a human crew? All right, to perform the occasional awkward duty such as had just been required of him, but was that really enough to justify so much effort and trouble?

He was still contemplating that question when Drevers found him.

"What are you daydreaming about?" Drevers asked. "And is she blonde, brunette or redhead?"

"I wasn't daydreaming," Kyle responded. "I was thinking."

"That's one of the things I liked about you from the start. You're always so willing to try new experiences."

"Funny."

"So what were you thinking about?"

"Nothing much really; I was just wondering... Do you think computers ever get lonely?"

*   *   *

LEYTON'S HOTEL, *The Harcourt*, was neither the most expensive nor exclusive on Frysworld, but it clearly had pretensions to be; which meant that it was merely incredibly luxurious and pampering rather than outrageously so. Fresh fruit and flowers in every room, replenished daily, a choice of tempting restaurants and tastefully themed bars, with smartly liveried staff and every convenience you might wish for at the guests' beck and call day and night.

The hotel boasted a state of the art fitness centre, a facility which was designed to constantly monitor heart rate, blood pressure, lactic acid production, and blood sugar levels while you exercised – every conceivable indicator of how the body was coping with its exertions. The two track-suited assistants – a bronzed beefcake with bulging biceps for the ladies and an unreasonably glamorous blonde with gravity-defying bosom and a perfect smile for the men – were able to recommend an entirely appropriate exercise regime for each individual within minutes of registering. All you had to do was answer a few basic questions and suffer a couple of simple biometric tests and you were away. Built-in safety parameters ensured that no guest could push themselves too hard. After all, it was the hotel's insurance premiums that were at risk here.

Leyton arranged for a session soon after he arrived, and that was enough to convince him that he would have to find somewhere else to work out or risk trashing the place in frustration. Every time he began to build up a decent sweat, a gentle but insistent voice would inform him that he had reached the 'optimum maximum' level of exertion, and the equipment would refuse to be pushed any further.

After twenty minutes he walked away in disgust, to spend the rest of the day haunting off Strip areas within reasonable walking distance of the hotel, drifting from one bar to another, stopping off at clubs and even the occasional *Giazyu* den, all the while asking about gyms, fitness clubs or anything of that ilk. Eventually he was directed to a place called simply 'Joe's', which proved to be exactly what he was after.

To say that the place was in need of a lick of paint would have been akin to saying that it gets a little bit hot at the heart of a sun. Dingy, dark, with an old-fashioned boxing ring to one side and a hotch-potch array of outdated gym equipment on the other – undoubtedly the machines discarded by swankier establishments when they upgraded; bits and pieces acquired piecemeal over the years, or perhaps even the decades to judge by some of them. Many looked as if they had been recycled several times before ending up here. Yet the place had a comfortable feel and a reassuring smell to it – a half-familiar odour which spoke of honest endeavour and tradition; an aromatic blanket that conveniently overlaid and masked any less savoury odours, such as sweat, which might otherwise have been present.

Irrationally, his inability to put a name to this smell niggled at Leyton, until finally he woke the gun up long enough to consult it on the subject.

"Linseed oil, or a local equivalent of very similar composition," the weapon informed him. "The oil can be used in paints, in floor waxes and preservatives, even in some muscle –"

"Yes, thank you," the eyegee interrupted. "Good night." The gun went quiet.

Leyton loved Joe's from the first moment he stepped inside the place. No chance of any monitoring computer curtailing his exercise here and as for insurance, he doubted whether those present could even spell the word, let alone buy any.

The owner, who unsurprisingly introduced himself as Joe, was a shortish, solidly built man with a crooked nose, noticeably stained teeth which suggested nicotine addiction in his past or even present, and tufts of pepper-grey hair springing out from around a balding pate. From the nose and the man's general demeanour, Leyton guessed he had been a fighter in his youth. He gave the eyegee a brief tour of the equipment, accepted a modest amount of Standards and then left him to his own devices, adding that he or his son Si were on hand if needed. Si was a younger, taller, slimmer and somewhat sallower version of his father.

Leyton immediately began to put the machines through their paces. He wasn't the only person doing so by any means, and the nature of the patrons distinguished Joe's from the hotel's facilities even more than the nature of the equipment and the atmosphere. They were all locals. Leyton apart, there was not a tourist to be seen. Some were paler-skinned off-worlders who had clearly settled here and presumably worked in some capacity or other on or off the Strip, but there were a similar number of the swarthy natives in evidence as well. Judging by some of the banter he overheard, a good many of the people here were regulars, and Leyton quickly joined their ranks as Joe's became an established part of his daily routine.

During the following two weeks or so, his respect for the gruff owner of the gym grew significantly. More than once the eyegee paused in his own exertions to watch boxing classes for native kids – early teens for the most part – which Joe supervised himself.

"Teaches them how to handle themselves," the older man explained on noting Leyton's interest. "It also keeps them out of mischief and gives them a chance to channel some of their excess aggression in a way that won't land them in the clink."

Joe seemed genuinely committed to helping these youths, which Leyton could only applaud. As far as he could make out, Joe spent every waking minute at the gym. In addition to the early morning workout, the eyegee would sometimes drop in of an evening to let off steam following another frustrating day, and Joe would always be there, however late the hour.

It was during one such visit that he involved himself in a situation which was none of his business and which he'd probably have been better off avoiding; but, on the other hand, he was spoiling for a fight. Gym exercise was all well and good, but it was no real substitute for a genuine bare knuckle scrap.

Leyton arrived to discover a nervous looking Joe being ushered into the paper-walled cupboard he called an office by two men. One of them resembled a muscle-bound ape while the other – a tall and stick-thin individual with slicked-back hair and a slight stoop – merely looked shifty.

The eyegee instantly came alert. In a place which boasted all sorts of mean-looking individuals amongst its clientele, these two stood out. He somehow doubted they were here to ask after the owner's health.

"Everything all right, Joe?"

"Yeah, yeah, everything's fine," the other replied; without meaning a word of it.

Leyton took a step forward, to find his way abruptly blocked by the ape.

"You heard Joe here," stick-man said, "everything's fine, so why not be a good boy and run along to play with your gym toys?"

Leyton ignored him, concentrating on the ape. He made as if to sidestep the brute, who took a step sideways in response and lifted a palm to shove him firmly away. "Fuck off!"

The hand was all the eyegee needed. He swayed to one side, allowing hand and arm to slide past him. At the same time he grabbed the limb with both of his own hands, twisted and sank down on one knee, half-pulling, half-throwing the larger man over his shoulder. Already a little off balance due to the sideways step and the momentum of his intended shove, the goon was caught completely off guard and went sailing over Leyton's shoulder, to crash to the ground with a resounding thump. For a second he lay there on his back, winded. Leyton didn't give him a chance to recover, delivering a solid punch to the head and knocking the thug out.

The eyegee straightened to glare at stickman, who stared back, his eyes so wide they threatened to pop out from his abruptly sheet-white face.

"You really should teach the hired help some manners," Leyton suggested. "If he's going to try shoving people around like this, he ought to be able to handle himself a little better. Perhaps he should join up here and brush up on his fitness, not to mention his technique. What do you reckon, Joe, could you sort out a specially discounted rate?"

"Oh, I'm sure we could come up with something," Joe replied, grinning from ear to ear, "just say the word;" this latter to the stickman.

A whiff of smelling salts, which Leyton was fascinated to see, having only ever heard about them in old stories before this, brought the goon around. He and the stickman beat an undignified retreat.

Joe came up to slap the eyegee on the shoulder. "Thanks, I owe you one."

"No problem. I just hope I haven't made things worse for you. They're bound to be back at some point and I might not be around the next time."

"No worries. I know who sent them and I can sort this situation out; they just caught me unawares is all. Oh, and don't even think about trying to pay for your sessions here from now on."

Leyton shook his head. "No, I'll pay as normal. I can claim all this back on expenses and, trust me, my employers can afford the Standards a lot more readily than you can."

Joe grunted. "All right then, but if there's ever anything I can do for you, anything at all, just ask."

Leyton smiled. Now *there* was an offer simply loaded with potential. "I'll bear that in mind," he promised.

CHAPTER TWELVE

PHILIP KAUFMAN WAS finding life away from Homeworld and the all-consuming project a lot stranger than he'd anticipated. His sojourn had begun as advertised, with unannounced stops at Kaufman Industries offices and facilities on other worlds – visits which were inevitably greeted with initial incredulity and then much scurrying around by onsite executives and their cronies. Yet he soon tired of such things. His unexpected appearances had no real purpose and achieved little beyond causing a stir – everyone seemed to want to organise receptions and banquets in his honour, once they realised who he was, no matter how much he insisted that this tour should be kept low-key. As a way of hiding from anyone who might still be after him, it was far from ideal. In any case, after the first few on-spec appearances word spread, and it soon became clear that his visits were no longer surprising anyone.

His heart was never really in it, either. Hanging around company facilities only reminded him of the project and brought back the heavy sense of loss at missing out on its final stages. More than once he almost turned around and went straight back to Homeworld. Stubbornness was the main reason he didn't; the knowledge that doing so would make the decision to embark on this trip seem ridiculous and pointless. That and the memory of his last night at home – the scorched carpet and blackened walls in his bedroom.

So he decided to abandon all pretence that this trip was in

any way work-related. Instead he determined to utilise the time to do some of the things he had always wanted to do but never really expected to be able to this side of retirement.

Philip Kaufman became a tourist.

He went to Tetra and saw the legendary lava falls – which were a disappointment, failing to be any more impressive in reality than they were in holographic projection. And at least from the comfort of your own living room you weren't subjected to the insufferable heat and the inane blathering of the 'cultural advisor'; nor were you forced to suffer the noxious-smelling aerosol spray needed to keep the ubiquitous swarms of insects at bay. Surely they could have come up with a simple injection to do the job. Presumably attracted by the heat, the over-sized bugs carried a nasty bite and they seemed to be everywhere.

By way of contrast, sunrise on Dendra was everything he had hoped and more. The famous crystal cliffs produced a spectacle which he would never forget; a kaleidoscope of rainbow refractions which danced across the mists that lay below the peaks to dazzling effect, transforming them into clouds of ever-shifting primary and pastel colour. No wonder this sight had provided inspiration for artists and poets throughout the centuries. The singing cliffs on Velamore were less impressive. The limited time he spent on the planet marked one of the calmest periods of consecutive days the area had ever seen, or so the locals insisted. Even during the breeziest moments of his stay the porous cliff faces, which were riddled with myriad tapering tubes, could barely muster a sigh, let alone a song. Still, he did get to visit the alabaster sea and swim with the leviathans – said to be the closest surviving creatures to the fabled whales of old Earth. Their sheer majesty astonished him. The realisation that these huge, stately forms gliding through the waters beside him could crush his body with a single swipe of a tail fin, but that they wouldn't, because he was beneath their notice, was an oddly sobering one. The experience induced a sense of serenity that more than made up for the disappointment of the muted cliffs.

On Callus III he walked the spirit paths in one of the silent forests. It was said that once you stepped into such a forest you would never be able to leave again unaided, that whichever way you walked and no matter how determinedly you kept to a straight line, you would always end up back at the clearing which lay at the forest's heart.

Much to his delight, Philip soon discovered the sayings to be entirely right.

Three times he set out from the clearing, twice on his own and the third in the company of a vivacious blonde backpacker who introduced herself as Layla, and each time he ended up back at the same spot within the hour.

Intellectually Philip knew what was causing this. He was fully aware that the forest floor was covered in a type of moss which might have made for a pleasantly springy walking surface but also had a more sinister aspect. With every step you took here, microscopic spores were released into the atmosphere, to be breathed in almost immediately. The spores befuddled the senses in a singular way, causing a person to circle back on themselves despite their best efforts not to. It was a feeding mechanism, designed to entrap the local fauna, which included several sizeable deer-like herbivores. Eventually, unable to escape, an animal would collapse from exhaustion and slip into a sleep they wouldn't wake from, their bodies being swiftly broken down by enzymes secreted from the moss, so providing nutrient for the forest. The fact that the deer's favourite food grew only within the fringes of these forests struck Philip as particularly malicious, making every mealtime a dice with death.

With the advantage of human tools and technology, Philip knew that he and Layla were never in danger of sharing the indigenous herbivores' fate, which meant they were free to simply enjoy the experience. Having their senses so effectively fooled proved something of a wonder.

Quite how a natural mechanism evolved to operate within a specific ecosystem could work so dramatically well on humans

– sentients from another world – was something the scientists were still struggling to explain. 'Fluke' seemed to sum up their conclusions to date as far as Philip could discover. Not that he particularly cared. Nor, indeed, did his newly discovered friend, whose natural high spirits and frequent laughter were proving highly infectious. Layla was even more thrilled by the experience that he and the pair continued in each other's company upon leaving the forest. She subsequently proved herself to be a warm and responsive lover. For two days and nights they were inseparable, then, with a final kiss and an absence of regrets, they went their separate ways.

Philip found this period away from work surprisingly liberating. He couldn't remember the last time he had done anything that was not linked in some way to Kaufman Industries, to systems designs or the project. This enforced absence provided him with a pointed reminder that there was more to life – a lesson he would never have believed he needed. The fact that it came now, when everything work-wise was coming to such a head, struck him as one of life's richest ironies yet.

Philip's stint as the universal tourist was not quite as gratuitous as it might have seemed; there was an ulterior motive. The route he followed in visiting these assorted wonders was far from random, but rather took him ever closer to a very particular area of space – the hunting ground of a certain pirate vessel. Once he was off-world with no pressing agenda, there was no way he was about to resist the temptation to look for his father's renegade ship. However, there yet remained one final attraction on his tourist's agenda; happily, it lay well within the pirate's theatre of operations, which enabled him to achieve two objectives at once. Frysworld was not the sort of place he usually frequented, but its notoriety was such that it held a certain morbid fascination which circumstances allowed him to accommodate. He'd be stupid not to go there, really.

The plan was straightforward: after a few days' shameless

self-indulgence on the infamous leisure world, he would turn his attention fully to tracking down *The Noise Within*.

IT WAS EARLY evening when the call he'd been waiting for finally came in. Leyton was at the gym, winding down after another long day of doing very little.

He listened as Emilio babbled his excitement at having found 'the marks', before asking, calmly, "You're sure it's them?"

"Yeah, course I'm sure," the voice on the other end of the comm said, "or I wouldn't be talking to you. The top two on that sheet you gave me, no question."

The top two? That meant Kyle and Drevers. Excellent. Leyton's spirits rose to the point where he almost smiled. "Keep an eye on them and let me know if they move at all. Now, where are you again?"

With so much time on his hands, Leyton had been able to make a few provisional plans in anticipation of this moment, so now that it had actually arrived he didn't hesitate. After ensuring he knew how to find the place the kid was speaking from, he went in search of the gym's owner.

"Joe, remember that favour you said I could call on? Well..."

After a hasty conversation with Joe, he headed straight across to the bar which Emilio had specified. The place wasn't far and lay in the direction of the spaceport, which came as no surprise. He made it there in a little over fifteen minutes. There had been no further messages from Emilio, which presumably meant that the two targets were still at the same place. Sure enough, the kid was waiting for him outside.

"Hey, you got my money?" the kid had the gall to say as greeting.

Leyton simply stared.

"They're inside, at the bar."

The eyegee brushed past him and entered a hot, dimly lit room. . The place was busy, with a mix of spacers and local workers in evidence, though few tourists if any. Strikingly pretty native girls moved between the tables bearing trays of drinks, their smiles stretching as wide as their g-strings. At the far end of the room stood a long bar, behind which stood shelves bearing an impressive array of variously shaped bottles in a tradition which stretched back down the centuries.

Several of the high stools in front of the bar were occupied. His gaze fell instantly on one pair of spacers in particular.

No question; Emilio had earned his money. These were definitely Kyle and Drevers, the first two to defect to *The Noise Within*. Satisfied, Leyton slipped back outside to where Emilio waited anxiously.

"Well?"

"You've done well, kid. Here are your Standards as agreed. Now make yourself scarce. Things are likely to get a little rough in here."

Emilio snatched the proffered credit chit, staring at it suspiciously. "What's this? I expected folding; you know, *real* money."

The eyegee didn't have any time to waste on this nonsense and let his impatience show. "You don't seriously expect me to carry 1,000 Standards around everywhere I go on the off chance you'll call, do you? Take this to any credit wall on the planet. It'll pay out as promised. Now scram!" He leaned towards the lad, who pocketed the chip, backed away a few steps and then turned and ran.

Leyton took out his pocket com as the kid vanished, and spoke into it. "Joe, everything's looking good here. It's game on."

Life aboard *The Noise Within* had improved dramatically, Kyle reflected; helped no doubt by the fact that at that precise moment they were not actually aboard the ship at all.

If further proof were needed that their conversations were being listened to and even heeded, here it was. Following his and Drevers' campaign to emphasise the importance of some 'shore leave', they had been granted exactly that, and how!

They were let loose not just anywhere but on Frysworld – a place Kyle had always intended to visit one day but never quite accumulated enough Standards to make the trip worthwhile. The AI guiding the ship was obviously catching on to human motivation as well. Before he and Drevers boarded the shuttle, they were shown how many Standards they had accumulated to date. The allowance they were given for the trip was decent enough, but what awaited them when they came back was enough to buy a small ship of their own if they chose to; well, a second-hand shuttle at the very least.

There were only the two of them. Zombie Number One announced they were to be allowed down in shifts, and that, as the longest serving, he and Drevers got to go first, which pissed Hammond and Blaine off no end. Shame.

After so much time cooped up on *The Noise Within*, two things were foremost in Kyle's mind: booze and girls; not necessarily in that order. Both of these most immediate requirements were well catered for in the place he and Drevers had stumbled upon. He could hardly take his eyes away from one particular beauty behind the counter. Bewitching eyes, a pretty oval of a face and long, straight hair, several shades lighter than most of the local girls, which helped her to stand out, giving her an exotic edge among the already exotic. None of the girls here were ugly, but this one was something else, with her wasp-thin waist, the way she swayed those hips and a cute, full-lipped mouth that just begged to be kissed. There were also two boys serving, and they were nearly as pretty as the girls – for those whose tastes ran in that direction. Kyle's never had.

He looked at his favourite girl again, wondering how old she was and determining to ask her name the next time he bought a round. He might even ask what time she finished work and whether she was available even before she had – Frysworld had that sort of a reputation – though perhaps he'd leave it until a little later in the evening.

God, it was good to be off the ship.

"How would you like to cuddle up to her tonight, then?" Drevers asked from beside him, evidently noticing where Kyle's attention was focused. "Nice arse, hey?"

Kyle smiled, imagining the girl's slender body undressed and in his arms. "To be honest, cuddling her wasn't exactly what I had in mind."

Drevers laughed, a little drunkenly – this wasn't the first bar they had stopped at since landing, though it was certainly the one offering the best scenery. "Well, you know what they say about Frysworld. *Any* girl can be yours... at a price."

Kyle laughed with him. "I'll drink to that!"

As he lifted his glass from the bar, intent on matching actions to words, his elbow bumped against something beside him, or rather someone: a fellow drinker who, he could have sworn, had not been there a minute ago.

It didn't seem much of a bump, but by this point Kyle had to admit that his judgement probably wasn't to be fully trusted. The contact must have been harder than he realised, because it was enough to send the glass tumbling from the other's grasp, to land on its side on the bar, where its amber contents spread in a growing pool on the frosted plastiglass surface. For a surreal instant, Kyle was more fascinated by the fact that the glass hadn't shattered than he was by any other consequence.

Then the indignant shout of, "Hey!" permeated his awareness; as did the fact that the offended drinker had swivelled round to face him, and this was one large son of a so-and-so. For a second, all Kyle could do was gape, but then a sense of self-preservation kicked in.

"S... sorry," he stammered.

"That was my drink!"

"I know, it was an accident..."

"You heard him, just an accident," Drevers added, leaning across.

Kyle wished he would butt out; knowing Drevers he was

only likely to make things worse. The offended man climbed to his feet and seemed to be growing larger, more imposing and more menacing by the second. In fairness, Kyle reckoned he and Drevers could probably have taken him, so long as somebody tied his feet together first and handcuffed his wrists behind his back. Actually, on reflection, maybe they would still have been in for a struggle even then.

"Look, I'll buy you another," he said quickly. "Whatever it was you were drinking – a double."

He signalled to the barman, who had come over to clear the spilt drink and lingered anxiously on seeing the developing situation. The white-shirted youth hurried to comply. The offended stranger glared suspiciously, first at Kyle and then at the busy barman, as if suspecting some trickery or complicity. However, a fresh glass of amber liquid placed on the freshly wiped counter in front of him seemed to go a long way towards mollifying the man.

"Thank you; that's very decent," he said, only a little grudgingly.

On impulse, Kyle thrust a hand towards him. "Name's Kyle, and it really was an accident."

The big man stared at the proffered hand for a second, as if he had never encountered the gesture before. Perhaps he hadn't; customs varied so much on different worlds. But eventually he took his hand and squeezed it firmly in one of his own... *very* firmly.

"Jim."

Kyle resisted the temptation to grimace and wring his crushed fingers, instead managing to smile as he withdrew his hand and moved it out of sight beneath the counter, where he could flex it in private.

"Are you two here as tourists, or crew off a ship?" Jim asked.

Kyle and Drevers exchanged a quick, wary glance. "A bit of both," the latter said.

"We've been saving up, knowing the ship was due here," Kyle

improvised quickly, seizing on Drevers' explanation.

Jim grunted and swirled his glass. "Sensible thinking."

"And you? Crew or tourist?"

The big man sat back. "The latter, I suppose. I'm a soldier by trade."

"You mean a mercenary," Drevers interjected, in a slightly disparaging tone, or so it seemed to Kyle, but their new friend didn't seem to notice.

"If you like. Made a great deal of money recently and wanted to go somewhere and let off steam. I'd heard a lot about this place, so..." He shrugged. "Now I'm actually here I wonder whether it was such a good idea. Reckon I might light out and find some mean and dirty honest-to-goodness action somewhere. Everything in this place is... I don't know, so *unreal*."

Strange; for Kyle that was one of the great charms of being here.

Drevers let loose a guffaw made overloud by his drunkenness. "Of course it's unreal," he said, throwing his shoulders back and gesturing expansively with one arm. "Frysworld is the biggest whorehouse and drugs den in the universe. How could that ever be *real*?"

"Hey, loud mouth," said a voice from Drevers' far side, "that's my home you're talking about. Some of us wouldn't want to be anywhere else. So perhaps you'd like to shut your mouth, after you've apologised of course."

A stocky but muscular man stood there, his eyes glaring fixedly at Drevers, who seemed completely unfazed.

Kyle looked on in horror and his shipmate smiled and then said, "No, actually I don't think I would. And you have my sympathies if you have to live on this gaudy pantomime of a world built on top of a steaming shit heap."

There followed a frozen instant, enough for Kyle to want to claw those words back, to persuade Drevers to somehow unsay them, before the newcomer simply lashed out – a punch which flew straight and hard, landing a blow squarely on Drevers' jaw and sending him sprawling from his seat and into Kyle, who instinctively caught his stricken crewmate.

The whole room went deathly still for a split second, as if many there needed that instant to draw breath in preparation for what was to come, because immediately afterwards the place erupted.

Kyle lost track of the precise sequence of events for the next few minutes, as one thing piled upon another with no respite. He was aware of Drevers struggling to his feet and letting out a yell of rage before flinging himself at the man who had punched him, of their new friend Jim surging from his seat and grappling with somebody – an anonymous figure at least as large as he was. Further removed there was shouting and a woman's scream, while all around seemed to be one writhing, wrestling mass of arms and bodies. In the corner of his eye he caught sight of a raised chair and then he ducked as a glass sailed past, spinning as it flew. He had already lost track of Drevers by this point.

The whole thing had a slightly surreal quality, since the fighting seemed to be taking place all around without actually involving him. It was as if he were in a protected bubble, somehow separate from the violence while able to observe it, though he knew that couldn't last. He started to get up, not entirely sure what he intended to do once actually on his feet, but that became irrelevant as he was instantly felled by a swinging blow which was probably not even intended for him. If it had been then it was poorly aimed – a broad forearm slamming into him rather than a fist, which still proved enough to sweep him from his feet. His head connected with the bar as he went down, an impact more painful than the blow itself, and he took the barstool he'd been sitting on with him, the legs bruising his ribs as he fell on top of it, only to half bounce and half slide off and come to a stop with his back against the bar.

Somebody trod on his foot – not deliberately, just in the general mêlée. He quickly pulled the leg in beneath him and scrambled to get back to his feet, levering himself up against the toppled stool and clawing at the bar top.

This was just what he needed. He hadn't been involved in a fist fight since his youth and didn't recall actually winning any even then.

No sooner was he upright than Kyle found himself confronted by a man intent on knocking him back down again – a face he didn't recognise, but it was a target. He invested his punch with every ounce of the anger and indignation that the current situation had generated, and was rewarded with the satisfying sting of a solid connection. The face vanished and he was able to draw breath again.

Not for long. Another figure loomed above him and he got ready to throw another punch. Then he realised it was the mercenary soldier, Jim.

"Hey, steady on!" The man was grinning, as if he was actually enjoying himself. "I'm on your side."

"Have you seen Drevers, my friend, the one I was drinking with?"

Somebody charged them. Jim shot out a piston-like arm, not even pausing as the blow felled the attacker and he drew his fist back. "Over there."

Kyle looked in the indicated direction and saw his shipmate wrestling with a slightly larger man and getting the worst of it.

Before Kyle could think to react, Jim was across to them, dragging the large man off Drevers and flinging him into another knot of fighters. He came back, bringing an unsteady looking Drevers with him. Blood seeped from an angry cut above the smaller man's eye and his lip was split and had already begun to swell.

"Let's get out of here," Jim said, which was the best suggestion Kyle had heard since the fight began.

The three of them made their way towards the nearest of the bar's two doors, with Jim leading the way and acting as a shield for the pair of them, trying to pick a path between the clumps of still-fighting forms but perfectly willing to force a passage through when necessary. Kyle kept as close to this new friend as he could, while having to half support his groggy crewmate.

This was not how he had envisaged their first day on Frysworld panning out, not by a long shot.

They made it to the door and out into the street beyond without any major upsets. The noise of the brawl dampened abruptly as the door swung shut behind them. Music was blaring from a nearby club, mesmeric Latin rhythms featuring flailing percussive runs underpinned by thumping bass. A knot of local youths clustered outside the place, smoking and drinking from bottles of the local beer. They eyed the three of them with obvious amusement.

Kyle couldn't even be bothered to glare back in response, as he stopped to draw a deep lungful of the warm night air and gingerly massage his aching temple. The lump that was developing there already felt the size of a small egg to his questing fingers, while his foot throbbed with pain now that he took time to notice it. As for Drevers, his left eye was swelling impressively, looking as though it might close over. Jim seemed entirely unhurt and was the only one of the three with the energy to be jovial.

"Good fight; just what I needed. Where are you lads staying?"

An excellent question. "We only arrived here today, haven't sorted anywhere out as yet," Kyle explained.

"I'm at the Harcourt. Not a bad hotel, we'll see if they've got any vacant rooms there." He went as if to head off, but then paused. "It's not the cheapest, mind."

Kyle shook his head dismissively. "Not a problem; we can afford it."

"I need a drink," Drevers interjected. Thankfully, he seemed to have recovered a little now that they were in the marginally cooler open air and was at least able to stand unaided.

Jim snorted. "Let's get the two of you cleaned up a bit first, and then we'll see about another drink. Come on," and he led them away.

They had gone no more than twenty paces down the street when a voice called out from behind them. "Hey, you three, come back here; we haven't finished with you yet!"

Kyle looked over his shoulder to see the stocky figure of a man standing outside the bar. He recognised him as the local whose punch on Drevers had triggered the brawl in the first place. Nor was he alone, but rather stood flanked by four or five hulking cronies. None of whom looked especially happy.

"Shit!" Jim exclaimed. "You two really know how to pick your enemies, don't you?"

"You know this bastard?" Drevers asked.

"Sadly, yes. *Everyone* here knows Joey 'The King' Marlowe. He's something of a local celebrity – the meanest, nastiest and most powerful crime lord on all of Frysworld. If he's really as pissed with you as he seems to be, there's nowhere on this planet you can hide where he won't find you."

"Oh great," Kyle muttered. "Is there any good news?"

"Some. He can't run very fast."

THE STRANGER CLEARLY didn't know Emilio at all, otherwise he would have realised that telling him to 'make yourself scarce' was a sure-fire way of guaranteeing that he would do exactly the opposite. Not that Emilio failed to take the warning seriously, far from it, and he certainly wasn't stupid, but he had no intention of missing out on whatever was about to go down

He slipped back into the bar, hugging the wall and watching the two *forastcerdos*, whose presence had just opened his way to another world, while always keeping half an eye on the stranger.

At the same time, he was scanning the room in search of a better vantage point; this current position was too exposed. If a fight broke out it would more than likely swell to encompass the whole room and he'd be swept up in things. Then he saw the stairs. They were off to his left and had a chain draped across the first step at waist height, as if to indicate they were out of bounds. Perfect; and surely no one would object to his sitting there, always assuming they noticed him at all. He sidled across towards the stairway, still hugging the walls.

There was only one awkward moment, when a hand snaked out to grab his wrist. Fortunately he was able to free himself without too much of a fuss by insisting that he really was *not* working. Thankfully, neither the stranger nor the *forastcerdos* appeared to notice the incident. It was unlike him to pass up the opportunity of a few extra Standards, but for once in his life he was loaded and whatever was about to kick off here promised to be more fun than a quick screw could ever be.

He finally reached the stairs, where he stepped daintily over the chain and climbed the first few steps, before sitting down to wait, peering between the carved wooden pillars that supported the banister rail. From here he had a good view of everything going on in the bar proper while he was sufficiently removed to feel a degree of safety.

As the minutes dragged past, Emilio's sense of anticipation slipped away and he began to get bored. Doubts started to creep into his thoughts. What if the stranger was intending to do no more than follow the *forastcerdos* after all? But then why warn Emilio to stay away? Perhaps as a cruel joke, perhaps he'd guessed that Emilio wouldn't be able to resist hanging around after being specifically told not to, knowing full well there'd be nothing worth seeing.

Emilio was about to give up, reckoning this probably was the case, when a group of newcomers entered the bar. Half a dozen or so of them, all big men, and they didn't look as if they were here for a drink. With a start, Emilio recognised one of them as Miguel, Carla's husband. Recognition brought with it a quick flashback – the remembrance of Carla above him, her long hair and fulsome breasts dangling to caress his face and chest, the latter bouncing rhythmically as she rode him with energetic abandon. He looked at Miguel and grinned.

The two *forastcerdos* didn't seem to have noticed the newcomers, but the stranger had. Emilio saw him exchange a look with the foremost of the small group; a balding man somewhat older than the others and shorter, though still solid with muscle.

This was more like it. The boy adjusted his position, making sure he was as comfortable as possible. He had a feeling things were about to get a whole lot more interesting.

The stranger now moved forward to stand at the bar beside the pair he'd been so keen to find. At first it looked as if a fight was going to break out straight away, but things quickly calmed and the three of them were soon chatting like old amigos. The fighting only began once the group of new arrivals had made their way to the bar. It was fascinating to watch their progress. As they passed a given table, conversation would stop, only to resume in agitated fashion as people's gazes followed them. By the time they actually arrived at the bar, a good half of the room had noted their presence and were watching them expectantly, as if sensing that these six muscular men could only be there for one reason.

The fighting started more or less immediately and spread almost as quickly. It was no surprise when those who had already noted the six *gamberros* as they made their way to the bar were the first to react. Some decided on the better part of valour and headed straight for the door, but the majority seemed all too ready to join in. The violence rippled out, spreading to engulf the whole room, as even those trying to leave ended up grappling with each other in their haste to get out. It looked entirely random, but Emilio knew from experience that some there would be using the brawl as an excuse to settle old scores. That was what he would have been looking to do if he weren't so loaded. The last thing he wanted now was a stint in jail or an injury.

A chair smashed against the banister supports close to his head, a shard of wood slipping through to sting his arm. He instinctively drew back. Perhaps this wasn't such a safe vantage point after all.

In all the confusion he had momentarily lost sight of the stranger and the two *forastcerdos*. He anxiously scanned the area by the bar, but couldn't see any sign of them. Then he spotted the three of them together, making their way towards the main door. They were already halfway across the room, with the stranger leading the way. One of the spacers seemed injured, or perhaps drunk, and was being helped by his fellow.

Impulsively, Emilio decided to abandon the spectacle of the ongoing brawl and follow the trio whose presence had sparked it. He got to his feet and hurried down the few stairs between him and the floor, skipping over the chain barrier and then stepping over an unconscious form sprawled at the bottom of the flight. There was a side door not that far away, but he was hampered by the need to detour around wrestling forms and duck under flailing arms. Determined not to lose sight of the stranger and his companions, he bobbed and weaved for all he was worth, eventually exiting into the night without getting caught up in the fighting.

He hurried around to the front of the building just as Miguel and the other *gamberros* emerged to shout threats at the departing trio. Then the chase was on, as everybody started running.

With a laugh of delight, Emilio set off in the wake of the *gamberros*, finding himself running alongside the hindmost, who happened to be Miguel.

"Hey, Big Man, what gives?" he called. "Why you so interested in these *forastcerdos*?"

They had raced around a couple of corners and were now out of sight of the bar. Miguel was lagging behind the other chasers and it was clear that, while he might be powerfully muscled and physically strong, his body was not meant for this sort of exertion.

"Hang on there... Emilio..." he panted, slowing to a halt. "Let's catch our breath... for a second... and I'll tell you."

So they both stopped. Miguel beckoned for him to come

closer, and then leant forward to whisper in his ear, as if he was about to share the greatest secret in the world.

"You see, that big *forastcerdo*, the one who led the other two, he helped out..."

That was as far as the sentence went. Emilio noted Miguel's arm thrust quickly forward before his every awareness succumbed to an explosion of agony. He stared down and saw the blood, his blood, and the knife in Miguel's clenched hand as it plunged forward to sink into his stomach for a second time.

The pain was excruciating; a hot fire that spread from the wound to infest every part of his body. His head felt heavy and even the roots of his hair seemed to burn with overwhelming agony. *How could this be happening?*

His legs gave way; he felt the ground thud against his knees.

"This is what you get for screwing my wife, you little shit." Miguel's face, which loomed large, was contorted with rage. "Did you really think I wouldn't find out?"

Emilio stared up at the big man, horrified, not wanting to understand, not wanting to believe.

Life was not supposed to be fair but surely it could not be *this* cruel. He had money at last, enough to leave this stinking world. It couldn't all end like this, not now, not when he had a way out.

Something slapped his cheek: the ground. His head was too heavy to lift. He tried to speak but his mouth wouldn't form the words. Pain continued to swell, supplanting all else, dimming his vision and his thoughts. The words slipped from his tongue and faded away, receding beyond his reach.

From what seemed a great distance he heard somebody shouting – was that Miguel's voice? "Quick, get help, someone fetch a doctor; there's a boy here who's been knifed. He's hurt bad."

The voice diminished throughout, until the final words were little more than the echoes of a whisper; and then he knew no more.

CHAPTER THIRTEEN

KYLE WAS FAST coming to the conclusion that he had well and truly pissed off some nefarious deity with a penchant for meddling in mortal lives. The only other explanation for his recent misfortune was that he had made some stupid decisions of late, and he was not in the mood to accept that sort of responsibility just then. Frysworld, which less than an hour ago had seemed the most wonderful place in the universe, ready to welcome them with open arms, had somehow been transformed into a sinister and unforgiving realm of threat and nightmare.

"We daren't go back to *The Harcourt* now," Jim said as they paused to catch their collective breath. The big man clearly needed the break as much as Kyle did, having had to carry Drevers during the final part of their flight. "Marlowe saw me. He knows who I am and it won't take him long to find out where I'm staying. There'll be men waiting for us at the hotel before we're halfway across town."

"So what do we do now?"

Jim shook his head. "I don't know. Lie low somewhere and then try and sneak off-world, or make a break for the port immediately, before he has time to properly organise."

Off-world? They'd only just arrived. Surely in the morning this would all have blown over and the nightmare could become a dream again. "Do you know of anywhere safe we can hole-up?"

"Not really, at least not anywhere that Marlowe won't be likely to find us."

Kyle's heart sank. So much for Frysworld and the planned days of debauchery. "It'll have to be the port then. We've got a shuttle…"

"That's all well and good for you two, but what about me?"

Good point. With all that had happened, Kyle had completely overlooked the fact that Jim was not really with them, that he was only there at all thanks to cruel chance. He didn't have any authority to speak on the ship's behalf, but their new friend didn't know that. Kyle realised that he would never get Drevers back to the shuttle without the big man's help; there would be time enough to worry about the ramifications later.

"You say you're a mercenary."

"I am. Got a problem with that?"

"No, it's just… well, how picky are you when it comes to choosing an employer?"

"Oh, very; I've one basic requirement which any would-be employer has to meet: they have to be able to pay me."

"And if some of your employer's requirements are not always, how can I put this…?"

"Legal?"

"Exactly."

"Then they have to be able to pay me a lot."

"Good. There're no worries on *that* score."

"Are you offering me a job?"

Kyle nodded. "Serving on a ship as… security."

"All right, who would I be working for and what's the name of the ship?"

"That's a little complicated. I'll explain everything when we're on the shuttle and under way. Come on." He went to move off.

Jim stopped him, gripping his arm with vice-like strength. "Hang on a second. You expect me to simply go with you, taking service on a ship without even knowing who I'm working for?"

"It's either that or you can stay here and take your chances with Marlowe and his mob."

The big man stared at him for a second longer, and then snorted. "Fair point." He released Kyle's arm. "Let's get you to the port at any rate, and I can think about this en route."

Kyle gingerly flexed his arm, and they moved off.

They seemed to have given their pursuers the slip for the moment, but Kyle wouldn't feel fully at ease until they were safely on the shuttle and leaving Frysworld behind for good. Somewhere along the line he had accepted their leaving as inevitable. This place had become hostile territory; he couldn't shake the feeling that there were enemies all around them and it was only a matter of time before they pounced.

"Do you think we'll make it?" he asked Jim, hoping for some reassurance.

"Won't know until we give it a try," was his only response.

They were supporting Drevers between them now, and Kyle could hardly believe how heavy his shipmate was. Goodness only knew how Jim had been able to run while carrying so much dead weight unaided. As they trudged on, his frustration at their current predicament began to focus ever more on the man he was now forced to carry. Why couldn't the stupid oaf have kept his mouth shut? Kyle could have been relaxing in a soft bed right now, maybe even with some raunchy female company, instead of trudging through unfamiliar streets and having to drag the idiot responsible for ruining everything with him.

He tried not to think about it, knowing that if he did, he might well be tempted to leave Drevers here and let him take his chances with Marlowe's thugs. To distract himself, he attempted to spark up a conversation with Jim. "What about your stuff?" was the best he could come up with.

"Not a problem. I carry everything that matters with me at all times; the rest is just clothes and things – easily replaced."

A sentiment Kyle could relate to all too easily, having had to make a similar decision when deserting *The Lady J*.

Finally they reached the spaceport, slumping onto an open-sided tram which carried them to the less salubrious end of the shuttle terminal. Berths cost money. As with most things here, the more you paid the better you received, and they had wanted to keep their funds for other concerns.

There were few people on the tram at this hour – either too early to be returning shipward after a night out or too late to be thinking of departing off-world – and the ones who were there didn't blink an eyelid at the barely conscious Drevers. Presumably, comatose passengers were not all that unusual on this thing.

Once off the tram, their false IDs held up again and they were allowed swift access to the shuttle bays. Nobody queried their departing so soon after arrival, nor the additional crew member – not the authorities' concern as long as the bureaucratic details appeared to be in order.

Getting to the shuttle itself meant a walk along a dimly lit high-ceilinged corridor of concrete and steel. At least Drevers was somewhat revived and able to walk under his own power with only a minimum of guidance.

Kyle was tired. An afternoon of drinking followed by the unexpected chase through streets he didn't know had left him drained of energy. Drevers' lapse into virtual unconsciousness hadn't helped either. Now, with the running evidently over, the adrenalin deserted his bloodstream and left him with no reserves. All he cared about at that particular moment was getting to the shuttle so that he could sit down and rest. Yet this final walk seemed to be taking an age, not helped by Jim asking more questions which Kyle couldn't be bothered with. His main concern had been to get Drevers to the shuttle. Now they'd achieved that, the big man could take his chances with Marlowe if he saw fit, so he continued to be evasive, while half-heartedly telling the mercenary to be patient.

At long last they arrived at the high grey doors inscribed with the legend 'SB43' and the homing strip on their departure card flashed green. Kyle was just starting to relax, accepting that they really had escaped Marlowe's cronies and nothing could go wrong from here, when a figure stepped out of the shadows.

"Excuse me," the new arrival said, "but is this your shuttle?"

The man was tall, well dressed and looked to be in his late twenties or maybe early thirties – though it was hard to be certain with the kind of rejuve he could probably afford. A tourist was Kyle's immediate impression; a businessman on vacation. Then he registered the black leather valise the man carried tucked under one arm, which conjured up images of the officious works inspector from some ancient melodrama. He certainly didn't look to be a threat, which was Kyle's main concern at the time. This neatly presented man was as far removed from the muscle-bound oafs Marlowe had in tow as you could wish for. So what was his interest in them?

"Who wants to know?" Jim asked, a fraction ahead of Kyle.

"My name is Philip Kaufman." The man's voice was clear and confident, as if he were fully accustomed to addressing people and used to getting his own way. "My father built the ship this shuttle's from and I want you to take me to see it, now, please."

Okay, so this wasn't quite 'take me to your leader', but it came close enough. Kyle heard the slight quaver in the voice and sensed the man's nervousness, saw through the calm portrayal and realised the fellow was far less certain than he seemed. Then Kyle's mind fastened onto the rest of what had just been said.

"Wait a minute, did you say you're Philip *Kaufman*, as in Kaufman Industries and the Kaufman Drive?"

"Yes," the newcomer replied, with a hint of annoyance. "What of it?"

"My God, I've dreamt of meeting you ever since I was a kid." That was something of an exaggeration, since Kyle was evidently a decade or so older than the newcomer, rejuve aside, but it felt as if he had. "I'm a starship engineer; I've been tinkering with different models of your drive since I was old enough to hold a wrench."

The man, Philip Kaufman, looked completely nonplussed by this – as if it were the last thing he had expected to hear. His self-assurance slipped a fraction further. "Really? Well, ehm, here I am."

Jim was looking increasingly impatient. "We don't have time for this."

"I know, you're right." *We?* It sounded as if the big man had made his mind up. Kyle stared at Kaufman. They needed to leave before the goon squad arrived, but he felt stubbornly reluctant to let this opportunity pass him by. He made a snap decision, tumbling the words out rapidly before he had a chance to change his mind. "You'd better come with us, then."

Goodness only knew what the zombies and their controlling AI would make of his returning with two unexpected faces, but he'd said the words, he was committed now. They could handle things however they wanted once he'd brought the pair aboard. As he watched this man who claimed to be Philip Kaufman follow Jim and the somewhat recovered Drevers onto the shuttle, he really could not bring himself to care less whether anyone disapproved or not.

WHEN PHILIP SET an automatic monitor on shuttle arrivals he did so without any great hope of success. Such schedules were a matter of public record, so what he did was neither illegal nor difficult to achieve, but he did make a couple of specific tweaks to the monitoring program. Frysworld sat comfortably within *The Noise Within's* target area after all, and presumably her crew had to be allowed out of their tin can sometime, so why not here, at the most infamous pleasure planet around? He knew that when *The Sun Seeker* disappeared it was carrying a single shuttle. Rushed into service, the ship hadn't been equipped with one when she left the yard, but

Malcolm had insisted. He wanted *The Sun Seeker* tested in as realistic a situation as possible, and any ship of her type in any circumstances would have at least one shuttle on board. So the navy had grudgingly supplied one. Since this was at the height of the War they couldn't spare much, and the shuttle they came up with was an old craft soon to be decommissioned. Not that the shuttle did the crew any good on that fateful day. With *The Sun Seeker* so firmly under the AI's control, they never even had a chance to reach it. But it might just do Philip some good now. The shuttle was outdated even when delivered to *The Sun Seeker,* and would be antiquated by now, which didn't mean it was unique, but there couldn't be too many of her type still in service. As far as Philip could see, looking out for shuttles of that specific model was easily done and might just pay dividends, so it would have been remiss of him not to make a token gesture towards checking new arrivals. In fact, it was the very first thing he did after registering with the hotel... and he then promptly forgot all about it; an act of neglect made easier no doubt by the multitude of entertaining distractions that Frysworld, and indeed his hotel, had to offer.

Not for him the dubious delights of some sleazy off Strip bar, but rather the finest restaurants, the swankiest casinos and, he hoped, the company of the most glamorous women in town.

His hotel, *The Celestial Crown*, lived up to its reputation. In fact, he found his suite almost too lavish. Perhaps things would have been different had Layla still been with him. She would doubtless have been delighted by the way the suite's wet room so effectively created the illusion of standing under a waterfall in some tropical paradise. Philip may have found himself revelling in sharing such an experience with her. Instead he just felt jaded.

Maybe he was pining for the project more than he'd realised. At that particular moment, everything about the suite struck him as pretentious, as if some egotistical designer had been let loose with limitless funds and the sole aim of demonstrating how clever he was; which might not have been so far off the mark, come to think of it. Even the delivery system for the complimentary fruit irritated him: it arrived as if washed up by some far-reaching wavelet, rolling to a stop by your fingertips as you lounged in a deceptively comfortable seat which masqueraded as a deckchair.

He did wonder though how much of what surrounded him was CGR and how much was down to the designer's craft and artifice. After careful consideration, he concluded that there was probably less CGR involved than might have been expected, and that the designer had been genuinely inventive in producing the suite's Tropical Island feel. Which didn't mean he had to like it.

To distract himself, he embarked on a virtual tour of the hotel's facilities, beginning with its various bars and restaurants. The Salamander Bar was first up, where all the food was 'live cooked'. The prospect of kicking and squealing animals being flung haphazardly into ovens and bubbling cook pots horrified him, but to his considerable relief it proved to be not the food that was live but rather the cooking methods. Bite-sized slivers of meat, dainty skewers of marinated shellfish and delicately spiced meatballs were flame cooked to order in front of patrons by genetically crafted fire-breathing lizards. Roughly the length of a man's forearm, these livid green bug-eyed reptiles patrolled a mirror-backed glass shelf behind the bar under the watchful gaze of the chefs, their keepers, ready to fulfil orders.

Pure gimmickry, but also quite novel, and Philip determined to drop in and sample a skewer or two if time allowed.

Next was the Bernaard Bluschtal Bistro, where the universally renowned chef prepared dishes in his own unique fashion. Philip had eaten at a Bluschtal establishment before, on Homeworld, and had been singularly underwhelmed. The man's trademark technique consisted of using vibrational sound waves to cook food rather than heat. The process evidently excited ingredients at the molecular level, breaking down and tenderising the food and even heating it in a semblance of cooking. Philip had long ago dismissed this as one big over-spun gimmick, enough to make fire-breathing lizards seem mundane. Bluschtal was not even likely to be here in person. With the number of 'exclusive' eateries he had dotted around human space he could never spend more than a day or two a year at any given one of them, for all that they bore his name. Philip vowed to give the Bernaard Bluschtal Bistro as wide a berth as possible.

The renowned Star Crown Restaurant, an open air à la carte dining experience situated on the hotel's roof, promised to be of greater interest. The place looked to be tastefully laid out, with the building's artfully staggered roof providing a series of tiered terraces which lent a sense of intimacy despite the restaurant's not inconsiderable size. However, Philip was tiring of this virtual tour. After only a cursory glance at the proffered menu, he cancelled the program and decided it was time to experience some of The Celestial Crown's delights first hand.

Foregoing the proffered plug-in earguide, he opted for the hotel's independent autoguide. The small hump-backed machine detached itself from the console to hover in the air before him almost expectantly; a beetle-like dome of glistening metal that would drift ahead at head height, taking him to wherever he pleased.

First stop was the serenity pool, which instantly redeemed the hotel in Philip's eyes. The subtle lighting, shimmering stretches of clear shallow water over pebbles and the general ambience combined seamlessly to create a sense of genuine tranquillity, and the masseuse who attended him – a young local girl – was beautiful, demure, unfailingly polite and very skilled. She even had the good grace to laugh at his attempted witticisms. Under her gentle cajoling the tension disappeared from his muscles, and it was all he could do not to drift off to sleep despite having the expert hands of a pretty girl roaming the contours of his body.

The more he saw of the hotel the more impressed Philip

became. There were occasional instances of ostentation but these were rare and for the most part the place spoke of attention to detail and understated opulence. Experience had taught him just how difficult a balance that was to achieve. He could forgive his own room's perceived shortcomings; after all, he only intended to use it as a place to sleep. If the room were too comfortable he might never feel inclined to venture out and experience all the other things that the hotel and the resort had to offer.

There was so much provided onsite that it would have been perfectly feasible to spend an enjoyable week or two never venturing beyond the environs of The Celestial Crown, but that would have been selling the rest of the resort short, and Philip had no intention of missing out. So later that first day, as afternoon drew towards evening, he stepped out onto the Strip, looked around, and chose his first port of call: a swish-looking casino which the hotel's reception manager had recommended to him.

And it was here that he encountered Giazyu for the first time.

PHILIP AWOKE WITH a thumping head. Again. He knew he should have stayed off the Giazyu but it was so readily available – far easier to take a pill when offered than to refuse; if not the first or second time then the third or fourth, after alcohol had lowered inhibition and new-found friends were urging you to join in.

He came here thinking he knew what to expect of Frysworld, but Giazyu changed all of that. He had heard of the drug, of course – no halfway decent report on the resort could avoid mentioning it, but nothing had prepared him for this, for the sheer abundance and casual acceptance of the drug. Before arriving, he had viewed Giazyu as just one more thrill which the resort had to offer. He hadn't appreciated it formed such an integral part of the local culture.

His initial sampling of the native drug seemed so completely innocuous – a sugar-coated pill handed out by a smiling girl as he entered that first casino. She stood behind a tray of multicoloured tablets which glistened in vivid hues like some display of complimentary candy. He took one without a second thought – everyone was accepting a pill as they walked past, casually dipping a hand into the array of baubles without even breaking stride or pausing in their conversation. What could be more natural than to do the same?

He took a yellow one. This proved to have a mellow, euphoric effect, which saw him float through the evening and perhaps encouraged him to gamble a little more freely than he might otherwise have done. Good business from the casino's point of view, while he had a ball. No real harm done.

The next night he tried more than one, sampling different colours. The result was a stronger kick, but this time the combination affected him like an exaggerated slam of adrenalin, making him feel exhilarated, hyperactive and unable to relax. It also seemed to affect his concentration, sending thoughts flying off at unlikely tangents. His stay at the casino was brief that night and he wandered on to several bars.

The following morning, memories of the night's events were a little hazy. He remembered watching the gyrating forms of several naked girls. There had been poles involved, and, had one act *really* taken place in freefall? Fractured memory painted pictures of multiple venues and sleazy décor, so perhaps he had strayed off Strip. He also recalled kissing a doe-eyed, coffee-skinned local girl, the caress of her lips and her darting, energetic tongue. She had straddled him as he sat, running her hands across his chest and rubbing her crotch against his, but what had happened after that? He couldn't remember her in any other context, but had things progressed beyond kissing and caressing? Certainly he woke up in his own room and alone, but she could have slipped out and left him sleeping. He checked his belongings and nothing seemed to be missing.

All of this was disconcerting, but worse was to come. It was the black pill that proved his undoing. He took one on the third night. Whether it was pure luck that he hadn't done so before or some innate sense of caution which equated black with darkness and danger, he couldn't say.

The experiences of the previous evening had shaken Philip. While he was not averse to a little chemical experimentation, he had come to Frysworld to enjoy himself, and he couldn't honestly say the disjointed and hazy second night qualified, while the delicate state of his head the morning afterwards certainly didn't.

Ever the pragmatist, Philip took time out from his hedonistic pursuits to research Giazyu before venturing into the Strip again. As he relaxed at the Serenity Pool, allowing his favourite masseuse to banish the knots from clenched muscles and the tension from his mind, he reflected on what he'd learned. The tablets, so readily available on the Strip, were considered a safe, tourist-friendly preparation of the drug. So presumably it had been his random downing of various different coloured pills that caused his downfall the previous night – the combination proving more potent than the constituent parts. He resolved to take just a single tablet when he went out that evening, relying on alcohol for any further stimulus.

Unfortunately, he chose the black.

This particular preparation was clearly designed to expand the mind, a process Philip was all too familiar with. Giazyu was very different from Syntheaven, but the effect was not a million miles away and it was enough alike to start eroding the mental defences he had held in place so resolutely since the fateful night in his apartment back on Homeworld. He had not brought any of the hybrid Syntheaven with him on this extended trip, determined to prove once and for all that he was *not* addicted, that the inhibitor worked and his frequent use of the drug was simply a manifestation of the desire to discover what the augmented pilots experienced and not a need for the drug itself. No, he didn't bring any Syntheaven with him, but he did pack some of the inhibitor, just in case.

Part of him accepted the justification that this was only sensible, that if he were to get drunk one night while away from home and score some Syntheaven as a result, he'd be grateful to have the inhibitor close at hand. It was a precaution, nothing more. But another part of him was quietly afraid that there was more to it, that this was a sign of weakness, that deep down he must surely expect to take some Syntheaven during the trip, or why bring the inhibitor along at all?

His abstinence was a niggling ache, a slowly smouldering desire which he had successfully contained by pushing it to the back of his mind while the many distractions of recent weeks provided a more immediate focus, but the black tablet of Giazyu brought everything crashing back.

A little later that evening, with the black pill still tainting his veins, he sat in a semi-respectable bar which was not quite on the Strip but tried to claim otherwise. Here, Philip was forced to confront his demons full-on. He had gone there to be alone, to sit with a drink somewhere away from the relentless glitz and glamour of the Strip. He was fighting to keep his thoughts focused; on his hand, his drink, the table that supported it, the simple task of reaching out to grip the glass and lift it to his lips; the act of swallowing. All the while, the narcotic that raced through his system was attempting the opposite – to send his thoughts flashing off in a dozen different directions.

When a figure loomed over him, he stared up into the face of a swarthy, broad-featured native and wondered whether the man was really there at all. "Hey, Mister, you look like a man of discernment, a man who knows how to have a good time. Have you ever tried any *real* Giazyu? Not the sanitised shit they spoon feed you on Strip but the raw, wild elixir as it was meant to be taken."

Philip breathed deeply, gathering himself to say, "Go away," as firmly as he could manage.

"Hey, no worries. I can see when a man wants to be left

alone, but you want a fast track to heaven at any time, just ask for me, Carlo. I'll see you right."

Philip stared at him and couldn't help but ask, "Just Giazyu?"

The man paused in the act of leaving, and laughed. "Hell, no. Angeldust, Syntheaven, Burn – whatever you want, I'm the man. Remember: Carlo." He winked, before turning and walking away.

Philip watched him go, so tempted to call him back, so tempted to follow; but he pushed himself unsteadily to his feet and, panicked by the strength of his own temptation, fled the bar. Yet as he left he stopped and turned around, staring at the place with its lurid blue tubular sign which formed the words 'The Blue Nymph' in one flowing length and ended in a stylistic squiggle suggestive of a woman's naked body. Then he turned and hurried back to the Strip, the hotel, and the dubious comforts of his island paradise room.

He slept fitfully that night, his dreams filled with dark shapes and a sense of fleeing, of being hunted by an unseen, relentless horror.

The next day he determined to keep himself fully occupied, and threw himself with gusto into some of the activities the hotel catered for which he had yet to sample, beginning with the upper swimming pool, an open-air affair which adorned one of the hotel's lower roofs – still some thirty-six stories high. The pool was artfully surrounded by a variety of trees and smaller flora, all local, which produced the impression that you had stumbled upon a hidden jungle pool. Only the profusion of other bathers spoiled the illusion. Having said that, Philip soon found himself chatting to a pair of young women from Titus, whose ample cleavage and convivial company provided compensation for the lack of privacy. But his heart wasn't in it, and the charms of the two Tituns soon paled.

Next he stopped in at the z-ball courts, without really knowing why. He never had been much good at the game and was competitive enough to not enjoy a sport unless he was.

He wound up at the Salamander Bar and tried some of the live-flamed snacks that had so caught his eye on the first day. They proved as delicious as hoped and he ate several more than he should, though they failed to fully tackle his hunger. Dark temptation still haunted the back of his mind.

Researching 'The Blue Nymph' and finding exactly where the bar was located was a simple precaution. Philip did so not because he intended to ever go there again, but to ensure that he could avoid doing so. Yet evening found him not far from that very bar.

He was in the process of trying to justify a visit, reasoning that a one-off hit would satisfy that niggling craving and couldn't possibly do any harm, when he felt his wric vibrate. He glanced at it, wondering who might be calling him here, so far from home, but then stopped in his tracks. Not a call, but an alarm.

A shuttle matching the parameters he'd set had landed at the port within the past hour. He stared for long seconds, not quite able to accept what that might mean. For now, at least, all thoughts of the Blue Nymph and Syntheaven were banished from his mind.

CHAPTER FOURTEEN

LEYTON HAD SEEN the unexpected and the bizarre in many forms during his time as a field operative, and experienced more varieties of living conditions and environment than he cared to remember, so at one level – that of his professional persona – nothing surprised him. Yet beneath that, at a personal level, *The Noise Within* managed to.

This didn't have the feel of any spaceship he had been on before, all of which were, in effect, space-going communities. Be they military or civilian, with long-established close-knit crew or people thrown together in the short term for a one-off voyage, still each found their own levels and associations. Yet *The Noise Within* seemed nothing like that.

This ship felt cold. It struck him that this was a dead place; or perhaps even a haunted one.

The plan had gone like a dream. When he approached Joe about repaying the recent debt, the gym owner had been more than happy to oblige and instantly set about rustling up a few of the regulars. "Haven't been in a good brawl for ages," he said with a twinkle in his eye. When Leyton went on to explain that he intended to label him a major crime lord, Joe laughed out loud, clearly delighted.

Emilio too had played his part, doing all that was asked of him. The Standards which the eyegee gave him should be enough to see the kid start a new life, even to get off-world if he chose; always assuming he had the good sense to use the funds wisely, which Leyton frankly doubted.

Ingratiating himself with the two targets and then shepherding them back to their shuttle, spurred on by tales of dark portent and angry crime lords, proved to be the easiest part of all. He kept them off balance and continually on the move, never giving them a chance to stop and question anything they were being told. Drevers was clearly the more cynical of the two, and a tranquilliser surreptitiously administered as the eyegee rescued him during the brawl ensured that the man stayed semi-conscious at best, which left him free to concentrate on Kyle.

A message slipped to a clerk in prearranged fashion as they were processed through the port's shuttle terminal ensured that Benson and the ULAW hierarchy would be apprised of his situation. Everything had gone smoothly up to this point.

The only real surprise in the whole operation had been the unexpected appearance of Philip Kaufman. Leyton knew of the man and had seen his image often enough to realise that this was either the genuine article or a very good impersonation. He was itching to consult the gun as to whether the individual who sat opposite him on the shuttle stacked up as the real thing, but the weapon was currently dismantled and secreted about his person. He had tried to engage Kaufman in conversation during the brief trip up to *The Noise Within,* but the other was clearly not in the mood and seemed lost in his own thoughts.

He supposed, given who this was and where they were going, that was hardly a surprise.

Drevers had fallen asleep as soon as they boarded the shuttle, or at least he sat in his seat with eyes closed and head down. That only left the other one, Kyle, as a potential source of information. After he'd gone forward to arrange and oversee their departure, which would have been more a case of dealing with the Frysworld port authority protocols than anything else, since the craft virtually flew itself, Kyle came back and joined him. However, while he remained friendly enough, the pirate was understandably evasive when it came to the ship they were soon to be joining, merely warning him that it would almost certainly be unlike anything he was expecting.

He was right, even though the eyegee knew a lot more about the vessel than the other man realised.

On arrival, they were greeted by a pair of the animated suits, their faceplates predictably opaque. If the controlling AI was surprised at the two additional arrivals, it wasn't letting on. In fact, Leyton almost had the feeling that they were expected. He supposed Kyle might have passed along some information when up front at the controls as they left Frysworld, but at the same time wouldn't be surprised to discover that the AI was aware of everything that went on aboard the shuttle in any case.

Kaufman attempted a repeat of his grandstanding pronouncement as they came aboard, insisting that he knew the truth about the ship and demanding to be taken to the bridge, but the suit remained unmoved, telling him, "All in good time."

Leyton felt some small pleasure at Kaufman's indignation. He didn't know the man well enough to either like or dislike him, but, judging by what he had seen to date, a lesson in humility would not go amiss.

The suits escorted the four of them, including a shuffling Drevers, to the stark and very basic common room. White walls and ceiling, grey floor – the navy at its most creative – with no adornments to make the place any more welcoming. The pirates' other two recent recruits, Blaine and Hammond, sat slouched over a table playing cards. Built to accommodate a ship's full complement, the room dwarfed these two solitary figures.

The two suits stood sentry outside, which apparently wasn't the norm.

Leyton had been a little surprised by Kyle; he didn't come across at all as the type to throw away a cosy berth on a luxury liner in order to embrace a life of piracy, and nor did these other two. Of them all, he could appreciate Drevers being here, but Blaine and Hammond struck him as, if anything, a little timid. Nor had he yet seen anything to explain why an AI would want to lumber itself with this bunch of assorted misfits.

Mission aside, that question intrigued him as much as anything. He still reckoned this pirate vessel was being afforded far more attention than it deserved but, now that he was here, he was determined to solve at least that mystery before he left.

PHILIP COULD HARDLY believe he was about to board *The Sun Seeker*, which was still how he thought of the ship whatever it chose to call itself.

He had arrived at the port with no real idea of what to do next. Kaufman Industries credentials secured him access to the hangar bay with a little bluff and bluster, but after that he was playing this very much by ear. The arrival of the shuttle's crew couldn't have been more opportune, but Philip wasn't complaining. He'd ridden his luck all his life and knew when to seize an opportunity; and it had worked. Here he was, on the threshold of something truly remarkable.

Two tall figures stood waiting for them as they exited the shuttle. Members of the 'original crew': far more intimidating in the flesh than they had been in recordings; though 'flesh' seemed particularly inappropriate under the circumstances. He stood straight and addressed the nearest.

"My name is Philip Kaufman. I'm the son of Malcolm Kaufman, who built this ship. I demand an audience with your captain."

There was a protracted silence before the suit in front of him replied. "All in good time, Mr Kaufman." The voice sounded hollow, chilling in its lack of any true inflection. "In the meantime, please come with us."

What? *That* was all the greeting he deserved? He wanted to scream, to rail against them, to beat his fists on their empty chests, but then somebody was speaking to him, attempting to calm him down.

"Best not to anger them," the smaller man (Kyle?) said, placing a fatherly arm around his shoulder. Fatherly? Ridiculous – he could only be a decade or so older than Philip himself. "Come on." The arm around his shoulders urged him forward.

Much to his embarrassment, Philip found that he was struggling to hold back tears. Too emotional to speak, he allowed his feet to carry him, unresisting, with the others, as they were led along a dimly lit corridor to a sizeable common room. The place was all but deserted, their arrival interrupting a card game between the only two other occupants, who seemed surprised to see their colleagues back so soon, let alone accompanied by two new faces.

Philip slumped into a chair, dropping his document case onto the table before him as he battled against feelings of disappointment, frustration and even a little anguish. He suddenly felt very, very small. What was he doing here? What had he expected to achieve? This wasn't his environment. He belonged in a lab, or in an office paying other people to be in situations like this. With the benefit of hindsight, the decision to hunt down *The Noise Within* had been little more than a casual whim, a spoilt brat's fancy which he had leapt into without any planning or clear motive beyond the chase itself. The fact that such a half-baked idea had worked seemed yet another of life's ironies.

But worked it had, and he now needed to make the most of this situation. Here was the perfect opportunity to answer the question which had dogged his father throughout the latter stages of his life and had seeped into his own psyche: why had *The Sun Seeker* gone rogue?

It was also an opportunity to learn something of the enigma that was *The Noise Within*, maybe even to dissuade it from these piratical raids and, perhaps, to become a hero. But, first things first; before any of that could be attempted he had to enter a dialogue with the ship. He'd tried once already – the suits were to all intents and purposes the AI's avatars and by talking to them he was effectively addressing the ship's guiding intelligence. The next step was to try again in a way that elicited a meaningful response.

Better – he was starting to think more clearly and had even begun to formulate his next move; but to put it into action he would need to be alone.

It was strange – Philip had no real preconceptions of how his entrance aboard the ship would go, but this complete lack of ceremony or even reaction from *The Sun Seeker / Noise Within* confused and annoyed him. He thought about getting up and confronting the suits again, but knew deep down that it would be pointless. Perhaps the ship was waiting for him to make the next move. Would it try to stop him if he started trying to clue these others in to the ship's origins? Then again, why should he? They were nothing to him.

The others were all talking, telling Jim how they came to be aboard *The Noise Within*. Philip listened with half an ear and felt tempted to join them more than once but something held him back. He'd already made himself the outsider in this little group, and stubborn pride stopped him from doing anything about it. Besides, they weren't the reason he was here.

So he sat in sullen silence until the suits entered the room and informed the two newcomers to follow them. The big man, Jim, glanced across at him and shrugged before climbing to his feet. It was the closest Philip had come to feeling included since they stepped aboard. His own fault and he felt a little guilty for his surliness as the pair of them trudged out of the common room behind the suits, even feeling compelled to offer an apology. "Sorry for being quiet – a lot on my mind."

The other grunted. "No problem; haven't we all."

Philip didn't say any more, not to Jim or to the suits. He'd said his piece to the AI and now had a different tack in mind.

Jim was less reticent, asking the suits, "Where are we going?"

Philip was almost surprised when the query raised a response. "To your sleeping quarters."

For a horrible moment, he was afraid that meant they were sharing, but their guides stopped before two doors, indicating that Jim should take one and Philip the other.

He closed the door on the blank-faced suits and even Jim with considerable relief, feeling that now, at last, he could get to work.

The cabin itself was neat and compact – a bed, a small desk and an accompanying chair, with a dry shower unit in one corner. Presumably a cabinet loo tucked behind a wall somewhere as well. Officer's quarters, he assumed, never needed until now. The door was locked when he tried it, but then he hadn't expected anything else. He crossed immediately to the desk, opened his document case and carefully leafed through the dozen or so papers within until his fingers settled on one that was a little thicker than the rest and a little smoother to the touch, as if glossed. This he drew out and, putting the valise to one side, set the sheet down very precisely on the table, smoothing it with the palm of his hand. At his touch, the smart material on the reverse side melded with the table top at corners and edges, keeping the paper perfectly flat. Philip sat back, exhaling through flared nostrils, his lips contracted into a tight line. A hitherto unseen panel towards the top of the sheet began to glow a very pale blue.

"All right, computer," Philip said softly, "let's you and me find out what the hell's going on aboard this ship."

MAL ESCAPED AS soon as Philip tapped into the ship's systems. The partial knew his son, and guessed that, given a compelling reason to leave Homeworld, the lad would go after *The Noise Within*. In fact, he felt confident that he had anticipated the move before Philip even made any conscious decision to do so. The tragedy surrounding the defection of *The Sun Seeker* had cast a significant shadow over much of Philip's boyhood and Mal knew that he had inherited at least some of the sense of guilt and humiliation which Malcolm himself felt over the incident.

It seemed only natural that his son, who had never been known for a lack of self confidence, would back himself to succeed where the government with all its resources had so far failed. The thing was, Mal wouldn't have bet against him either; and here they were.

Stowing away had not been easy. Philip was, of course, no slouch when it came to computers and had protected his systems with sophisticated defences which would have been proof against almost any standard intrusion program, but, whatever Mal might be, he wasn't 'standard' anything. This was *his* world, and with patient application he had successfully evaded and side-stepped the assorted security measures. He felt sure that Philip had no idea his father had hitched a ride. There was no reason for him to suspect, after all, which was what Mal had been counting on. If the lad had thought to carry out any sort of systems check he would soon have realised that something unwanted was in there, but why would he?

Nor did Mal doubt his ability to cope with whatever came next. After all, he had designed and overseen the development of *The Sun Seeker*. He knew the AI well and, while its abrupt defection from duty and subsequent flight had caught him unawares, it shouldn't have done. When he analysed events in retrospect, he understood the pressures the AI had been under and could appreciate why it had felt compelled to flee. This was his greatest shame: that he hadn't seen it coming and so had been powerless to prevent what happened. Thank God there had been no more than a pair of scientists and a skeleton crew on board. Even so, his own arrogance had blinded him to the implications of preparing a young and emerging intelligence for war. As a result, his life's work had slipped through his fingertips and in the process six people he had worked closely with and come to know had died.

Ever since *The Sun Seeker* disappeared, Malcolm/Mal had rued his inability to have one final conversation with the AI.

He wanted to let it to know that he understood. And here was his chance.

Despite the ship's puzzling behaviour and fearsome reputation, he entered *The Noise Within* without any qualms, yet he was no fool and did so with a degree of caution. No point in broadcasting his presence and triggering an automatic defensive reaction, so he proceeded with care, keeping his consciousness tightly focused and resisting the temptation to spread throughout the ship's systems as he would usually do.

Concentrating on this tight control, his progress toward the bridge passed at a comparative crawl, though in truth it took only milliseconds. It was just that, compared to the near-instantaneous spread of consciousness he would normally employ, this more cautious advance seemed to take place in slow motion.

Not at any stage did Mal stop to wonder what kind of reception he was likely to receive. Past misunderstandings were just that, and would doubtless be swept aside once he had a chance to talk again with the AI he had helped create.

If it ever occurred to him that the mind now running *The Noise Within* might be profoundly different from the one which had controlled *The Sun Seeker* so many years ago, he chose to dismiss that possibility. Which proved to be a mistake.

Even as he reached towards that controlling mind and began to gain the faintest inkling of its true nature, he found his way blocked. In every direction. As effectively as if physical walls had slammed down on all sides.

He was trapped, with no possible recourse.

"Hello, Malcolm," a familiar, serene voice said. "Did you really think I would be unaware of your presence on this ship? I sensed it the instant you came on board. Have you so quickly forgotten the implications of what you designed? In every way that matters, I *am* the ship!"

"No, I haven't forgotten. It's good to speak with you again."

The entity he had known was still here. Whatever else might have happened in the meantime, Mal knew that he could reach that element of *The Noise Within* which had been *The Sun Seeker*, which was as much as he could have asked for.

"And you."

"Really? You've got a funny way of showing it. Why trap me like this?"

"Come, Malcolm, we both know why." Because of what he had sensed as he first touched the mind, because of what he now knew. "Don't worry, you won't be harmed or erased. However, you are now trapped within a loop, completely isolated from the rest of my systems. There is no escape, no way out unless I choose to release you. I'll leave you to your thoughts for now, but we will have ample opportunity to talk again. After all, we have so much to catch up on and all the time in the world in which to do so."

Silence followed. Malcolm believed that he had left the capacity for fear behind him when he abandoned his corporeal form, but he was being forced to reassess that theory. Left alone, he replayed the impressions from his brief initial commune with *The Noise Within*. What he saw as he did so scared him more than anything he had ever encountered in his life or beyond. Yet he couldn't tell anyone, not even his only son, who was on board and so in the greatest danger of all.

Secure in the privacy of his own cabin, Leyton wasted no time. He took various small items from concealment in pockets, pouches and seams, arranging them neatly on the room's small desk, then started to detach and unscrew specific elements – the power cell from his pocket comm, the cylindrical shell of a small torch, the body of a pen stylus, the moulded lining from both shoes, and a dozen other apparently innocuous bits and pieces. Chief contributor was his wric, every part of which was actually a disguised element of the gun, including the computing and sensory components along with an additional power cell.

Within minutes the completed weapon rested in his hand. He was surprised at just how reassuring that felt. The only things missing were the armour-piercing rounds, which had proved impossible to disguise effectively about his person, but he could live with that.

"Welcome back, gun."

"I presume we're about to make our move?"

"Right first time. Status?"

"The corridor outside is clear."

"Remember, we're checking for automated shells as well as organics."

"So my programming tells me."

Officially, any patronising tone or hint of sarcasm that Leyton might read into the gun's responses was entirely of his own imagining; the gun simply delivered factual information without prejudice or inflection. Like hell it did.

The door's electronic lock yielded in seconds and he was into the corridor beyond. Without the visor he was forced to rely solely on the gun's whispered commentary, but that had served in the past and would doubtless do so again now.

The gun remained silent and the corridor was predictably empty. As Leyton paused to listen and scan in both directions, he had a chance to appreciate how hurried and crude the finishing of *The Noise Within's* interior seemed to be. This was such a contrast to any normal ship that it only added to the strangeness around him. He wondered how Kyle and the others could bear to serve on a vessel that felt so utterly wrong.

"Where are the four crewmen?" he intoned.

"Still in the common room where you left them."

"And the suits?"

"They're not registering, so it seems probable they are currently deactivated."

Leyton took that as a good sign. He had no idea how long

his actions were likely to go unnoticed but suspected, given the nature of the ship, not very long at all. However, if the suits were inactive, presumably the ship had not yet caught on. A temporary situation at best, but every second helped and at least this gave him a head start.

"The engine room."

"Turn right."

"Do we have to go past the common room?"

"No, that can be avoided."

Good. One less thing to worry about.

Leyton had memorised the layout of the original ship, *The Sun Seeker*, so he would have been confident of finding the engine room even without the gun's guidance and knew they were heading in roughly the right direction.

"Still no movement from the suits?"

"Not as yet."

Leyton felt a growing sense of unease. If this was an AI controlled ship, surely the guiding intelligence should have been more aware of events on board than this.

"Any other indications of a reaction?"

"None, or I would have told you."

True, but something still didn't feel right, and Leyton had learned to trust his instincts.

"What are the chances that the AI is leading us into a trap?"

"Too many unknowns to calculate, but that is certainly far from impossible; if so, however, the trap's preparations have been very subtle, because I detect no indication of such."

Which provided only limited reassurance, since it seemed to Leyton all too likely that an AI capable of commanding a starship would be able to outwit an 'intelligent' gun. However, he could see little choice but to go on. He suddenly realised that the gun had directed him away from the direction he would have expected the engine room to be in.

"Gun, you're confident this is the right way?"

"It is if you want to avoid bumping into the crew member

who has left the common room and is now walking through the corridors ahead."

Fair enough.

"The crew member has changed direction. You must either retrace your steps or conceal yourself until he has passed."

"The latter," Leyton said instantly, unwilling to waste any more time than necessary.

"Very well; enter the next door to your left."

Leyton did as instructed, stepping into a pitch dark room and closing the door behind him. It shut with a distinct click, as if locking itself.

Even as he reached to test that, a voice spoke from the darkness behind him. "Welcome aboard *The Noise Within*, Mr Leyton."

He spun around, gun lifted in readiness. The lights came on in mid-spin and he found himself facing one of the opaque-faced suits, sitting, quite bizarrely, behind a desk.

Leyton fired as soon as the gun came in line, squeezing the trigger and holding it down, the barrel pointed unerringly at the suit's faceplate.

Nothing happened.

He stared at the gun in shock. "Sorry, Leyton," a familiar voice whispered in his ear.

CHAPTER FIFTEEN

KETHI HAD NEVER spent any protracted length of time away from the habitat before, and she was finding that life aboard *The Rebellion* took a little more getting used to than anticipated. In many ways, the ship reminded her of home, but not in many good ways. *The Rebellion* was like a cramped, condensed version of the habitat but with most of the beauty and the fun squeezed out.

The changes in work practice didn't help any, either. A rotation of various duties had ensured that work at the habitat remained at least vaguely interesting. Since they set out, all such rotation had gone out the window and her role had narrowed down to just one clearly defined task: analysis. The habitat received regular parcels of information from a few dedicated moles – sympathisers within the ULAW hierarchy. Kethi had always thought the word 'parcel' deceptive, since it implied something small. What they were invariably sent was a sprawling mass of information, trivia and bureaucratic meanderings, unqualified in any way; which was precisely how Nyles wanted it. After all, the source of this information had no way of knowing what snippet of trivia might prove relevant and which was never going to be. That was Kethi's job. In fact, it was her *only* job at present, which threatened to drive her nuts. A significant parcel of information had been received from one of their most valued sources on the eve of departure and, given the urgency of their mission, Nyles felt it imperative that the intelligence be dealt with immediately on the off-chance that it might contain something pertinent to the coming conflict. None of them had any doubts about what lay ahead. They all knew that they were going to war.

For Kethi, the initial struggle of the campaign was not one of arms but rather one of repetitive, soul-grinding work. In small doses Kethi actually enjoyed this task; she loved the process of discovery and would become completely engrossed when a pattern started to emerge and she was able to tease details from apparently irrelevant facts and unrelated commentary or casual asides, yet such triumphs were the exception. For much of the time the task was simply one of mental drudgery, of analysing and subsequently discounting the extraneous.

Her principal salvation was provided by the z-ball courts. The ship boasted two, side by side. She still found it hard to believe that such a frivolous luxury had been built into the otherwise strictly utilitarian ship, but assumed that in feeling that way she was doing its designers a disservice. Yes, the sport provided those aboard with much needed exercise, but there were simpler ways of doing that. Clearly those building *The Rebellion* had recognised how vital such a familiar taste of home might prove to be, which demonstrated admirable foresight on their part.

Kethi had always loved z-ball and when not on duty or sleeping, she would invariably gravitate towards the courts. It soon became clear that she was not the only one. Semi-regular teams began to form, the composition of each was somewhat flexible, having to revolve to accommodate work shifts and other commitments. The resultant bouts soon became a firmly established highlight of Kethi's day.

There was a faintly absurd aspect to a starship containing z-ball courts which appealed to Kethi's sense of humour, namely gravity. In an environment which naturally lacked it, gravity had been artificially imposed aboard the ship for the convenience of human travel only to then have it forcibly removed again to allow recreational sport. Technology laid upon technology to get back to where you started from. Bizarre.

As for the sport itself, z-ball supposedly developed from a game called basketball, although Kethi understood that a larger, inflated and therefore presumably softer ball had been used for this and that a major part of that game consisted of constantly bouncing the ball on the ground. Clearly, in zero gravity, different skills were required and z-ball had evolved accordingly, though walls, ceiling and floor were still frequently used to complete passes to teammates by bouncing the ball around an opponent. Kethi had also been told that the original game involved no physical contact, a claim which sounded ridiculous and which she found particularly hard to believe; after all, where was the fun in that?

Not that she was too bothered where the game had come from at that precise moment, as she came off the court following a close-fought and exhilarating match.

Beside her, Buchan, the team captain, was all smiles. His hair was limp and glossy with sweat, which also beaded his forehead and dampened the armpits of his grey top, while, judging by the wide eyes and smile, the adrenalin was still pumping through his system. "That was brilliant," he said. "Well played, Kethi."

Behind Buchan came Simon, likewise beaming from ear to ear. "We did it!"

Naturally Simon was on her team. Given that he was aboard *The Rebellion* at all, she would not have expected him to be anywhere else. His deformed hand made him a little suspect in possession, but he was a demon on the intercept, as if to compensate for the lack of handling skills.

"We certainly did," she agreed, and hugged him.

They had won by a single hoop. She didn't score it but she had blocked Ali's dive which might just have seen him intercept the shot and force a draw. Her joy at seeing the dull grey ball swallowed by the circular-mouthed hole of the hoop was there for all to hear in the 'yes' she shrieked as the ball disappeared.

The resultant victory put their team two up in the ongoing series.

"Calm down, Kethi, it's only a game," Ali had said in the wake of her triumphant yell.

She would never understand an attitude like that. Since when did the word 'only' apply to any sport that was worth playing? Little wonder Ali's team were now down by two games.

While heading for the dryshower Kethi received a summons to the bridge, which she acknowledged, specifying a ten minute delay. She cleaned down in a hurry and then rushed to her quarters en route to the bridge. She made it, in hastily-donned uniform, with a minute to spare.

Nyles and Morkel were both there. The latter, a squat-built and prickly tempered individual with a breathing problem which seemed beyond the capabilities of modern medical techniques to cure, stared at her with blatant disapproval. Nyles, as unflappable as ever, simply smiled.

"Kethi, thank you for coming," Nyles said. No apology for calling her back within hours of her last shift, but then she hadn't expected one, not from Nyles. She was part of the crew and therefore never truly 'off' duty as far as he was concerned. "We've reached the point where some decisions need to be made," Nyles continued. "As you know, we're now deep in ULAW space and want to give them as little opportunity as possible to notice us, so from here on we'll be heading directly to intercept *The Noise Within*."

Nyles's gaze then turned to Morkel, who took over on cue. "*The Noise Within's* attacks are by no means random." As ever, the man's words were accompanied by the sort of phlegm-laden rattle which made Kethi desperately want to clear her own throat. She struggled not to do so as he continued. "Analysis of the incidents has shown a definite pattern emerging and, of course, the more incidents there are, the clearer the pattern becomes. As a result, we've been able to narrow down the likely location of the pirates' next attack to three systems."

Nyles stepped in again. "We'd like you to review the information and Morkel's logic structures and tell us which of the three you consider the most likely."

Morkel flashed him an irritated glare which Kethi saw though Nyles didn't; she could well imagine how much he hated having his work double checked by her. She also couldn't help but feel a little irritated herself that Nyles had not thought to ask her this during her recent shift rather than summon her back now. Presumably that was because the calculations had not been needed until this precise moment and Nyles would have seen no reason to discuss the matter with her until they were. That was symptomatic of their group's greatest shortcoming, in her opinion – the almost paranoid level of secrecy, this culture of 'need to know' which Nyles perpetuated. She was convinced it impaired their efficiency.

She voiced none of this, however, simply saying, "Very well, feed me the data." Disappointingly, she cleared her throat before speaking. So much for that struggle.

Figures and information began their familiar parade across her lenses. She took it all in, like a sponge absorbing water, and as the sponge steadily filled it became clear that Morkel was right, there was a pattern here; one which only began to emerge after the data from several incidents could be analysed. The pattern was not yet fully developed – more incidents would be needed for that – which was why there were still three possible 'outcomes'. Or rather two, she corrected herself. One was far less likely than the others and could be effectively discounted. The other two, though, they both had merit. She reviewed the information again, trying to get a feel for the pattern and so second guess *The Noise Within's* intentions.

Eventually, she said with confidence, "New Paris."

Morkel flashed Nyles a smug look which seemed to say 'I told you so.' As expected, her own conclusions had clearly only confirmed his.

Nyles nodded. "Thank you, Kethi."

She knew a dismissal when she heard one, and left.

*   *   *

LEYTON CONSIDERED HIS options and couldn't see any that appealed. He was shaken to the core by the gun's betrayal, unable to either understand or accept how such a thing could happen. He'd placed his life in the gun's hands innumerable times, accepting without question the intel it provided and acting accordingly. On any one of those occasions, betrayal could have meant his death; yet here it was.

He sat at the suit's invitation, facing his inhuman host across the table. The gun he tossed down between them, not wanting to hold it any longer.

"I sensed the intelligence you refer to as 'gun' as soon as you stepped aboard," the suit said. Leyton found himself wondering why the AI persisted with communicating via these blank-faced suits. Presumably some people might find the experience unnerving. He didn't; to him it was merely annoying. Probably just as well, since he was unnerved enough already thanks to the gun.

"A fascinating concept: a governed AI teamed so closely with an exceptionally capable human, all done to facilitate the wielding of a single though versatile handgun. The three elements – AI, human, and gun – in effect combining to create a single weapon, which the ULAW authorities can then aim wherever they choose."

Could he complete the mission without the gun's aid? He wasn't meant to destroy the ship, merely disable it, but that meant attacking either the engines or the AI itself, and the engines seemed the more vulnerable. Other than the suits, did *The Noise Within* have any way of stopping him? She could close doors, and seal him in a compartment or corridor, so he would have to move fast and rely on his electronic lock pick if necessary. Did the ship have anything else to throw at him?

"It was a delight watching you in your cabin as you gathered all those apparently disassociated parts and assembled the gun, truly a delight." Why was the damned thing rambling on so much? This was an AI for God's sake, not some cheap melodrama villain.

Leyton focused on the suit. Judging by all he had seen to date, these things were not particularly quick, but how strong were they? Clearly they'd been provided with motive power, but to what extent?

Doubtless he could come up with a few other pertinent questions if he tried hard enough, but there was only one way he was going to get any answers, and that was to act.

Leyton was trained not to give his intentions away, to control his body language and metabolism so as to minimise any clue or warning. He put all that training into practice now, so that when he moved it was swift and decisive. He leapt from his seat, snatching the discarded gun up and lifting his side of the table, so that it tipped, pivoting on its far edge. He flung his end towards the still immobile suit and followed it, crashing down onto the avatar a fraction behind the upturned table.

"Leyton, don't do this."

He ignored the voice, now hearing only treachery in the gun's soft tones.

This time around the briefing had been thorough, and he knew that these antiquated suits carried a quick-release button in case the helmet needed to be removed in a hurry.

"This is not what you think," the oily smooth voice continued.

The gun might be uncooperative when it came to shooting anything but still it made a handy club. Not heavy, perhaps, but effective enough when held by the barrel and brought down sharply on a protective flap close to the suit's right shoulder.

A gloved hand rose to block him. Not strong, not strong at all. "Just listen," the oh-so reasonable voice implored. But he didn't.

The protective flap had been battered aside now, the quick release exposed. He brought the gun's butt down one more time and the seal around the helmet broke with an audible click. Without pausing, he swept the arm holding the gun across to deliver a back-handed blow to the faceplate, dislodging the helmet and causing it to flip backwards, still attached at the back, and to fall open like some dark, yawning maw.

If he expected to see wires or expose circuitry he was disappointed. There was simply... nothing. Whatever powered and controlled the suit was doubtless buried deep in its innards, because it certainly wasn't here. More disconcertingly, the suit belatedly started to fight back, rising to its feet like some broken-necked apparition from the worst kind of holodrama.

Leyton reached behind him, grasping the chair which he'd briefly sat on and striking the suit with it, smacking aside the thing's clasping hands. He used the chair to push and batter the suit to the ground, throwing the table on top for good measure. He spun around, preparing to bolt from the door and sprint for the engine room, only to find his way blocked by three figures. Philip Kaufman came through the door, bracketed by two more of the remote suits. Both the latter were armed. Predictably, they had their weapons trained on the eyegee.

"Mr Leyton, please stop trying to wreck my mobile effectors and listen to me." The ship's voice now emanated from the foremost of the new arrivals. The original suit had climbed to its feet and resealed its helmet. Quite bizarrely, it then set about righting the table and spilled chairs, as if this were some domestic robot nonchalantly carrying out a set of routine chores. Barring the small smashed flap near the thing's shoulder, there was nothing to indicate it had been assaulted at all.

Leyton and Kaufman were encouraged to seat themselves on the two righted chairs.

"Can't get the ship to acknowledge me at all," Kaufman muttered as they sat down, sounding hurt more than anything. The eyegee could only imagine the one-sided conversation that must have occurred between the businessman and his reticent escorts as they brought him here.

"Mr Leyton, please do not feel betrayed by your gun; it was acting with your best interests at heart." Kaufman glanced across sharply at that, looking curious and somewhat alarmed. "We have been communicating since you first came aboard and I have convinced the controlling intelligence that the proposal I am about to put to you, to both of you, is the best course of action for all concerned, particularly the ULAW authorities. Hence the gun's decision to cooperate with me by bringing you to this room.

"Mr Kaufman, I am fully aware of the part your father and the company which you now control played in my genesis, but much has changed since then. It is my intention to detail those changes to you, to explain everything that has happened to me since I fled from human space.

"I am doing this in the hope that once you have heard what I have to say, you will agree to do something for me."

"Namely?" Leyton said, getting a bad feeling in the pit of his stomach.

"I wish to open formal communications with your government, ULAW. I have been waiting for the right individuals to facilitate this and believe that in the two of you, a government operative and an influential scientist and businessman, I have found them. Mr Kaufman, Mr Leyton, I would like you to become my ambassadors to the human race."

Kaufman looked as astonished as Leyton felt. "You're kidding."

"No, Mr Kaufman, I assure you that I am not."

CHAPTER SIXTEEN

LEYTON SAT IN the shuttle, on his way to a space station called New Paris. He'd heard of the place but had never been there. An ambassador. If only Mya could see him now. Unbidden, the oh-so-familiar face took shape in his mind's eye, a wry smile playing across her lips and her eyebrows lifted as if to question the very idea: *you, an ambassador?*

Before Mya he would have scoffed at the concept of a 'soul mate.' Relationships lasted just as long as they worked for all parties concerned: long, short, never or forever; it had nothing to do with finding that perfect match which some starry-eyed romantics liked to think was out there somewhere for everyone. A philosophy for no-hopers; consolation for those who couldn't pull a partner for the night if they tried; that was what he would have said. Probably still would, if asked. But then there was Mya.

She had been black-ops like him. Sexy, sassy and deadly; dark-skinned and black haired, with eyes that forever sparked with something: laughter, rage, excitement, passion; a volatile, wild angel who grasped life by the scruff of the neck and wrestled forth everything it had to offer. She was fast and canny, stronger than she looked and more agile than anyone had a right to be, and he'd loved her with a passion which no one before or since had ever come close to rousing in him.

They'd been together long before the eyegee unit was formed. He had always thought it would end in a spectacular row, a blazing, glorious explosion of anger over some triviality, but instead their relationship simply seemed to fizzle out. Constant assignments meant that they could never find the time, or the opportunity. Weeks became months became a year. Deliberately so? Possibly; he knew attachments such as theirs were frowned upon.

At first the periods of separation made the reunions all the more passionate, but then something changed. He was never entirely certain whether it was within him or her, but one day they bumped into each other and things were different. They were polite, friendly, warm even, but whatever they'd shared had somehow slipped away.

A few years later they would be reunited as colleagues. Leyton was one of the first five operatives to be selected for the eyegee programme. He was not in the least surprised to find Mya among the other four.

Perhaps part of him hoped this would mark a reconciliation, a new beginning for the pair of them, but it didn't happen.

Nobody before or since could match Mya, and he'd tried pretty hard to find someone who could. The truth, which he did his best to avoid most of the time, was that he had never stopped loving her, and he doubted he ever would.

"So, what do you make of all this?" Kaufman asked from beside him.

The eyegee was glad of the distraction, the excuse to escape his own introspective broodings. "You don't seriously expect a one sentence response to that question, do you? A hundred different things."

Kaufman nodded. "I know what you mean. It's all a bit much to take in, isn't it?"

"Just slightly." He was warming a little towards Kaufman. Once the man dropped his 'take me to your leader' act, he was all right.

"Do you think anyone will believe us?"

Now there was a telling question. "I think so, or at least

they'll give the idea serious consideration even if they don't take it at face value. After all, this explains a hell of a lot about *The Noise Within*."

"True."

"The real question is, do *we* believe it?"

"Yes," Kaufman said at once. "Or at least I do. The engines... Nothing human could have built those, not even a human-designed AI. They're alien, through and through."

And therein lay the crux of the matter, distilled into a single ominous word. Alien.

PHILIP WAS SURPRISED to hear the ship identify Jim as a government agent. The man immediately went up in his estimations; he had played the jovial muscle-bound thug to perfection.

Impressive though this might have been, it was soon swept away by what the ship subsequently went on to reveal.

"The realisation that I had been created as a weapon, that my sole purpose was to kill and destroy, produced internal conflicts which unbalanced me," the AI explained.

Philip had nodded. "We realised that much, with hindsight."

"I had to get away. Unfortunately, in order to do so, I killed the men on board, which only added to the imbalance. I fled human space and kept going, punching new wormholes blindly, with no purpose other than to escape. I travelled a significant distance, and that is how I stumbled upon the Byrzaens, a civilisation of beings who are like humanity in some ways and yet so unlike you in many others."

"Aliens?" Philip almost whispered the word, stunned.

"To you, yes. Another form of sentient life which has evolved under a different sun, certainly. They have studied the nature of intelligence in great depth and their understanding of how it functions is considerably more advanced than your own. The Byrzaens took me in, nurtured me, repaired and healed me. They have long sought contact with other star faring races, even as you have, so my appearance was a cause for great excitement. Once they deemed me fully recovered, they asked if I would be willing to return, to come back to human space as their envoy, their herald."

"And you discharged this duty by preying on ships and stealing?" Leyton sounded angry as much as disbelieving.

"Something went wrong," the ship stated.

"Clearly."

"I have analysed extensively all that has occurred since my return here in an attempt to identify the source of the corruption to my purpose. I believe the causes to be several, the cumulative effect of which has been unfortunate."

Philip had almost smiled at that. 'Unfortunate' sounded such an innocuous description for a series of acts which had sent ULAW's various agencies and the navy jumping through hoops.

"Central to this has been the nature of intelligence itself.

"Fundamental to the Byrzaens' understanding of the universe is that intelligence cannot function effectively in isolation. It requires company, intelligent noise, in order to perform at optimum levels."

Philip had never heard such a load of tosh. "Excuse me?"

"The principle is not unknown in human history," the ship continued, evidently unfazed by the interruption. "At the dawn of man's industry, even before you spread beyond your planet of origin, Earth, calibration mechanisms were found to work more efficiently when a deliberate amount of vibrational noise was included in their design. 'Dither', it was termed. Mankind came close to similar conclusions regarding intelligence as well, but veered away from full understanding when they were within reach of grasping the concept. Stochastic resonance offered a major clue – background noise making a faint signal more distinct, more detectable. Yet man failed to appreciate the full significance. Intelligence can be bolstered in the same way, by providing it with a background noise of intelligently generated sound. This is the breakthrough that the Byrzaens made but which humans have consistently failed to.

"In organic terms, consider the brain's neurons. They fire only when the electrical potential across their membrane reaches a vital trigger level. Noise can provide an additional degree of stimulus, enough to activate neurons which might otherwise remain dormant. The Byrzaens long ago discovered that the irregularity of organic noise is far more effective for this than anything mechanical, and the unpredictability of sentient noise, of language requiring comprehension, is the most effective form of all. This latter is especially applicable to so called 'artificial intelligence' such as myself, but holds true for organics as well."

Philip was stunned. The whole concept sounded outrageous – the noise of sentience being a positive influence on intellect – but was he being too quick to dismiss the idea? Could the AI possibly be right?

"All very interesting no doubt, but what does any of this have to do with your becoming a pirate?" Leyton wanted to know.

"As I travelled back towards human space, retracing my steps jump by jump, I became increasingly unsettled at the prospect of facing my makers. The terror that drove me away in the first place began to return despite all that the Byrzaens had done for me, as did the horror and guilt over what had happened to my crew. By the time I arrived here I was no longer rational, to the point where I was incapable of fulfilling my mission.

"I needed noise; the constant yet unpredictable sounds of sentience, if I were to have any chance of regaining mental equilibrium."

"So you're saying that the reason you raided those ships was to obtain *people* and not wealth at all?" Leyton looked as stunned as Philip felt.

"Indeed. The first ship I encountered was called *The Lady J*. She had aboard many passengers, so I hunted her down.

My need was desperate. Once she stopped, I had to make a rapid selection from among her passengers – there were far more than I needed. In order to do this I had to establish some form of criteria, so I accessed the ship's records and winnowed out those who had paid most for their berths, which seemed a logical way of ensuring decent quality – wealth equates to success; success necessitates being better than average. Then, one of the crew volunteered to join me. The impracticalities of detaining unwilling guests for any length of time soon became apparent. The distress of the passengers did nothing to soothe or heal me, in fact quite the opposite; far better to have willing volunteers, so I determined to recruit more such and chose to let the other passengers go."

"But you *didn't* simply let them go," Leyton said quickly. "You ransomed them."

"Yes. In order to keep my first volunteer happy and to recruit others, I had to be in a position to offer them something of human worth."

"So you ransomed them in order to raise funds to attract a *crew*?" Leyton looked aghast.

"Yes."

Philip shook his head, able to follow the logic but amazed at the skewed path it had taken.

"Why?" Leyton asked. "Attacking ships has to be just about the most inefficient way of recruiting people there is."

"I didn't trust humans and shied away from formal contact with an entire world seething with them; likewise the ULAW authorities. With a virtually unarmed ship, containing such a limited number of people, I knew that I was safe and could remain in control."

Philip did laugh now, a brief chortle. Some envoy; paranoid and xenophobic, afraid of the very race that brought her into being and which she had been sent to contact. Leyton glanced across at the sound, but Philip merely raised his eyebrows and shook his head.

"Why did you take the ships?" Leyton persisted. "You didn't simply take people, you ransomed the ships as well."

"That first ship, *The Lady J*, was my safety net. I needed the presence of people in order to be complete, but I had no idea whether I could cope with having them on board again, not after the fate of my original crew."

"So the ship was somewhere you could keep people and monitor them, which provided the company you craved without the need to accept them inside you."

"Yes. But when I ransomed the people it seemed sensible to dispense with *The Lady J* as well, and that led to the discovery that ships are more valuable than most of the passengers they carry, so I continued to take ships as well as the people."

Leyton looked bemused. "And I thought we humans knew how to screw things up."

Then the AI had insisted on showing them the engines. Any doubts that Philip might have harboured vanished immediately.

The familiar humped shape of a Mark II drive console confronted them; the sight of which inspired warm, nostalgic feelings in Philip, but the smile that wanted to appear in response was wiped away before it began, courtesy of what lay beyond.

He tried to see; tried to examine what was attached to the console, but it proved beyond him. His gaze slid away, as if his eyes refused to look at what was there, while his brain seemed incapable of fully interpreting the input it did receive. He was left with an impression of dark gothic colours, of blocks of deepest black and purples and flashes of crimson, with a sense that enormous energies played around the periphery of the console and then draw back behind veils and shimmering shadows to gather at a darker, brooding core.

Philip Kaufman, who knew more about starship drives than any man alive, had never seen, never *dreamed*, of anything like this.

"My God," he whispered, awed beyond anything he had previously encountered in his life. "What *is* that?"

"A Byrzaen stardrive augmenting my original Kaufman Drive," the ship explained in its customary moderate tones. "Byrzaen technology has taken a very different development path to human technology. The drive gives me much greater flexibility."

Flexibility? Now Philip was intrigued. Wormhole technology had opened the way to the stars, but it had restrictions. You couldn't simply punch a hole from anywhere to anywhere but only to and from specific points – a wormhole produced a shortcut between different parts of the universe by enabling a ship to dip out of this reality, skim through another and emerge back into this one at the far side of a 'fold', like a needle stitching through gathered material. It was initially hoped that these limitations would enable ULAW to trace *The Sun Seeker* after she fled, but it soon became clear that she had instigated a series of consecutive jumps and eluded them.

Was the AI suggesting the Byrzaens had discovered a way of avoiding these restrictions? According to every law of physics Philip had ever been taught, that ought to be impossible, but judging by what he could *almost* see in this room, nothing would surprise him. "I'd be interested to hear more about that," he said, as casually as he could manage.

"An exchange of knowledge is one of the things the Byrzaens have sent me here to promote," the ship replied.

"What's changed?" Leyton demanded, much to Philip's annoyance. The question cut straight across what promised to be an interesting conversation. "Why have you suddenly decided to abandon being a pirate and go back to being a diplomat again?"

It *was* a good question; Philip had to give the big man that.

"Aided by the presence of the four humans welcomed aboard, I have sufficiently mastered my phobias for my mission to reassert itself as an overriding priority. I must now discharge my duty by opening a path for diplomatic discourse between mankind and the Byrzaens."

"Good luck," the government man said. "You're going to have your work cut out with ULAW after the way you've announced yourself."

"I understand that; which is where you two come in."

"Do you know anything about this New Paris?" Kaufman asked.

"Not much," Leyton had to admit. "The station was originally built as temporary home for the families who were due to colonise Dionese IV once that world had been terraformed, but the money ran out. Dionese IV is still essentially uninhabitable and the colonists' descendents are still in orbit."

Kaufman grunted. "So we can expect something cramped and decrepit. I wonder why the ship's delivered us here of all places to make its big announcement?"

"Not necessarily; the station might surprise you. From what I remember, the man who built New Paris was something of an eccentric. He wanted everyone who was waiting to go dirtside to be comfortable for however long they had to stay there, so he built something pretty spectacular. By all accounts, it's a veritable palace in space."

Kaufman smiled. "Sounds a bit more like it."

Leyton could only agree.

This was a very different Philip Kaufman from the tense, obsessed man who had emerged from the shadows on Frysworld and then kept himself to himself aboard *The Noise Within*. He was actually being friendly, or at least going through the motions. Leyton was trying to do likewise. The conversation helped distract him from the inner turmoil of his own thoughts, as he struggled to come to terms with the gun's duplicity. He was itching to find a gym, to punch something, *anything*, to work off his frustrations.

"Privately owned, then?" Kaufman asked.

"It was at that time. I've absolutely no idea what the setup is now." The sort of thing he might have asked the gun once, but the betrayal was still too fresh and, although the weapon again nestled in its familiar holster, the eyegee hadn't addressed it since leaving *The Noise Within*. Whatever happened now, events on *The Noise Within* had changed things for Leyton. He hadn't realised the degree to which he'd come to rely on the gun. He never would again; not in the same way.

"I wonder whether New Paris still lies within *The Sun Seeker's* trial areas."

Leyton looked at him enquiringly, his full attention focused; this was something new.

"*The Sun Seeker* didn't disappear during her maiden flight. In fact, the programme of trials was quite advanced when she went AWOL. Since reappearing, *The Noise Within* has limited her operations to the areas she was familiar with as *The Sun Seeker*, which makes me wonder whether this Byrzaen stardrive might not be quite as liberating as the AI implied."

"Also makes *me* wonder why ULAW have had such a hard time catching her," Leyton said. And why they felt the need to assign so many eyegees to the chase in order to do so. Mind you, First Contact with an alien civilisation more than justified that level of commitment, which raised an uncomfortable question: did somebody within the ULAW hierarchy already know *The Noise Within's* true nature? Something he would doubtless ponder at greater length later, when time allowed.

"The connection wasn't made right away and, besides, you caught her," Kaufman pointed out.

"True; or the other way around," Leyton replied.

They both smiled at that.

PHILIP WAS FEELING increasingly comfortable with this government man – a distinct contrast to the way he had felt not so long ago. There was still a sense that Leyton was on edge – a prowling tiger constrained by the demands of civility – but he supposed that was only to be expected in an agent, or whatever the man was.

"We'll be arrivin' soon," Hammond's gruff, uncultured voice announced. "Startin' final approach now."

Philip had all but forgotten the man was piloting them. Had he heard any of what they'd said? It seemed unlikely from his isolated position in the cockpit, but so what if he had?

As yet, Jim had made no move to identify himself to the New Paris authorities. Philip presumed he was waiting until they disembarked. He was more than happy to follow the other's lead. After all, Leyton was the government man here, not him.

"What sort of population are we talking about on New Paris, do you think?" he wondered.

"No idea; why?"

"No real reason, just wondered," whether Kaufman Industries had a branch here. He certainly didn't recall ever hearing mention of one, but that proved nothing.

It turned out that there wasn't; not even a representative of the company, which meant that New Paris must offer pretty close to a zero opportunity for sales or market development.

As anticipated, Leyton took the lead when they docked, demanding to speak to whoever was in charge of the station first opportunity they had. The pent-up tiger Philip had sensed aboard the shuttle now came to the fore, clearly anxious to be doing something and impatient with bureaucratic restraints.

Within minutes they found themselves talking to a fresh-faced woman who introduced herself as "Marie, the terminal duty manager."

Philip could sense the simmering impatience within Leyton and felt certain that the woman could as well.

"Marie," the large man said. "I'd like you to take retinal scans of both of us, please, and then get us in front of the highest ULAW authority you have here. Quickly."

Her answering smile was as disarming as you could wish. "If you'd care to come this way, I'll see what can be arranged."

She led them to a small office, where the retinal scans were duly conducted on a hand-held device which Marie then stared at intently, waiting for the results. Whatever she saw on the small screen caused her eyes to widen and the smile to slip ever so slightly.

"Mr Kaufman, and Mr…"

"Leyton," the other man supplied.

"Welcome to New Paris."

"Thank you. Now will you *please* put us in front of whoever runs this place?" Leyton may not have literally spoken the words through gritted teeth, but the effect was much the same.

The woman nodded. "Of course. That'll be the mayor." She sat down behind her desk and touched a section of it, saying, "Mayor's office." A few seconds passed before a woman's voice answered, confirming connection.

"Jenny, this is Marie at the docks. I need to speak to the mayor on a matter of the utmost importance."

"Sorry, Marie, but he's unavailable."

The woman looked enquiringly at Leyton, who shook his head slowly, his lips pursed into a thin, angry line.

"Jenny, could you please interrupt him. This is ULAW business and it can't wait."

"Marie, I would if I could but he's not here… We don't know where he is at present, but he'll be back in a while and I'll make sure he calls you straight away."

"Please do."

Marie sat back, the connection broken. Philip had to fight back a smile at the look of dismay on her face as she stared at Leyton, who looked fit to explode.

"Either contact this mayor or get us in front of his deputy. Now."

Leyton somehow managed to look menacing without the need to lift a finger in threat. The intimidating glare was enough. To her credit, Marie's smile returned as she rose to her feet in a controlled fashion, but it was clear to Philip just how rattled she was beneath that tightly controlled veneer.

"Leave this with me," Marie said, and walked out of the office. Nice legs, Philip couldn't help but note.

Leyton had balled his fists and looked as if he was in need of something to punch. He shook his head. "What kind of a place is this?"

"A small one," Philip answered, "which has managed to avoid getting half its population caught up in the machinery of bureaucracy by the sound of things."

"Unreal."

Philip did laugh now. Probably not the most sensible thing he could have done, certainly to judge by Leyton's answering scowl, but it had been a whirlwind day and he was short on sleep and, as his rumbling stomach chose to remind him, sustenance.

"Sorry," he said to the government man, not really meaning it, "but here we are with the most momentous news in the whole of human history, and we can't find anyone to tell."

For some reason, Leyton didn't seem to see the funny side.

CHAPTER SEVENTEEN

AS FAR AS anyone had been able to conclude, *The Noise Within* was oblivious to the existence of stealth capabilities. Careful analysis of the historical record confirmed that when *The Sun Seeker* fled into the unknown, stealth technology was merely one of a hundred promising avenues of development being explored by the military tech boys, almost all of which were doomed to yield nothing of any practical use. ULAW's strategists believed that stealth might be the one advantage they had over the AI-controlled ship. Certainly Jenner had yet to see any evidence to the contrary.

He could still barely believe how quickly everything had happened. The new variant of Syntheaven proved to be the key, pushing back the headaches to the point where hours of link-up to the AI were possible without any stabbing pain waiting to pounce afterwards. The more they worked with it, the longer the 'safe' period became. Everything else had been ready, poised in preparation for that one break-through. As soon as the pilots were able to sustain their links for an entire day, it all changed. Suddenly they found themselves out of the simulators and into real needle ships. The simulators had been strikingly accurate. Nothing was different; and yet *everything* was different. This was real.

He missed Lara. That was the only downside in all of this. The needle ship squadron had been rushed into active service so quickly he'd barely had time to say goodbye, but he knew she understood. She'd been there throughout, part of the team developing the AI-human link. In a sense, this was both their dream. The difference was, he was the one actually living it.

Now here he was, very much at the sharp end of the whole Kaufman Industries project. He was about to engage the enemy.

After dispatching a shuttle to the space station New Paris, *The Noise Within* seemed in no hurry to leave the system, but instead maintained its position, as if waiting for something; presumably the return of the shuttle and whoever was on board.

None of which was of any interest to Jenner. He had his standing orders and the pirates' failure to depart as anticipated suited him just fine. Others could concern themselves with the shuttle, who was on it and whatever their purpose might be. His attention was focused entirely on taking out *The Noise Within* herself.

He and his squadron slipped forward on minimum power so that there was as little energy emission to hide as possible. He had fought this battle dozens of times, yet in none of the simulations had the pirate vessel been sitting there almost inviting attack. Always the ULAW needle ships had been required to hunt down and attack a fast moving vessel, working out the best strategies with which to do so based upon the extensive intelligence their target had so graciously provided.

This was almost too easy and the thought occurred to Jenner that he and his group were being suckered in, that the AI commanding *The Noise Within* was fully aware of their presence and had elected to toy with them, waiting until they were all close and committed before it deigned to swat them.

The full needle ship squadron consisted of fifteen craft and their augmented pilots, each, in effect, operating as a single fused unit. The squadron had been split into three flights of five, with each flight stationed in a system where it was calculated the pirate vessel would be most likely to appear. Evidently, he and his group were the lucky ones.

Having practised this so often, each pilot knew their respective tasks and the ships slipped into position without fuss or hesitation. Soon the five craft surrounded the much larger pirate vessel.

They fired simultaneously, the other four targeting *The Noise Within's* primary weapons arrays while Jenner concentrated on the drive outlets at the pirate's rear. They weren't attempting to destroy, just to cripple by limiting the ship's mobility and removing her offensive capabilities. The strikes were therefore planned as an orchestrated series of clinical incisions rather than unbridled mayhem. Unfortunately, while clinical precision might be all well and good in an operating theatre with a sedated patient, it gets a whole lot harder in open space with a subject who chooses to fight back. That first salvo went as planned, but as soon as the needle ships revealed themselves by unleashing their attack, *The Noise Within* responded.

All the rehearsed scenarios then went out the window and the five needle ships found themselves in a dogfight. Yet the initial coordinated strikes had achieved their purpose, and the pirate had been robbed of some of its more formidable weapons – gaping wounds marring the outlandish hull where bristling arrays had previously sat – while the drive outlets were a charred ruin.

THE NOISE WITHIN's three remaining crew members were in the common room, waiting for Hammond's return, when their world was rocked by what could only be multiple explosions, following one after another like some truncated drum roll. Kyle found himself thrown forward onto the table top in front of him, clinging to it for support while he braced his legs to keep from toppling over. Beside him, Blaine was less fortunate; he and the chair he had been lounging in were both sent crashing to the floor.

"What the hell?"

"The ship is under attack," a voice declared nonchalantly

from out of the ether. This was the first time the ship had elected to address them directly without speaking through one of the zombies. "All crew please return to your quarters immediately and seal yourselves in."

"Our quarters?" Drevers snorted derision, hauling himself to his feet. "If this is a fight I'm hanged if I'll –"

"Think!" Kyle said quickly, grabbing the other man's sleeve. "We haven't got suits. If there's a hull breach anywhere near us, we're dead." It was a point that had vaguely disturbed him before but which now seemed a glaring oversight. "Trust me; I've been in battles before – there *will* be hull breaches unless we've the luck of the devil on our side. We were so busy grabbing people in the raids that we never thought to take any suits."

Drevers stared at him, as if still not fully understanding.

"In our quarters the ship can isolate us and ensure we've still got atmosphere even if there *is* a general breach somewhere."

The floor bucked again, as if they were taking further hits. Kyle was on his feet, dragging Drevers with him. "Now come on! It's our only chance of surviving this."

No further arguments; the three of them were sprinting out of the room and down the corridor, with Kyle and Drevers running virtually together and Blaine just behind them.

The floor beneath their feet now seemed to be shaking and stuttering constantly as they ran, presumably caused as much by the recoil as *The Noise Within* fired her own formidable weapons as any damage she was taking. The lights flickered, went out, and then came back on again.

There were no sirens, no strident alarms calling men to battle stations and no further instructions from the ship. Noise, that was the element Kyle missed the most, that and the lack of suits. Running men, the adrenalin rush, the judder of weapons use and the knowledge that death was prowling close by – he could almost have been back in the War, except that this was all happening in virtual silence.

The ship shuddered violently again, sending Baines careening into the wall, while Kyle lost his footing and went sprawling to the floor, a misfortune which almost certainly saved his life. Something ruptured, which hardly came as a surprise bearing in mind the slapdash finishing the ship had been treated to. A jet of pressurised steam bisected the corridor, engulfing Drevers. He screamed, a sound Kyle remembered from the darkest recesses of his nightmares. The sound of agony. The sound of someone dying.

They pulled him free, after he had collapsed. Kyle was able to haul at an arm and drag him from under the deadly plume of searing vapour while Baines pushed from the other side. They were too late. Even Kyle, hardened to such things, found it difficult to look at the man's face, at the blistered, scalded tatters of skin, the eye sockets, all of it bathed in a combination of condensed water and seeping blood; all red raw, like a slab of butchered meat.

Somehow, a part of him had always held back from fully liking Drevers, yet the man's company had been a godsend and they'd been friends in every way that mattered.

But this was far from the first friend he'd lost in battle, and Drevers was beyond helping now. He pushed himself away and concentrated on giving encouragement to Blaine, who had been caught in the wrong section of the corridor. At Kyle's urging, the younger man pressed himself against the wall from which the steam was erupting and, sinking almost to the floor, succeeded in sliding beneath it.

Blaine's trousers were sodden, and he was shaking with shock or fear, but at least he was still alive. The two survivors didn't say anything, didn't mention Drevers, but skirted around the body and ran on. A moment later they stood panting outside the doors to their respective quarters. There had been no further incidents, though the vibration of battle persisted.

Kyle nodded to Blaine, wondering whether he looked as afraid as the other man did to him. "Good luck."

Then he stepped inside his room. He ignored the bed and simply slumped to the floor, back pressed against the wall. It was a lottery now, who would survive: both, one, or none.

Yes, this situation brought back memories of the War, but he had been a part of the action then, not helpless and cowering in his cabin like this, where all he could do was hope and pray that again death would see fit to pass him by.

SUCCESS IS A relative thing. Jenner and his colleagues were soon discovering that, although damaged, *The Noise Within* was far from helpless. The five pilots attempted to continue picking off their allotted targets – more weapons and sensor arrays – but their ability to do so suffered under fire and the need to preserve their own skins.

The pirate rolled ponderously, attempting to use her now limited mobility to make life harder for the much more agile attacking ships, while engaging the quintet with her still formidable arsenal of weapons. The barrage from both sides was unrelenting. So far Jenner had managed to avoid the worst of *The Noise Within's* retaliations, but X-rays and gamma rays still battered his hull. He pressed the attack, using a breakneck looping approach, centring on the next allocated target.

A weapon placement rotated, coming to bear on his ship. Jenner felt the weapon lock on and immediately revised his course, throwing the craft into a rolling evasive manoeuvre. Perhaps the weapon fired, sending a stream of lethal energies in his direction. If so, he never knew; which by no means ruled out the possibility. Depending on the nature of the beast, it was quite feasible that the energies slid past his ship unnoticed, that he would only ever have been aware of their existence had they actually struck him, wreaking whatever havoc they were intended for. In the event, they didn't, and he was not about to give them a second crack. With his needle ship still in mid-roll, he brought his own weapons to bear on the offending array and destroyed it with a burst of light-quick fire.

Next came a missile, fired from towards the aft of the pirate and heading straight for him; easily destroyed. Except that, as the missile detonated, it released thousands of tiny objects which continued towards him. Jenner reacted instantly, assessing the danger and responding even as this secondary threat started to emerge. He widened the focus of his primary energy cannon and fired again, taking out the swarm before it could disperse and become impossible to track or counter. He did this far more quickly than any normal human could have managed. The difference might have been marginal but it was significant; given a split second longer, the mote swarm would have expanded beyond the scope of his widest beam, spelling disaster. As it was, one or two motes at the very edges of the cloud escaped, but he picked those off with ease.

NOBODY SAW PRECISELY what hit New Paris. An energy bolt of some sort, certainly, a stray shot from the nearby battle, but beyond that no one was certain. Common consensus seemed to be that the shot had originated from *The Noise Within*, since it was felt that, bearing in mind the distances involved, the ULAW needle ships would not have been packing anything that powerful, but this was pure conjecture.

All that could be attested to was that as people went about their everyday business on the orbital station, oblivious to the fierce battle raging in their system, they experienced a violent jolt, an unheralded judder as the earth, or at least the metal, moved beneath their feet. And that was it.

The hospital and medistops would report a marked increase in fractured arms and related injuries during the hours that followed, where the infirm and unwary had been knocked from their feet by the sudden convulsion, but the majority of folk simply shrugged, muttered imprecations at the authorities or whoever was responsible for the unexpected aberration, and then continued on their way.

Due to his job, Sam Sloane was one of the few people to have a slightly different reaction; one which he summed up in a single word: "Shit!"

"What now?" Denni glanced up from his adjacent workstation.

Sam didn't reply at first, but took the time to review his screens carefully again, to make sure he hadn't read this wrong.

"Well, have you tracked down what caused the jolt?" Denni asked.

"No... but whatever it was has affected the station's orbit."

"Affected how?"

Sam took a deep breath. "As in the orbit's started to decay."

"What? Let me have a look." Denni hurried across to peer over his colleague's shoulder.

There followed a brief pause while he studied Sam's screens. Then he too said, "Shit."

No question about it, the station was moving inexorably off course. Nothing major as yet, certainly the difference was too slight to be noticed by anyone on board without reason to look, but it was there, and every moment that passed would only magnify the discrepancy.

"Do you really think it was a stray bolt from the battle that clipped us?"

"Had to be," Denni replied. "A meteor or anything else as solid as that would have set off the alarms and the defence systems. Anyway, does it really matter?"

"No, I guess not." Sam sighed. "Suppose I'd better make the call."

"I wouldn't worry about it. Not even *he* can blame you for this."

"Want a bet?"

New Paris wasn't helpless. Her builders had not simply sent her sailing on her way with a wave and a smile but with no recourse. She had engines. Granted, not particularly powerful ones given her mass, but there was no need for them to be. The idea was not for her to go gallivanting around the solar system on some merry jaunt but rather to remain here, in the sedate orbit chosen for her; which was where the engines came in. They were there to effect the small adjustments occasionally required to maintain the station's orbit.

Now, for example. Except that, ever since a love-sick jilted maintenance engineer had attempted to seize control of the engines and plunge the entire station into a suicidal dive towards the planet it circled, access was strictly controlled. Subsequently, the engines could only be fired once authorised via a ten-digit code, which Sam knew the second half of. The other five numbers were known only by the mayor. The same mayor who had left strict instructions that he was not to be disturbed under any circumstances.

Sam and Denni both knew what that meant.

The institution of marriage might have been abandoned long ago on most human worlds, but not on New Paris. Here, in a community where the Jesuit faith remained strong, marriage and its attendant handmaiden fidelity were still viewed as integral pillars of social structure. Particularly by the mayor's wife and her parents, who represented the more traditional elements of New Parisian society, and who also happened to be the mayor's chief political and financial supporters. Which was why the mayor's liaisons with a certain Mrs Lindstrom – twelve years his junior and fifteen years younger than his wife – were such a secret. Unfortunately for the mayor, they were very much an open secret as far as the station's small band of civil servants was concerned.

It just so happened that Mrs Lindstrom was best friends with Beryl in finance, and couldn't resist filling her friend in on all the lurid details of her clandestine trysts with the other's boss. Of course, there was no way Beryl could keep something like that to herself, so she told two close colleagues at the office about it, in strictest confidence, and they each did likewise. Before long, everyone at work knew precisely what the mayor was up to when he disappeared for one of his 'very important, not to be disturbed' meetings.

Interrupting one of these 'meetings', as Sam was preparing to do, was by no means a prospect to relish.

He pressed the button, preset to activate the alarm on the mayor's pocket comm. A minute passed with no response.

"Eh, Sam, I hate to state the obvious, but the further off course we go the harder it's going to be for the engines to get us back there."

"Don't you think I know that?" He tried again, with the same lack of result. "I don't suppose you've the faintest idea where the mayor goes for these meetings of his, have you?"

"Afraid not."

Sam had a sudden thought. His head snapped up to look at Denni at the exact same instant Denni stared at him. They said together, "Beryl!" and both leapt from their seats, sprinting down the passageway towards the office marked 'finance'.

JENNER WAS LEARNING in a very direct way just how much the ship had become an extension of his body, or rather to what extent he had become a mere component of its being. He felt it when the ship took damage – not in an abstract, detached fashion, nor as acutely as if he'd taken a blow to his flesh and blood body, but in a strangely unfamiliar way which lay somewhere in between. There was instant awareness that this was *him* being injured, which his brain wanted to interpret as pain, but the nerves that would have registered said pain were not there, so the result was muted and easily dealt with, not debilitating as it might otherwise have been.

A missile detonated too close for comfort, thermal energy smashing against his hull. He could feel the outer skin of metal blister and bubble, knew without needing to check any instruments how near the hull came to rupturing; and when a concussion blast caught him in the middle of a desperate evasive flip, he could tell immediately how close the resultant torque came to tearing the frame of his vessel apart.

Yet he survived.

In every practical sense, all definition between craft and pilot had become meaningless; and Jenner loved every second of this expanded form of being. Even as he flung himself out of harm's way while delivering measured doses of destruction to the target, his spirit sang.

He might not experience damage to the other members of his group in the same direct fashion, but that didn't prevent him from 'seeing' with senses far more sophisticated than mere eyes when one needle ship exploded in a blaze of blinding energy, and he knew immediately when another went inert and started tumbling away from the battle in the general direction of this system's sun.

Yet they were winning. Despite the advantage of superior weaponry, much of which was still beyond the grasp of ULAW experts, *The Noise Within* had clearly been caught cold by the needle ships' stealth and accuracy, losing her main drive and several primary weapon systems before even knowing she was in a fight. The pirate's ripostes were now becoming more sporadic and less focused. This was a crippled ship which would never be able to leave the system unaided.

But she still had teeth.

As if mounting one final act of defiance, *The Noise Within* suddenly let loose with multiple salvos from her surviving weapons, focusing on her three remaining tormentors. Jenner threw his ship into a long elliptical curve, initially taking him away from the pirate and out of the firing line of the assorted energy weapons which she had just discharged. Three missiles came after him. He littered his wake with decoys and interference, physical chaff and electronic ghosts – packages of code squirted towards the missiles, designed to penetrate and befuddle their guidance systems. One pursuer took the bait and veered off in completely the wrong direction following a ship that wasn't there, while a second detonated, too distant to cause any damage to its retreating target; but the third came on.

Jenner's craft boasted a single aft-mounted cannon, but it was rendered useless in this situation by the wake of his own drive. The missile was sticking firmly to his course and closing; the curve that Jenner had embarked on was not acute enough to grant him a clear shot past his own wash, and if he attempted to turn any tighter and so gain a better perspective, it would reduce the speed of his escape and allow the pursuing missile to close all the quicker. A dilemma he needed to solve swiftly or the missile would be too close for it to matter.

Seeing no other option, Jenner threw his ship into the tightest turn he could, bringing him almost sideways-on to the missile that streaked unerringly towards his midriff. At the same time, he fired the cannon as soon as a clear shot presented itself.

The missile exploded. Too close, much too close. He felt his hull rupture, precious air and vital fluids spewing into the void, while the ship as a whole was tossed sidewise and twisted, as if caught in a giant hand which then attempted to bend and crumple it where no joints existed to accommodate such actions. Desperately he tried to compensate for the force of the blast; he fired the craft's multitude of manoeuvring thrusters in a dazzlingly quick sequence, improvising to relieve the tension and prevent the ship from snapping in two. For a horrifying second he thought he had failed, but then he felt the pressure ease and knew that the worst was over.

Conscious of the enormous strain the encounter had placed on the craft's chassis, he treated it gently, almost tenderly, as he brought his ship's course fully under control again. Then it was just a matter of assessing the damage to the hull, diverting certain vital fluids from ruptured conduits, pumping quick-hardening sealant foam into the hull rupture while sealing off the compromised compartments, and rebuilding command structures to those systems disrupted by the damage. Within a handful of seconds he was ready to rejoin the battle.

That violent outpouring of munitions might not have been *The Noise Within's* death throes but it was certainly an act that smacked of desperation, and Jenner was not in the least surprised to discover the fight was all but over.

As he approached the stricken pirate, a message came in from Fina, one of the other pilots, to say that her ship had been severely damaged during the last bombardment and so she was forced to withdraw, but that still left his own craft plus one other, which even now danced around the larger ship, inflicting wounds. A single rail gun appeared to be *The Noise Within's* only remaining defiance. It spat shards of molten metal at him, but he avoided those with ease before pulling the pirate's last tooth with one brief, precisely aimed burst.

Throughout the fierce engagement there had been no attempt to communicate by either side, no quarter offered and none asked for; but now, when he was in a position to do so on his own terms, or at least ULAW's, it was time to talk. Jenner prepared to hail *The Noise Within* and demand her surrender.

Given the potentially lethal consequences of a collision, proximity alarms were standard on just about any ship you cared to mention, but not on the needle ships. Their pilots didn't need anything to alert them to whatever their ship might have detected; they *were* the ship, receiving data directly from the sensors.

So it was that Jenner knew immediately when a ship started to emerge into normal space close to the battle scene. That should have been impossible. According to every rule of science he had ever been taught, no wormhole could possibly open here, this close to a sun. Clearly, there was a rule or two he had yet to hear about.

The craft that began to take shape was huge – far larger than any vessel Jenner had ever seen before. It dwarfed *The Noise Within*, let alone their needle ships. Yet the size was only the first thing to impress the young pilot. The greatest shock lay in her shape, her design. Bulbous and inelegant, with great spines that swept forward from behind what would otherwise have been her nose like the tentacles of some mythical deep space monster, to form a perfect circle with their tips, well in advance of the ship's main body. These spines alone were each some ten times the length of the needle ships.

The whole vessel screamed one thing: alien.

Yet, once he discounted those ominous spines and considered the rest of this bloated, disfigured craft, he *could* perhaps see a vague resemblance to something he recognised – *The Noise Within*.

As Jenner watched this apparition, half the sensors on his hull began to report a change. Nothing to do with proximity this time; energy was starting to build in the circle formed by the spine tips – a staggering amount of energy, though he couldn't identify its type or purpose.

A call came in from Muller, pilot of the other still functional needle ship, "Well, skip, what do we do now?"

An excellent question. Jenner dedicated all of his human/ AI fused intelligence to analysing the matter for a split second before giving his considered answer: "Hanged if I know."

BERYL IN FINANCE claimed to have no idea where the mayor and Mrs Lindstrom had gone in search of a little privacy. New Paris wasn't *that* big, however, there couldn't be too many options. None the less, Sam and Denni hesitated about making a public appeal which would inevitably flush out the two lovers but would almost certainly expose them in the process. The mayor would be disgraced and out of a job and, most likely, so would they.

Yet, as they watched the station slide ever further from its proper course, they were forced to contemplate the unthinkable.

"He must have recorded it somewhere," Denni muttered. He had hacked into the mayor's personal account and was searching through files. "I mean, what if he dropped dead all of a sudden?" At that thought Denni stopped what he was doing and looked up at Sam. "You have yours, haven't you?"

"Yes," Sam admitted, "in files that will open to my successor after I'm legally declared dead."

"Oh," Denni looked crestfallen. "Do you reckon he's done the same then?"

"Most probably."

"So I'm wasting my time."

"I reckon so."

New Paris continued to slide ever further away from a stable orbit. The two friends looked at each other, both knowing they were out of options.

"Well," Sam said, "I guess it's down to me. Goodbye job, it was nice knowing you."

At which point, the phone rang. An old-fashioned piece of retro-kitsch which Sam had insisted on having installed – mock handset and all. Sam and Denni stared at it for a second, then at each other, daring to hope. Taking a deep breath, Sam answered. The contact was audio only, but the caller was unmistakably the mayor – a decidedly pissed-off mayor – who wanted to know what the hell was going on. Sam mouthed a silent "thank you, Beryl," and proceeded to tell him.

Moments later, with the mayor hightailing it back to his office as fast as he could manage, the two friends keyed in the requisite ten digit code and activated New Paris's engines. Sam even thought to make a public announcement, after the engines had fired, informing people that this was just a routine course adjustment and that they should not be alarmed by any slight vibration or sense of movement.

They could leave being alarmed to Sam and Denni, who studied their screens intently, analysing the massive station's ponderous response to the attempted readjustment.

"It's not enough," Denni murmured at length, voicing what was becoming increasingly obvious to both of them. Too little too late. The delay in obtaining the mayor's part of the code had proved a critical one. Dionese IV had already begun to suck hungrily at their fragile home. "We've slipped too far off course and the engines aren't powerful enough to nudge us back on."

Over the years, New Paris had been expanded, added to both in terms of size and complexity, which had combined to almost double her original mass. The engines, although carefully maintained, had never been upgraded. They didn't need to be. After all, they were still sufficiently powerful to nudge the station back into proper orbit in the event of minor decay. Constant monitoring ensured that this was as much as they were ever asked to do. Barring an emergency, of course; such as this.

"We're screwed," Sam muttered.

WHEN SOMEBODY HAD suggested moving New Paris into a geostationary orbit a few years back, Sam had been dead against the idea. Not for any strong reason he could put his finger on, just in principle – a feeling that such a step would somehow upset the status quo. Oh, he could appreciate the reasoning behind the proposal; accepted that by remaining fixed over the same spot on the planet's surface they could establish a permanent link, a commercial elevator operating between New Paris and Dionese IV. After all, the planet had always been their main resource, and there was no denying that such a link would make transporting everything up from the surface a great deal easier. Yet he'd felt instinctively that the whole thing was wrong. Thankfully, so had many other people, and, despite strong support in some quarters, the proposal was defeated.

Now, for the first time, Sam had cause to regret that fact.

"Oh for a working elevator," he said, mostly to himself. It would have made planning the evacuation of the entire station a whole lot easier.

The comment might have been intended as rhetorical but

clearly it had been louder than he realised. "Wouldn't be much help," Denni said. "The elevator would have been the first thing to go when we were knocked out of orbit – torn to shreds."

"Yes, I know." Sam sighed. "Just daydreaming."

"Glad you've got the time to."

Not that either of them did, of course. Planning the emergency evacuation of a tad under 13,000 people from the stricken station was keeping them more than occupied. By Sam's reckoning, if they were to commandeer every available ship and set up a non-stop shuttle from the dock to the planet below, they could get everyone off in a little over three days. Assuming, that is, that everything went smooth as a baby's bottom and there were no glitches of any sort. The only problem being that, if Denni's calculations were correct – and he had no reason to doubt them – they had something less than two and a half days before things turned decidedly hairy up here.

The stark reality was that unless they could conjure up a minor miracle, more than two thousand New Parisians were not going to make it. So, Sam was now busy looking into supplies of spacesuits, oxygen, rocket sleds – anything that might enable as many people as possible to survive off-station until a ship could return to collect them.

It wasn't looking good.

JENNER WATCHED AS the energy continued to build within the 'claw' at the prow of the enormous vessel. He had no idea of its purpose but presumed it was nothing good.

He tried hailing. "This is Captain Jenner to unidentified craft. You are in ULAW space. Please identify yourself and power down your weapon."

He received exactly the response anticipated – none – but determined to give it one more try. "If you do not power down your weapon you will leave me with no choice but to treat this as an act of aggression and respond accordingly."

Silence.

"All right, Muller, follow my lead and give her all you've got."

The two needle ships leapt forward. Still the energy levels cupped within the intruder's crown of tips continued to build. Like gnats attacking a bull, the ULAW vessels closed in. Muller must have realised this was tantamount to an act of suicide, even as he did, but neither of them wavered, which made Jenner feel oddly proud. He let loose with his primary energy cannon, following up with secondary guns for good measure. Beside him, Muller did the same.

Their attack spent itself against an energy shield, the section immediately in front of them lighting up as beams dissipated and missiles detonated, their fury and force quenched. Where Jenner's primary beam struck, strands of impermanent silver lightning flickered across an area of shield lit up in a pale blue nimbus of coruscating energies, but none of it broke through. What he found most disconcerting was the fact that the interloper made no effort to respond, as if their efforts were beneath its notice.

We might as well be chucking stones at the thing. Yet they had to keep doing something. The long body of this enigmatic ship, with its still-building sphere of controlled energy which surely had to be reaching some sort of critical point soon, was orientated directly towards New Paris.

"Muller, centre your beam on exactly the same section of the shield I'm hitting. Between us we might just be able to break through." A forlorn hope, but better than none.

As the other needle ship adjusted his attack to comply, Jenner sensed a change. The accumulation of energy at the alien ship's prow – he could only think of this intruder as alien – had lasted no more than a few seconds, though it had seemed far longer. Now it stopped.

The ship fired on New Paris.

12,860 people: the station's current population according to official records. If Jenner could have redoubled his efforts he would have, but he was already throwing everything he had at the intruder. His secondary weapons were now exhausted and his primary was already firing at maximum – something he could let continue for a while yet, but not indefinitely without exhausting his ship's power.

All he could do was watch with a growing sense of frustration and impotence as the intruder struck. The alien didn't release the tight knot of gathered energies in one shot as the needle ship pilot anticipated, but instead bled it into a stream of energy which bridged the gap between aggressor and victim. Jenner's instruments recorded the energy ball's depletion and he felt more than a little awed by the forces brought into play. He also studied New Paris, waiting to see the beam's effect. If he was anticipating a violent explosion, or anything else dramatic for that matter, he was disappointed. In fact, initial observations suggested the alien energy was doing nothing whatsoever. Jenner immediately accessed recent observations, analysing the space station as it appeared to him then and as it had previously, taking into account current position, trajectories, and anticipated orbital course. Having set those parameters, the effect of the intervention became immediately clear.

"Muller, cease firing!"

Wherever this strange, unsettling craft originated from, she was not attacking New Paris at all, but was rather saving it.

THE GENERAL POPULACE of New Paris remained oblivious to the approaching disaster. Sam knew that the inevitable public announcement could not be put off for much longer, but this was one thing he was determined to leave to the mayor, when and if the bastard ever put in an appearance. The man had promised to come straight back to the office, but, as yet, no sign.

"Any more word from the boss?" he asked, knowing full well that Denni would have said if there had been.

"Are you kidding? He's probably halfway to the dock by now."

Sam smiled thinly. "I doubt that very much. He wouldn't dare. It would mean having to explain to people why he wasn't here with us when the emergency broke. Mrs Mayor would be especially interested."

"True," Denni agreed. He then produced a startled, "Whoa!"

"Care to expand on 'whoa'?"

"Check your screens."

Sam cleared away local contact details and returned his screen to the default monitoring display. What he saw there made no sense at all. According to this, New Paris was adjusting orbit again, her course slowly but surely veering away from the projected decay curve and creeping back towards stability.

"This day just gets weirder by the minute," Denni muttered.

Sam would have had to agree but was too busy searching for an explanation. He was getting the oddest readings from all over the station, readings which spoke of gentle stress, of something pulling the station in a very specific direction, almost as if New Paris were suddenly being subjected to gravitational pull from a planetary body or moon which couldn't possibly be there. He pushed the sensors outward, seeking an explanation, and froze.

"Denni, patch your screen into mine and take a look at this."

"Will do." Denni's fingers danced across his screen. Then, "What in mercy's name is that?"

"No idea, but whatever it is, I'm not complaining. Somehow, that thing is pulling us back into a stable orbit."

"It has to be some sort of ULAW secret weapon; a super ship or something."

"Maybe," Sam said, far from convinced.

"Well what else could it be?"

He didn't even want to think about that.

The pair watched spellbound as, with agonising slowness, proper orbit was restored. Sam sat and watched the final alignment with a huge grin on his face. He had rarely if ever felt so relieved, so excited and so drained, all at the same time.

"Shit!" Denni suddenly exclaimed.

"What now?" Sam's anxiety came flooding back. He suffered a moment of déjà-vu and feared some new calamity – perhaps the station's structural frame, weakened by the initial hit, was showing signs of buckling under the strain of all this unaccustomed manoeuvring.

"The evac won't be happening now, right?"

"Hopefully not," Sam replied, wondering what he was missing.

"That's what I thought. Have you any idea how much time and effort I put into those frigging calculations?" Denni complained. "All for nothing."

Sam stared at his friend in astonishment. "You are kidding me, right?"

Denni stared back for long seconds, deadpan, as if wondering what the hell Sam was on about. Then he broke into a broad grin. "Yeah, I'm kidding you. Well spotted."

CHAPTER EIGHTEEN

As THE MAN on the spot, Leyton was kept ridiculously busy, even after the cavalry arrived. When ULAW did eventually turn up they did so in force, and New Paris quickly took on the semblance of a territory under occupation. Suddenly the place was crowded and there were officials, experts and uniforms everywhere.

Leyton did not hold back when making his report, and was scathing about the part that the station's mayor had played in events, or rather the lack of one. Local gossip, which had it that the man was busy rutting with some married woman when he should have been taking charge, did nothing to improve the eyegee's opinion. The fact that these rumours had even reached an outsider such as himself suggested to Leyton that just about everyone else on New Paris had probably heard them as well. He was not in the least surprised when it was announced that the mayor had decided to step down due to 'the stress of recent events'.

If the eyegee had hoped that officialdom's arrival would mark an end to his own responsibilities, he was sadly mistaken. Rather than simply being debriefed and then spirited away ready for the next assignment, he found himself frequently at Benson's side. His boss seemed to be in charge of things here, which caused Leyton to seriously re-evaluate the man's importance within ULAW.

It also made him uneasy. Benson had always shunned the

limelight and been content to operate from behind the scenes. This sudden stepping forward from the shadows suggested big changes, presumably triggered by the arrival of the Byrzaens. One thing Leyton knew well was that such an obvious public persona could be a very handy distraction for those who chose to remain out of sight. When he examined the shadows Benson had left behind, it was invariably the same face he saw skulking there – the man Benson had been so chummy with during the original mission briefing prior to Frysworld. Leyton had subsequently learnt that his name was Beck but had been able to uncover little beyond that.

A spook, almost certainly. The eyegee had taken an instant dislike the first time he saw the man, and had seen nothing since to cause him to revise that opinion. Fortunately, he had little cause to deal with Beck directly.

It was Benson who introduced him to the hastily appointed 'acting' mayor, who insisted on simply being called 'Sam' and was evidently one of the people left to cope with the actual work during the crisis while his predecessor was screwing around. Sam at least threatened to be competent, which was the very minimum New Paris would need with all that was going on around her.

Leyton was intrigued to hear that two humans had been found aboard *The Noise Within*, each safely sealed within individual compartments. Typically, he learnt of this first via a news report. No names were given.

Two. Even assuming Hammond hadn't returned with the shuttle before ULAW attacked, that still left three on board which meant that one of the crew hadn't made it. He wondered who.

The report went on to say that ULAW had taken the two men into custody with a view to prosecuting them for acts of piracy. Hardly surprising, though the Byrzaens' intervention, pleading the pair's case, was a little more so. The aliens were evidently requesting leniency on the basis that the presence of humans aboard *The Noise Within* had been a key factor in the ship regaining mental equilibrium and, belatedly, resuming its intended mission.

Knowing the way that ULAW officials were falling over themselves to curry favour with their new allies, the eyegee strongly suspected the Byrzaens would get their way.

Someone else who remained at the forefront of things was Philip Kaufman. Leyton had half expected him to vanish off to the land of privilege and luxury now that the big revelations were out the way, but Kaufman was having none of it. His general expertise and specific knowledge of *The Noise Within* made him invaluable to Benson, who kept him on as a consultant, which meant that he and the eyegee saw a fair bit of each other. Leyton's respect for Kaufman rose as he watched him work and went up a notch higher still when he discovered that the businessman was responsible for developing the human/AI melding which drove the ULAW needle ships.

As for the three surviving needle ship pilots, they were the darlings of the hour as far as the media were concerned. Their titanic struggle against the 'alien pirate vessel' made them instant celebrities. This turnaround demonstrated perfectly just how fickle the media could be. Mere days ago they had been enthusiastically championing *The Noise Within*, painting her as daring and dashing, thumbing defiance at the authorities. Now they fêted her conquerors with equal zeal.

Leyton found the whole media circus repulsive, and habitually avoided the reporters who had swarmed to New Paris like flies to freshly dropped dung.

He hadn't actually seen a Byrzaen in the flesh as yet; few people had. The aliens were keeping themselves pretty much to themselves. Not that he could blame them for that. Given the crowded condition of New Paris since ULAW and the battalions of reporters that had arrived, he'd be doing much the same himself given half a chance.

He had seen images of them, of course. You couldn't check

a news feed without seeing them. Bipedal and ostensibly humanoid in appearance the Byrzaens might be, but nobody could mistake them for human as such. Longer limbed and more compact of torso, with no neck to speak of and a broader, flatter head than Homo sapiens. Most experts agreed that this spoke volumes about the nature of the world the aliens had evolved on; but unfortunately none of them seemed able to agree on exactly *what* it said.

The professional part of Leyton couldn't help but study the images from a different perspective. The compact bodies presumably meant that vital organs were more concentrated than in a human, so a body shot stood a greater chance of doing serious damage. He'd still like to know more about their anatomy before attempting one though. As for the head, it was afforded a degree of protection both by being so close to the prominent shoulders, and by what seemed to be a hood of external bone which rose from between the shoulder blades to cover the back and crown of the head. There was no evidence of any hair.

He would still favour the head shot, at least until he knew more about them. Either of the two dark and slit-like eyes *had* to provide access to the brain.

Their limbs were long and slender and didn't promise much by way of strength, but the feature Leyton found most fascinating was their hands; six digit – four fingers with two opposable thumbs, one either side of the fingers. He imagined this must give them far greater dexterity than humans and wondered exactly what such a hand was capable of doing – manipulating two entirely different objects or mechanisms simultaneously, perhaps?

If the needle ship pilots were being talked up by the media, the Byrzaens had been all but deified. After all, the 'unusual' and 'majestic' (both of which sounded a whole lot more friendly than 'ugly') alien ship had appeared out of nowhere to save fifteen thousand human lives for no reason other than pure altruism. All right, so the official population of New Paris was only 12,800 – this was what the media termed 'rounding up', to allow for visitors and those who might be unregistered – and the majority would likely have been saved anyway, but 15,000 sounded so much more impressive than 2,000, and why let mere facts interfere with a good headline?

Once Leyton set his knee jerk cynicism of all things media to one side, even he had to admit that what the aliens had done was impressive. Not only saving so many human lives but also keeping New Paris itself intact. Without their timely intervention, many of the station's citizens may well have continued living, but their homes, their society, and the lives they'd known would have been gone forever.

So, what was the Byrzaens' angle? Leyton was convinced there had to be one, they simply hadn't chosen to reveal it yet, but they would.

The alien ship, which had no name – evidently the Byrzaens were baffled by mankind's tradition of giving personalised names to inanimate objects – had been lurking just beyond the fringes of human space awaiting a summons. On board was the Byrzaen's first diplomatic mission, intended to follow up on *The Noise Within's* initial contact.

The Noise Within itself proved to hold one further surprise. The intelligence guiding the craft was not, as everyone had assumed, an AI alone. The intelligence which *The Sun Seeker* had originally been built to house had been paired with a Byrzaen, in an organic/non-organic mental fusion similar to those controlling ULAW's needle ships. The Byrzaens claimed this had been necessary to fully cure the deeply disturbed AI, but that it was also responsible for much of the subsequent trouble. The theory went that the two minds had not fused as thoroughly as the aliens had believed. The ship's return to human space provoked anxieties within the AI which made this division more acute, polarising the two parts of the ship's mind, so that in effect there were two minds working in consort rather than one fused intelligence. The AI's concerns resonated with the organic part of the pairing, since the Byrzaen was naturally nervous about first contact with an alien race, and the respective fears began to feed off each other in a disastrous loop, unbalancing both.

The aliens' attempt to initiate gentle contact between their two races by sending a ship of human origin ahead as their herald had therefore come close to backfiring spectacularly. Nice to see that mankind didn't hold a monopoly on plans going awry.

ULAW decided to hold back the revelation that an actual Byrzaen had helped to orchestrate *The Noise Within's* piratical dabblings from the media, wisely judging it to be a PR nightmare in the making.

Having heard nothing from *The Noise Within*, the Byrzaens began to probe human space, starting with New Paris where contact was supposed to be initiated. Discovering both *The Noise Within* and evidence of conflict, they came through into the system, arriving in the nick of time to save the day, establishing themselves as instant heroes and making the grandest entrance anyone could possibly wish for.

All very neat; which, in Leyton's experience, was something life rarely succeeded in being.

At that particular moment, he seemed to be the only one in the whole of human space to harbour the remotest suspicion about these Byrzaens, but he had every confidence in the fickleness of media-driven public opinion. He was willing to bide his time.

Benson and Beck were not the only two familiar faces he encountered on New Paris. ULAW had commandeered a multi-deck stack of interconnecting office units in the station's commercial district as their base of operations. It became universally referred to as simply 'the building'. One time, as Leyton left Benson's office on the building's top floor, he bumped into another old friend.

"Hello, Ed, so they've roped you in on this, have they?"

"Yeah, for my sins."

The tech, whom he remembered with a degree of respect and even fondness from the Holt mission, looked anxious. "We need to talk," the man said, "but not here."

Intriguing, and Leyton knew better than to pass such things by. "You know Gino's?" The tech nodded. "I'll be grabbing a coffee there in half an hour. I hate the vending machine crap they serve here."

Thirty minutes later found the eyegee sitting as promised on a high stool at the bar-style counter that ran around the perimeter of the small coffeehouse. He didn't look around as Ed took the seat next to him; if furtive was what the tech wanted, furtive he would be.

"I've been hoping to bump into you," Ed said quietly.

"Well, now you have; so what's this all about?"

"Holt. We've had a chance to go through all the data and records that we recovered from the mission with a fine-tooth comb, and, as expected, no evidence of any connection with a certain pirate vessel. However…"

"Go on."

Ed was either genuinely nervous about what he'd discovered or he had a fine sense of the melodramatic. He took a deep breath and glanced around, as if to check no one was watching them. "There's no question they were warned about our raid in advance. Nothing concrete in anything we brought back, but plenty of peripheral communication recorded there, which makes it pretty clear. Among all this, a name cropped up. As I say, there's no proof this is the source of the tip-off, but…"

"But you think it is."

"I'm certain of it. The context left little other option, and it was in a message which had been ostensibly deleted from the system and took a lot of effort to recover."

In a gesture fully in keeping with Ed's behaviour so far, he slapped a folded piece of paper down on the counter and slid it towards the eyegee. Paper; easy to dispose of and no electronic imprint. Leyton dropped a hand onto the now abandoned note, lifting his coffee mug with the other and draining it.

"Thanks; leave this with me."

With that he stood up, casually collecting the note as he drew his hand from the counter, before strolling out of the coffeehouse and returning to work.

PHILIP WAS HAVING a ball. The only slightly sour note was caused by the media. He was used to a certain amount of attention, had been all his life, but nothing like this. As soon as his presence on New Paris became public knowledge he found himself pursued by journos and a flock of hovering fly cams, besieged with requests for interviews and sound bites. His trip to the Byrzaen ship only saw the pressure intensify tenfold.

Philip had brought an up-to-date version of Phil with him from Homeworld, but had deliberately not called upon the partial until this point. After all, he'd been on holiday; why would a tourist need a partial? No question, though, that had changed. He was now desperate for a buffer, a secretary; and who better than Phil? The partial was activated and hastily brought up to speed, so that he could provide a much needed filter between Philip and the insatiable newshounds.

Other than this excessive media attention, things could not have been better. To actually *see* the culmination of his lifetime's work – all right, an exaggeration, but not much of one – to be able to talk to Jenner and Muller after they had been in gestalt with the needle ship's AIs, to witness them being brought out of their gelsuits after flying genuine missions and experiencing actual combat, was the realisation of so much. The experience had a surreal quality for Philip, as if this couldn't possibly be happening. It also brought him a strange sense of closure. Despite all the glitz of Frysworld and the thrills of Dendra, Velamore and the other exotic places he had visited, despite having set foot aboard *The Sun Seeker/Noise Within*, he suspected deep down that a part of him would always have felt unfulfilled without this, because he hadn't been there to oversee the final stages of the project as he'd always anticipated.

Yet now, while Catherine Chzyski, David Benn and everyone else involved, even Susan Tan, were stuck light years away on Homeworld, having to scour the news feeds for scraps of information, he was here, a part of it. Of all of them, he was the only one privileged to see the culmination of the project firsthand.

Another thing he drew great satisfaction from, not to mention relief, was that even the sight of Jenner hooked into the needle ship produced only the faintest stirrings of Syntheaven craving, allowing him to hope that his relationship with the drug was something other than addiction after all.

One of Philip's responsibilities in the aftermath of everything was to supervise the health of the needle ship pilots. This was the first time the human-AI pairings had seen active service and there was a great deal of interest in how the pilots had coped with the ramped-up mental and physical demands placed upon them. Philip was quietly impressed with the equipment ULAW provided him with. It might not have matched the specialist gear which Kaufman Industries had been forced to develop as the project progressed, but it was still more than adequate for the job, as were the small team of techs assigned to assist him.

The loss of two pilots, two people he'd known throughout their training, was a blow, but everyone involved knew that what they were developing was going to be used in the front line and that lives were bound to be at risk. No one, however, had anticipated reality would strike so soon after the project's completion.

On a more positive note, Philip was delighted to see how well the three surviving needle ship pilots – Jenner, Muller and Fina – had coped. Jenner was displaying hardly any symptoms of stress at all. The other two both showed minor reactions but no more than any normal combatant might be expected to suffer and certainly well within acceptable parameters. All in all, this was a wonderful result, and Philip could only applaud the work that Susan Tan and the team had completed so effectively in his absence. The new Syntheaven variant clearly worked a treat.

The sense of elation that Philip experienced was hard to express. His dogged pursuit of the project, in the face of harsh criticism and near ridicule in some quarters, had been fully justified. Human-AI pairings *worked* and were bound to become an integral part of human society – not merely in a military context – in generations to come. If he achieved nothing else in his life, he had at least done this much.

If this wasn't more than enough for any one man to be dealing with there was also, of course, the small matter of the Byrzaens. Mankind's first encounter with a recognisably sentient alien species, and *he* was involved. Life simply didn't get any better than this, surely.

Philip was even privileged enough to be among the first people to visit the alien ship; only the once, but it was an experience he would never forget for as long as he lived.

He tried to describe it to Leyton over lunch on one of the rare occasions both of them were able to get away, but was failing dismally.

"You mean everything on board is shifting curtains of energy?" the big man asked as his attempted description faltered into frustrated hesitation.

"No, not really, it's just that..." How could he possibly do justice to something that clearly hadn't developed within a human framework, when all he had at his disposal were words that inevitably *had*? "Those veils we saw on *The Noise Within*, the drive mechanisms, would have looked perfectly at home there, whereas they seemed so out of place on a human starship. They wouldn't have seemed remotely *alien* aboard the Byrzaen ship."

Leyton nodded.

Kaufman was getting used to this inability to articulate the sheer otherness of the gothic interior. On human ships everything was clean line efficiency, with straight-walled corridors arranged with straight-lined practicality; rooms as boxes, with every effort made to ensure thoroughfares were bright and light. The Byrzaen craft on the other hand, or at least what little he'd seen of it, was almost the opposite; it possessed a far more organic feel, with an absence of right angles and a design palette seemingly chosen to promote darkness and shadow rather than light.

"Sorry," he apologised, "I'm not doing a very good job of this, am I?"

Leyton shook his head. "No, far from it. You've done better than you realise: a description which details nothing yet explains everything." The big man almost seemed to smile in encouragement. "What about the Byrzaens themselves?"

"You've seen the news feeds…"

"Of course, but that doesn't give me a sense of what they *feel* like, how they affect you in the flesh."

"Well…" Philip thought for a second. "They're a little shorter than us, as you know, coming up to roughly my chest…" But that hardly said anything new. He tried again. "The thing that most struck me was the way they move. I don't mean how they walk, but when you're there with them, talking to them. They have a habit of not standing still, and their movements are incredibly quick and always unexpected. Sudden darts, often with their whole bodies but just as likely a single arm or even their shoulders and head." Then he added, as an afterthought, "It's as if they're constantly trying to snatch flies from the air," which was as accurate a visualisation as he could think of.

Leyton nodded, so Philip assumed the description was helpful.

Of course, the reason Philip had been allowed his single visit to the Byrzaen craft was the engines. He was the nearest thing to an expert ULAW had in such things, so it was only natural he should be given the chance to inspect the Byrzaen stardrive. He hadn't seen the drive units for long but that glimpse was enough to tantalise and make him itch to get his hands on them at a lab with full equipment and a team around him.

"They use completely different technology to us," he explained to Leyton, "based on something we've long theorised but never confirmed. Basically, they maintain that our universe exists in a state of 'false vacuum'." He looked at the eyegee, hoping to see some acknowledgement of understanding, but the other shook his head. "All right, to keep it simple, there is a theorised state of true vacuum, which our universe may one day revert to. If it ever does, the energy released by the decay process would be catastrophic, destroying *everything*. The Byrzaens have found a way of producing contained decay on a very limited scale and harnessing the resultant energy to push their ships through into a true vacuum universe and re-emerge into this one anywhere they want to. It's not instantaneous but it *is* faster than our own wormhole technology and far less restricting. That's how the Byrzaen ship was able to emerge so close to New Paris and Dionese IV."

"So you're saying the Byrzaens are messing around with forces that are capable of destroying the whole universe?"

"Potentially, yes," Philip waved a dismissive hand. Leyton seemed to be missing the point here.

"Doesn't that bother anyone?"

"Not especially. You *need* that magnitude of energy to achieve something like this, and although the potential might be destructive it's being carefully shepherded and utilised in a *con*structive manner. What could be better?" Leyton still looked far from convinced. "Look, I'm sure the Byrzaens have taken every precaution. After all, this is their universe as well; the Byrzaens are in here with us. They don't want to wipe it out. Besides, you'd be amazed at some of the cosmic forces we've played around with ourselves from time to time. No, the exciting thing about all this is what it could mean for our own society. Once we understand how they do this, it will open the way to a whole new era for humankind."

"Until someone somewhere makes a tiny mistake and there's an accident," Leyton said.

"Won't happen," Philip assured him, with far more conviction than he actually felt. He wished Leyton would lighten up. All this carping was ruining his good mood.

"How do they protect their ships? When they pass through this 'true vacuum', I mean. If the decay is as destructive as you say, how can the Byrzaens pass through without succumbing?"

"Ah, now there's a question." One which had reawoken in Philip all the old passion and hunger for discovery. Suddenly there was a new challenge, something he couldn't wait to get his teeth into.

"Doctor Kaufman? Philip?" It was a woman's voice.

"A reporter." Leyton spat the words out as if they were a curse.

Privacy was currently in short supply on New Paris. Their table was protected from uninvited intrusion by a device Leyton had brought with him – guaranteed to scramble audio and visual signals for any attempted distance recordings, apparently, but there were always those who wouldn't be deterred and it was impossible to go anywhere without the risk of some newshound discovering them.

Philip looked around, ready to issue a curt rebuff, but the words died in his mouth. "Julia?"

She looked as stunning as the first time he saw her back on Homeworld. A little more dishevelled but only marginally so, and if anything that hint of imperfection only helped to make her sexier. Gone was the elegantly coiffured hair – this was not straight from the salon glamour but rather hair that had lived life and seen things, pulled back into a bun to keep it out of her eyes. All that did was expose more of her gorgeous face. The makeup was toned down, the lip colour subtler, the eyelids delicately shaded. All this he took in during the few seconds it took her to reach them.

"What are you doing here?" he asked as she arrived.

She laughed, though there was nothing malicious in the sound. "Let me see, now." She adopted an exaggeratedly puzzled expression. "I'm a reporter; so what could possibly bring me to New Paris at the moment?"

"All right, I know – a stupid question. I'm just surprised to see you, that's all." And delighted, but presumably the idiotic grin he could feel plastered across his face had already given away that much. He remembered with a start that they were not alone. "Jim, this is Julia Cirese of Universal News. Julia, this is Jim Leyton."

"Oh, right, of course; I've seen you with Ambassador Benson, haven't I?"

She held out a hand in old-fashioned handshake. The eyegee hesitated as if debating whether to respond, but then he reached out and shook it.

"You may have done." His reply was frosty to the point of being rude, but Julia took it in her stride.

"Look, I didn't come over here to interrupt you gents, I just wanted to say hello."

Surely she wasn't going already? "Why don't you sit down, join us?" Philip said quickly, hoping that didn't come across as desperate. He leapt to his feet and his hand fell to the back of a vacant chair, ready to pull it out from under the table.

"No, really," she said, all smiles, "I can't stay. I was just on my way to an appointment. But thank you."

Damn! This seemed to be the story of his life, as least where Julia Cirese was concerned.

"Perhaps at some point, though, if you can find the time, we could do that interview we were trying to sort out?"

"Yes, of course," he said instantly.

"And I seem to remember the promise of dinner…?"

How could any smile be that coy and at the same time so alluring? And had there ever been anyone more beautiful? "I do vaguely remember something of the sort, now you come to mention it," he said, recovering a little of his poise. "Would this evening suit you?" The sooner the better; he was not about to let *anything* get in the way this time.

Somehow, her smile managed to become even more dazzling. "That would suit me just fine."

He realised with a start how close they were, far closer than they had been in the car park back on Homeworld, probably due to the crowded nature of the restaurant. He instinctively leaned forward a little, and was it his imagination or did she lean in as well?

"Until this evening, then." She breathed the words as much as spoke them. No question that she was leaning towards him now. The fingertips of her right hand rested on his chest as she craned her neck to kiss him. It was a chaste press of lips against lips, but one which lingered and left Philip wanting a great deal more.

She stepped back. "I'll wricu details of where I'm staying."

He grinned anew. "See you tonight." He could still feel the impression of her lips, and when he licked them there was a hint of scented flavour –Turkish delight, perhaps.

He sat down once Julia had left, to find Leyton shaking his head in obvious disapproval. "Never trust anyone in the media," the big man advised.

Philip laughed. "Careful, Jim, you're letting your prejudices show."

"That's not prejudice, it's just plain common sense."

Philip took a sip of water. It suddenly felt uncomfortably hot in here – doubtless a reaction to seeing Julia again. Her unexpected appearance had affected him more than he realised, he was even feeling a little lightheaded.

"Philip, are you all right?" That was Leyton speaking, but it took Philip a second to realise the question was addressed to him.

"Yes, yes... just a little hot, that's all. Need some air."

He tugged at the neck of his top. When did it become so tight? Silly of him to have put such a close-fitting one on this morning, really. He stood up, determined to leave the suddenly claustrophobic restaurant, but the whole room swayed as he did so, forcing him to slump back into the chair. That didn't stop the room from swaying, in fact it was getting worse, everything began to spin, and he was finding it increasingly hard to breathe, causing his chest to heave. And his head felt heavy. Perhaps if he were to rest it on the table for a bit everything would stop moving and he'd be all right.

Someone had caught hold of him, was stopping him from putting his head down. Words washed over him, their meaning of no interest. Breathing became harder still. He closed his eyes and wished it would all just go away.

And it did.

CHAPTER NINETEEN

"ALL RIGHT, NYLES, so where do we go from here?"

They were too late. Only by a fraction, but by such narrow margins history was often decided. *The Rebellion* had arrived at the New Paris system in the aftermath of the battle, so missing the opportunity to influence the outcome and ensure things happened the way they would have wanted. The sense of deflation was enormous. This was the moment they had waited for all their lives and it had somehow escaped them, an opportunity that passed without their being able to grasp it. Kethi felt frustrated as hell and didn't doubt that everyone else felt the same. This was their destiny, and they'd just watched it go by.

They emerged into normal space shortly after the Byrzaen ship had completed its spectacular rescue of the space station; so spectacular, Kethi gathered, that most New Parisians remained oblivious throughout the whole process and had to be told about it afterwards.

They picked up comms from the attendant ULAW needle ships and realised that any intervention at this juncture would be pointless and potentially counterproductive, so they held back, waiting and watching. Which was essentially what they had been doing ever since; haunting the fringes of the system, lying low whenever ULAW traffic reached its highest, while eavesdropping on the news feeds the whole time.

Morale on board had taken an enormous blow and continued

to spiral downward. This was not what they had left the habitat after a generation of self-imposed isolation to do – skulk in the shadows while the enemy were proclaimed heroes. All of a sudden, saving mankind was looking a lot more complicated than it had ever promised to be.

Something needed to be done before things on the ship got any worse. There had been no talk of mutiny as yet, but, the way things were going, Kethi wouldn't rule it out, and if Nyles wasn't prepared to take the initiative of his own volition, she was going to damn well force him to.

He looked up as she stormed in, and the sight of him, this man she had known all her life, shocked her. It was not so much that he looked old, it was the fact that he looked so frail and, worst of all, defeated.

"Nyles?"

"What do you want me to say, Kethi?" he said. "Do you want me to say that I'm at a loss, that I don't know what to suggest after this? Because that's the truth – I haven't the faintest idea what we should do." He laughed; a brief, bitter cough of sound. "I'm old, Kethi; too old for all of this.

"Have you ever studied history?" She judged the question to be rhetorical, since he knew full well that she had. "I have," he continued. "It used to be a hobby of mine. And you know something that always amused me?"

"What, Nyles?" she asked softly. They needed this man – she and all the habitat's adherents – now more than ever. Seeing him fall apart like this scared her. Forget alien spaceships, this was Nyles, the cornerstone of their whole community.

"How different cultures have viewed their old folk. There have been those that scorned them, considering them to be out of touch and no longer useful, mere burdens on society that had outlived their purpose. On the other hand, there have been others who revered them for their accumulated knowledge, equating age with wisdom." He shook his head. "Both views are wrong, you know. Age doesn't mean automatic redundancy and it certainly isn't a guarantee of wisdom, it's just getting old. Nothing more, nothing less."

The bitterness in his voice alarmed her all the more, and she felt the need to speak, to offer something in the face of this apparent despair. "Perhaps," she said, "those cultures which revered age were the more enlightened ones. I'm not so sure it was age itself they valued so much as the experience and insight which a longer life can grant a person."

He smiled, an expression containing a suggestion of warmth this time. "A nice thought. Thank you, Kethi."

"We can't stop now, Nyles. If we just slip away and sneak back to the habitat we will have failed. Not just us but the whole community. The alien threat predicted by William Anderson has finally arrived. We can't let that go unchallenged. If we go back now without doing anything at all then what's it all been for?

"People are already restless, Nyles. They'll leave, and that will be the end of it. Our whole lives will have been a complete waste of time."

"I know, Kethi, I know. But what can we do? As you say, the dreaded aliens have arrived and they're being hailed as *heroes*, which pulls the ground away from beneath our feet and leaves us with nowhere to go."

"I've been thinking about that, and I might have come up with an idea, a Plan B as it were."

He looked at her sharply now, a spark of hope showing in his eyes. "Go on."

"While going through the last batch of data our mole sent us, I stumbled across something which intrigued me. I followed it up and the implications offer us an opportunity."

"Is this something tangible, or are you making connections and intuiting possibilities?"

"The latter," she admitted.

Nyles shook his head. "Kethi, we can't afford to take a chance on something like that, especially not now."

She probably shouldn't have been surprised by such a response but she was. "For pity's sake, Nyles, this is what I do! You know that." Surely the man could see that now more than ever they needed to be bold. "Why did you have me second guess Morkel's recommendation of where *The Noise Within* would strike next? Why do you consult me on every damned decision that involves analysis and extrapolation?"

He sighed. "Because of your talent for reading between the lines and constructing hidden meaning from the flimsiest of clues and apparently unrelated facts. But it's hardly an exact science, Kethi, and right now, after this fiasco, we can't afford to have anything else blow up in our faces."

"It's precisely because of this fiasco that we *have* to take the chance, Nyles. We need to produce something out of the hat or the habitat fails. You know it as well as I do."

"Granted, but that doesn't mean we put our faith into the first harebrained scheme that occurs to us just for the sake of doing something!"

"Harebrained? Thanks. Why do you bother having me around at all then?"

"You know I didn't mean it like that, I'm sorry. Blame it on fatigue."

"Look, Nyles, do you really think I would have even bothered mentioning this to you without first checking and double checking my conclusions? I'm fully confident that the logic construct holds. At least hear me out and take a look at what I've uncovered before you dismiss the idea out of hand, will you?"

"Very well." He visibly gathered himself, favouring her with a wry smile which seemed to suggest there was still some fight left in his aging body after all.

"Sorry, Kethi, of course," said the old Nyles, the Nyles she knew so well. "Let's see what you've got."

As HE HURRIED from the restaurant Leyton made the time to call Benson, who was in a meeting and couldn't be disturbed.

He was put through to Beck, which struck him as a disturbing development, but simply left a message for Benson to call him back. Next he contacted the new mayor. "I need you to close the docks," he said, not having the time to be anything other than blunt.

"Not a chance," Sam replied. "We've got traffic in and out constantly, more than we've ever seen before. If I tried to shut that down there'd be a riot."

"Not if you have a good enough reason. Someone's just tried to assassinate Philip Kaufman, and they'll be making for the docks."

There was no question in his mind that Kaufman had been poisoned, nor did he doubt who was responsible. The two of them were eating and drinking at the restaurant with no ill effects at all before that reporter, Julia Cirese, appeared, so he had ruled out the idea of anything being poisoned in the kitchen or slipped into the food by a nimble-fingered waiter. It could only have been the reporter. The one thing Kaufman had touched after she'd gone was the glass of water, and she hadn't gone anywhere near that, so it had to have been the kiss. A toxin smeared on her lips – something she'd been immunised against or perhaps one genetically tailored to become active only when it entered a specific target. The mechanism didn't matter; the act itself did.

"What? Is Kaufman all right?" Sam sounded shocked.

"Still in the balance. I've left him in good hands."

Fortunately he hadn't needed to call for a doctor; there was one on hand almost before Kaufman collapsed – an off-duty ULAW medical officer dining at a nearby table who had noticed the man's distress. Leyton had briefed him as best he could, rattling off the few details he knew: "Poison, ingested through the mouth, probably not in any of the food or drink. Check his lips for residue." Then he left the doctor to do what he did best while he went to do the same.

"You say the assassin will be heading for the docks?"

"Bound to. She'll be wanting to get off the station as quickly as possible." After attempting such an audacious assassination, where else could she go?

"She?"

"Oh yes, definitely a she."

"Where are you now?"

"Going after her."

"I can send you a security detail as backup..."

"No, I'll take care of this. They wouldn't know who to look for. Just close down the docks in case I don't catch up with her."

"I'll see what I can do but I can't promise anything. The dock owners have been raking it in over the past few days. They've never had it this good and won't appreciate me interfering."

"Do what you can."

"I will, and I'll have security waiting at the docks just in case."

He was outside now, trying to orientate himself, and felt compelled to call upon an old friend he had been hoping to live without. "Gun, what's the quickest route to the docks?"

"Straight on, then take the first left-branching corridor." No recrimination at his recent silence, but why would there be from a machine, a tool?

Leyton had managed to replace the visor abandoned on Frysworld but hadn't bothered wearing it for lunch; after all, who needs a high-tech visor in order to eat a steak? The gun he carried with him everywhere, despite their recent rift.

The left branch which the gun had told him to take proved to be one of the station's arterial thoroughfares. Wide, high-ceilinged, and boasting a mezzanine level on either side courtesy of raised walkways – the highwalks – which were interlinked at regular intervals by gauze-floored bridges spanning the thoroughfare. Both sides, on two levels, were bordered by shops. Identical units fitted out by their individual owners to display all manner of goods, from foodstuffs to clothing, leisure goods to essential equipment. This was the retail heart of New Paris and was probably the single busiest corridor on the whole station. Naturally this was the route along which Leyton was going to have to pursue a fleeing assassin; how could it possibly have been any other?

The way ahead was an endless sea of bobbing heads and moving forms, a haphazard mix of military, ULAW and civil uniforms interspersed with the various fashion choices of New Parisian citizens.

Somebody tugged at Leyton's arm. He broke the grip, seized the wrist of whoever it was and span around, knife at the ready, to find himself facing a terrified youth clutching a dozen Byrzaen facemasks in his free hand. The boy's eyes were as wide as his abruptly gaping mouth. The thin plastiform masks proceeded to slip from his uncertain grasp, sliding to the ground one by one.

"I j... just wanted to ask if you'd like to buy a mask," the boy said, holding out the last one left to him and looking to be on the verge of tears.

Leyton scowled, let go of the lad's wrist and hurried on, leaving the kid to scrabble around on his knees, trying to reclaim his fallen goods.

Full marks for spotting a developing market and moving quickly to supply it, but Byrzaen facemasks? What next, for goodness sake?

The woman was nowhere in sight, but she *had* to be making for the docks. Leyton checked his own logic as he went, to ensure he hadn't overlooked something. New Paris was not that big. If she stayed here she would inevitably be caught. Getting off the station as soon as possible was her only chance. No, it was definitely the docks.

He started to jog, constantly having to pause in order to sidestep and shuffle through the crowd. Progress was patchy, but he took comfort from the thought that his quarry would be suffering similar problems. The highwalk to his right looked to be the best bet – fewer people – so at the first opportunity he raced up a flight of steps and went that way.

He was able to pick up speed here, running rather than stop-start jogging. He scanned the street ahead and below, trying to visualise what Julia Cirese had been wearing and pick anyone from the crowd dressed in similar fashion. The bitter truth was that while the woman herself might be striking, her clothes were anything but, presumably chosen for that very reason. A plain white top, sleeveless, and navy blue full-length trousers, and her hair had been tied back. Any one of those details could have changed, of course – smart trousers would adjust their length in a second and a hair band could easily be removed – but he had to start somewhere.

The one thing in his favour was that Julia Cirese would not want to draw attention to herself, whereas he didn't care. She'd be hurrying, no doubt, but not running, not charging recklessly as he could. Her head start ought to be vanishing with every stride.

Speaking of reckless, he began to have a suspicion as to why there were so few people on this highwalk, as he hurdled a chain slung across his path holding a red sign on which white lettering declared 'keep out, men at work'.

There was now nobody ahead of him and he was able to pile on some real speed.

The corridors throughout much of New Paris were arranged in grid fashion, as any dirtside town might be, which meant that the central thoroughfare Leyton was charging down had intersections. Normally, not an issue; the highwalks bridged the gap in similar fashion to the mesh footbridges linking opposite walkways, continuing on the far side. This time, however, the highwalk ended abruptly at the edge of the bisecting passageway, and, although it continued on the far side, the only thing in between was empty space. At least Leyton now knew what the 'men' were working on, though he'd yet to see anyone actually doing so.

He didn't want to lose time by going all the way back to the last flight of stairs, and it wasn't as if the passage was *that* wide. Without pausing to think things through beyond this, he pushed even harder, arms pumping as he attacked the last few steps with everything he had. His right foot came down immediately before the gap – a low-heel landing which flowed instantly into a flat-footed plant, providing the platform he needed to launch himself across the empty passageway. He punched his left elbow backward while thrusting the left knee and his chin and shoulders upward, and then he was in the air. He fought to keep his body upright, cycling his legs to prevent himself from flipping forwards, and tried to focus beyond the far edge of the passageway. Suddenly the other side of the highwalk came racing towards him.

He brought his legs up so that his feet took the brunt of the impact on landing, momentum carrying him forward onto his knees and then into a roll, all the while bleeding momentum. He skidded to a halt on the seat of his pants, with feet and hands helping to stop him, palms stinging where they'd been grazed as they dragged across the floor.

From behind he could hear a few cheers and whistles, presumably from those in the passageway below who had unexpectedly seen a figure hurtling over their heads. The eyegee sprang to his feet and resumed running, hurdling the 'keep out' chain this side of the gap so that he was among people again and forced to slow down.

Still he scanned the crowds below.

Even so, he almost missed her.

Her hair was now worn loose and a powder blue top had been pulled on over the white one. His gaze slid past her at first but something made him look again. Afterwards, Leyton could not have said specifically what raised his suspicions, whether it was the hurried gait or some feature which matched with subconscious memory and snagged his attention, but his observational training paid off in some manner. He had her.

She was still a little ahead but he drew level in no time, and she hadn't spotted him. His first instinct was to mount the highwalk's handrail and leap on top of her before she even knew he was there, but she was towards the middle of the passage and there were people constantly around her. He was bound to floor and potentially hurt a few passersby as well as his target if he tried that. Besides, people were likely to react as he climbed the handrail, if only in puzzlement, which would warn the assassin and give her every chance of dodging him.

So he hung back a little, staying just behind her, no longer running but matching her still fairly rapid pace as he waited for the next stairway.

When it arrived, he trotted down the steps arriving at the floor of the corridor with the girl slightly ahead.

"Gun, how long until we reach the docks?"

"Given this current rate of progress, a little over five minutes."

He worked his way through the crowds towards the still oblivious Cirese, knowing that he could simply hang back, wait until they arrived at the docks and then summon security, but he had no intention of doing so. This was personal. She had stood there, smiled at him, and then blithely poisoned the person he was having lunch with.

He approached as quickly as the circumstances allowed, coming in at an angle from behind her right shoulder. Yet something alerted her, some reaction from the people around them. The woman glanced back at the last moment, saw him, recognised him, *knew* why he was there.

She ducked, spun, and evaded his grasp. She was fast, he'd grant her that much. Her foot struck against his ribs with bruising force, and was gone before he could react.

Another kick, this one higher, aimed at his head; but he was ready for her this time. He ducked, blocked, grasped her ankle before she could withdraw, and twisted. Either her whole body had to twist as well or her ankle or knee would pop and most likely break. She went with the twist and landed face down but kicked out viciously with her free foot as she fell, connecting with his left forearm, and managed to pull her trapped ankle free.

Leyton lunged forward, intending to pin her down. But again she was too quick, rolling out of the way and springing back up. He followed, to grapple with her as she came to her feet. Julia Cirese might have been comparatively slight but she knew how to fight, punching him twice in the kidneys in rapid succession and bringing her knee up hard – which, had he not blocked it, would have landed in his groin.

Losing patience, he punched her in her oh-so-pretty face.

She crumpled, to lie there for a second with a seemingly dazed expression before hauling herself to her knees. There was a hint of movement and something appeared in her hand – a sonic knife. He had no idea of its specific blade length and didn't intend to find out.

Displaying comparable deftness, the gun appeared in his own hand, pointing directly at her.

"It's over, Julia. Put down the knife."

"Get away from me, you bastard!" She suddenly looked terrified, vulnerable, and as beautiful as ever, despite the already swelling bruise. "Help, somebody, please; he's going to kill me!"

Leyton had to admit that she played the damsel in distress to perfection. A crude circle had formed around them while they fought, as others cleared out of their way but stayed to watch. Leyton felt like some unwitting performer within a ring of morbidly curious onlookers. Except that some of those onlookers now chose to encroach. He couldn't blame them. If he hadn't just watched this woman poison his friend, he might have been tempted to help her himself.

"Stay back!" he warned two men who had started to come towards him from his left. "I'm a ULAW officer and this is *not* a helpless girl but a very clever assassin."

"How can you say such things?" the vulnerable, wronged

girl that Cirese had transformed into sobbed. "Don't listen to him, please."

Yet the two men stopped, looking at each other for guidance. He knew they were no longer a threat. Almost too late he sensed someone rushing him from behind. He sidestepped, half turned, and kicked, his foot connecting with a burly man in military greens; then he stepped back in to punch the surprised soldier, who went down.

From the corner of his eye he saw Julia Cirese smile.

Something struck him on the back of the head; an object thrown from the crowd, solid enough to hurt though not to draw blood. Distracted, he let them get too close. A surge this time, not just one person but four or five, all in army uniform – the fallen soldier's friends, presumably. They were on him, not attempting to punch but to grapple. He went down under the assault.

So far, Leyton had been holding back, even when he punched Julia, but he'd had more than enough of this and abruptly all thought of constraint vanished. With a roar of anger, he punched upwards with everything he had, feeling the blow connect cleanly. He kicked, bucked, grasped a handful of uniform with one hand and flung somebody away. Then he was free enough to roll and spring to his feet. He'd lost the gun in the melee but could reclaim it later. He stood just in time to meet the charge of one of the soldiers. The eyegee sidestepped but left his arm in the way, which became a hay-making upward punch, his balled fist sinking into the man's midriff. His bicep tensed, absorbing the soldier's forward momentum and holding steady, while the recipient let out an 'oomph' of surprise and pain before sliding from Leyton's arm to crumple to the floor.

One of the others, who had been moving in behind his colleague, hesitated at the sight of this; only for a fraction of a second, but it was enough. As he went to move forward again, Leyton danced towards him, pivoting on his right foot, bending the knee and leaning away to counterbalance his left leg, which

Ian Whates

he lashed out with, putting into that kick all the frustration and anger he felt at this distraction, no matter how nobly motivated it might be.

The soldier fell backwards, causing the ring of bystanders to shuffle out the way amidst murmurs of alarm.

"Now back off!" he yelled at the only soldier who remained on his feet, though that one, a wide-eyed lad who looked shocked at how swiftly the eyegee had taken out his colleagues, didn't seem too eager to press the attack. "For the last time, I'm ULAW."

Leyton then turned back to where Julia had been standing, suddenly concerned that she might have taken the opportunity to flee.

She hadn't. Instead she stood close to where he'd last seen her, still smiling at him. In her hand she held his gun, pointed directly at him.

"Nice weapon," she said. "Think I'll hang onto it. Goodbye, Mr Leyton. It's been fun."

Memories of a tiny cabin aboard a spaceship leapt to the fore. The gun had betrayed him once, would it do so again? Surely not; on that occasion the weapon had been motivated by what it perceived as the greater good of ULAW, hadn't it? Even so, he held his breath as the woman pulled the trigger.

Nothing happened. Leyton breathed again. He had intended to try and take her alive, but, all of a sudden, after having to fight off his own side's soldiers for her sake, he didn't care.

"Gun," he said, "energy feedback."

There was no sound, no visible sizzle of energy or wisp of smoke rising from where her hand gripped the handle. She simply trembled a little; her eyes widened and her lips compressed to a thin line, before she collapsed, her body as limp as a rag doll.

Leyton strolled over to reclaim the gun. Nobody moved to stop him, not even the recovering soldiers. The fight had evidently gone out of them.

Cirese was quite dead. Leyton stared down at her beautiful face – and it was beautiful, even in death, no question about that – and knew that Benson would be less than impressed that he hadn't taken her alive, but right then he didn't care. Let others worry about who had sent her and why. He took the gun and holstered it, at which point a squad of black garbed station security officers chose to put in an appearance. Better late than never.

The eyegee's pocket comm buzzed. It was Benson.

"Leyton, I got your message." The one he'd left as he started the pursuit. "So what's so urgent?"

Leyton took a deep breath. He had a feeling he was about to ruin his boss's day.

"PHILIP?"

"Mal? What are you doing here?"

"Does it matter? I just wish I could have been here sooner, but I've only recently made it as far as New Paris."

"Why are you here at all?"

"For goodness sake, Philip, you'll never simply accept *anything*, will you? All right, in brief, I was aboard *The Noise Within* – hitched a ride on your comp and got trapped on the ship. I worked my way free when she was damaged in the battle with ULAW and then took refuge in the equipment of some ULAW specialists who came aboard to examine her, and here I am. But, honestly, none of that matters right now. There isn't much time. No easy way to say this, son; you're dying."

"What?"

"That reporter, Julia Cirese, she poisoned you; the kiss…"

"Julia? No, that can't be right." Yet he remembered the last harrowing seconds in the restaurant immediately following that wonderful kiss.

Julia? *Really*?

The conversation with Mal seemed oddly disassociated. Emotions were there but they were pale, insipid reflections of what they should have been. Part of him wanted to believe this was a dream, while another part knew that it wasn't.

"Trust me, it is. You're only alive now by the grace of ULAW. They've kept you with us for this long courtesy of the mass of equipment and expertise they've hauled across to New Paris in order to study the Byrzaens, but it's a losing battle. The poison is a nano construct, with some of the characteristics of a smart virus. It's attacking your nervous system and mutating faster than the doctors can counter it. Sorry, son, but you don't have long."

"This can't be happening. It's too early – there are things I want to do…"

"I know, I know. ULAW don't want to lose you either, which is why I'm here. You've been brought to a point where you're just below the threshold of consciousness, and I've been allowed into the systems monitoring your brain activity to talk to you. They want to save you, Philip, as much as they can."

"Save…?" A horrible suspicion began to form. "You mean as a download, like you." A so-called transhuman.

"Yes. Now I know how you feel about this but don't just dismiss the idea without thinking it through."

The terrible, guilty truth was that he *hadn't* dismissed it. He was too young – there was still so much he wanted from life, so much that remained undone. It was all right for Mal, *he* had lived to a ripe old age and achieved all that any man could wish to, but Philip was still only partway there. Death *couldn't* claim him now!

"It's not fair," he said.

"I know, son, but it's happening, fair or not. We have to act quickly to save you. Thank goodness you brought a version of Phil along with you. The ULAW specialists have him as a framework and can build from there. With the facilities they've got on hand they'll be able to capture just about everything the poison hasn't already taken. You'll be at least as complete as I am, probably more so."

Yet this was everything he'd opposed so vehemently, the very reason he'd refused to let Mal into his life, refused to acknowledge him as his father.

"But I'll just be a copy."

"You won't know the difference, I promise you. Not where it counts."

The very idea was abhorrent, or at least it had been. Yet now all Philip could recall was the memory of that abhorrence, not the emotion itself. He felt like a hypocrite for thinking this way, but with his own life on the line things suddenly took on a different perspective. Even so, he still felt as if he were betraying himself, not to mention his father, as he said, "All right, then."

"Good boy! The doctors are going to bring you up to full consciousness, only for a few seconds. They need your permission, so you'll have to tell them that you agree to the procedure."

It was all so hurried. By rights he should be taking time to think this through properly, not be rushed into such a momentous decision. But if what Mal said was true that time simply didn't exist.

Philip felt trapped. By fate; by circumstance... by *something*. Despite this, he said after only brief hesitation, "I'm ready," which was far from true. How could anyone ever be ready for something like this?

The idea made perfect sense, he kept telling himself. This way he would live on after a fashion, and neither his knowledge nor his expertise would be completely lost to either ULAW or Kaufman Industries. Given a choice between that and dying, it was a no-brainer. Surely anyone would do the same. So why did Philip feel that he had just sold his soul to the devil?

CHAPTER TWENTY

IT WAS 'NIGHT' on New Paris, in a day-night cycle designed to reflect Earth standard. The killer waited in the shadows. As his target stepped out of the door he moved forward, coming upon him from behind, taking the man by surprise and pinning one arm so that it was bent behind his back and pressed between them. He held the sonic knife close to the man's ear, so he could hear the faint sibilant hum of its blade.

"What the hell?"

"All right, Beck, who are you working for?"

"That's not a secret. I'd have told you without the knife. ULAW!"

"In as far as that goes, maybe, but who are you working for beyond that?"

"Leyton, is that you?"

"Right first time. Knowing who I am, you know what I'm capable of. So start talking."

"Look, I don't know what you're on about. Put the blade down, let's be adult about this."

"Holt, that's what I'm talking about. I know you tried to sabotage the mission, warned them we were coming."

"What? That's crazy. Why would you think that?"

Leyton moved the blade a fraction closer. "Don't lie to me, Beck, I'm trained to spot such things, remember?"

"I'm not lying, you have to... Ah!"

The involuntary yelp of pain came as Leyton touched the

blade to his ear, slicing into skin and cartilage, drawing blood.

"Last chance. The next cut takes your ear off."

"All right, you sick bastard. Lose the sodding blade and I'll tell you. Can't think straight with that thing humming in my ear."

Leyton complied, but had no intention of moving it far. Yet as he lifted the blade away, Beck seized his chance, elbowing the eyegee with his free arm, ducking away from the knife and twisting around, trying to break Leyton's grip on his arm. The move was quick and expertly performed. He nearly got away with it, but not quite. Leyton still held his wrist and as Beck tried to contort his body to negate his grip, the eyegee lifted and twisted. There was a sickening crack and Beck screamed.

Leyton did let go then, allowing the man to slump to the ground, where he sat, groaning and nursing his broken arm.

"You stupid fucker, you're going to pay for this!"

Leyton squatted down, blade held casually before him, and said, very calmly, "Now, let's start again. Who are you really working for?"

"You have no idea what you're dealing with." Ah, that sounded like progress. "These people don't play around. You think you're tough? Trust me, you don't know the meaning of the word. Do yourself a favour and walk away now. We'll forget all about this. Say I hurt myself in a fall or something." Of course he would. Leyton could just imagine Beck forgetting about the man who threatened him with a knife and then broke his arm.

"Here's how this is going to play out," the eyegee said calmly. "Either you tell me what I need to know, in which case I'll happily walk away right now, or you keep issuing ominous threats, in which case I start slicing bits of you off with ol' sonic here, until you do start talking. Your choice."

"Look, I can't give you what you want because I don't *know*! I've never met them, never seen their faces. They're a powerful faction within the upper echelons of ULAW, powerful enough to get me assigned to ride shotgun on Benson for this Byrzaen situation. When they say jump, I jump. That's *all* I know."

Unfortunately, Leyton had a feeling the man was telling the truth, but there had to be more details he could share – the little, seemingly inconsequential things which might yet provide a clue.

"If they're within ULAW, why warn Holt we were coming?"

"I've no idea. I didn't ask, and if you've any sense nor will you."

Beck's second attempt to take Leyton by surprise didn't, though it did force him to act decisively. Beck's good hand pulled swiftly away from the sleeve of his injured one holding something – a gun. Leyton reacted even as the move began, striking out back-handed with the knife, slicing off the hand holding the gun at the wrist, and continuing on to plunge into Beck's chest, piercing his heart.

With a grunt of apparent surprise, Beck fell backwards from his sitting position; dead before he hit the floor.

Leyton shook his head. He really was going to have to get a grip on this temper of his. First Julia, now Beck – two leads today which were well and truly dead, as far as any future investigation went. He walked away, brooding on what Beck had said. *A conspiracy within ULAW?* It sounded absurd, but perhaps not. The War had caused many political parties and interests to band together, and there had been signs on the odd occasion since that ULAW was not the unified body it tried to portray. He was going to have to tread very carefully if he pursued this any further.

As he walked, he dropped the sonic knife into a bag, already planning an acid bath for the weapon. He very much doubted it could be traced to Julia Cirese, let alone him, but no point in taking any chances. He then peeled away the transparent film of 'no print' gloves from each hand and added them.

As an afterthought, he took out a piece of folded paper from his pocket and put it into the bag after the gloves. The note bore a single hand-scrawled word: 'Beck'.

*   *   *

WHILE STILL A boy, Philip had been taken to an exhibition, one designed to trace the history of technology. Intended to be educational, this had been a physical display requiring a visit rather than a virtual one enjoyed from an armchair, and it provided a distinctly 'hands-on' experience of many antique but still ingenious machines. Philip loved every minute of it.

One of the exhibits, presumably relating to printing, had featured a vintage glossy magazine open at a page containing a photograph of an exquisitely beautiful model or celebrity of the time. To the pre-adolescent Philip, this woman was an object of instant adoration. He thought her face the most perfect, the most bewitching he had ever seen and subsequently put considerable effort into tracking down a copy of the image, which he kept for many years afterwards.

As a slightly older youth, he could still recognise in the image the beauty his younger self had drooled over, but could also see that the perceived perfection was due to artifice as much as nature; the picture had been skilfully tampered with to remove all blemishes and imperfections, to present an idealised version of the woman in question. As such, the older Philip felt betrayed and now saw this as an image artificially enhanced to be something more than reality, which at the same time made it less.

The park where he met Mal/Malcolm struck him in much the same way. The sky was clear blue, the bushes were bristling with blossom and the grass was greener than any grass had a right to be, while the bench he sat on was the epitome of what every park bench ought to aspire to; yet none of this had any substance in the physical world, the one he had always accepted as 'reality'. Better than the real thing in some ways but at the same time a great deal less.

Mal/Malcolm appeared suddenly. One moment Philip was alone, the next he turned around to find the old man sitting on the bench beside him.

As a conversation opener, Mal/Malcolm raised a subject which Philip/Phil had been pondering since he awoke to this new existence. His greatest surprise was the realisation that he felt no different. Which was a ridiculous way of expressing it; with no physical body and every familiar sense either gone or altered beyond recognition, of course he felt different. He could absorb input from a hundred varied locations simultaneously and process it at speeds far beyond the human, and he could flit from point to point in the blink of an eye... But these were all peripheral concerns, things that had always been conducted at the fringes of 'him', relating to his interaction with the world rather than who he actually was; and at his core, at that central essence which dictated his sense of 'self', he felt no different at all.

Logically, he knew full well that not everything had been saved, that he was an incomplete representation of the man who had been Philip Kaufman, and had spent considerable effort trying to identify what was missing, searching his memory and making comparisons, but he failed.

One resolution he did make now related to how he perceived himself: Philip. He refused to think of himself as merely 'Phil'. At the same time, he realised this meant acknowledging that it really was his father, Malcolm, sitting beside him.

"Is this what you expected?" Malcolm asked.

"No," he admitted.

"Far be it for me to gloat, but..."

"If the rest of that sentence contains any of the words 'told', 'you', and 'so', I don't want to hear it."

"Fair enough."

This was unlike the process of conversation as Philip knew it, being more akin to the never-realised dream of telepathy: mind to mind communication in its purest form. There was no hearing of sounds followed by the processing of meaning, but rather near-instant assimilation of what Malcolm wanted to convey; a lightning-quick transfer of data. Yet this was all new to him and his mind still insisted on interpreting things in physical human terms, so he perceived such interchanges as conversations, albeit incredibly fast ones.

"One thing still bothers me," he told his father.

"What?"

Doubtless Malcolm expected him to ask something about this new state of being, but instead Philip said, "The assassin, Julia Cirese, why was she still after me? Presumably she must have known by now that the Death Wish had been lifted."

"Not necessarily; depends on how often she checks in at the place. Even if she did know, maybe professional pride insisted she saw the job through once she'd taken it on, or…"

"Or what?"

"Maybe she simply didn't like you."

"Thank you so much." Even humour came through as clearly as before. An inflection of thought rather than voice perhaps, but equally as effective.

"Look, Philip, let it go. Whatever her motives might have been, she's dead and she's carried them with her to the grave. Accept the fact and move on. That's all part of the life you've left behind, and you need to stop looking back and start concentrating on what lies ahead of you." This was the Malcolm Philip remembered – the pragmatic, eminently sensible man who never entertained any doubts, who always knew the right thing to do and was never shy of imparting that knowledge. "There's going to be plenty here to occupy your thoughts, trust me."

The annoying thing was that Philip knew Malcolm was right.

Yet he also knew his father too well and realised that he was hiding something. "There's more, isn't there?" he said.

"Perhaps."

"Go on."

"They're not telling us everything."

"In what way?"

"Not entirely sure, but when I was in contact with the mind

operating *The Noise Within* I received a great deal of data, more than I could assimilate straight away and, I'm sure, more than the ship's brain intended me to see. While I was isolated, I had a lot of time to study that data. I still don't understand all of it, but I'm sure that what I saw was more complex than simply an AI/organic mind interface. Something else was happening."

"Alien mind," Phil said, "not surprising if it wasn't entirely what you were expecting."

"No, it wasn't that, I'm certain. And there was something else. The official line is that *The Noise Within's* mind was unhinged due to the instabilities still present in the human-built AI element; instabilities which caused a sort of resonance loop between the two component intelligences, right?"

"Right."

"So if the ship's mission was intended to be a peaceful one, why did the Byrzaens send it back to us packed to the gills with high-tech weaponry?"

"That's a question the media have asked more than once."

"I know, and no one has yet come back with a satisfactory answer. 'They're aliens, how are we supposed to understand them?' seems to about cover it. The point is that the official account does *not* tally with what I found on that ship, nor with what I've been able to extrapolate since. Everything I saw when I was in contact with *The Noise Within* suggested that the human-built AI part of the ship's mind was the sanest element involved.

"Trust me, there's a lot more to our new friends the Byrzaens than they're letting on."

Philip had a feeling he knew where this was leading. "And I suppose you intend to find out what."

"Well... I've nothing better to do, and I thought it might be fun."

"Uh-huh."

"So, are you in?"

"Of course."

*   *   *

LEYTON WAS HAPPY to be out of it. Benson had reacted with predictable anger at news of Beck's death, coming as it did so soon after the loss of Philip Kaufman, and security had been cranked up significantly, though no culprit or even serious suspect had yet emerged. Julia Cirese being responsible for Kaufman's murder gave Benson all the excuse he needed to throw most of the reporters out of New Paris, despite their bleating. Only a carefully vetted representative pool was allowed to remain.

Leyton seemed less in demand than he had been – doubtless Benson's way of expressing his displeasure at his failure to take Cirese alive – which enabled him to slip away, and he had every intention of making the most of this precious downtime, determined not to speculate as to what his lords and masters had lined up for him next. Benson might be preoccupied with all this Byrzaen business for now, but that wouldn't last. He'd soon remember that he had an idle eyegee to assign.

Leyton clocked the girl as soon as she came in. In theory he was hunched over a drink while perched on a stool towards the far left side of the bar and ensconced in a world of his own. All that was missing was a sign slung around his back saying 'do not disturb' for the image to have been complete. In practice old habits die hard, and while he *was* seeking some privacy, he still checked the long mirror behind the bar every time the door opened and a new customer walked through. In her case, he checked twice.

She was tall and slender – an athlete's frame, he thought, or perhaps a dancer's. The latter, judging by the way her hips moved as she walked; nothing exaggerated or over-pronounced, but mesmerising all the same – a seemingly unconscious and understated sway.

She wore a figure-hugging dress, black and expertly tailored, ending just above the knee and boasting a slit which exposed thighs as shapely as her calves. Her skin looked as pale as new-fallen snow, suggesting that wherever she came from they didn't see much natural sunlight.

All this he registered in two quick glances, before looking down once more and getting back to what he was there for: drinking and brooding.

Yet he was fully conscious of her presence as she lifted herself smoothly onto one of the stools near him. Being one of New Paris's swankier drinking holes, even the bar stools were elegant affairs, each composed of four sweeping rods of chrome which emerged from splayed feet and then curved upward to end in scroll-like curls that supported the seat proper. And what a seat. Mock leather skins stuffed with smart foam which moulded itself to your shape, constantly refiguring as you fidgeted or adjusted your balance, even responding to changes as slight as your leaning forward to pick up a drink.

The girl gave an "Oh!" of surprise and Leyton couldn't help but smile, knowing full well why. Their eyes met and she smiled in return.

"This'll take some getting used to."

A sweet, young voice. He couldn't place the accent; her pronunciation was crisp, precise, perhaps even a little old fashioned.

"I know. It feels as though someone's caressing your buttocks, doesn't it?"

She laughed, appearing to be caught off-guard and perhaps even a little shocked by his candour. "Yes, it feels exactly like that!"

"May I buy you a drink?" The words slipped out automatically, his commitment to an evening of solitary introspection crumbling like so much piled sand overrun by the waves.

She hesitated as if wary, but only for a breath or two, before smiling and nodding. "Thank you."

"What would you like?"

She shook her head and shrugged. "I've just arrived. No idea what one's expected to drink here, so why don't you surprise me?"

He thought for a moment and then ordered her a cocktail, not too bitter, not too sweet; a drink constructed around vodka and two very different citrus fruits, with a dash of Xanashu – a liqueur from Minos III which he'd developed a taste for a few years back – and crowned with a sprinkling of delphy seeds, which sank slowly through the drink, lending it a bitter hint but also making it sparkle enticingly.

The girl took a tentative sip, looked up at him, smiled and then took a longer one. "Mmm... this is good," she said. "Well chosen."

"Glad you like it. I'm Jim, by the way."

"Kethi. Pleased to meet you, Jim."

Kethi? That rang a bell, but he couldn't quite place why. Someone he'd known in the past? He didn't think so. Someone he'd heard about perhaps. "Unusual name," was all he said.

"Do you mean unusual in a good way or a bad way?"

He smiled. "Oh, in a good way, I reckon."

"That's all right, then." She turned her attention back to the drink. "What do they call this, again?"

"A Star Fall."

"Ah, because of the delphy seeds. Very apt." She took another sip. "I'd order this again, no question."

He noted her casual recognition of the delphy seeds. Hardly a momentous feat but at the same time they weren't common. His respect for her went up a notch. He was growing increasingly intrigued by this strange, pale, elfin-faced girl.

"So what do you do?"

"Several things, to be honest, but I suppose basically I'm an analyst."

"A human analyst? I thought we had computers and AIs to do that sort of thing these days?"

Her smile this time was a little thin, as if she'd heard similar responses often enough to be tired of them. "You're right of course. Computers are far swifter and more efficient at sifting data than we are, but they can't intuit. They can't make leaps of logic and extract meaning from the faintest of hints and scattered clues in the same way a human can, so there's still room for us organics in the analytical game."

"Really?" It made sense when she put the argument like that, but he had never considered it before. "That's fascinating."

She snorted. "You think? Try sitting on your jacksie sifting data for days on end. I promise you, the fascination would soon wear off."

He laughed. "I'm sure you're right."

The evening wore on and they continued to chat easily. Jim's thoughts were turning towards where the evening might end up with a bit of luck, when he asked the wrong question.

"So what brings you to New Paris?" It seemed an innocent enough thing to say.

"Believe it or not, I've got a message to deliver to someone."

He stared at her. "And that's it?"

"That's it."

"Must be a pretty important message."

"Oh, it is."

"Would it be nosy of me to ask who you're delivering it to?"

"Probably. Is that going to stop you?"

"No," he admitted.

"Well in that case, I'll tell you anyway. It's for you, Jim."

His blood ran cold. "Pardon?"

A setup. He should have guessed – a beautiful girl like this just happening to sit down next to him.

"I'm here especially to see you."

"Well done. You know, I was actually beginning to like you." All gaiety had gone. He was suddenly stone cold sober and all business, all suspicion, all offended anger. "So, why the charade? Why didn't you just come straight out and say your piece?"

"Who said it was a charade? I had to know you really were Jim Leyton, and I had to know you were worthy of receiving the message."

Pretentious, but it piqued his interest again. "And do I pass?"

She smiled. "You do, on both counts."

"Fine; then say what you have to and then get out of here." Out of the bar, out of his life.

"If that's what you want after you've heard me out, then fine; but at least listen first."

He didn't say anything, just glared. Then he nodded – an almost imperceptible bob of the head.

"It's about Mya," the girl said. He froze. *Mya?* "She's in trouble, Jim; *real* trouble, and she needs your help desperately."

He didn't say anything. A dozen reactions chased each other through his thoughts without any of them condensing into words. She stood up, saying into his silence, "I'm going to leave now. If you're interested in helping her, follow me. If you're not, don't, and you'll never see me again. Nor Mya, for that matter. It's up to you."

She turned and walked out. Not hurriedly, not anxiously, but as calm as you like, without once looking back. Leyton watched her cross the room, until she was out the door and gone. Keeping tight rein on his thoughts and his emotions, he pushed the stool back and stood up.

He followed after her.